I0612847

Mr. Punch

Mr. Punch's Victorian era

Her Majesty the Queen

Mr. Punch

Mr. Punch's Victorian era
Her Majesty the Queen

ISBN/EAN: 9783741198915

Manufactured in Europe, USA, Canada, Australia, Japa

Cover: Foto ©Andreas Hilbeck / pixelio.de

Manufactured and distributed by brebook publishing software
(www.brebook.com)

Mr. Punch

Mr. Punch's Victorian era

JOHN TENNIEL.

MR. PUNCH'S
VICTORIAN ERA

An Illustrated Chronicle

OF

FIFTY YEARS OF THE REIGN OF

Her Majesty the Queen

FROM THE CONTEMPORARY PAGES OF "PUNCH"

VOL. II.

LONDON
BRADBURY, AGNEW, & CO., 8, 9, 10, BOUVERIE STREET, E.C.

LONDON :
BRADBURY, AGNEW, & CO., PRINTERS, WHITEFRIARS.

CONTENTS OF VOLUME II.

✦ 1860 ✦

THE year opened with the prospect of "plenty to do" in the political and diplomatic world. There was much talk of the proposed Congress, which has already been referred to, but it came to nothing. The Italian question was therefore before us in all its difficulty. There was war in China and in Morocco, and a dispute with the United States concerning the San Juan boundary. At home a Reform Bill had been promised, and the questions of Finance and of Naval Administration awaited consideration. The New Year therefore had his work cut out for him.

(See Cartoon, "Young 1860.")

JAN. 9.

THE remains of Lord Macaulay were on this day interred in Westminster Abbey. *Mr. Punch* had the following lines on the occasion :—

MACAULAY IN WEST-
MINSTER ABBEY.

JANUARY 9, 1860.

Among the men whose words
and deeds
He best has taught our time
to prize;
Macaulay's honoured coffin
lies,
'Mid hush of jeering cliques and
creeds.

A shadow falls upon his grave
Where morning lights the
modern prose ;
And one, whom sunset splen-
dours rain

THE CONGRESS PARTY.

By the Treaty of Villafranca, which had been signed at Zurich on the 11th November, 1859, it had been agreed that an endeavour should be made to assemble a Congress of the European Powers to consider the question of the pacification of Italy. Discordant views, however, on the part of the various Powers led to protracted delays, and ultimately to the abandonment of the scheme.

JAN. 17.

Mr. Cobden was appointed Plenipotentiary to negotiate a Treaty of Commerce with France. The Emperor had, on the 5th of the same month, intimated his intention to remove many of the existing restrictions on French Commerce. On the 23rd the Treaty was signed at Paris.

(See Cartoon, "Dame Cobden's New Pupil.")

JAN. 24.

Parliament was opened by the Queen in person. Mr. Punch thus summarised the Royal Speech:—

Great Peers of England, pillars
   of the State,   (I'm glad
And you, whom I may also call
   :Excuse the jest), because you
   do support it.
Right glad am I to meet you
   once again.   (advice,
And ask for your assistance and
Not being in the slightest need
   of either.   (amongst
With all Ten Tea-Pots (I'm at
Called from the Boy's Own
   Book, and, analysed,
Makes (vocatums) I'm on the
   happiest terms.

In August last I told you I'd
   been asked   (Congress
To send my envoy to the general
That was to settle the Italian
   quarrelsom.

There is a hitch about the Con-
   gress now,   (are known.
But if it meets, my sentiments
I've made a Treaty with the
   Emperor
For letting in French wines and
   other things
As a diminished duty—better for
To tap the Frenchman's claret
   in that way,   (happen
Than brilliantly, and so Mr.
In April means to try Herrick's
   tap.

Not so I mean to teach John
   Chinaman.   (my ships,
Who at the Peiho forts repulsed
That folks had better play no
   tricks with me.

Our expedition's getting ready now
(In concert with the French), and it will curb
The Chinese power right ceremoniously.
Touching that vexed question of San Juan,
We might have got into an awkward row
With Brother Jonathan, had not my own
Behaved with all forbearance.—I believe
That squabble will be pleasantly arranged.
Lord Clyde has tranken out the mutiny

DAME COBDEN'S NEW PUPIL.

   *   *   *   With Japan
And Guatemala compacts I have made,
Which, I dare say, will be enormous boons,
But leave it to yourselves to find out why.
   *   *   *
These islands must be guarded, O my Lords,
So, O my Commons, rumble out the tin,
There's no excuse for shilly-shally, then,
The revenue is satisfactory.
   *   *   *

And now, my Lords and Gentlemen, perpend:
You will be shortly asked to give your best
Attention to a measure of Reform.
Amendment and extension are your care,
I pray you tackle to the task in earnest,
And let's be quit of that many bothersome.
   *   *   *   Now, I have done.
The nation's tranquil, crime's diminishing,
And so is poverty; and everywhere

For which all thanks unto a Higher Power
Than mine. Be proud deliberations blessed !
    [*Exit* QUEEN, *attended by Court. Scene closes.*

FEB. 4.

THE New Treaty of Commerce between England and France was this day ratified.

Under it French wines were admitted to this country on cheaper terms, and it was expected they would come into much more general use. Coals were now exported into France free of duty.

[*See Customs,* "*The Next Invasion,*" *and* "*An Uncommonly Civil War.*"]

FEB. 6.

REFERRING to renewed reports of the Emperor's intention to annex Savoy and Nice to France, Lord John Russell wrote to Sir J. Hudson at Turin : " In speaking to Count Cavour respecting the rumoured annexation of

THE NEXT INVASION.

LANDING OF THE FRENCH (LIGHT WINES) AND DISCOMFITURE OF OLD GENERAL BEER.

Savoy, you will not disguise from Count Cavour that, in the opinion of Her Majesty's Government, it would be a blot on the escutcheon of the House of Savoy if the King of Sardinia were to yield to France the cradle of his ancient and illustrious House." The Emperor now temporised and equivocated, did not deny that " in certain eventualities he might think it right to claim a proper frontier for France," said that he believed the wish of the Savoyards was to be united to France, but disclaimed any intention of annexing them *against* their wish. The French Minister of Foreign Affairs also hinted that the annexation *might* " present itself as a geographical necessity for the safety of our frontier."

FEB. 10.

THE CHANCELLOR OF THE EXCHEQUER, Mr. Gladstone, introduced his Budget, which had been postponed from the 6th owing to his illness and loss of voice. As embodying the results of the French Treaty it was a Budget of special interest and importance, and portions of *Mr. Punch's* commentary on it may therefore be accounted.

THE BUDGET OF 1860.

OUT spake the gallant Chancellor, the Chancellor of X,
While all the listening Swells outstretched their sorrowful necks :

" At present, Mr. Money,—and I say it from my soul,—
We're all, financially at least, in what I call a Hole.

*   *   *   *   *   *

" Now, as we go to Turkey, and *abroad*, it seems to me
That I shan't touch the duties on sugar until on tea :
Coals would have liked to take them off, but as I've often said,
The real way to help the poor's by stimulating trade.

" Then comes the Treaty. *Inter alia, France* will soon let in

AN UNCOMMONLY CIVIL WAR.

Mr. Bull. *"Allow me, my dear Ravisson, to introduce to your notice three beautiful Diamonds!"*
Ravisson. *"And let me, cher M. Bull, offer you a glass of this excellent light Wine!"*—(N.B. We know who has the best of it.)

MARCH 1.

SPEAKING at the opening of the legislative session, the Emperor of the French, referring to the annexation of Savoy, said:— "Looking at the transformation of Northern Italy, which has put all the passes of the Alps into the hands of a powerful State, it was my duty, for the security of our frontier, to claim the French slopes of the mountains. This reassertion of a claim to a territory of small extent has nothing in it of a nature to alarm Europe, and give a denial to the policy of disinterestedness which I have proclaimed more than once; for France does not wish to proceed to this aggrandisement, however small it may be, either by military occupation, or by provoked insurrection, or by underhand measures, but by frankly explaining the questions to the Great Powers."

MARCH 1.

LORD JOHN RUSSELL introduced the Government plan for Parliamentary Reform, proposing to reduce the borough franchise to £6, thus, it was estimated, increasing the number of

THE NEW RUSSELL SIX-POUNDER.

voters from 440,000 to 634,000. The Bill was very coldly received.

(*See Cartoon, "The New Russell Six-Pounder."*)

THE NICE LITTLE BILL.

MR. DISRAELI, *Sir*, I'm obliged by these cheers,
And I beg that the House will extend me its ears,
While I try to set out to this best of my skill,
The reforms I propose by our Nice Little Bill.

I do not think that a fellow I view
In the Bill which I passed in the year XXXII.
As a retrograde, 'tis because it succeeded, I will
Amend in few faults by my Nice Little Bill.

That the Nation is rich and is happy, see forth—
No need to throw deeps for Lord Castlereagh's Acts;
We're conservative, loyal, progressive, and old
Is wanted on earth but my Nice Little Bill.

Occupation shall give £,—but that understood,
Though we don't value dwellings when coupled with land,
Or houses that dwellings—for instance, a mill—
There's demanded £5 by my Nice Little Bill.

For votes in the boroughs, I mean, Sir, to fix
The pounds in the rent at the figure of 6.
Then two hundred thousand out twist of our quill
To the Register adds, by my Nice Little Bill.

AN UP-HILL JOB.

MR. PUNCHEON PUNCH (*compassionately*). "Now, little 'Un, do you THINK you'll be able to shove that Perambulator up them Steps?"

MARCH 2.

COUNT CAVOUR, writing to M. Thouvenel, intimated that though the Sardinian Government would never willingly cede or exchange any part of its territory, it could not refuse to the King's subjects dwelling on the other side of the Alps the right of freely manifesting their will.

MARCH 7.

THE QUEEN received, at a special levée in St. James's, the officers of the newly formed Volunteer Rifle Corps. About 2500 were present, representing a force of 70,000 men, which Earl Grey, the Under Secretary at War, said he

though would be increased before the end of the summer to 100,000.

MARCH 8.

AN ultimatum sent from Shanghai to the Chinese Government, demanding an apology for firing on our ships, the ratification

A GLIMPSE OF THE FUTURE.
(A PROBABLE AND LARGE IMPORTATION OF FOREIGN RAGS.)

of the Treaty of Tien-tsin, an indemnity of 4,000,000 taels, and the reception of a resident magistrate at Pekin, was rudely rejected by the Chinese.

MARCH 11.

A VOTE taken in Tuscany and the Æmilia (in which was included the Duchies of Parma and Modena and the Legations) resulted in a very large majority in favour of annexation to Sardinia, as against being constituted a separate

REFUGEES AND RAGS.

WHAT, Tyrants, do you, wanting gap
For Britain's Press, deny us rags,
In order that you may, by dint
(Of paper famine, check our print)

The time will come when discontent
Will overthrow your government;
I If subjects where your ragged rims
Will rise, rebel, and kick you out.

Then, if your rags old England lacks,
You'll come, and bring them on your backs;
Yourselves and rags you'll barter sweet,
And bundle off to Leicester Square.

MARCH 24.

ON this day a Treaty was signed between the Emperor of France and the King of Sardinia, by which the latter consented to the annexation of Savoy and the arrondissement of Nice to France; the annexation to be effected "without any constraint of the wishes of the populations." This annexation was met by formal protests on the part of Austria and Prussia, and excited great indignation amongst the friends of Italy and of freedom. In the

it and the French Emperor in impassioned terms, and Lord John Russell, amidst loud cheers from both sides, spoke out upon the subject in words which Lord John Manners declared "would vibrate from one end of England to the other," and which Mr. Punch said

"descended like a thunderbolt upon the Spoiler of the Slopes."

MARCH 26.

The Pope pronounced the Major Excommunication against the invaders and usurpers of certain Provinces in the Pontifical States. Although not directly named, the Emperor of the French and the King of Sardinia were the personages chiefly aimed at in this fulmination, which, it was declared, "shall have the same power upon every one whom it

THE REFORM JANUS.

concerns as if they (the Letters Apostolic) had been presented *nominatim personaliter*." The Excommunication did not greatly trouble the peace of those against whom it was directed.

APRIL 16.

The House of Commons reassembled after the Easter recess. Mr. Massey, Liberal M.P. for Salford, gave notice that after the second reading of Lord John Russell's very unpopular Reform Bill he should move that it be referred to a Select Committee. The House indeed was

satisfied neither the earnest advocates nor the vehement opponents of Reform.

(*See Cartoon, "The Reform Janus."*)

APRIL 17.

On this day took place at Farnborough the great fight for the championship between Tom Sayers, the English Champion, and Heenan, alias the "Benicia Boy," an American. The fight excited unusual interest, as being invested with a sort of international character. The Prize Ring had fallen into deserved disrepute, and even this sensational contest could not revive its de-

talk of the town, and it was attended by persons of all ranks and professions, peers, members of parliament, poets, painters, and it was said even parsons. The disparity in the size of the pugilists added to the interest of the contest; Heenan was a colossus of 6ft. 1 inches in height, whilst Sayers, now 34 years of age, was but 5ft. 8½ inches, and weighed under 11 stone. Notwithstanding his inferiority in physique, and the fact that the loss gave him the lowest ground with the sun in his eyes, whilst early in the fight his right arm was so damaged as to be practically useless, Sayers maintained a gallant struggle

was inconclusive, the police appearing at a critical moment of the fight, and the ring being broken into. Heenan at the time was nearly blind, and many maintain men have lost the fight, though American partisans naturally took a slightly different view. Ultimately a belt was presented to each of the combatants.

APRIL 23.

At the close of the voting in Savoy and Nice it was announced that in Savoy there were 130,533 votes in favour of annexation to France and 235 against, in Nice 25,743 for, and 160 against.

MAY 5.

A Revolutionary outbreak had taken place at Palermo, and in Messina and Catania. Francis the Second had succeeded his father Ferdinand the Second on the throne of the Two Sicilies; he was as despotic and as unpopular as his detested predecessor. Guerilla bands traversed the interior, and the movements of the insurgents were directed by a secret revolutionary committee. In the meantime Garibaldi was collecting volunteers to take part in the insurrection. On the 5th May he sailed from Genoa with 1000 men. He issued a proclamation to the Italians. "The Sicilians," it said, "are fighting against the enemies of Italy and for Italy. To help them with money, arms, and especially men, is the duty of every Italian." Although the Sardinian Government officially expressed disapproval of the expedition, it took no active steps to prevent it, and Victor Emmanuel subsequently said, "The people were fighting for liberty in Sicily when a brave warrior devoted to Italy and me—General Garibaldi—sprang to their assistance. They were Italians. I would not, I ought not to restrain them." On the 10th of May Garibaldi effected a landing at Marsala,

GARIBALDI THE LIBERATOR; OR, THE MODERN PERSEUS.

the name of Victor Emmanuel and Italy. The next day he defeated 3,000 Neapolitans under General Landi, and on the 27th he attacked Palermo, drove the Neapolitans into the citadel and compelled them to propose an armistice, during which the Royalist troops evacuated Palermo.

MAY 7.

In a debate in the Commons raised by Mr. Horsman as to the construction of Mr. Walter, M.P., with the Times, Mr. Horsman made many insinuations regarding Lord Palmerston's relations with Mr. Delane, the

temperedly repudiating any relations with Mr. Delane but those of friendly appreciation, took occasion to pay some graceful compliments to the "gentlemen of the Press."

(*See Cartoon, " Pam's graceful recognition of the Press, or Fourth Estate."*)

MAY 6.

Mr. Government proposal to repeal the Paper Duty, a part of Mr. Gladstone's Budget, was this day carried by a majority of 9 in a House of 419. The Lords threatening to reject it, a public meeting was held at St. Martin's

Hall on the 15th to protest against such action, Mr. Bright being the leading speaker.

MAY 10.

On this day, at the meeting of the National Republican Confederation at Chicago,

PAM'S GRACEFUL RECOGNITION OF THE PRESS, OR FOURTH ESTATE

" *My Right Honourable friend has observed, that the Contributors to the Press are the foundation and the constituent of the social circles into which they enter. In that opinion to to, it seems to me, perfectly correct. The gentlemen to whom he refers are, generally speaking, persons of great attainments and information. It is, then, but natural that their entry should be agreeable.*"—LORD PALMERSTON in the House of Commons, Monday, May 7, 1860.

Abraham Lincoln was selected as the candidate for the Presidency.

MAY 21.

The House of Lords rejected the Bill repealing the Paper Duty by 193 votes against 104. This rejection roused much indignation amongst the more advanced Liberals, Mr. Bright in particular fulminating vehemently at Manchester against the privileges and prejudices of

JUNE 11.

Lord John Russell, at the end of a protracted debate extending over six nights, announced that the Government intended to abandon their Reform Bill.

JUNE 17.

On this day the "Great Eastern" left the

Atlantic, reaching New York in ten days and a half.

JUNE 21.

The town of Melazzo surrendered to Garibaldi. In the contest preceding the surrender he had personally engaged, and very narrowly escaped death.

JUNE 23.

ON this day the Queen, accompanied by Prince Albert and other members of the Royal Family, with the King of the Belgians, reviewed 21,000 Volunteers in Hyde Park. Of the men present 15,000 belonged to London, while 6000 came from the provinces. It was the first review on a large scale of the lately instituted Volunteer forces, and it excited much public interest and enthusiasm.

JUNE 26.

FRANCIS II., King of the Two Sicilies, being now anxious to appease the discontent of his subjects, promised certain concessions, such as a Liberal Ministry, the adoption of the national flag, and a Vice-regal and Liberal government for Sicily. It was however too late.

JULY 2.

ON this day the first meeting of the National Rifle Association was held at Wimbledon. The Queen fired the first shot — "a centre." The first "Queen's Prize" (the gold medal of the Association and £250) was won by Mr. Ross of the 7th North York.

(See Cartoon, "Best Rest for the Queen's Rifle.")

THE VOLUNTEER'S SONG.

Air.—"*I am a Simple Maiden.*"

I am a Rifle Volunteer,
And quite particular to rule;
Not much, not drill, however onerous,
My military ardour cools.
I am but in my country's cause,
To keep her from the Eagle's claws;
If they attempt a swoop to make,
Crack! crack! my cannon to class;
They'll find they've made a slight mistake—
I am a Volunteer!

I am a Rifle Volunteer,
And they who are not so are—males!
My nerve is firm, my sight is clear,

BEST REST FOR THE QUEEN'S RIFLE.

To face the art I'm not afraid;
And should the foemen dare invade,
Crack! crack! my shot they'll hear.
My money and my Queen to aid—
I am a Volunteer!

JULY 9.

THE PRINCE OF WALES left England on a

had received a special invitation to Washington from President Buchanan, who on the 4th June had written to the Queen saying that "the Prince would be greeted by the American people in such a manner as cannot fail to prove gratifying to your Majesty." Her Majesty in reply courteously accepted the invitation on behalf of

JULY 18.

O⁣ᴺ this day Lord Clyde, on his return from India after suppressing the Mutiny, was enthusiastically welcomed at Dover.

(*See Cartoon, " See the Conquering Hero comes."*)

JULY 23.

L⁣ORD PALMERSTON made a statement of the intentions of the Government with regard to the recommendations of the National Defence Commission. He told the House (says *Mr. Punch's* "Essence of Parliament") "that we really must Fortify. He meant no disrespect to Anybody anywhere, and Nobody had 'any call' to be offended, but it would not do for England to owe her safety to Anybody's forbearance, and she must be as strong as Anybody else. Therefore it was proposed to lay out about Nine Millions of money in the way recommended by the Fortification Committee. . . . About Two Millions of money were wanted at once." This Lord Palmerston proposed to charge on the Consolidated Fund, and raise by annuities for a term not exceeding 30 years.

The resolution excited some opposition, but was ultimately agreed to on the 2nd August.

JULY 25.

T⁣HE EMPEROR OF THE FRENCH, in a letter addressed to M. Persigny, complained of the unfounded suspicions entertained concerning the policy of his Government. "Affairs" (he said) "appear to me to be so complicated, thanks to the mistrust excited everywhere since the war in Italy, that I write to you in the hope that a conversation, in perfect frankness, with Lord Palmerston will remedy the existing evil." He declared that "since the Peace of Villafranca I have had but one thought—one object—to inaugurate a new

"*SEE THE CONQUERING HERO COMES.*"

era. I had renounced Savoy and Nice; the extraordinary additions to Piedmont alone caused me to resume the desire to see provinces essentially French reunited to France."

The Emperor's pacific assurances were not received in this country with implicit confi-

JULY 27.

G⁣ENERAL GARIBALDI, writing from Melazzo in reply to the King of Sardinia, who had urged him to suspend operations against Naples until Sicily had declared in favour of an united

said he was "called for and argued on by the people of Naples; that he endeavoured in vain to restrain them. But if I should hesitate now" (said the General) "I should endanger the cause of Italy, and not fulfil my duty as an Italian." He therefore pleaded for permission not to obey, promising that as soon as he had fulfilled the task imposed on him by "the wishes of the people which groan under the tyranny of the Neapolitan Bourbon" he would lay his sword at the King's feet and obey him for the remainder of his life. Words very significant of the situation in Italy. On the 28th, Garibaldi concluded a truce with the Neapolitans, who agreed to evacuate Italy, though retaining the Castle of Messina.

Aug. 6.

By a majority of 33 in a House of 499, Mr. Gladstone carried his resolution for removing "as much of the Customs duty on paper as exceeded the Excise duty at home."

Aug. 7.

The North Country Volunteers were to-day reviewed by the Queen at Edinburgh, in the park adjoining Holyrood Palace.

Aug. 23.

Parliament was still sitting, the session having been prolonged in a way which was then unusual. On this day, however, the Ministerial Whitebait Dinner was held at the Trafalgar Hotel, Greenwich.

(See Cartoon, "Retribution; or, the Greenwich Dinner.")

Aug. 24.

Lord Palmerston, in a debate on foreign affairs, spoke emphatically (amidst general cheering) of the "painful impression" which the cession of Savoy had produced in this country,

RETRIBUTION; OR, THE GREENWICH DINNER.

Lord John Russell. "This can't be Whitebait?"
Lord Palmerston. "Oh, yes! You would make it so late in the Season."

ceived formal acknowledgment by any of the Powers—certainly not by this country—and cannot, at present, be said to form part of the public law of Europe."

Aug. 28.

like a wounded snake had been dragging its slow length along since January the twenty-fourth, was this day put an end to."

Aug. 31.

SEPT. 6.

THE KING OF NAPLES issued a Manifesto to the Courts of Europe against him whom he called "a daring Condottiere," who had "attached our dominions in the name of one of Italy's sovereigns," and "with all the forces which revolutionary Europe possesses." After thus

protesting and denouncing, the King left Naples and retired to Gaeta. On the 7th, Count Cavour intimated to Cardinal Antonelli that unless the Pope's mercenary troops were disbanded, the King of Sardinia would feel himself justified in invading the Papal States. The Holy See indignantly protested, and the Emperor

Napoleon promised that he would oppose "such culpable aggression into the Pontifical territories."

On the 8th, Garibaldi, after twice defeating the Neapolitan troops, "entered Naples with a few of his staff, having reached it from Salerno by the railway train! He came, not at the head

THE MAN IN POSSESSION.

VICTOR EMMANUEL. "I wonder when he will open the Door."

of victorious legions with all the pomp and circumstance of war, but as a first-class passenger in a railway carriage. He had dethroned the Bourbon dynasty, and marched from Melito to Naples with hardly the loss of a single man since the moment when he first set foot on the Calabrian shore."

On the 9th, Victor Emmanuel was proclaimed King of Italy at Naples. On the 10th and 11th, fifty thousand Sardinian troops entered the Pontifical States. General Lamoricière was appointed

the 11th the fortress of Pesaro, with a garrison of 1,500 men, surrendered to the Piedmontese army led by Cialdini. Fano, Urbino, Perugia and Spoleto were shortly afterwards taken by assault.

SEPT. 28.

LAMORICIÈRE, having been worsted in several engagements, had fled for refuge to Ancona, his army having laid down its arms. On this date he surrendered with the entire garrison of Ancona as prisoners of war to the Garibaldians.

October the Royalist troops, commanded by the King of Naples in person, were defeated by the Garibaldians at the Battle of Volturno, although the Neapolitans numbered some 30,000 men, while the volunteers under Garibaldi did not exceed half that number.

"The state of Naples under Garibaldi" (says Mr. Punch's Summary) "was very unsatisfactory, and tumults had to be repressed and popular feelings controlled—not always with the best discretion on the part of the Dictator."

Oct. 9.

THE KING OF SARDINIA issued a Manifesto to the people of Southern Italy. "I have proclaimed Italy for the Italians," he said. "People of Southern Italy! my troops advance among you to maintain order. I come not to impose my will, but to make yours respected.

You may freely manifest it. Providence, who protects the cause of the just, will suggest the vote which you should place in the urn. . . . . My policy, will, perhaps, not be inefficacious in reconciling the progress of nations with the stability of monarchy. As for Italy, I know that there I bring to a close the era of revolution."

Oct. 12.

PEKIN, threatened with bombardment, surrendered to the Allies; "for the first time in history the flags of England and France floated victoriously on its walls." ("Annals of Our Time.") The Summer Palace, a collection of buildings in a huge park, and crowded with

THE NEXT DANCE!

LOUD PUNCH. "Now, my Boy! There's some pretty Uncle Columbia—you don't get such a Partner in that every day!"

the most choice and valuable objects of Chinese art, was burnt and plundered by the English and French troops. The Convention of Tien-tsin, the signature of which had been long delayed, was signed at Pekin on the 24th.

Oct. 18.

GARIBALDI issued a decree saying that Naples ought to be incorporated with the Italian Kingdom. On the 21st the Neapolitans voted in favour of annexation to the Sardinian States, an example shortly followed by the Sicilians.

Oct. 20.

THE PRINCE OF WALES, as before stated, was at this time paying a visit to the United States. He arrived at Detroit on the 20th September, visited Washington on October 3rd, Philadelphia on October 9th, New York on October 11th, and Boston on October 17th, leaving for home on October 20th.

[See Cartoon, "The Next Dance!"]

THE NEXT DANCE.

Yes, dance with him, Lady, and bright as they are,
Believe us he's worthy those smiles you confer.
We're o'er him the flag of the Stripe and the Star,
And gladden the heart of the Queen of the Isle.

We thank you for all that has welcomed him—most
For the sign of true love that you bore the Old Land;
Proud Heiress of all that his ancestor lost,
You restore it, in giving that crown, loving hand.

And we'll claim, too, the smart, Fate's looking askance,
And Fate, only, knows the term time she will play;
But if John and his Cousin join hands for the Dance—
Bad luck to the parties who get in their way.

OCT. 22.

To-day the Emperors of Russia and Germany met at Warsaw. The Imperial Conference gave rise to considerable conjecture.

(See Cartoon, " The Warsaw Conference.")

THE TRIO AT WARSAW.

When Virtue first began to reign
Without the Tyrants' leaves,
He much abused three mighty men :
And two of them were thieves :
The first he was a Russian ;
The next he was a Prussian ;
And the third he was a little Kal-set :
Three Despots altogether.

The Russian chafed with scorn ;
The Prussian spun a yarn ;
And the little Kal-set waxed red with wrath,
And all three Sovereigns warm.
The Russian was choked with self-will ;
The Prussian made another his yarn ;
And the Rebels did carry with the little Kal-set,
With his charter makes his era.

THE WARSAW CONFERENCE.

Lord Nap. (a Detective in Plain Clothes). "Oh ! You're up to a nice game : but I've got my eye on you !"

OCT. 26.

On this day occurred a memorable meeting between the King of Piedmont and Garibaldi. The interview took place between Teano and Speranzano. Victor Emmanuel had crossed the frontier into the Abruzzi at the head of his army, and Garibaldi with his volunteers advanced to meet him. The interview is thus described by a witness : "Seeing having recognised Garibaldi gave his horse a touch of the spur, and galloped to meet him. When ten paces distant the officers of the King and those of Garibaldi shouted " Viva Victor Emmanuel!" Garibaldi made another step in advance, raised his cap, and added in a voice which trembled with emotion, " King of Italy !" Victor Emmanuel raised his hand to his cap and then stretched out his hand to Garibaldi, and with equal emotion replied, " I thank you."

NOV. 3.

The Sardinian army laid siege to the fortress of Gaeta, whither Francis II. had retired.

NOV. 7.

King Victor Emmanuel entered Naples in triumph. He issued a proclamation to the people of the provinces over which, he said, "the results of the vote by universal

(he said) " this new award
of the national will, moved,
not by any monarchic am-
bition, but by conscientious
feelings as an Italian.

" We must show Europe
that, if the irresistible force
of events has broken
through the conventionali-
ties grounded on the cala-
mities by which Italy was
for centuries afflicted, we
know how to restore to the
united nation the empire of
those unchangeable prin-
ciples without which every
society is infirm, and every
authority is exposed to
struggle and uncertainty."

On the 10th, Garibaldi
left Naples and returned
to his quiet home in
Caprera.

Nov. 17.

Lᴏʀᴅ Jᴏʜɴ Rᴜssᴇʟʟ
having written a des-
patch to Sir James Hudson,
our Minister at Turin (with
reference to the disapproval
expressed by several Eu-
ropean Courts of the re-
cent action of the King of
Sardinia), in which Lord
John remarked that " Her
Majesty's Government can-
not pretend to blame the
King of Sardinia for assisting the people of Southern
Italy," *Mr. Punch* ex-
pressed his approbation of
Lord John's pluck and
popular sympathies in the
following lines :—

JOHNNY'S LAST.

Wᴇʟʟ said, Johnny Russell.
That latest despatch
You have sent to Turin is
exactly The Thing.
And again, my dear John, you
come up to the scratch
With a pluck that does credit
to you and the King.

All the Despots have spoken, you justly remark,
Abusing King Victor for blundered and grab,
So you can't suffer Europe to rest in the dark
Regarding the views of our tight little Isle.

Explaining that Naples is clearly as much
Entitled to ask the minisitive she claims,
As England was, then, to make use of the Dutch
To help her extrusion of bigoted James.

You're glad that King Victor had spirit and pluck
To set Bomba Secundus a cutting his stick ;
And you wish the New Italy every good luck—
Well said, Johnny Russell, you write like a Brick.

PUNCH.

RIGHT LEG IN THE BOOT AT LAST.

Garibaldi. " *If it won't go on. Sire, try a little more powder.*"

Nov. 24.

LORD ELGIN had enforced a completion of the Chinese Treaty, which the Celestials again displayed a disposition to shirk. A sum of 3,000 taels was especially appropriated to those who had suffered from Chinese barbarities, and the survivors of those who had succumbed.

(*See Cartoon, "New Elgin Marbles."*)

Nov. 25.

ON this date the Emperor Napoleon issued a decree the effect of which was to permit greater freedom of discussion in the Chambers.

Nov. 27.

THE army of Garibaldi was to-day finally disbanded.

Dec. 1.

KING VICTOR EMMANUEL II. on this day made a public entry into Sicily.

Dec. 1.

"CONSIDERABLE anxiety (says an article of *Mr. Punch's* in the Number bearing this date), "has been of late prevailing in the monetary world, by reason of a little squabble between these highly informal and respected personages, Madame la Banque of France and the Old Lady of Threadneedle Street."

THE MONEY MARKET AND THE FUNNY MARKET.

So far as we can gather, the row arose in consequence of the behaviour of Madame, who, on finding her long purse was getting short of gold, created what is called an artificial run for it. This she partially achieved by laying up in so many bills to London as she could lay her hands on, and sending them over here to be prematurely discounted; an operation that occasioned the Old Lady of Threadneedle Street considerable annoyance, and made her more than usually testy when applied to. Matters were at length indeed brought to such a pass that she tied up her old stocking in which she keeps her gold, and

declared that she'd be "dewered" if she'd send out any more of it; adding, that if her neighbour wanted gold, she ought to mint her rate of discount, and not cross bothering over here and running off with all the gold that she could grab from us. For her part the Old Lady said she wouldn't have demeaned herself by stooping to such practices, and if Madame did not know the proper way to go to work, it was high time that she were taught, and while she was about it, the Old Lady was determined to give her a good lesson.

Madame la Banque of course felt some amazement at this, which she tried her best to hide by affecting indignation. She knew too well, however, that it would not suit her interest to quarrel with the Old Lady, and so she compromised the matter by begging for a loan of two millions of gold to be secured by a deposit of an equal sum in silver, of which it seems that she has plenty stored away in two or three old china teapots in her safe. The request, as is well known, was graciously acceded to; but those behind the scenes are aware there was some

NEW ELGIN MARBLES.

ELGIN TO RUSSIA. "*Come, humbly down! No shooting this time!*"

THE TWO OLD LADIES.

Quoth Madame la Banque, "De l'or qui je manque!
But my notes for discounting I mossu't serve high,
By way of restraining the gold that keeps draining
From strong room and till, till I'm nearly run dry!

"I've funcs here in plenty, but can't loan twenty
Against a Napoleon; so ere I get shorter,

Perforce to my old I must call the Old Lady
Who lives in Threadneedle Street, over the water.

*   *   *   *

So Madame La Banque called a cab off the rank,
And tipping the driver a handsome four-livre
Took the tram, and to Dover from Boulogne steamed away,
In spite of sea-sickness, and other felto noises.

MUTUAL ACCOMMODATION.
MADAME LA BANQUE AND THE OLD LADY OF THREADNEEDLE STREET.

Her courteous stoore'd with a cumbersome load
Of sure five franc pieces, to change for de l'or
In the street of Three-boodle, she hoped to the bodle,
Who sports his red cloak at the Old Lady's door,

He ushered her in to the sanctum within,
Where sat the Old Lady, sedate and serene;
With Punkins eno, Dame La Banque made a curtsey,
That expanded the skirts of her vast Crinoline.

"Chère Madame, if you would—be as kind—so ver' good,
A neighbour to help in a pinch, if you please,"
(Here her silver she tugged from the bag which she lugged,)
"Donnez-moi, chère Madame, English sovereigns for these."

Quoth the Old Lady, "Well—I have bullion to ar'?—
But as for exchanger, they can't well be but,
With Victoria and porter, on our side the water,
On poor L. Napoleon and I'm refluzen.

"And you'll pardon my saying, this game you're been playing
Of laying up gold at a low source can pay—
If your discounts you'll brighten the market you'Brighton,
And we have to beg for help over the way.

"Still, though I can't swop, I agree to a 'pop;'
Take my gold, and in pledge have your silver instead!
And still may we serve our scores in such metal,
Instead of poor Emperor's coin—steel and lead."

Dec. 13.

The health and spirits of the Empress Eugénie (says a Note of Mr. Punch's) "had suffered so much from sorrow for the death of her sister, the Duchess of Alba, that some total relaxation from Court state and complete change of scene were recommended. Her Majesty, with the promptitude that distinguished her earlier days, decided on a visit of the most unceremonious character to England and Scotland. Her Majesty therefore crossed the Channel on the 21st (of November) in the ordinary packet-boat, attended by the Marquess

of La Grange and two
ladies in waiting, and
took first-class tickets for
London. Arrived at
London Bridge the party
engaged the ordinary street
cabs, and drove to Cla-
ridge's Hotel, where they
were fortunate enough to
find apartments disengaged.
. . . After a rapid tour
through Scotland, on the
4th of December the Em-
press was received by Her
Majesty at Windsor Castle,
and arrived in London on
the same day. The Em-
press returned to Paris on
the 13th, greatly improved
in health."

(See Cartoon, "A Friendly
Visit.")

Dec. 18.

Tнɪs dispute between
North and South in
America, concerning the
Slave Trade and other
matters, was now fast verg-
ing to a crisis. Mr. Punch
thought he saw therein

THE BEGINNING OF
SLAVERY'S END.

Thus far shall slavery go, no
    farther :
  That tide must ebb from this
    time forth.
So many righteous Yankees are
    there,
  Who Good and Truth hold
    something worth,
That they remember the immoral
  Throughout the States, on that
    old quarrel
That stands between the South
    and North.

The great Republic is not entire
  So much in half ; the rest is
    tamed.
Most of her sons have not for-
    gotten
  Her own foundation ; holy
    ground !
The better party is the stronger,
  And by the worse will now no
    longer
Brow to be bullied, ruled, and
    banned.

  The nobler people of the nation
    The better sort the more will quard,
  Not cringe to truculent slavedom
    Enforced, with strength of court)eous hand,
  By ruffians, for example, brawling
    In Congress, who knock statesmen sprawling,
  To back slave-call against free land.

Their higher-minded fellow creatures

Of slavery's blaspheming practices,
    That smells taints with small relish,
  To justify the abomination
  That's cherished by their congregation,
    Whose feet those cursing portions lick.

  This is America's decision,
    Awakening, she begins to see
  How justly she brews derision
    Of tyrants, whilst she shames to free :

Then may London Empire grooming,
    Or ground beneath the Papacy.

  Come, South, accept the situation ;
    The change will grow by safe degrees.
  If any talk of separation,
    Hang all such traitors if you please.
  Brook up the Union ? Brothers, never !
  No ; the United States for ever,

A FRIENDLY VISIT.

ENGLAND. "How friendly ! Why don't your Husband call in this quiet way ?"

DEC. 16.

M. DE PERSIGNY, in a circular addressed to the Prefects of the Departments, announced the abolition of the Passport system so far as concerned visitors from this country. The Emperor had decided, he said, " that from the 1st of January next, and by reciprocity, the subjects of the Queen of Great Britain and Ireland coming into France will be admitted to circulate on the territory of the Empire without passports."

(*See Cartoon, " A Sensible Move."*)

DEC. 20.

ON this date South Carolina announced that it seceded from the United States. The election, on the 4th November, of Abraham Lincoln as President had pushed matters to a crisis, and long growing disaffection issued in secession. The Governor and his Executive Council were empowered to issue a proclamation asserting " that this State is, or else has a right to be, a separate sovereign, free, and independent State, and as such has a right to levy war, conclude peace, negotiate treaties, leagues or covenants, and to do all acts whatsoever that rightfully appertain to a free and independent State."

Punch's view of this disastrous division in the Great Republic is well expressed in the following extract from some lines published at the moment of the announcement.

THE STAR-SPANGLED BANNER.

THE Star-spangled banner that blows broad and brave,
O'er the home of the free, o'er the hut of the slave—
Whose stars in the face of no foe e'er waxed pale,
And whose stripes are for those that the mutineers small—

Can it be there are parricide hands that would tear
This star-spangled banner, so broad and so fair?
And if there be hands would such marriage try,
Is the banning too weak the attempt to defy?

Now Heaven guide the same! May Freedom's white hands
Ere too late, from the flag pluck those blood-nursed strands,
And so battle and bruise fling the banner in pawn
That 'tis all her own fabric, so warp as is woof.

If this may not be. If the moment be nigh,
. . . .

To make strong division of brains and of bars,
Let the South have the Stripes and the North have the Stars.

DEC. 24.

ON this day Victor Emmanuel issued decrees formally annexing the Marches, Umbria, Naples and Sicily to his own Italian dominions.

A SENSIBLE MOVE.

EMP. "*There, Monsœur Beef! No more nonsense about Passports. Here's a little key, and come and go when you like!*"

✦1861✦

"THE condition of the manufacturing and agricultural interests" (says *Mr. Punch's Political Summary*) "was apparently sound and satisfactory at the beginning of the year 1861, notwithstanding the Civil War in America, and the deficiency of the harvest at home. The benefits of Free Trade were sensibly felt by the people, a very large importation of grain had been received both from America and Europe, and the cost of the staff of life was thus kept within moderate bounds, and within reach of the poorer classes.

"Home politics were almost stagnant, as the demand for Reform, which had created a temporary excitement at the close of the last year, had subsided, and for a time appeared to be abandoned by mutual consent of all parties."

JAN. 1.

PRINCE FREDERICK WILLIAM IV., King of Prussia, died at Potsdam, and was succeeded by his brother the Regent, Prince William, a sovereign destined to an extraordinary career.

JAN. 9.

MISSISSIPPI seceded from the United States. This example was followed by Alabama on the 11th, Florida on the 11th, Georgia on the 19th, Louisiana on the 28th, Texas on the 1st February, Virginia on the 17th April, Arkansas on the 6th May, Tennessee on the 8th May, and North Carolina on the 20th May.

[*See Cartoon, "Divorce à Vinculo."*]

On the same date (9th January) in his Message to Congress, President Buchanan referred to secession actual and projected as a serious

DIVORCE À VINCULO.

MRS. CAROLINA ASSERTS HER RIGHT TO "LIBRUP" HER NIGGER.

policy requires us still to seek a peaceful solution of the questions at issue between the North and South."

In Charleston Harbour, on the same day, the troops in Fort Sumter fired on the "Star of the West," which came with reinforcements for the batteries. This was the first actual collision

FEB. 4.

THE EMPEROR OF THE FRENCH at the opening of the Chambers said that he had thought it necessary to augment the garrison at Rome when the security of the Holy Father appeared to be menaced; and had despatched his fleet to Gaeta refuge of the King of Naples. "After leaving it there for four months" (he added),"I have withdrawn it, however worthy of sympathy a royal misfortune so nobly supported might appear. The presence of our ships obliged us to infringe every day that principle of neutrality which I had proclaimed, and gave room for erroneous interpretations."

The Emperor had in fact abandoned the King of Naples, and his support of the Pope was regarded as of a very equivocal character.

FEB. 5.

PARLIAMENT was opened by the Queen in person. The Royal Speech made a friendly reference to the American dispute, saying, "My heartfelt wish is that these differences may be susceptible of a satisfactory adjustment." Measures were promised for simplifying Land Transfer, improving the law of bankruptcy and insolvency, and for establishing a uniform system of rating in England and Wales. There was no mention of a Reform Bill,

WHERE'S THE BABY?

an omission upon which Mr. Bright commented severely.

(*See Cartoon*, "*Where's the Baby?*")

FEB. 8.

DELEGATES from the Southern States assembled at Montgomery, Alabama, under the presidency of Mr. Jefferson Davis, to arrange a form of constitution.

FEB. 13.

AFTER a siege which had lasted since the 3rd of the preceding November, the fortress of Gaeta, the last refuge of the King of Naples, surrendered to the Sardinian troops led by Cialdini. On the 18th the new Parliament of Italy met at Turin. "Opportunity matured by time," said Baron Ricasoli, "will open our way to Venetia. In the meantime we think of Rome. This is for the Italians not merely a right, but an honorable necessity. We do not wish

unreasonable, rash, mad attempts—which may endanger our former acquisitions and spoil the national enterprise. We will go to Rome hand in hand with France."

FEB. 18.

JEFFERSON DAVIS, at the assembly of Southern delegates at Montgomery, Alabama, was chosen as President of "the Confederate States," as those States which had seceded from the Union called themselves. "If," said he, "passion or influence the ambition of the North, we must prepare to meet the emergency and maintain by the final arbitrament of the sword the position which we have assumed among the nations of the earth. We have entered upon a career of independence which must be indexibly pursued through many years of controversy with our late associates of the United States."

MARCH 3.

On this day the Czar Alexander issued his memorable decree emancipating the serfs throughout the whole of Russia.

MARCH 4.

Abraham Lincoln, the new President of the United States, this day entered upon his term of office. In his Address he said, "I have no purpose, direct or indirect, to interfere with the institution of Slavery in the States where it exists. I believe I have no lawful right to do so, and I have no inclination to do so." He, however, emphatically declared that "No State can, upon its own mere motion, lawfully get out of the Union: resolves and ordinances to that effect are legally void, and acts of violence within any State or States against the authority of the United States are insurrectionary or revolutionary according to the circumstances."

MARCH 4.

Mr. Gladstone in an eloquent speech in defence of a foreign policy sympathetic with Italian efforts at freedom, denounced the rule of the ex-King of Naples, and said, "The miseries of Italy have been the danger of Europe. The consolidation of Italy, her restoration to national life—if it be the will of God to grant that boom—will be, I believe, a blessing as great to Europe as it is to all the people of the Peninsula. It will add to the general peace and welfare of the civilised

JACK'S "NAVY ESTIMATE."

Mr. Bull. "Come, bless me! What a price I pay for my Navy!"

Jack. "As perhaps, sir 'cause bon't almost d'un fighting' buggers, it's three Trouser buggers."

MARCH 11.

Lord Clarence Paget brought in the Navy Estimates. The money wanted for the Navy was £12,029,475. France, it was declared, was making every effort to bring her naval force up to ours, and Lord Clarence Paget emphasi-

plated vessels similar to the French "La Gloire" and the English "Warrior." This led to a lengthy debate on the comparative advantages of iron and wood warships. The former were now in the earlier stages of a development however to proceed to such marvellous lengths, a development which this debate greatly stimulated.

MARCH 13.

A VOLUME of theological essays entitled "Essays and Reviews," had been lately published, and had created much excitement owing to what was considered the startling heterodoxy of the views it put forth. To-day a large clerical deputation waited upon the Archbishop of Canterbury, urging him to banish the authors of such heresies from the Church. The Archbishop advised them to wait patiently for the conclusive replies which would be forthcoming from the Church.

MARCH 16.

THE DUCHESS OF KENT, mother of the Queen, died this day at Frogmore House, in her 75th year.

THE 'LATEST ARRIVAL.

MARCH 17.

TO-DAY the Italian Parliament declared Victor Emmanuel "King of Italy." Protests were subsequently made in form both by the Pope and the King of Naples. On the 19th the Sardinian Ambassador was recognised by Lord John Russell on behalf of the Queen as "Envoy of Victor Emmanuel II, King of Italy."

[See Cartoon, "The Latest Arrival."]

MARCH 31.

THE remains of Napoleon I. were this day interred in the tomb which had been pre-

APRIL 8.

THE Census of Great Britain and Ireland was taken this (Sunday) evening.

Population at previous Census 1851.

England and Wales	17,927,609
Scotland	2,888,742
Ireland	6,552,385

Population Now.

England and Wales	20,061,725
Scotland	3,061,329
Ireland	5,764,543

The total population of the British Isles was

1851, showing a net increase over the entire kingdom of 6 per cent, and over England and Wales alone of 12 per cent.

In Ireland only the population had diminished since the last decennial enumeration, showing a decrease of 787,842.

APRIL 10.

MR. BAINES proposed to reduce the Borough franchise to £6, but his motion was negatived, a majority of the House voting for "the previous question." The advocates of Parliamentary Reform could, for the moment,

APRIL 13.

The Pope had issued an Allocution in which some of the characteristic features and tendencies of modern civilisation were unreservedly condemned.

(*See Cartoon, "Papal Allocution."*)

MODERN CIVILISATION.

Air—"The Viva of Shop."

His Holiness the Pope of Rome
Has launched an Allocution
At Reform abroad and Reform
at home,
Which he calls Revolution;
He heaps abuse, pronounces
blame,
And deals out condemnation
Heart, without reserve, by
name,
On Modern Civilisation.

For other times than Pontiff sighs,
And groans for other ages,
While he scolds, and screams,
and shrieks, and cries,
And rants, and raves, and
rages,
For the palmy days of Interdict,
And Excommunication,
All which have been to Rome
kicked
By Modern Civilisation.

The Holy Rome will grow too
hot
To hold the Holy Father;
He'll have to seek some other
spot,
To rule and govern, rather;
Jerusalem now looks suggest;
And that's a diversion
Where he would not be much
distrest
By Modern Civilisation.

'Twere better if to Jericho
He went, with all his band,
Or his Cardinals and he might go
Among the Indian Red Men;
The Pope and Conclave could
amass
The native population;
Let them fly to the far Ojibbe-
ways,
From Modern Civilisation.

APRIL 13.

Charleston was this day surrendered by its Federal garrison to the Confederates.

PAPAL ALLOCUTION.—SNUFFING OUT MODERN CIVILISATION.

APRIL 15.

The Chancellor of the Exchequer introduced his Budget. Mr. Punch said:—

"It may suit Mr. Gladstone to take three hours to detail the contents of his Budget, but Mr. Punch has no intention whatever of being so wasteful of words. Here is the Budget:—

"Though the Lords choose to repeat, call, Duty on Paper!
One penny I resent from Income-Tax trickery;
Divers Licenses meanben, not worth your attention;
And, lastly, I double the Duty on Chicory.

"Add that he says he shall have a surplus of £1,911,000 instead of the deficiency which his enemies had been predicting."

The expenditure is estimated at £70,000,000, the income at £71,823,000, this (says "Annals of Our Time") being the largest estimate of revenue ever made.

APRIL 15.

President Lincoln by proclamation called out the Militia of the various States of the Union, amounting altogether to 75,000. On the

14th the Confederate Congress passed an Act empowering the President to borrow fifteen million dollars on the credit of their own States, by the issue of bonds at 8 per cent., the principal and interest being secured by an export duty on cotton of ⅛th of a cent per pound. ("Annals of Our Time.")

APRIL 17.

To-day the breach between North and South was further widened. President Lincoln declared the Southern ports in a state of blockade, and President Davis, on the other hand, issued letters of marque.

(*See Cartoon, "The American Difficulty."*)

MAY 3.

President Lincoln by proclamation called out 42,000 Volunteers to serve the United States, and directed the regular army to be increased by 22,714 officers and men, and the navy by 18,000 seamen. Mr. Secretary Seward, writing to the American Minister at Paris, said, "There is not now, nor has there been, nor will there be, the least idea existing in this Government of suffering a dissolution of the Union to take place in any way whatever.

"There will be here only one nation and one government, and there will be the same Republic and the same constitutional Union that have already survived a dozen national changes, and changes of government in almost every country. These will stand hereafter, as they are now, objects of human wonder and human affection. You have

THE AMERICAN DIFFICULTY.

President Abe. "What a nice White House this would be, if it were not for the Blacks!"

energetically defended it. After a debate extending over several nights it was carried, but only by a majority of 296 to 181.

MAY 8.

LORD JOHN RUSSELL announced to the House of Commons that the law officers of the Crown were of opinion that the Southern Confederacy of America must be recognised as a belligerent Power.

(See Cartoon, "'Cæsar Imperator!' or, The American Gladiators.")

MAY 13.

A PROCLAMATION of Neutrality warning all subjects of the Queen against lending aid of whatever kind to either of the belligerents in the American quarrel was issued by this country on this date.

MAY 15.

GENERAL BUTLER occupied Baltimore with 1,000 men and proclaimed martial law there.

MAY 24.

THE Gorilla was, as *Mr. Punch* called him in a Cartoon, "The Lion" of the season. A book on African Travel by M. de Chaillu (upon the strict accuracy of which doubts had been thrown by Dr. Gray, Keeper of Zoology at the British Museum, and other scientific men,) had drawn attention to the colossal monkey; Professor Owen had lectured upon it at the Royal Institution (on the 14th March), and in fact the Gorilla was just now the talk of the town.

MONKEYANA.

Am I satyr or man?
Pray tell me who can,
And settle my place in the scale.
A man in ape's shape,
An anthropoid ape,
Or monkey deprived of his tail?

The Vestige taught,
That all came from naught
By "development," so called "progressive;"
That insects and worms
Assume higher forms
By modidcation successive.

"CÆSAR IMPERATOR!" OR, THE AMERICAN GLADIATORS.

Then Darwin set forth
In a book of much worth,
The importance of "Nature's selection;"
How the struggle for life
Is a struggle in strife,
And results in "specific distinction."

Let pigeons and doves
Select their own loves,
And grant them a million of ages,

Then doubtless you'll find
They've altered their kind,
And changed into prophets and sages.

Learned Homer relates,
That Biblical dates
The age of the world cannot trace;
That Bible tradition,
By Nile's deposition,
Is put to the right about face.

Then there's Pengelly,
Who erst will tell ye
That he and his colleagues of late
Fossil-eeks and shaped stones
Of contemporaneous date.

Then Prestwich, he prig
With lancet-jaws and refer
All who do now believe his relation,
That the tools he exhumes
From gravelly bottom
Date before the Mosaic creation.

Then Huxley and Owen,
With rivalry glowing,
With pen and ink rush to the scratch;
'Tis Brain versus Brain,
Till one of them's slain;
By Jove! it will be a good match!

Says Owen, you can see
The brain of Chimpanzee
Is always exceedingly small,
With the hindermost
"horn"
Of extremity shorn,
And an "Hippocampus" at all.

The Professor then tells 'em
That man's "cerebellum"
From a vertical point you can't see;
That such "convolutions"
Contains a solution
Of "Anthropophalic" degree.

Then apes have no mens,
And thumbs for great toes,
And a pelvis both narrow and slight;
They can't stand upright,
Unless to show fight
With "Sir Charles," that chivalrous Knight!

Next Huxley replies,
That Owen he lies,
And garbles his Latin quotation;
That his facts are not true,
His mistakes not a few,
Detrimental to his reputation.

"To twice slay the slain,"
By dint of the Brain,
(Thus Huxley concludes this matter)
Is but labour in vain,
Unproductive of gain,
And so I shall bid you "Adieu!"

Zoological Gardens,
May, 1861.   GORILLA.

[See Cartoon, "The Lion of the Season."]

MAY 30.

INSINUATIONS having been made that the action of the Government with respect to the Galway Packet Company's contract had been influenced by a desire to secure the Irish vote on the Budget, Lord Palmerston gave an account of his interview with Father Daly of Galway, who had waited on him to urge the claims of the Company. Seeing that the request to him to receive a deputation of Irish members covered the desire to bring

interested pressure to bear on him, the astute Premier had declined to see any of them.

THE INDIGNATION OF O'MELANIL.
(THROUGH HIS HIMSELF.)

WHAT! Oirishmen yield to the base love o' bribe?
The mighty Miletian be bought and be sould?
No! though Ould England fall thro, when the bason furnush her,
Welsh sweine the bare brutal looks of his sould.

Isn't meself, ye say, offered to vote for the Budget,
If his mane Galway subsidy Pam would renew?
I fling the foul calumny back, where I judge it,
Wid sich—in their throats that are bould the taia threat.

Who dares say that I a'n't to a job showed a brain—
That blush is the white of my deep rollin' eye?
Let the dastard but say't, and, when class of his mania's,
It's meself will be kickin' the ruffian sky-high.

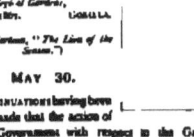

THE LION OF THE SEASON.
ALARMED FLUNKEY. "MR. G-g-g-o-o-o-rilla!"

Would I deny the hand that in
  days of old unsinking
Stood the days of Mac Mur-
  rough and Brian Boru?
Would I scorn the proud head,
  that the shams disdaining,
Hew still bid his love, evils
  and bailiffs, "go to!"

If the purse of the Saxon was
  lyin' afore me,
With its cursed comfort
  showin' brought on the floor,
D'ye suppose that I'd stoop?
  By the mother that bore me,
I'd pass by, wid contempt, and
  lash them as she lore.

When you gave us your help,
  in the hour of our famine,
'To throw thin we dhreuht out
  our hands for your dole;
But the very same months that
  your victuals was crammin'
Was steel tin' a curse on the
  boor Saxon's soul.

And now, if your subsidy Galway
  accepted,
D'ye think 'twas to curry your
  love they said?
No' the money she got, and
  small blame if she kept it,
Though the terrors of contract in Leeping she had.

Was one grand Celtic nature—
  that's pu'they incarnate—
To be held to your best bums
  belum, Saxon bolder?
Go mantle the ocean, your gag
  it will spare o—
Go force the word, that poor
  feither damskm!

JUNE 3.

O^N this day (says *Mr.
Punch's* "Essence"),
"the Paper Duty Abolition
Bill passed the Commons
amid a great cheering from
the Liberals." It had been
strenuously opposed by the
Tories, and was carried by
Mr. Gladstone with much
difficulty. Mr. Disraeli had
proposed that instead of
taking off the Paper Duty,
the duty on tea should
be reduced. "And the
whippers whipped with their
whips, and the members
were gathered together in
tremendous force." Mr. Disraeli had rather hoped—so
at least it was thought—on
this point to put the Government in a minority.
He did not succeed.

(See Cartoon, " A Derby Spill.")

JUNE 6.

"S^{UMMERLY}" (so *Mr. Punch* writes), "and so
human apprehension at an unfortunate

out her liberation expires. After a brief illness,
reported to be terminating favourably, Count
Cavour died this day. The melancholy event
was befittingly alluded to in the House of Lords
by the representatives of all sides in politics."

Count Camillo Benso di Cavour, one of the
greatest of the Italian Liberators, died at Turin

his countrymen and the world, a grief not lessened by the prevailing belief that but for the error
of his physicians in bleeding their patient more
than in his debilitated condition his constitution
could bear, the great and wise champion of his
country's cause might have recovered.

He was succeeded at the head of affairs by

A DERRY SPILL.

JUNE 10.

THE Federals under General Butler were defeated by the Confederates at Big Bethel.

"The American press at this time" (says one of *Mr. Punch's Notes*) "contained some strangely contradictory articles. Whilst one writer blamed England for not assisting the North to crush the South, another repudiated all aid from the Mother Country, and declared any interference on the part of England would be an insult to the United States."

(*See Cartoon, "Naughty Jonathan."*)

JUNE 11.

THE Bill repealing the Paper Tax passed the Lords. Sang *Punch*:—

And joy to every scribbling cuss
Who creates the midnight taper,
On this eleventh day of June
The Lords they danced to Gladstone's tune,
And smashed the Tax on Paper.

NAUGHTY JONATHAN.

"I'm MEAN'T interfere, Mother—as I you ought to be as my wife—and it's a great shame—and I don't care—and you SHALL interfere—and I won't have it.

The Bill received the Royal Assent on the 12th. "Mr. Gladstone" (says *Punch's* "Essence") "immediately burst into song in the character of the Peri:

"Joy, joy for ever, my task is done,
The Bill is passed, and the game is won:
Oh, am I not happy, I am, I am,
To thee, dear Paper, here dark and red
Are the war-taxed Tom from Chesginmgunm.
Or the crystal Sugars from La Trinidad.
Joy, joy for ever, my task is done,

JUNE 23.

THE Emperor Napoleon recognised Victor Emmanuel as King of Italy.

JUNE 25.

THE new Order of the Star of India instituted. It comprised the Sovereign as Grand Master, and twenty-five knights (European and native), exclusive of honorary knights. ("Annals

JUNE 25.

ABDUL-MEDJID Sultan of Turkey, died, aged 38. He was succeeded by his brother Abdul Aziz.

JUNE 29.

THE greatest of English poetesses, Elizabeth Barrett Browning, wife of Robert Browning, a woman of fine genius and lofty character, died this day at the Casa Guidi,

JUNE 30.

On this night suddenly appeared in the heavens an extremely brilliant comet, which remained visible for some time and attracted much attention.

JULY 10.

The *Times* of this date said, "The Emperor puts down the Slave trade carried on on the coast of Africa by French agents under the pretext of hiring and service."

(*See Cartoon,* "*Cæsar et Imperator.*")

JULY 20.

The Congress of the Confederate States met this day at Richmond, which had been chosen as the capital of the new Confederacy. On the next day was fought the Battle of Bull's Run, otherwise called Manassas Junction, the first important engagement of the war. The Federals were defeated and fled pell-mell to Washington. The cowardly conduct of the Northern troops on this occasion naturally exposed their side to much derision, which subsequent events however proved to be but little deserved.

THE RUN FROM MANASSAS JUNCTION.

Yankee Doodle went to war,
On his little pony,
What did he go fighting for,
Everlasting gawry!
Yankee Doodle was a chap
Who bragged and swore terrible,
He stuck a feather in his cap,
And called it Federalism.
    Yankee Doodle, &c.

Yankee Doodle, in sworn forth
To conquer the Secedors,
All the journals of the North,
In most tremenduous bunkers,
Breathing slaughter, fire, and smoke,
Especially the latter,
    His rage and fury to provoke,
    And vanity to flatter.
        Yankee Doodle, &c.

Yankee Doodle, having flavored
His reiterated bauthers,
He reckoned, his victories crowned
Would turn against no others.

And afterwards, from Britain's crown,
The Canada would wrest.
    Yankee Doodle, &c.

England offering neutral sauce,
To gunas as well as gander,
Was what made Yankee Doodle cross,
And did inflame his dander.
As though with shorter sword, he found,

Senator Old England had presumed
To stem a course imperial,
    Yankee Doodle, &c.

Yankee Doodle bore in mind,
When warfare England harassed,
How he unblushingly, and unkind,
Beset her, and embarrassed;

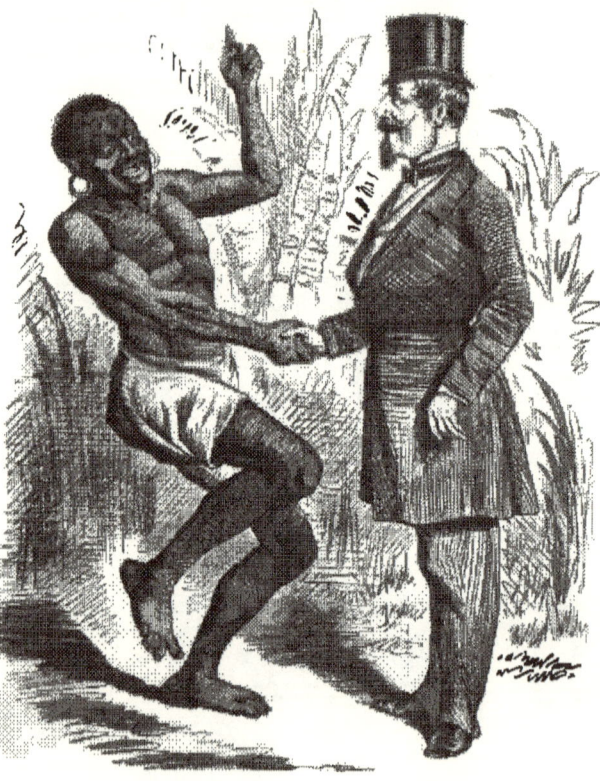

CÆSAR ET IMPERATOR.

"*Ah, Massa Napoleon! You alʼays was de Friend ob Freedom—Now you am a Man and a Bruder.*"

Most earn this trouble with a latter
Vindictern revolution.
  Yankee Doodle, &c.

We be North and South alike
  Entertain affection :
These for negro Slavery strike :
  These for forced Protection.
Yankee Doodle is the Pot :
  Southerner the Kettle :

Equal mostly, if not
  Men of equal mettle.
    Yankee Doodle, &c.

Yankee Doodle, near Bull's Run,
  Met his adversary :
First he thought the fight he'd won,
  Feet proved quite contrary.
Panic struck he fled, with speed
  Of lightning glib with marrтом

Of slippery grease, in full stampede,
  From famed Manassas junction.
    Yankee Doodle, &c.

As he looked, no ways slow,
  Yankee Doodle blubbered
"We are whipped !" and fled, although
  No enemy followed.
Nerved and gun right shirk he threw
  Both away together.

HOW THEY WENT TO TAKE CANADA.

"*For the Outrage offered on the Queen's Proclamation, the United States will possess itself of Canada.*"—"*New York Herald.*"

In his cap, to public view,
  Showing the white feather.
    Yankee Doodle, &c.

Yankee Doodle, Doodle, Do,
  Whither are you flying,
"A cursed hot we've been licked too
  And knocked to Hades," crying?
Well, to Canada, fit-см,
  Now that, by Secession,
I am driven up a tree,
  To seize that three possession.
    Yankee Doodle, &c.

Yankee Doodle, be content,
  You've had a lenient whipping :
Court and further punishment
  By transporter of scalpping
These neighbours, whom if you would.
  They'll surely whip you hollow :
Meantime, whom you've turned your tail,
  Won't hesitate to follow.
    Yankee Doodle, &c.

The Federals on this occasion lost 462 men
and 19 officers, 947 men and 64 officers being

wounded. The Confederate loss, on the contrary, was comparatively slight. When the flying Federals appeared in the streets of Washington, grave fears were entertained for the
safety of that city. There had been some wild
talk at the time of America's intention to seize
Canada.

(See Cartoon, "How they went to take Canada.")

JULY 24.

Lord John Russell, who had been elevated to the House of Lords as Earl Russell, gave up his seat for the City of London, and delivered a parting address to the electors.

(See Cartoon, "Retiring into Private Life.")

JOHN RUSSELL, EARL LUDLOW.

Air—"John Anderson, my Jan."

John Russell, Earl Ludlow, John,
When we were first acquaint,
You would have entered the harem
On which you now are bent.
But times are s80 times changed, John,
From thirty years ago,

Then from the Lord John came I knew
Will be the Earl Ludlow.

John Russell, Earl Ludlow, John,
We cried " Reform " together ;
But Reformers now-a-days, John,
Have all chopped on the tether :
The Big Reform Bill pass'd, John,
The Small one proved No Go ;

RETIRING INTO PRIVATE LIFE.

And you can boast a bard in both,
When you are Earl Ludlow.

John Russell, Earl Ludlow, John,
A gallant course you've fared,
spiks of letters, now and then, John,
That had kept better spared,
The British Constitution——, John,
You've talked out long ago ;
You'll drop your common places,
I hope, as Earl Ludlow.

John Russell, Earl Ludlow, John,
I can't refrain a groan,
Contrasting your new sphere, John,

The House of Lords I fear, John,
You'll find uncommon slow,
And for the Commons, gipsy-like,
You'll sigh, when Earl Ludlow.

John Russell, Earl Ludlow, John,
You'll miss that field of fight,
Where each day brought its combat,
Its struggle every night.
At night your business done, John,
Home from the Pees you'd go,
And, like Pat, "for want of baiting,"
You'll sneak, my Earl Ludlow.

John Russell, Earl Ludlow, John,

Who to put on Peer's ermine
Laid down their earlier honor—
Of Chathams, Holland, Palmay—
Whose ghosts in warning row,
Within the House of Lords, John,
Wring hands o'er Earl Ludlow !

AUG. 3.

Victor Emanuel had recently ceded Savoy to France, and it was now rumoured that

expressed his opinion upon the projected plan, which however was never carried out.

(See Cartoon, " Above that sort of thing.")

ROCK AGAIN!

(*An old Story newly applied, apropos of a late Debate in the House of Commons and a late Communiqué in the Patrie.*)

ONCE on a time, in Kilda's Isle,
Where Nature seldom deigns a smile
To ripen aught that grows,
Where hoods of kail are precious things,
And gooseberries devoted fruit for kings,
And thistle stands for rose,

ABOVE THAT SORT OF THING!

AUG. 6.

PARLIAMENT was prorogued by Commission.
Mr. Punch thus summarises the Royal
Speech:—

MY LORDS AND GENTLEMEN,
                    The Session done,
You have your Queen's true leave to cut and run :

For services, from all degrees and ranks,
Your Sovereign tenders you her heartiest thanks.
With foreign Powers she's on good terms, just now,
And trusts there'll be no European row,
Italia has started on anew
Under King Victor's sway. May all go right !
In Turkeydom is raised the tunble-cry :
We mean to put no finger in that pie.

The Powers have quashed that horrid Syrian riot,
Withdrawn their troops, and hope for peace and quiet.

India's improving hugely, and expresses
Hope to be lifted from financial messes.

BELOVED COMMONS,
                    Thankfully is noted
The willingness with which the Tin was voted.

"DOTH NOT A MEETING LIKE THIS MAKE AMENDS!"

HER MAJESTY THE QUEEN. "My dear Ireland, how much better you look since my last visit. I am so glad!"

MY LORDS AND GENTLEMEN,
                    The Queen trusts
The noble spirit of the Volunteers.

Gladly she wills the measure that effects
The forfeit wages of two most wicked sports.

Gladly she wills the Bill (my Bill) that deals
Justice where now the Bankrupt Harpy steals.

And gladly welcomes (are before ye drew)
Consolidation of the Law of Crime.

Henceforth, the ladies with well-trained mind
May serve his Sovereign in the East, he'll find.

You've trusted properly, the Queen is sure,
Harbours ; and Sea Tolls ; and the Settled Poor.

Not one like you unearthed the stifling fact
That you have passed a decent Drainage Act.

Pleased, she beholds throughout her wide domain
Order, contentment, and obedience reign.

Now to your Commons. Do your duties there.

(*The Speech concluded with the usual prayer.*)

AUG. 21.

THE QUEEN, Prince Albert, the Prince of
Wales and Prince Alfred paid another—
their third—visit to Ireland, landing at Kings-
town on this day. The Royal party were enthusiastically welcomed wherever they went.

(*See* CARTOON, *"Doth not a Meeting like this make
Amends ?"*)

AUG. 27.

LORD PALMERSTON was this day installed at Dover as Warden of the Cinque Ports. In his address he spoke very characteristically. "The security for peace" (he said) "arising from a perfect state of defence unconnected with any notion of aggression, not coupled with hostility towards any one, but confined solely to a manly determination to protect and maintain what we have, is a security which I trust this country will long continue to possess." *Punch* addressed to him the following complimentary verses on the occasion:—

PAM UPON THE HEIGHTS.

[After Aytoun Townson.]

Not old, stood Pam upon the Heights,
The Commons meeting at his feet,
And Bumbledom, with antique rites,
Did him the homage meet.

Punch, in his place, did much rejoice,
Not for the title then assigned,
But glad to hear the brave old boy's
Name shouted on the wind.

Admiring much his British pluck,
His sturdy tongue, his cheery jest,
His never dawning on his luck,
But keeping for the best.

His hate of humbug, saving such
As should to humbugs still be flung,
His speeches, void of mortal touch,
Yet racing English tongues.

His deeper hatred for the gang,
Who, praising of our Right Divine,
Down freedom's friends to starve, or hang,
Or in foul dungeons pine.

Three for the Constable! Our foes
Find him the nightmare of their dreams!
We, the wise Englishmen, who know
The Falsehood of Extremes.

SEPT. 16.

A PAMPHLET was published, written by Father Passaglia, against the maintenance of the temporal power of the Church of Rome, which he said was no longer expedient, and had now become a source of dissension and irreligion in Italy. The Italians and their stout-hearted King were quite ready to strike a further blow for its total abolition, but the Emperor of France, with whom Victor Emmanuel had declared his intention to act, hung back and delayed, to the considerable disgust of the more ardent friends of freedom.

THE GERMAN FLEET.

Mr. Punch (to small German). "There's a Ship for you, my little Man—now cut away, and don't get in a mess."

OCT. 1.

AT this time the Germans were developing a strong desire for the possession of a Fleet, with the view of becoming an important Naval Power. Their aspirations in this direction were then pretty generally ridiculed.

[See Cartoon, "The German Fleet."]

OCT. 6.

On this day took place at Compiègne a meeting between the Emperor Napoleon and the new King of Prussia, William I. The latter was crowned at Königsberg a few days later, on the 18th October. The Compiègne meeting greatly excited the curiosity of the political quidnuncs.

(*See Cartoon, "The Cover-side at Compiègne."*)

THE CHANT OF COMPIÈGNE.

(*With a Fashionable Burden.*)

There's a drowsy cove at the Tuileries,
But at President's to throw a care :

And Louis is not more anxious to do,
Than William not to be done.
As the Baden Conference proved a sell,
Let's try what Compiègne will do :
With dinner and dance, with pic-nic and play,
The Germans won't come to !
So we'll rogue the trick, and we'll harass the week,
But the fly only says, says he,

THE COVER-SIDE AT COMPIÈGNE.

King of Prussia. "I'm a young man from the country. But you don't come over me !"

" ' I'm a young man from the
country,
For you don't come over me !'

" Your hon'rable intentions all
With gratitude I hail ;
But promises to pay are not
Quite payments on the nail.
If financiers stand be terrified,
And trustees overburdened,
Suppose we dropped our *little*
Me,
And had a Congress called ?
But as things stand between us
two !
Ah ! I say is, d'ye see, —
" ' I'm a young man from the
country,
But you don't come over me !'

" If you have frontiers to round,
I've frontiers to maintain ;
Without my loss I don't quite see
How I can help your gain.
My German wits they may be
dull,
And yours are sharp, I know ;
But if upon our ropes we pull,
I fear you might let go ;
Then level o'er limb where I was
buried,
No more my song would be,
" ' I'm a young man from the
country,
But you can't come over me !' "

Oct. 21.

ON this day the Northern
army suffered another
reverse, the Federals under
General M'Clellan being
defeated by the Confede-
rates at Ball's Bluff.

Oct. 25.

SIR JAMES GRAHAM died
at Netherby, at the
age of 64.

Nov. 2.

THE blockade of the Con-
federate ports having
very greatly diminished the
supply of cotton to this
country, distress was already
beginning to make itself
felt in Lancashire, a distress which a little later
was to assume the serious
shape of a national afflic-
tion. *Mr. Punch* thus early
called attention to the danger in the following lines :—

KING COTTON BOUND; OR, THE MODERN PROMETHEUS.

(*See Cartoon,* " *King Cotton Bound.*")

KING COTTON BOUND; OR, THE NEW
PROMETHEUS.

FAR across Atlantic waters
Groans in chains a Great King ;

Needs but Fancy's pencil plume
Fresh to paint till both agree ;
For King Cotton is a giant,
As Prometheus claimed to be.
Each give blessings unto men,
Each disburnest reaped again.

Should be equal honour claim ?
You and life to millions giving,
That, without him, had no living.

And if they are one in blessing,
So in suffering they are one ;

LOOK OUT FOR SQUALLS.

JOHN BULL. "You do what's right, my Son, or I'll blow you out o' the water."

Nov. 8.

ON this day Messrs. Slidell and Mason, with two other gentlemen, Commissioners despatched by the Confederate States to Europe, Mr. Slidell being bound for France and Mr. Mason for England, were forcibly seized on board the packet-ship "Trent," belonging to the British Mail Steamship Company, by Captain Wilkes, commander of the United States war steamer "San Jacinto."

This was held to be a breach of international law, and the British Government demanded the liberation of the Commissioners.

(See Cartoon, "Look out for Squalls," page 41.)

The incident created much excitement in this country, war preparations were vigorously commenced and troops were despatched to Canada, where also the militia and volunteers were promptly and spontaneously called out by the Colony.

(See Cartoon, "Waiting for an Answer.")

WAITING FOR AN ANSWER.

BRITANNIA waits on power.
　Sad and stern,
Her weapons ready, but un-
　sheathed they lie :
In her deep eye, suppressed, the
　lightnings burn,
Still the war-signal waits her
　word to fly.

Wrong has been done that they
　whose stainless folds
Have carried freedom where-
　soe'er they flew :
She knows sharp words to slaves
　and shrewish scolds,
She but bids those who can,
　that wrong undo !

She that bears patient ; will be
　patient still,
Who more than she knows
　war, in curse and woe ?
Harsh words, poor courtesy,
　hard-mouthed ill-will
She meets, as rocks meet
　ocean's fretful flow.

All that she knows drags honors in its train,
Whate'er the foes, the cause for which they stand ;
But worst of all the war, that leaves the stain
Of brother's blood upon a brother's hand.

The war that brings two mighty Powers to shock,
Powers, 'twere when late Commerce shared her crown :
By kinship knit, and interest's golden lock,
One blood, one speech, one past, of old renown.

All this she feels, and therefore, and of cheer,
She waits an answer from across the sea ;
Yet loath her sadness to allay of fear,
No thought to count the cost, what it may be.

Dishonour lack an equipoise in gold,
No equipoise in blood, in loss, in pain :
Till they whose force has ta'en from 'neath the fold
Of her proud flag, stand 'neath its fold, again

She waits in arms ; and in her cause is safe ;
Not fearing war, yet hoping peace the end,
Not hurrying those her sword who'd check or chafe ;
THE RIGHT SHE SEEKS : THE RIGHT GOD WILL DEFEND !

After some little delay, however, our demands were yielded to by the United States authorities. The four Commissioners were placed on board a ship-of-war and arrived in this country in January. The American Congress nevertheless passed a vote of thanks to Captain Wilkes for his action in the matter.

Nov. 30.

MR. JEFFERSON DAVIS was elected President of the Confederate States for a term of six years.

DEC. 2.

PRESIDENT LINCOLN opened the Congress of the United States. He spoke of the Federal reverses at Bull's Run and other places as "the natural consequences of the premature advance of our brave but undisciplined troops which the impatience of the country demanded."

DEC. 14.

ON this day, after a brief illness, to the great distress of the Queen and to the surprise and sorrow of the country, died the Prince Consort. A feverish attack from which at first no serious results had been anticipated, rapidly developed to a critical stage, and a failure of vital power in the Prince prevented the possibility of rallying. He died at Windsor Castle at ten minutes before 11 P.M., at the comparatively early age of 42.

The Queen, who was deeply devoted to her husband, felt the most passionate grief at her sudden and unlooked-for bereavement, which however she bore with exemplary fortitude, though it saddened her life and cast a shadow over many future years of her now lonely reign. The country, which had learned to appreciate more fully than at first the fine character and sound intelligence of this accomplished Prince, sincerely mourned his demise, and earnestly sympathised with the widowed Queen in her great sorrow for an irreparable loss.

DEC. 19.

WHEN the peremptory demand for the surrender of Messrs. Mason and Slidell

COLUMBIA'S FIX.

COLUMBIA. "Which answer shall I send?"

reached America there was some hesitation in acceding to it, and for some weeks the tone of the American Press (says *Mr. Punch's* Summary) was so hostile that the most energetic preparations were made by the English Government.

(*See Cartoon, "Columbia's Fix."*)

DEC. 23.

ON this day the remains of the Prince Consort were interred in St. George's Chapel, Windsor. The ceremony was not a public one, but the people marked their sense of the occasion by a very general cessation of business and wearing of mourning.

Thus gloomily closed the year 1861.

✦1862✦

THE year opened with anticipations of trouble. What became known as the Cotton Famine was imminent, owing to the blockade of the Confederate Ports, by which the supply of cotton to this country from America was so greatly lessened as to throw increasing numbers of the operatives engaged in that industry in Lancashire out of work. On the 3rd of January meetings were held at Blackburn, Preston, Wigan, and other towns to consider measures of relief.

JAN. 8.

THE "Europa," which had arrived off Queenstown on the 6th, and had now reached London, brought the welcome news that the American Government had determined on the release of Messrs. Slidell and Mason. The two Commissioners were subsequently set at liberty, and arrived in this country on the 19th January.

(See Cartoon, "Up a Tree.")

JAN. 16.

ON this day occurred the memorable Hartley Colliery accident. Owing to the snapping of a beam the whole of the pumping apparatus, weighing upwards of twenty tons, fell down the shaft, cutting off all communication with the workmen, to the number of over 200, engaged in the shaft and cuttings. For seven days and nights would-be rescuers worked, labouring strenuously to get at the imprisoned victims. When they were reached, on the 22nd, they were all found lying in rows, as though asleep, men and boys, some resting on and embracing each other, but all dead, suffocated by the foul accumulation known as a "stythe." Memoranda and messages scratched on planks, etc., showed that they had met their lingering fate manfully, with patience and prayer. It was a touching sight, a pitiful story, and the whole country from the Queen downwards was moved to sympathy and to practical aid. Scarcely a cottage in the hamlet but had its dead—some had lost several, some all the males of their family, men and boys, fathers, brothers, sons, at one fell swoop. A public subscription on behalf of the survivors was raised, and reached the amount of £61,000. *Mr. Punch* said:—

"UP A TREE." COLONEL BULL AND THE YANKEE 'COON.

'Coon. "Air you in arnest, Colonel?"   *Colonel Bull. "I am."*   *'Coon. "Don't fire—I'll come down."*

ONLY ONE WORD.

Thorns and Survivors! Make them Miners too,
To work through his a gold mine oped by you.

JAN. 18.

THE new Legislative Council for India held its first meeting on this date.

JAN. 25.

The inquiry instituted to ascertain the mental competency of William Frederick Windham, of Felbrig Hall, Norfolk, to manage his own affairs had been opened in the Court of Exchequer on the 16th Dec., 1861, and did not close until the 30th Jan. following, thirty-four of the intervening days having been occupied by the inquiries, upwards of 150 witnesses having been examined, and almost all the leading talent of the English Bar having been heard in support of the various interests involved in the investigation. The costs amounted to something like £20,000. Windham was found capable of managing his own affairs, though his conduct was that of a great fool. He died 2nd Feb., 1866, aged 29. (Note to Vol. XLII.)

[See Cartoon, "Law and Lunacy."]

LAW AND LUNACY; OR, A GLORIOUS OYSTER SEASON FOR THE LAWYERS.

JAN. 30.

Achille Fould, who had, on the 14th November, 1861, been appointed Minister of Finance by the Emperor Napoleon, had recommended retrenchment.

"PULLING UP IN TIME."

There was a little man,
And he had a little gun,
And he spent too much on powder and on lead, lead, lead;
And the constable so far
Ottawa for ships of war,
And soldiers, that upset dry his purse he bled, bled, bled.

Then his neighbours all began
To abuse this little man,
For a nuisance and a mischief and a pest, pest, pest;
And his tenants they all swore
They would mend the screw no more,
And "L'Empire c'est la paix" was taught but jest, jest, jest.

Till at last this little man,
Not a bit too soon, began
His in-comings and out-goings to o'erhaul, haul, haul;
And this truth he did perceive,
Those who spend ere they receive,
Will wind up with no revenue at all, all, all.

Then he summoned Monsieur Fould,
An Israelite well schooled
In Dabies and in Creditor accounts, 'counts, 'counts;
And he said, "Pray let me know
Exactly what I owe;   ['counts?"
I'm afraid to something knavish it amounts, 'mounts,

Monsieur Fould went through his books,
With extremely serious looks,
And a long face at the balance-sheet did pull, pull, pull;
"Forty millions, Sir," said he,
"As far as I can see,
Is the sum to pour discredit, stamp full, full, full.

"There's the funded debt beside,
But o'er that a man can ride,

As witness Mr. Bull, across the way, waj, wayi ;
But you sadly ought to get
Rid of all this deseeing debt,
And pull up if you ever mean to pay, pay, pay."

"Oh, dear, it costs a wrench,
One's expenses to retrench !"
The little man exclaimed with a tear, tear, tear :

"But if I must, I must ;
So I'll e'en down with the dust,   [rust,
Which in Europe I've kicked up this many a year, rust,

"I'll give up my drums and mobs,
And my military toys,
I'll do with fewer soldiers, ships and guns, guns, guns ;
And I'll buy a nice new tax.

On my loving subjects' backs,   [down, down,
And 'twixt two screws, up and down, pay off my debts,

"Wars and war-leagues I'll cease,
Take to trade and arts of Peace,
So a moral, mild and quiet little nation, nation, nation ;
Till even Mr. Bull
Gives me confidence as full
As beloved 'Le Vol de l'Aigle' first began, 'gun, 'gun."

THE HOLIDAY TASK.

Dr. Punch (Head Master). "I am much pleased, my dear young friends, that you have employed the vacation to such good purpose!"

FEB. 6.

PARLIAMENT was opened by Commission. The Royal Speech of course made reference to the death of the Prince Consort, and expressed the consolation Her Majesty had experienced under her irreparable loss in the sympathy of her people with her great sorrow. Eloquent expression to the sympathy of Parliament was given by the Earl of Derby, Earl Granville, Lord Russell, Mr. Disraeli and Lord Palmerston.

Concerning the rest of the Speech Mr. Punch...

Lord Westbury informed us, That we are at peace with all European Powers and "trust" to remain in that pacific condition.

That we have had a "question" between us and the United States, which has been satisfactorily settled by the restoration of the mischief-makers and the disavowal of the "act of violence,"

That the conduct of our North American colonists on this occasion had been admirable.

That we have entered into a conversation with France and Spain for regulating a combined operation on the coast of Mexico, in order to obtain redress for wrongs upon foreigners in that country.

That the Chinese are behaving very well, and do not want so much looking after as heretofore.

Morocco to pay his debt to Spain, and we could more fighting with the Infidelious Spaniards.

That the Estimates, &c. &c. &c.

That some Law reforms will be introduced, especially one for rehearsing that which the wise call Conveyancing, though Shakspeare mentions a shorter means for it.

That, despite local discord from temporary causes, the general condition of the country is "sound and satisfactory."

Briefer speech was never spoken, and it is only to be hoped—certainly not to be believed—that such brevity will be the characteristic of the speeches which will throng the next six months with the tidings of stories of Parliament.

(See Cartoon, "The Holiday Task.")

FEB. 6.

THE PRINCE OF WALES started on a tour in the East, in the course of which he visited Egypt and the Pyramids and Jerusalem, spent several weeks in Syria, and returned through Smyrna, Constantinople and Athens, &c. He travelled as Baron Renfrew, and was accompanied amongst others by General Bruce and the Rev. A. P. Stanley, afterwards the celebrated and beloved "Dean Stanley."

MARCH 1.

THE Pythoness at the Zoological Gardens had at this time laid about 100 eggs which she was incubating, but which were ultimately all addled in consequence of the creature

THE PARLIAMENTARY PYTHON.

leaving them whilst casting her skin. *Mr. Punch* applied the incident to Parliamentary prospects.

[*See Cartoon, "The Parliamentary Python."*]

MARCH 1.

LORD ELGIN, who had been appointed Governor-General of India, in place of Earl Canning retired, reached Calcutta. He was installed on the 12th, and Earl Canning left for England soon after.

MARCH 6.

ON this day the "Merrimac" (a vessel originally belonging to the United States, but which had been seized by the Confederates and afterwards named the "Virginia") attacked the Federal squadron in the Hampton Roads, sunk the "Cumberland," burnt the "Congress," disabled the "Minnesota" and drove her ashore, and drove the "St. Lawrence" and "Roanoke" to take shelter under the guns of Fortress Monroe. On the next day the Federal iron-clad "Monitor" attacked the "Virginia" (or "Merrimac"), but the engagement was short and indecisive.

MARCH 12.

ANNOUNCEMENT was made by Mr. George Peabody, a wealthy American merchant resident in London, that he intended to make over a gift of £100,000 to be applied "to such purposes as may be calculated directly to ameliorate the condition and augment the comforts of the poor who, either by birth or established residence, form a recognised portion of the population of London." Mr. Peabody, without

finding the discretion of the trustees, suggested
that "at least a portion of the fund might be
applied to the construction of such improved
dwellings for the poor as would combine in
the utmost possible degree the essentials of
healthfulness, comfort, social enjoyment and
economy."

APRIL 3.

"G̲ᴇᴇɴ" (says *Mr. Punch's* "Essence of
Parliament") "came the Budget for 1862.
"Its features are mild, not to say inexpressive,
and when Mr. Gladstone, after talking pleasantly
through three columns, came to the statement

that the probable revenue for next year would
be £70,190,000, against an expenditure of
£70,040,000, the Commons began, as he said,
to hear. However, he explained everything to
the hearers :—

First. There are to be no new Taxes at present.
Secondly. Our financial condition is healthy.

THE "BRITISH TAR" OF THE FUTURE.

Thirdly. French commerce is approaching when
Navarino, and that greatest of petty Ministers, Mr. Pitt,
intended it should be.

Fourthly. We must shut the wine ducks à Turtle,
making two classes instead of four. (N.B. No fear lest
the purchasers should handle by this.—P.)

Fifthly. There can be no remission of taxes now.

Sixthly. Yet the duty on playing cards must be reduced
from one shilling to threepence, because the present
duty is evaded.

Seventhly. We can lay on a Scottish probate duty.

Eighthly. We can lay on an eighth per cent. on public
loans.

Ninthly. We can grant little licenses to sell drink at Fairs.

Tenthly. We must uphold the Spirit duties.

Eleventhly. We will consider the Hop duties—the
Grower shall not pay them, and the Brewer shall.

Twelfthly. Everybody who leaves twenty his seat is
under £100 must take out a License, price twelve and
sixpence.

Thirteenthly. Our National expenditure is not increasing
but diminishing.

Fourteenthly. But if you want relaxation in taxation,
you must Economise.

APRIL 4.

"G̲ᴏᴠᴇʀɴᴍᴇɴᴛ" (says "Essence of Parliament") "have been fairly worked up at
least upon the subject of the ships, and a rumour
that got about, we have no idea how, that Mr.
Punch intended to make a demonstration upon

the subject in the shape of a marvellous Cartoon
representing Jack in Iron finally decided the
Premier's course. . . . . Then Pam, choosing
the right moment, as he always does, rose and
declared that Government were intensely alive
to the importance of the subject ; that Captain
Cowper Coles's cupola was a capital contrivance ;
that the forts would be suspended, and the float-
ing defences should be taken in hand. . . . So
on the whole *Mr. Punch* thinks himself justified
in closing the chronicle of the present work with
the remark ' Hooray ! ' "

(See Cartoon, " The ' British Tar ' of the Future.")

APRIL 16.

PRESIDENT DAVIS issued a conscription calling to arms all men between the ages of 18 and 45.

The question of Slavery as between the North and South was coming every day more to the front. On the 4th April the "domestic institution" had been abolished in the district of Columbia. On the 7th was signed what was known as the Seward-Lyons Treaty between Great Britain and the United States for the suppression of the Slave trade. It was ratified on the 20th May. As Mr. Punch's "Essence of Parliament" for 8th May said, "Mr. Layard informed the Commons that King Abraham Lincoln had concluded a new treaty with Queen Victoria for the suppression of the Slave Trade, and that such treaty was really valuable, because it gave us the right of search. The Union Flag is no longer to be hoisted to save the slaver

From the dread English cruiser's shattering guns."

Virginia (which was a chief seat of the war, and into which General McClellan had advanced on the 5th April, with the view of taking Richmond, and besieging Yorktown which was held by 50,000 Confederates) was vehemently opposed to the abolition of slavery.

(See Cartoon, " Oberon and Titania.")

APRIL 24.

ON this day New Orleans surrendered to the Federal fleet commanded by Admiral Farragut. General Butler occupied the city on the 26th, and issued a proclamation declaring that women who expressed any contempt for his troops should be treated as prostitutes plying their vocation.

"The infamous proclamation of General Butler at New Orleans" (says Mr. Punch's

OBERON AND TITANIA.

OBERON (MR. PRESIDENT LINCOLN). "I do but beg a little Negro Boy, To be my Henchman."

TITANIA (MRS. ENGLAND). . . . "Set your heart at rest, The Northern Land buys not the Child of me."

who showed any disrespect towards the flag of the United States, furnished occasion for comments in Parliament, and Lord Palmerston declared that no man could read this infamous proclamation without a feeling of the deepest indignation. Englishmen must blush to think that it came from a man of the Anglo-Saxon

himself to the rank of a General, but he was of opinion that any interference of England in the affairs of America would only serve to aggravate the sufferings of those now enduring privations in consequence of the war in their country."

The conduct of General Butler greatly prejudiced the Federal cause in the minds of

MAY 1.

On this day was opened by the Duke of Cambridge, representing Her Majesty, the second of the International Exhibitions—this time at Brompton. The design by Captain Fowke was far less graceful and fairy-like than that of the memorable Paxton-designed "Crystal Palace" of a decade before; but the Exhibition itself was a grand one, and attracted large crowds until its close at the end of October. It was visited altogether by 6,117,450 people, only 50,000 less than the number attracted to the Great Exhibition of 1851. Of foreign visitors to this there were 16,456, as compared with 6,566 in 1851.

(See Cartoon, " The May-day Present.")

OUR ANCHOR AT THE EXHIBITION.

A Kindred War, an Italian Motley
By strong arm, fire, and crushing usurl apparent,
The fight for Freedom waged in Italy,
Which Austria's Volume partly dispossessed,
And now America's inhuman strife,
Brothers with brothers warring in the halls,

THE MAY-DAY PRESENT.

Mrs. Britannia, "Oh, thank you, Mr. Bull, very much! I can't think it quite so pretty as the one you gave me eleven years ago."
Mr. Bull, "Ha! Perhaps not, dear Madam—but you should see yourself!"

These horrors, following on our first World's Fair,
When sanguine prophets bade us to prepare
For the Millennium's near approaching edge,
Forbid us to prophet the like again;

No tale of Universal Brotherhood,
To date from this, our annual vast Work-Show!
Far evil still divides this world with good.
As when Cain murdered Abel long ago.
Nay, rather come, ye Nations, and behold
Our shattered truest mistrust unfolded.

From their impression on our Fellow-men.
Yet did we fail so meanly below,
As Earth of violence full, would meet to try?
Much misery and blood might have been more;
We still have tried to lead the brutes away.
Of peaceful toil the fruit if we have lost,
What from below is safe from blight and frost?
Our little efforts meet at village stop;
We plough, sow, irrigate—implore the crop,
At last the needful aid we may obtain.

MAY 11.

The Confederates, having been repulsed at Williamsburg, and having surrendered their naval depôts at Norfolk, Virginia, blew up and burnt their iron-clad "Merrimac" to prevent her capture by the Federals.

MAY 24.

MAY 24.

THE Federals, after many reverses, had, by the capture of New Orleans, and some other successes, somewhat redeemed their character, and revived the spirits of their sympathisers.

(See Cartoon, "The New Orleans Plum.")

MAY 26.

HENRY BUCKLE, author of that remarkable work the "Introduction to the History of Civilisation in England," died at Damascus, aged 40, leaving his colossal undertaking incomplete.

JUNE 2.

AT Lord Derby's home, St. James's Square, was this day held a meeting of the Opposition. Mr. Stansfeld, the Radical Member for Halifax, had made a Retrenchment Motion. Lord Palmerston "had met the tactics of his antagonists by giving notice of an amendment to Mr. Stansfeld's economy resolution. . . . . The Tories then sought to trump Pam's card by another amendment. They wanted to damage and discredit the Government, but by no means to force Pam to extremities." Mr. Walpole was selected to move this amendment. "There was a gathering of some hundred and eighty-six Delegates in St. James's Square, and they agreed to support Mr. Walpole." On the 3rd "as soon as the deck was cleared for action, the Premier rose, and with a mischievous glance at the Opposition ranks, calmly intimated that inasmuch as Mr. Walpole's amendment, if carried, would be equivalent to a vote of Want of Confidence in the Government, the best thing would be to throw over other questions and fight out the battle on the real point between parties. Then Lord Palmerston sat down.

When this was said, no Congreve rocket Discharged into the Gallic trenches,

E'er appalled the trembresome shock It Produced upon the Tory benches,

Mr. Walpole withdrew his amendment. Mr. Stansfeld's was rejected by 367 to 65. Mr. Disraeli described Mr. Walpole (it was the eve of the Derby) as "a Derby favourite who had bolted." Lord Palmerston's amendment was agreed to, "the Government thereby

carrying a Vote of Confidence in itself, and the House rose at 1·15 on the morning of the Derby Day."

PAM AND THE MATCH.

(A Trooper's Ballad of the Great War of the Parliament.)

OH, of all the gallant captains that ever I did see,
There's none like gallant Captain Pam, where'er the others be,

THE NEW ORLEANS PLUM.

Big Lincoln Horner,
I'p in a corner,
Thinking of humble pie:

Posed under his thumb,
A New Orleans plum,
And said, What a 'cute Yankee am I!

He'll laugh and chaff before the fight, and, the battery-barley done,
He'll laugh and chaff as gaily as before the fight begun.

Black Ben he was a captain that Rupert's colours wore,
But little cared which side he fought, or what the flag he bore;
A wily blade that never stuck by honest post and guard.

But have some weapon secret thrust to get beneath your ward.

* * * * *

Before their host up to our post Black Ben he rode alone—
"Now yield the place, and look for grace: how 'tis inside is known.
Of Rupert's stalwart cavaliers ill may't thee bear the brunt,

With the muskets to gall thy rear, while we assail in front."

A scornful laugh laughed Captain Pan—"Who talks of weakness?
What boots Black Ben from Rupert's men, if e'er he opes his maw?
But enormed wrath, and unfilled snore, and sunbeams

BEN THE BIRD-CATCHER. (OUT OF LUCK.)
"It's no use! I can't get hold of 'em nohow."

Here had he tried their ranks of one, detached but too late.

"I parley not with such as these—but, Captain Walpole, hark!—
I know you for a gentleman! Ware, ere you ride too near.
Thought you to catch the old weasel asleep upon his watch?
The platform that you stand upon is mined: I hold the match.

"Be warned; retire, or else I'll fire!" And, oh! 'twas awe to mark
How from man to man a paleness ran, and Ben's own face grew dark;

"Now charge for Rupert i—charge!" he cried, but none struck upon in flank;
And deaf the ears they turned on him, and paled the looks and blind.

Then answered Captain Walpole, a civil-spoken man,
"Or weak or strong, you do us wrong, we'll not swerve, if we can;
We would but ask a parley, and exhort you beat your ears
To friendly counsel; much may come, from force or confusion.

"Put up your match, a spark might catch—to you, where we retire?
Tramp! throw thsem short!" Vain Black Ben's charge, "Stand, cowards! Stand! or fire!"

They never looked behind them . . . the fired the hind-most catch!
The ground was cleared . . . and loud we cheered, as old Pan blew out the match!

JUNE 3.

At this time (says a Note preceding Vol. XLII.) the Member for Buckinghamshire had been "soft soldering" the extreme Liberals, the Irish, and the Priesthood, but with little practical result.

(See Opinion, "Ben the Bird-Catcher.")

BEN THE BIRD-CATCHER.

Lay your nets—bird-catcher—
widely and warily ;
Spread chaff for young banks,
and lay salt on young tails ;
Teach your decoy-birds to
warble it merrily.
New tunes may do, when the
ancient can fails.

With "Retrenchment! retrenchment !" some gull you may
gobble,
Who adore *Bright* plumage
with quakerly brown ;
Sing " Reduction of armaments,"
and with a gobble,
Some today *White*-th…es on
your chaff may light down.

Chant " *Salmon for Popes !* "
in good Roman metre,
The Irish black birds of ill-
omen to charm,
Snaroy proverb that *screams* round
the bark of St. Peter,
Portentous of tempest and
shipwreck and harm ;
Sing " Up with King Lucuts !"
and " Down with king
Virtue !"
Thus the Mormonby dew may
be drawn to your bow,
As the fascinate pray of the bun-
con-victron,
Where first duly skreened, is
gulped slow and sure.

Net your twigs, limed with rhe-
torie's glue, close together,
'Neath your fair flowers of
speech, hide your sophistry's
snare,
Spread widely your clap-traps,
for birds of all feather,
From the drab to the red that
the cautious wears ;
But remember the while, Papa
gives the foremost,
That only young birds can be
gammoned by chaff ;
That decoy-songs, though genuine music they're reck-
oned,
By scolders and troubles, make
wiser fowls laugh.

JUNE 9.

On this date the United States Senate decreed the abolition of Slavery in all territories of the Union ; and ten days afterwards the Federal House decreed the confiscation of all slaves held by rebels. (" Annals of Our Time.")

THE "SENSATION" STRUGGLE IN AMERICA.

The war proceeded with varying success, but at enormous cost in money and men. Stonewall Jackson had defeated Banks at Winchester on the 16th May, McClellan took Hanover Court House on the 27th, a severe but indecisive battle had been fought at Fair Oaks … recreated from Corinth, Tennessee, pursued by Halleck and the Federals. On the 16th June, on the other hand, the Federals were defeated near Charlestown. The United States debt at this time was estimated at £100,000,000.

(*See Cartoon, " The "Sensation" Struggle in America."*)

JUNE 17.

Died at the early age of fifty, Charles John Earl Canning, son of the celebrated George Canning, and Governor-General of India during the time of the Mutiny (1855-62).

JUNE 25.

COMMENCEMENT of a seven days' conflict on the Chickahominy, attended by great slaughter, undertaken by General McClellan with the object of hastening the fall of Richmond. Ultimately, however, the Confederate General Lee, with the aid of General Jackson, compelled McClellan to abandon the siege, and retreat with the army of the Potomac to Harrison's Landing, a protected bend on the St. James's River 17 miles distant.

A little later President Lincoln paid a visit of encouragement to McClellan's army, and called for 300,000 volunteers. On the 16th July, Halleck superseded McClellan in the chief command.

JUNE 25.

THE British Embassy at Jeddo was removed to Yokohama, owing to the danger incurred at the former place from the attacks of natives.

JUNE 26.

AT this time the Italians abolished the passport system, so far at least as concerned travellers from England.

JUNE 27.

THE Triennial Handel Festival at the Crystal Palace, Sydenham, was this year celebrated with great effect, nearly 4,000 performers, vocal and instrumental, being engaged in the great Handel orchestra.

JULY 1.

ON this day took place the marriage of the Princess Alice Maud Mary, second daughter of the Queen, to Prince Louis of Hesse-Darmstadt. It was understood that the young pair were to reside in this country during a part

AU REVOIR!

MR. PUNCH. "Bless your Royal Highness! I am glad we are not going to lose you."

TO THE PRINCESS ALICE.

DEAR to us all by those calm earnest eyes,
And early thought upon that fair young brow;
Dearer for that where grief was heaviest, thou
Wert sunshine, till He passed where tears shall rise
And art no more: thou, in affection wise
And strong, wert strength to her who even has now
In the sad presence of the lost bid . . .

Too full of love to own a thought of pride
In aught thy gentle bosom: on his best:
Yet noble is thy choice, O English bride!
And England hails the Bridegroom and the guest,
A friend—a friend well loved by Him who died;
He blessed your troth—your wedlock shall be blessed.

(See Cartoon, "Au revoir!")

JULY 7.

IN a discussion on going into Committee on the Fortifications (Provision for Expenses) Bill, Mr. Cobden made a personal attack upon Lord Palmerston, whom he charged with "incessantly misrepresenting the Emperor of the French as a bellicose personage," and thus being responsible to a considerable extent for invasion panics which periodically disturbed the country. Lord Palmerston in reply said (says *Mr. Punch's "Essence"*) "that he was proud of being attacked by Mr. Cobden, who never had an idea that England ought to be defended, who was in a state of blindness and delusion on that subject; who understood Free Trade, but that was his Last, to which he ought to stick, for when he went beyond it, he went into matters which he could not understand."

(*See Cartoon, "The Old Sentinel."*)

JULY 17.

THE first of a series of scientific balloon ascents made by Mr. Glaisher in Coxwell's new balloon took place on this date. The balloon was 55 feet in diameter, 60 feet high, and contained 95,000 cubic feet of gas. On this occasion they reached a height of nearly 5 miles (26,177 feet). Several further ascents were subsequently made, and on the 5th September, starting from Wolverhampton, the aëronauts reached a height of over 36,000 feet. They were nearly frozen to death, the temperature at 5 miles high being 2° Fahr. Mr. Glaisher lost consciousness, and Mr. Coxwell had to pull the valve with his teeth in order to lower the balloon, the aëronauts gradually regaining consciousness and power as they neared the earth again. The chief object of these ascents was to ascertain facts connected with the decrease of temperature and the distribution of mois-

THE OLD SENTINEL

Pam. "Don't you meddle with things you don't understand, young feller."

JULY 19.

AT a meeting held in Bridgewater House and presided over by the Earl of Derby, the Cotton District Relief Fund was this day constituted, with the object of assisting the distressed operatives in Lancashire now suffering comes from America. £11,000 was subscribed by those present at this meeting, the Queen contributing £2,000. On the 22nd Mr. Villiers, President of the Board of Trade, obtained leave to bring in a Bill empowering distressed Parishes and Unions to claim contributions from the common fund of the Union in the one case,

other. The Bill as passed also enabled Unions to raise money by loan, and resort to a rate-in-aid, when the expenditure exceeded 3s. in the pound.

Said *Punch's "Essence."* "The relief is confined to Lancashire and Yorkshire, and the plan is to work out the noble old plan of the Elizabethan Statesmen. A parish overweighted by poor-rate is to be able to call on the Union, and an overweighted Union is to be able to call on other Unions. . . . It is at present forbidden to England to mediate between those whose fratricidal strife is the cause of the distress, but at least it is is permitted to her to interpose between starvation and those who have hitherto bravely borne the hardest form of sorrow."

DUNDREARY ROW—HYDE PARK.

Said one Dundreary to another Dundreary—"By Jove! It's awfully jolly: ain't it ?"

JULY 26.

At this time, what was known as the Dundreary cut of whiskers and of dress made fashionable by Mr. Sothern's "get up" in the character of "Lord Dundreary" was very prevalent amongst the "swells" of the metropolis.

[See Cartoon, *"Dundreary Row, Hyde Park."*]

JULY 28.

Discovery of the Source of the Nile. Speke and Grant the African Explorers arrived at in his Journal) "had now performed its function. I saw that old Father Nile, without any doubt, rises in the Victoria N'yanza, and, as I had foretold, that lake is the great source of the holy river which cradled the first expounder of our religious belief. . . . The most remote waters or top-head of the Nile is the southern end of the lake situated close on the third degree of south latitude, which gives to the Nile the surprising length in direct measurement, rolling over 34 degrees of latitude, of about 1,500 miles, or more than one-eleventh of the circumference

JULY 29.

On this day occurred an event which led to much subsequent difficulty between this country and the United States. The steamer "Alabama," built by Messrs. Laird of Birkenhead, under pretext of going for a trial trip, left the Mersey, proceeded to Terceira, where she took on board Captain Sumner, and started on her privateer cruise against the shipping of the United States. "The local authorities at Liverpool had received instructions to detain her pending an inquiry as to her ultimate destination." ("Annals

instructions involved this
country in a long dispute
and heavy final damages.

AUG. 2.

EARL RUSSELL, writing
to Mr. Mason con-
cerning the claim made by
the Confederate States to
be recognised as a separate
and independent Power,
said that a State claiming a
place among the indepen-
dent nations ought not only
to have strength and re-
sources for a time, but afford
promise of stability and per-
manence. "Should the Con-
federate States of America
win that place among
nations, it might be right
for other nations justly to
acknowledge an independ-
ence achieved by victory
and maintained by a successful resistance to all attempts
to overthrow it. That time
however has not, in the
judgment of Her Majesty's
Government, arrived."

AUG. 4.

PRESIDENT LINCOLN
called for a second
levy of 300,000 men, to be
draughted from the militia
for a service of nine months.
At this time volunteering
was very slow, and the
public debt was estimated at
1,284,000,000 dollars.
(*See Cartoon, "Lincoln's Two
Difficulties."*)

AUG. 7.

THE Thames Embank-
ment Bill received
the Royal Assent. It em-
powered the Metropolitan
Board of Works to em-
bank the river from West-
minster to Blackfriars, and
to make the needful ap-
proaches thereto.

AUG. 10.

PARLIAMENT was pro-
rogued by Commis-
sion.

AUG. 22.

A LETTER addressed at this time by President
Lincoln to Mr. Horace Greeley furnishes a
significant commentary upon the real character
and ruling motive of the struggle between North
and South. Mr. Lincoln said, "My paramount

LINCOLN'S TWO DIFFICULTIES.

Dix. "What? No Money! No Men!"

save the Union without freeing any slave I would
do it, and if I could save it by freeing all the slaves
I would do it; and if I could save it by freeing
some and leaving others alone, I would do also
that. What I do about slavery and the coloured
race, I do because I believe it helps to save the

AUG. 29.

ON this day occurred the melancholy affray
at Aspromonte. Garibaldi had long been
fretting under disappointed hopes. The lame
and impotent ending of the much-vaunted

almost murdered this fervent patriot. His heart's desire was the entire emancipation of Italy from all foreign dictation, whether of Austria or France or of the Pope, and its establishment as an united independent nationality, with Rome as its capital. The slow measures of princes and diplomatists estranged the patience of the patriotic soldier. Acting (says *Mr. Punch's Political Summary*) "under some extraordinary infatuation, he attempted to lead a band of adventurers to the walls of Rome. He issued at Palermo an extravagant address, and carried many of his old followers to join him. The Royal troops, however, put down this gathering, and Garibaldi and his son Menotti having been wounded, their followers were dispersed." This regrettable contest between the impatient hero and the soldiers of the King he had so splendidly served, occurred on the 29th August at Aspromonte. Garibaldi received a bullet wound in the ankle. He was conveyed to Spezzia, where after much delay and great suffering the ball was extracted by Professor Partridge of King's College, sent over for that purpose by Garibaldi's friends in England. He disclaimed any intention of opposing Victor Emmanuel or fighting his troops, but complained bitterly of Ratazzi's Government for standing in the way of the liberation of Rome.

[See Cartoon, "*Garibaldi surrenders his Sword.*"]

GARIBALDI SURRENDERS HIS SWORD.

GARIBALDI DOWN.

Alas! the love of Italy lies bleeding,
But not in vain: his wounds are mouths, that speak,
With an ungenerous Patron strongly pleading.
The stronger that the Prisoner's voice is weak.
He fell, a forlorn hope of patriots leading,
Whose cry for Rome had fallen on ears unheeding.
How long! And were they Rome still longer seek?
A hero's ransom, and a madman's freak.

It has not failed, a captive though he lies,
If niggard France relent. Napoleon, hear
The nobly blood that out again thou criest
And thy hand policy, which right denies
To Italy, if not thy tears first.

The sympathy of people in this country was strongly displayed on the side of the wounded hero.

AUG. 30.

DEFEAT, a second time, of the Federal army at Bull's Run. The Confederates under Lee and Jackson invaded Maryland. On the 14th September, however, General McClellan defeated the Southern troops and compelled

SEPT. 22.

O^N the 22nd September, President Lincoln announced by proclamation his intention to recommend to Congress a decree emancipating all slaves in the United States, such decree to take effect on and after the 1st January, 1863, compensation for the loss of their slave property to be made to all owners who had remained loyal to the Union.

(*See Cartoon, "Abe Lincoln's last Card; or, Rouge-et-noir."*)

ABE'S LAST CARD; OR, ROUGE-ET-NOIR.

BRAG's not game: and awful losers
We've been on the *Red*,
Under red above the table,
Awfully we've bled.
Ne'er a stake have we advanced,
But we've lost it still,

ABE LINCOLN'S LAST CARD; OR, ROUGE-ET-NOIR.

From Buff's Run and mad Massacre,
Down to Sharpsburg Hill,

When luck's desperate, desperate ensure
Still may bring it back;
So I'll chance it—neck or nothing—
Here I lead THE BLACK!

If I win, the South must pay for't,
Pay in fire and gore;
If I lose, I'm no't a dollar
Worse off than before.

From the Kneps of Smoketown rebels
Than I strike the chain;
But the chains of loyal owners
Still shall slaves remain.

If their owners like to stop 'em,
They to stop are bounden;
Or if they prefer to swop 'em,
I have here one shin-plaster!

There! If that 'are Proclamation
Does its holy work,
Rebeldom's annihilation
Is did somehow work;

Back in Union, and you're welcome
Each to stop his nigger;
If out, at White let thy darky—
Guess I an't that vigour!

SEPT. 22.

O^N this date General Forey, who had entered Mexico with 2,500 French troops on the 18th August, issued a proclamation promising the Mexicans entire liberty in their choice of a new Government.

"Mexico" (says Mr. Justin McCarthy, "A History of our Own Times," ch. xviii.) "had for a long time been in a very disorganised state. The Constitutional Government of Juarez had come into power, and got into difficulties with several foreign States, England among the rest,

over the claims of foreign
creditors, and wrongs committed against foreign subjects. Lord Russell, who
had acted with great for-
bearance towards Mexico
up to this time, now agreed
to co-operate with France
and Spain in exacting repa-
ration from Juarez. But
he explained clearly that he
would have nothing to do
with upsetting the Government of Mexico, or impos-
ing any European system
on the Mexican people.
The Emperor of the
French, however, had
already made up his mind
that he would establish a
sort of feudatory monarchy
in Mexico. He therefore
persuaded the Archbishop
Maximilian, brother of the
Emperor of Austria, to
accept the crown of the
monarchy he proposed to
set up in Mexico. The
Archduke was a man of
pure and noble cha-
racter, but evidently wanting in strength of mind,
and he agreed after some
hesitation to accept the
offer."

The melancholy sequel
of this enterprise will be
seen later.

SEPT. 23.

At this time, under the
conflicting influ-
ences of the more politic
advisers of Victor Em-
manuel, and the enthusi-
astic admirers of Garibaldi,
complicated by the cla-
morous claims of the
Papacy, and the equivocal
action of the French Em-
peror, affairs in Italy were
in an unsettled state. Louis
Napoleon had notified that
he proposed to withdraw
his soldiers from Rome, an
announcement which of
course greatly perturbed the Pope. *Punch*, in a
Cartoon entitled "Relieving Guard," represents
"Mr. Nap," in reply to the appeal of "Mrs.
Pope "—not to leave a poor old 'ooman," saying,
"You will be quite safe with your friend Victor
yonder. He's a capital officer." Victor Emmanuel's conduct was indeed at the moment
viewed here with some, perhaps undeserved

FAUST AND MARGUERITE.

Faust . . .	MR. V. Emmanuel.	Mephistopheles . .	MR. L. Nap.
Marguerite .	Miss Italy.	Martha . . .	Mrs. Pope.
	Marguerite. "He loves me—He loves me not."		

suspicion, a suspicion aggravated by the unhappy Aspromonte affair, and Italy herself
seemed uncertain who was her truest lover
and sagest adviser in this the hour of her
perplexity.

(*See Cartoon, "Faust and Marguerite."*)

FAUST AND MARGUERITE.

hath idea her charm by plucking off the petals,
(As loverish English maids by ten or dozen do:)
But when her tempter's changeful will unmasks,
Who is the Third Napoleon's *Mephistopheles?*
Is it the cruel swaggering *Arimanes*,
Who Frenchmen ever unto mischief egg'th on,
Is it *La Gloire*, that god of godless *Louis?*
Down with that dream, down to burning Pluto then:

SEPT. 23.

In consequence of the rejection by the Prussian Chamber (by 308 to 11 votes) of the Government proposals for the military defence of the Kingdom, Herr Otto von Bismarck-Schoenhausen, afterwards so marked a figure in modern history, succeeded, upon the resignation of Van der Heydt. On the 13th October, owing to a continued dispute between the Chambers, the King of Prussia (William I., who had been crowned at Königsberg on the 18th October, 1861) closed the session, and announced his intention to govern independently of the Constitution.

SEPT. 24.

Earl Russell advised Denmark to give self-government to Schleswig, and yield to the demands of the Germanic Confederation as regarded Holstein and Lauenburg.

A dispute had arisen between Denmark and the German Confederation respecting the Schleswig-Holstein succession. Schleswig Holstein and Lauenburg were Duchies attached to Denmark, but to a large extent Germanic in nationality. "Put into plain words," (says the "History of our Own Times") "the dispute was between Denmark, which wanted to make the Duchies Danish, and Germany, which wanted to have them German."

Much was to arise out of this dispute.

OCT. 22.

The Greeks rose in revolt against the government of King Otho, who was very unpopular. On the 24th he announced that to avoid bloodshed he would leave the kingdom, and a little later he quitted Greece on board a British man-of-war. Considerable discussion at once arose as to the choice of a successor to the throne of Greece.

Emperor Napoleon.   *Empress Eugénie.*

HERCULES AND OMPHALE.

OCT. 30.

"The Empress Eugénie" (says a Note prefixed to Vol. XLIII.) "was thought at this time to greatly influence the Emperor in the settlement of the Italian difficulties."

(*See Cartoon, "Hercules and Omphale."*)

OCT. 31.

The Lancashire Cotton Famine was now productive of great distress, which baffled the best efforts of public and private philanthropy fully to deal with. Lord Lindsey, writing on this date to the Mayor of Wigan, said, "We

to show that we are no laggards in providing for the wants of those who are now dependent upon us for relief and assistance. And when we think of the noble patience with which the operatives endure this adversity—an adversity not brought on by their own fault, but by external circumstances over which they have had no control—I think we shall consider, not how little, but how much we can each of us supply towards the great and crying necessity before us."

Nov. 13.

THE EMPEROR OF THE FRENCH had for some time past been inclined to favour intervention in the American quarrel. He had through his Ambassador proposed to Her Majesty as well as the Emperor of Russia, that the three Courts should endeavour both at Washington and in communication with the Confederate States to bring about a suspension of arms for six months. Lord Russell, writing to Earl Cowley on this date, said in reply, "After weighing all the information which has been received from America, Her Majesty's Government are led to the conclusion that there is no ground at the present moment to hope that the Federal Government would accept the proposal suggested, and a refusal from Washington at present would prevent any speedy renewal of the offer."

Nov. 26.

AT this time there was an outbreak in the Metropolis of what became known as Garotting. The roughs and robbers of London, many of them ticket-of-leave men, hunting in couples, and lurking in dark places, attacked the unwary wayfarer, one getting behind and throttling him by "putting on the hug" as it was called, whilst his rascally "pal" in front robbed him with no accompaniments of

THE GAROTTERS' FRIEND.

"Let go, Bill, that per—it's our kind non-interfering friend, Sir George Grey!!!"

bludgeoning if deemed needful. It was felt that special measures were demanded to abate this plague of ruffianism, though Sir George Grey, at that time Home Secretary, did not favour flogging. On this day, the 26th, however, the Sessions of the Central Criminal Court commenced, and Baron Bramwell resolutely tackled the growing danger by the infliction of severe sentences, which had the effect of scaring the ruffianly garotters, and abating the mischief.

(See Cartoon, "The Garotter's Friend.")

In the next Session of Parliament an Act was passed to punish this class of criminals with the—by them—much dreaded "Cat-o'-nine-tails."

DEC. 1.

The Greek Government directed a *plébiscite* to be taken to decide the election of a King for that country in place of King Otho who had abdicated. The Hellenes pretty generally agreed in a desire that Prince Alfred of England should be called to the throne, but of course this invitation was not accepted. England, France, and Russia informed the Greek Government on the 13th December that their desire was to exclude the dynasties of the three protecting Powers.

(See Cartoon, "Alfred refuses to Burn his Fingers.")

ALFRED THE LITTLE AND ALFRED THE GREAT.

Prince Alfred, however keen
    equals or from shot
As a true British tar he may
    scorn to recoil,
Let us hope won't go meddling
    with Greece kissing hot,
When such meddling is cer-
    tain to end in a broil.

Then following this caution of
    Alfred the Great's,
Let Alfred the Little, should
    Hellas rumbling
To ask our young tar to take
    charge of her cates,
To blister his fingers politely
    decline.

Philhellenes are we all : Greeks
    and Greece we admire ;
But lending her sovereigns
    we've dabbled enough in !
Rest leave her to pluck her own
    nuts from the fire,
And at cost of Greek fingers
    to roast the Greek snuffin.

DEC. 13.

On this day took place the Battle of Fredericksburg. General Burnside had crossed the Rappahannock on the 10th with the Federal army, and on the 11th proceeded to bombard Fredericksburg. On the 13th, after obstinate fighting, Burnside was completely routed by the Confederates, admirably led by Generals Lee, Longstreet, and "Stonewall" Jackson. Three days later he was compelled to retreat, with the remnant of his army, across the Rappahannock.

ALFRED REFUSES TO BURN HIS FINGERS.

DEC. 18.

The Queen had caused to be constructed in Frogmore Park a Mausoleum for the reception of the remains of the Prince Consort, which this day at an early hour, and with only private ceremonial, were transferred thither from their temporary resting-place in the vaults of

DEC. 24.

A Memorial to the Provisional Government of Greece, presented this day at Athens by Mr. H. G. Elliot, British Plenipotentiary, indicated the conditions upon which the Ionian Isles would be ceded by the Protecting Powers.

DEC. 27.

At the close of the year, in wintry weather, and with no prospect of improvement in the American Cotton supply, the distress amongst the Lancashire operatives was at its worst. The number of persons shown by the relief lists of this week to be dependent on charitable or parochial funds (says "Annals of Our Time"), was 494,816, and the weekly loss of wages was estimated at the enormous sum of £168,000. The pitiful cry of "Welly Clamming" (nearly starving) heard everywhere in the afflicted districts, appealed forcibly to the feelings of the country, and ready response was made by the public.

WELLY CLAMMING.

"Everywhere we hear this, the Lancashire Cants for 'Nearly Starving.'"—*Correspondent.*

Hear the Plaint, 'tis not a cry.
Here's no whining, wailing, shamming,
Think what sorrows underlie
"Welly Clamming."

JOHN BULL PREPARES TO SPEND A MERRY CHRISTMAS.

Mr Bull, "There, my friend, I've done my best to make you comfortable; a nice, I think, I must enjoy my Christmas."

In our prisons vermin sleep
Amply fed, well-nigh to cramming,
Honest hearts in silence weep,
"Welly Clamming."

Slumberous beggars before loud,
Thoughtless benefactors humming;
These by foeless chimney howled,
"Welly Clamming."

Shameless paupers enter bold
Workhouse doors behind them slamming,
These all shivering in the cold,
"Welly Clamming."

Clothe them; blankets, jackets, hose,

Into bags sent off to those
"Welly Clamming."

Feed them. Round us Union dues
They stand jeering, jostling, jamming,
Send them food, as I hear no more
"Welly Clamming."

Were the stream of gold, I sit,
E'er so near to check and damming,
It must flow in flood at this
"Welly Clamming."

Help them. Spring will next be here,
Smiling, greeting, flowering, lambing
You'll be said to woo this dame

There are longed and loable rhymes—
Let the faintest praise fall damming
On them, as these moral chimes
"Welly Clamming."

At the Manchester Distress Meeting the Earl of Derby headed the list with £5,000, and £70,000 altogether was subscribed. £80,000 being subsequently added; a worthy and well-deserved dole for the season of good-will and cheer, which this year was saddened by suffering at home and difficulty abroad.

[See Cartoon. "John Bull ventures to Spend a Merry

✦1863✦

JAN. 1.

ON the first day of the new year President Lincoln issued the memorable Proclamation which practically put an end to Negro Slavery in the United States. It declared that "all persons held as slaves within the Confederate States are and henceforth shall be free, and that the Executive Government of the United States, including the military and naval authorities thereof, will recognise and maintain the freedom of such persons." The Proclamation enjoined upon the people so declared to be free to abstain from all violence unless in necessary self-defence, and, when allowed, to labour faithfully for reasonable wages. It continued:— " And I further declare and make known that such persons of suitable condition will be received into the armed service of the United States, to

SCENE FROM THE AMERICAN "TEMPEST."

CALIBAN (SAMBO). "YOU beat him 'nough, Massa! Berry little time, I'll beat him too."—SHAKSPEARE. (Nigger Translation.)

garrison forts, positions, stations, and other places, and to man vessels of all sorts in said service. And upon this, sincerely believed to be an act of justice warranted by the Constitution upon military necessity, I invoke the considerate judgment of mankind and the gracious favour of Almighty God."

(See CARTOON, " Scene from the American ' Tempest.' ")

Earl Russell, commenting on the Proclamation in a letter to Lord Lyons of January 17th, principle adverse to Slavery in this Proclamation. It is a measure of war, and a measure of war of a very questionable kind." He remarked that " it made slavery at once legal and illegal," by emancipating slaves in some places " where the United States cannot exercise any jurisdiction or make emancipation a reality;" whilst "it does not decree emancipation of slaves in any States or parts of States occupied by Federal troops, and subject to United States jurisdiction; and where, therefore, emancipation if " I venture to say" (continued Earl Russell) "that I do not think it can or ought to satisfy the friends of abolition, who look for total and impartial freedom for the slave, and not for vengeance on the slave-owner."

JAN. 7.

THE absurd and inconvenient fashion known as " Crinoline," which *Mr. Punch* had so plentifully ridiculed, still reigned; and he now

in painting a moral to
England with respect to
the rapidly increasing national expenses.

(*See Cartoon, " The National
Crinoline.*")

**TAKING IN, AND
LETTING OUT;**

OR, THE RIVAL CRINOLINE.

Who ever knew two belles of
one mind as to toilette?
" *De gustibus,*" (moderavit,
'twere ill) " non disputan-
dum."

Yet Crinoline craves still never
tool, though you on too
you call it,
Till all ask " *Crino-line* " (not
Cato-) " *quousque tandem ?*

Both Britannia and America
have managed to improve
Their weak lords till they let
'em back so swell out their
surroundings,

Thus the earl that's said to
keep you thus inflated costs
a fortune,

And both are mostly ruined
by their spunglings and
their frouings.

But John Bull, if so may, is a
prudent spouse at bottom ;
And Britannia's State bills at
last have grown to such
dimensions,

John, summing up their totals,
exclaims in wrath, "'Od
rot 'em,

These red-taped, steel-ribbed
petticoats are ruinous inven-
tions.

"So look out, Pam and Gladstone, Russell, Somerset &
Co.,
For Britannia's Crinoline, I'm
determined on retrenching it.
It's no use your telling our ladies'
papers are worn so ;
I shall have that poor thing's
skirts on fire, to burn myself in quenching it.

"Britannia must take in a
reef, and cut down her expenses—
In housekeeping and dressing,
in guiding and gunnionary ;
I know Folly may lose pounds,
while Wisdom saving pence
is,
But I want my savings real
ones, and waste sincalled
economy.

Meagre bills, across the Atlantic,
Uncle Sam, John Bull's relation,

Exhibits quite a different view of *Woman and her Master*,
Where go a-head America, by way of a retrenchment,
" *For* King Dollar, find," proclaims the reign of Queen
blue-plaster.

And Uncle upon looks on and bids Europe join in praising,
While his strong-minded lady, all vanity and vapour,
Along Wall Street and Broadway flaunts like a meteor
blazing.　　　　　　　　　　　　[paper.

"Shortest the greenbacks left and right, run up the ticks
of Abitrar :
Spread, spend, 'tis only paper, and there's more on't
where that came from ;
When poor bills whip all creation, so glorius we'll es-
tablit 'em,
And undo the worn old country in the debt it won he

" Let John Bull bid Britannia square her bills and mind
her guineas,
Uncle Sam says to America, swell out both ems and
t'other ;
Leave payment to the Britishers, those meek and sneakby
varmints—
America republicate, and, sirry, whips her mother."

THE NATIONAL CRINOLINE.

MR. PUNCH. " Tell you what it is, MARM, all your guards won't keep you out o' the fire, unless you reduce some of THAT."

JAN. 9.

A BANQUET was held to-day at the Farringdon Street Station of the new Metropolitan Railway in honour of the opening of the first Underground Railway laid in London. The line was opened to traffic on the following day, when 30,000 people travelled thereon.

JAN. 14.

GREAT rising in Poland against the Russian conscription, whose cruelty (says *Mr. Punch's* "Political Summary" in Vol. XLV.), "excited universal condemnation in this country. Men had been seized for their political opinions, and while the peasantry had been exempted the

townspeople had been solely chosen for the army. In fact, as Lord Napier, the British Ambassador at St. Petersburg, observed in a despatch to Lord Russell, 'it was a design to make a clean sweep of the revolutionary youth of Poland, to shut up the most energetic and dangerous spirits in the restraints of the Russian army; it was simply a plan to kidnap the

A GROWL FOR POLAND.

Mr. Bull. "Ah, old Dog—you'd like to have another row at that Bear, wouldn't you; but it won't do this time."

opposition and send it off to Siberia or the Caucasus.'"

(*See Cartoon, "A Growl for Poland."*)

Enraged beyond endurance by the carrying off by the police agents and soldiers of 2,500 victims in one evening, the Poles rebelled, and entered once more on a further fight for freedom under the direction of a Central Committee sitting at Warsaw. The rebellion soon spread over the whole of Russian Poland.

JAN. 14.

AT the opening of the Prussian Chambers on this day, in reply to the protest of the deputies against the Ministers carrying on the Administration against the Constitution, Count Bismarck made the characteristic and significant retort that "While the Ministry in England was the Ministry of the Parliament, in Prussia they were known to be the Ministry of the King". (The King refused the claim of the deputies to

so much of the masterful German statesman's subsequent policy.

JAN. 31.

THE MARQUIS OF LANSDOWNE died in Bowood in his 84th year. *Punch* said of him :—

He fought with Pitt, he served with Fox ; he shared
The struggles of a fiercer than those days,
When party severed chiefs and sundered powers
By gulfs, set thick with sharp lines, barbed and bared

Fear in the heat of party strife
he kept
That gentler mood, which
calm o'er conflict brings;
Avail o'er stormy waves spreads
smoothing rings,
Till wise by this old feuds and
passions slept.

*   *   *

And so passed slow and nobly to
its end,
Serene and summer still, his
long-drawn day,
While England mourns a
Nestor past away.
How many, high and low, lament
a friend !

Feb. 5.

PARLIAMENT was opened
by Commission.
"The Speech from the
Throne" (says *Punch's*
"Essence of Parliament")
"was interesting only from
its reference to the Princess Alexandra."

Lords and Commons here in-
vited,
How d'ye do?
You will hear, I'm sure, de-
lighted,
This news for you :
Wales and Denmark are united,
Alexandra's faith is plighted ;
And a treaty is indited
That links the two.

This referred to the im-
minent nuptials of the
Prince of Wales with the
Princess Alexandra, daughter of the King of Den-
mark.
At the afternoon sitting
of the House of Lords on
the same day the Prince of
Wales took his seat as a peer
for the first time. A little
later (on the 19th), in response to a Royal Message,
the House of Commons
unanimously agreed to Lord
Palmerston's proposal to
settle £100,000 per annum
on the Prince of Wales.
As £60,000 accrued from
the revenues of the Duchy
of Cornwall, only £40,000
had to be drawn from the
Consolidated Fund, making
with £10,000 a year also voted for the separate
use of the Princess of Wales, what *Mr. Punch*
called "The Dowry" of an additional £50,000
per annum. In the event of the Princess sur-
viving the Prince, a provision of £30,000 per
annum was made for her.

(See Cartoon, " The Dowry.")

THE DOWRY.

Mr. Bull. " There, Pam there's the trifle of Money for the Marriage. Ah ! how much better than some United States, eh ?"

Feb. 6.

RUSSIA and Prussia concluded at Warsaw
a Treaty for "united action in suppressing
the Polish insurrection."

Feb. 9.

ON this day the "George Griswold" arrived

visions, a gift from Americans to the Lancashire
Relief Fund. She was followed on the 14th by
another vessel, the "Achilles," similarly laden.
The Chamber of Commerce at Liverpool pre-
sented an address to the commander of the
"George Griswold," conveying thanks to
America for "the munificent and well-timed

Feb. 23.

The Polish Insurgents, under their leader Louis Mieroslawski, were beaten and driven to flight by the Russians.

March 7.

The Princess Alexandra of Denmark, on her arrival in this country, received a splendid reception at Gravesend, which was continued in every form that cordiality and loyalty could devise, all along the route of her journey to London and thence to Windsor.

March 10.

On this day the marriage of the Prince of Wales and the Princess Alexandra was solemnized in St. George's Chapel, Windsor. It was a happy occasion and a splendid ceremonial. It was said of it that "From the first to the last, one event followed another with a certain ease of action and unity of design which left nothing to be desired." The Queen, as was natural, considering the mingled emotions roused by her motherly interest in the occasion, and memories of her own recent irreparable loss, was deeply affected, and during the Primate's benediction" was observed to kneel in her private closet, and bury her face in her handkerchief." The Prince and Princess, after a short interview with the Queen at the Castle, started for Osborne.

The pageantry and illuminations in London and elsewhere were very general and exceedingly brilliant.

PROBABLE EFFECT OF MR. SOMES'S SUNDAY CLOSING BILL.

Workman. "Look, Betsy, if they won't let us get any refreshment of Sunday out of doors—we must buy in a shed, and drink at home, like the poor Swell!"

March 11.

On this day died, at the age of 61, the gallant and generous-hearted Lieut.-General Sir James Outram, the British Bayard, most chivalrous of Indian heroes, friend and comrade of Havelock, and described (says " Annals of Our Time ") even by an opponent as *sans peur et*

March 17.

" Pen " (says Mr. Punch's " Essence ") " almost fails to describe the horror of this night, and *vide* Cartoon for the assistance rendered by pencil. Mr. Somes asked leave to bring in a Bill for closing all Public-houses all Sunday. Resistance was offered—we should think so—

and next day but one brought his Bill in. Patrician champagne and plebeian beer are alike foaming at this fanatical outrage; but Mr. Punch's picture will settle the question, and the ridiculous Somes will be smashed on the Second Reading." He was.

(See Cartoon, " Probable Effect of Mr. Somes's

MARCH 30.

Prince George of Denmark, brother of the Princess of Wales, was proclaimed King of Greece.

MARCH 31.

The French Army in Mexico entered Puebla after bombarding it for some days.

Santa Anna had a short time before landed at Vera Cruz, and declared himself on the side of the French.

APRIL 13.

Sir George Cornwall Lewis, War Secretary in the existing Ministry, a statesman and

scholar of sound ability and high character, died at the age of 57.

APRIL 16.

Mr. Gladstone introduced his Budget. He came out (says *Mr. Punch's* "Essence") with a three hours' speech of pleasing elaboration

THE SCOTCH WITCHES' CAULDRON.

1st Witch. *Round about the cauldron go,
In the best materials throw.
Porridge, that stuff alone
Were a feast for any sow.*

2nd Witch. *I offer, clear and not obscure,
Beef, the workman's third to slake,
Bowl of Milk, to mend his prog,
Is he not a bo-lo dog?*

3rd Witch. *Beef—no better feeds the Pork—
Potter worthy of respect—
Fork a breakfast offers cold Tom,
Such the requisiteths of our cauldron.*

and unbroken eloquence. He let three cats and several kittens out of the bag.

He has got a surplus of £3,791,000.

1. Tobacco has been extended to.
2. He equalises the duty on coffee and chicory.
3. Clubs are to take out liquor licence.
4. Certain beer licences to be charged like spirit licences.
5. Anybody shall sell any quantity of beer.
6. Omnibus and stage-coach duty to be so arranged.
7. Railway Excursion exemption from duty to be abolished.

9. Charities and Corporation Trusts to pay Income Tax. All these changes will bring up the surplus to £3,874,000.

10. He abolishes his own little changes on parcels and bills of lading.

11. He relieves Minor Incomes from some Income Tax.

12. He takes off Five pence from the Tea Tax, henceforth to be One shilling.

13. He takes off Two-Pence from the Income Tax, henceforth to be Seven-Pence.

All these changes will get rid of £3,163,000 of surplus.

APRIL 16.

"A Working-man's Dining-room" (says a Note to Vol. XLIV.) "had been opened in Glasgow, and an excellent meal of meat, vegetables, and pudding provided for a very small charge. The undertaking had proved of great value to the working-man and remunerative to the projectors." Precursors this of many plans for feeding cheaply the very poor.

APRIL 20.

A Bill introduced by Sir George Grey for allowing to the inmates of prisons, who were not members of the Established Church, the offices of ministers of their own religious faith, was debated on second reading. It ultimately passed into law, receiving the Royal assent on the 25th July; one more of those concessions to humanity and toleration which have illustrated the reign of Queen Victoria.

APRIL 22.

On the 30th March the King of Denmark had issued a proclamation for the better consolidation of his kingdom, a Constitution being granted to all his dominions except those attached to the Confederation of Germany. It decreed the annexation of Schleswig and independent rights to Holstein. On this date the King announced to the Rigsraad that this ordinance had been opposed by the great German Powers; but that he intended to adhere to it.

" BEWARE !"

KINDER. " He ain't asleep, young JONATHAN ; so you'd best not irritate him.

MAY 2.

At this time a good deal of strong feeling was excited in Parliament and the country by the language held in America concerning our conduct in the quarrel between North and South. On the 24th April, in an American debate in the Upper House, Earl Russell said " he was acting with the utmost caution in reference to the proceedings of the Yankee cruisers, for what was illegal, and also for the conduct of Mr. Adams in granting gracious protection to certain English vessels, thereby implying that others were liable to be seized " (" Essence of Parliament "). In the Commons on the same night, Mr. Roebuck hotly denounced the Federals, whom he declared to be " unfit for the government of themselves, and for the courtesies and the community of the civilised not to be subject to the overbearing domination and insolence of a race like that." A more temperate and conciliatory tone was of course adopted on the part of the Government, but American demands and denunciations, combined with the loss to our commerce and the sufferings to our Lancashire operatives caused by the unhappy conflict, could not fail to produce considerable irritation in this country.

MAY 2.

The Federals under General Hooker, and the Confederates under General Lee, engaged in various conflicts in the neighbourhood of Chancellorville. In one of these (on the 5th May) the gallant and much-beloved Confederate leader, General (Stonewall) Jackson was mortally wounded. He died on the 10th May, a great loss to the Confederate cause. The Confederates nevertheless got the best of the series of fights, Hooker being again compelled to recross the Rappahannock.

MAY 3.

The Polish Central Committee declared itself a Provisional Government. Russia had offered a conditional Amnesty, but the Poles rejected the terms, which included a stipulation that they should lay down arms before 13th May. In reply to an intervention on the part of England, France, and Austria, Russia had returned what *Mr. Punch* called an "Evasive Answer."

(*See Cartoon, "Russia's Evasive Answer."*)

RUSSIA'S REASON: or, THE PLEA OF POLAND ANIMIZED.

Pot and soldiers of the triangles,
Rent and ran from head to
heel,   [triangles,
While the Russian Knouter
Every inch that you can feel.
Fenton and England, Austria
ever,
Looking on in wrath and shame,
Call on Russia, nor she's driven,
To give up the bloody game.

Gortschakoff, with cool assurance,   [and grimace,
Answers:—"Poland within
Not for sufferings past endurance;
Not for wrongs to whom we serve;

" Not for slaughter of her martyrs;
Not for terror of her sons;
Not for pikes of Russia's Tartars,
Not for groups of Russia's guns

" But because, in mad impatience,
She will twitch and turn and toss,
Turning mutual cessations

RUSSIA'S "EVASIVE ANSWER."

ENGLAND. "It seems to mean—eh? Eh?"
FRANCE. "I think it means—eh? ha!"

AUSTRIA. "I expect it means—eh? ha!"
CHORUS. "And we don't know WHAT it means."

" Let her take her haunting coolly,
And not strain the cords that bind,
She will find the Czar most duly
Liberal, indulgent, kind!

" Till she hears the ropes that cord her
Without struggle, stress and stands,
Agitation and Disorder,
As we are, in Warsaw reign."

MAY 4.

That part of Mr. Gladstone's financial proposal involving the taxation of Charities was this night abandoned in deference to influence too strong to be withstood. Mr. Gladstone however defended his plan in what *Mr. Punch*

hissing speeches." "En-
dowed Institutions," he said,
"laugh at public opinion.
The press knows nothing
of their «expenditure»; Parliament knows nothing of
it. It is too much to say
that hospitals are managed
by angels and archangels,
and do not, like the rest of
humanity, stand in need of
supervision, criticism, and
rebuke. Therefore, even in
the case of St. Bartholo-
mew's, I object to an ex-
emption which, by its very
nature, at once removes the
principal motives for economical management."

MAY 7.

THE state of the traffic
in the City, especially
with regard to loitering cabs
and furiously driving vans,
had for some time past
caused well-grounded dis-
satisfaction. A Bill had at
length been introduced,
which (as *Mr. Punch* said)
"gave the Lord Mayor most
tremendous power over the
traffic." It passed through
Committee in the Commons
on the 12th May.

(*See Cartoon, "Gog and Magog
Clearing Out the Van-
Demons."*]

MAY 8.

REPLYING to Mr. Disraeli
in an Italian debate
in the Commons, on this
day, Mr. Gladstone said
with emphatic earnestness
and amidst loud cheers, "It
won't do for him, it won't
do for his friends, to inculcate equivocal doctrines
(*cheers*), to utter these am-
biguous sounds in the face
of a nation, which, if it has
made up its mind upon
one thing upon earth, has
made up its mind that Italy
ought to be its Own, and ought to be FREE."

MAY 11.

IN the Prussian Chamber of Deputies, on the
occasion of the debate on the Ministerial
"Army Reconstruction Bill," which was

GOG AND MAGOG CLEARING OUT THE VAN-DEMONS.

"*The City is now taking itself in hand, and a Bill, giving the Lord Mayor the most tremendous power over the traffic, went through Committee in the House of Lords to-night. The Van-Demons told, we hope, to no purpose.*"—*Vide* "*Punch's Essence of Parliament.*"

occurred the exciting episode immortalised in
Mr. Punch's lines entitled "Bockum Dolffs his
Hat." Herr von Bockum Dolffs, second President
of the House, was in the chair, and when the
Minister of War, Herr Von Roon, was describing
the utterances indulged in against the Cabinet
as "no more than a piece of arrogance," the

hon ensued, the Minister protesting against inter-
ruption, the President persisting in it. "Should
my commands be disregarded by the Minister,
I shall order my hat to be brought," cried
Bockum Dolffs. Ultimately he did so, put it on,
and amidst ringing cheers left the chair, the
members rising also. The President declared

ROCKUM DOLLY'S HIS HAT.

The world has wondered, while Prussia blundered,
What knew thee would bring,
Would King crush Constitution,
Or Commission King?
Would Ministers put down Members,
Or Members by Ministers fix;
But may 'tis plain the question has been
Is Rockum Dollfs his Hat.

Let 's hope that this intrepid tile
Hereafter may prove to be
The genuine Palladium
Of Prussian liberty.
And the spirit of Freedom in Berlin
Shall sit, where old Free sate old,
Not in a Phrygian bonnet-rouge,
But in Rockum Dollfs his Hat.

Perhaps you suppose as Syrian freedom rose
From Gesler's planned chapeau,
That after a while from the Dollfuss tile
Press liberty may grow.
But you must be aware, if you mean to compare
This case of redoubtate with that,
That from hat to man Swiss resistance ran,
While Prussian may still in HAT.

BRITANNIA DISCOVERING THE SOURCE OF THE NILE.

BRITANNIA. "Aha, MR. NILE! So I've found you at last!"

Mahomedites, yours are 'gainst Commons and Laws
You wilfully run amuck,
Blind chief of the blind, with a martinet mind,
Which you mistake for pluck.
With the odds as they are far press our war,
I should think twice—perhaps say—
E'er I lashed the Holstenhorsts their graves,
'Gainst Rockum Dollfs his Hat.

A little later (May 27), in reply to an address from the Chamber of Deputies, the King of Prussia declared his entire confidence in the Ministry, and his intention to carry on the government of the country without a Parliament.

The Crown Prince expostulated with his father on his imperious and arbitrary conduct in dissolving the Deputies. Mr. Punch again sang ("Rockum Dollfs Bounsered"):—

Dissolve the Chamber, gag the Press!
An eagle, out a bat,
Is Prussia's badge, and down it sweeps
On Rockum Dollfs his Hat.

The hour of deeds is come, quite by
The time for idle chat,
King William has flung down his glove
To Rockum Dollfs his Hat.

MAY 28.

AT the Meeting of the Royal Geographical Society on this day, the discovery by Messrs. Speke and Grant of the long-sought source of the Nile was formally announced by the President, Sir Roderick Murchison.

On the 17th June Captains Speke and Grant arrived in this country, and on the 22nd they made a short statement of their wonderful discoveries before the Geographical Society.

(See Cartoon, "Britannia Discovering the Source of the Nile.")

JUNE 8.

THE Prince and Princess of Wales visited the City in state and were entertained at a banquet in the Guildhall, the Prince being presented with the freedom of the City.

On the 10th June the Albert Memorial at the Horticultural Gardens, Kensington, was publicly inaugurated by the Prince and Princess of Wales.

On the 15th the House of Commons voted £123,000 for the purchase of the 17 acres of land at South Kensington where the Exhibition stood. A proposal to purchase the Exhibition Building also was negatived.

Mr. Punch, in a Note to Vol. XLIV. says, "The frightful building erected for the Great Exhibition of 1862 at South Kensington was proposed by the Government to be retained at a cost to the nation of nearly half a million, and Lord Palmerston had said that 'a little stucco' would hide all the blemishes complained of by the opponents of the building."

(See Cartoon, "Putting a Good Face on it.")

JUNE 24.

THE "Alexandra," a vessel of the same class as the more notorious "Alabama," and built in an English yard, had been detained by our Government under the Foreign Enlistment Act. The legality of the seizure had, however, been disputed, and on this day, in the Court of Exchequer, a verdict was returned for the owners of the "Alexandra." Lord Chief Baron Pollock directing the jury that "if there was to be a conviction under the Act, it must be upon evidence and not suspicion." The judgment was afterwards appealed against, but (says Mr. Punch's "Summary") "the verdict of the jury was regarded by the anti-English party in America as another instance of an unfriendly

PUTTING A GOOD FACE ON IT.

Pam (the Plasterer). "Lor bless you! a little bit o' stucco will make it perfect!"

JUNE 24.

A new provisional Government, called "The Regency of the Mexican Empire," was set up in Mexico.

JUNE 26.

THE Prince and Princess of Wales at-

by the Guards, in the Picture Galleries of the International Exhibition Buildings. It was a most brilliant display of opulence and female loveliness.

At the same time was under discussion the case of Mary Ann Walkley, a seamstress in the employ of a fashionable milliner in Regent

succumbed miserably to cruel overwork, and sleeping the short sleep allowed her by the exigencies of fashion in an ill-ventilated room amidst unsanitary surroundings. The case excited much indignation. *Mr. Punch* combined the two events of the Guards' Ball and the Sempstress's death, in pointing with pen and pencil the moral of the incident.

(*See Cartoon*, " *The Haunted Lady ; or, "the Ghost' in the Looking-Glass.*")

THE GUEST AT THE GUARDS' BALL.

" WHAT am I doing here, with my ribs so blank and bare ? " [*stare ?*
What business is it of yours, under canopy and heritic to
" What am I doing here with my chin and thighbones clean ? " [*Crinoline ?*
Who are you dares push your question past the bounds of

THE HAUNTED LADY, OR "THE GHOST" IN THE LOOKING-GLASS.

Madame La Modiste. " We would not have disappointed your Ladyship, at any sacrifice, and the robe is finished by WEDNESDAY."

It's true I wasn't invited,—not, at least, in my own name ;
But I must presume that *Madame la Mort* is welcome all the same. [*See*,
And not at the Guards' Ball only, but wherever twinkling bright eyes, and glossy tresses, and brilliant toilettes meet,
But sure love so welcome as when with their diamonds, lappets and plume, [*come ;*
I creep past our Gracious Princess in the crowded drawing
And some deeps a graceful curtsey down to the crimson floor ! [*la Mort !*
Then *La Grande Maîtresse des Robes de la Cour*, Madame
Entre nous, 'tis I who have never to do these most people are sorry [*crammers over ;*
With those ...

There's scarce a house of business, that a West End connection boasts, [*their pets.
But *Madame la Mort* is there to keep the young ladies at

I'm at home in the crowded work-rooms, where my pupils their needles ply ; [*lie.
Let pulses throb and brains go round, as on fingers idle
I'm at home in the up-stairs dormitory, where the sharp five hours' sleep at level ; [*two to a bed.
Snug—isn't it ?—each six feet of space with its sleepers,

Poor dears ! Where're they either while thus they work and sleep, [*camp.
To my house of business, after all, they're but too glad to

To visit the sewers which I furnish with their tailored rich and rare.

The old painters—women die for speaking of artists as fair— [*long ago ;
Had a subject they used to call " *La Danse Macabre* "
In which—but nowever so they are, these artists—they made her

With all conditions of life, as, at last, being led away by me,

I should like to suggest to our painters—(we've some clever ones they say) [*day ;
A *New Dance of Death*, adapted to the fashion of the
On the one side the House of Pleasure ; sweet, the ball-room ; and next door, [*of Madame La Mort,
The House of Business ; and far across, the Work-room

JUNE 27.

A DISPUTE between Brazil and this country respecting reprisals taken by our envoy there for alleged insults to our flag, led to the suspension of intercourse with that country. Lord Derby had declared the proceedings of the representatives of the Crown unjustifiable, but Earl Russell had defended them. The question having been referred to the arbitration of the King of the Belgians, he decided against this country on the ground that in the mode in which the laws of Brazil had been applied to the English officers concerned, there was neither premeditation of offence, nor offence given to the British Navy. Earl Russell was dissatisfied with the verdict, but of course had to accept it.

(See Cartoon, "Humble Pie at the Foreign Office.")

JUNE 30.

GREAT debate in the House of Commons on Mr. Roebuck's motion to recognise the Southern States as an independent Power. The acidulous member for Sheffield, known, from his pugnacious tendencies, as "Tear 'em," was strongly, almost fiercely in favour of that course, which was as hotly opposed in a magnificent speech by Mr. John Bright. "Mr. Gladstone" (says Mr. Punch's "Essence") "urged the necessity of having punctilious, testified to English admiration of the heroism of the South, but adverted to the counter-current of anti-slavery feeling. He had not been afraid of the Union, nor desired its destruction, and at all events, he deprecated any argument based on selfish grounds." Mr. Bright implored the House not to aid the South in "the most stupendous act of guilt which history had recorded."

Mr. Roebuck, in the course of his speech, gave an account of his recent interview with

HUMBLE PIE AT THE FOREIGN OFFICE.

BRITANNIA. "Now, JOHNNY, you know that these Brazil-nuts have disagreed with you, and King Belgium says you did wrong, and that a little humble pie will do you good, so eat it like a man."

made some important statements of opinion, and given him permission to communicate them to the House. Generally they amounted to the declaration that the Emperor had not changed his opinion as to the desirability of recognizing the South, which course he was still in favour of. "Tear 'em" was much chaffed

considered his credulous subserviency to the Emperor he had elsewhere so virulently denounced.

The debate was adjourned, but on the 13th, on the motion of Mr. Roebuck himself, the order for resuming it was discharged.

JULY 1.

Fighting in America still proceeded with varying success. After the death of "Stonewall" Jackson the Federal General Grant had carried on a successful campaign in Tennessee, defeating Johnstone and Pemberton in May, and investing the strongly fortified Vicksburg, Mississippi. In June, on the other hand, the Confederates under Lee had invaded Maryland and Pennsylvania, and taken several towns. On the 27th June the Federal General Hooker had been superseded by George H. Meade, who at the beginning of July advanced against Lee, and fought the furious though indecisive battle of Gettysburg. The Confederates, however, evacuated Pennsylvania and Maryland, and on the 4th July Vicksburg was bombarded and was surrendered by Pemberton to Grant and Porter.

JULY 10.

The Mexican Assembly (says "Annals of our Time") resolved to adopt an hereditary monarchical government under a Roman Catholic Emperor, and to invite the Archduke Ferdinand Maximilian, eldest brother of the Emperor of Austria, to accept the Imperial title.

JULY 28.

Parliament was prorogued by Commission.

AUG. 14.

Field-Marshal Lord Clyde, hero of the reconquest of India after the Mutiny, died, aged 71 years.

AUG. 18.

The "irrepressible Nigger," as he had been called by President Lincoln, still gave much trouble. "It was thought" (says a Note to Vol. XLI.), "and thought rightly, by Mr. Punch, that the Negro would prove the great

BRUTUS AND CÆSAR.

From the British edition of Shakespeare:
The Tent of Brutus (Lincoln). Night. Enter the Ghost of Cæsar.
Brutus. Well, now! Do tell! Who's you?
Cæsar. I am thy ghost, Massa Lincum.
Du child a awful bad presumed.

nuisance of the Civil War then raging in the States."

(See Cartoon, "Brutus and Cæsar.")

BRUTUS AND CÆSAR.
(From the American Edition of Shakespeare.)
The Tent of Brutus (Lincoln). Night. Enter an Ethiopian Serenader with a Banjo.
Serenader. You want for me, my lord?

I calculate, Steve, I did that same.
Canst thou hold up thy heavy eyes awhile,
And touch these instruments a strain or two?
Serenader. Ay, my lord, in't please you.
Brutus. It does, my b'hoy,
I trouble thee too much, but thou art willing.
Sing me a soothing song, yet trembla.

Serenader sings.

THANKSGIVING.

AUG. 17.

A CONGRESS of German Sovereigns assembled at Frankfort, with a view to unification. The Emperor of Austria presided. The King of Prussia declined to attend, saying that before doing so it was necessary that " the proposed changes in the Federal Constitution should be harmoniously discussed in their relations to the just power of Prussia, and the just interests of the nation." The Congress sat until the 1st September, and carried resolutions in favour of the formation of a Chief Directory of Sovereigns, a Federal Council, and a Federal Court of Justice.

SEPT. 9.

EARL RUSSELL, who was on a visit to Dundee, in a speech at Blairgowrie said that so far as Reform was concerned, we were entitled "to rest and be thankful." The phrase was ever afterwards associated with the noble Earl, and passed into the political currency.

THE PIG AND THE PEASANT.

PEASANT. " Ah! I'd like to be cared tor half as well as thou be

SEPT. 19.

AT this time the miserable condition of the English rural labourer attracted some and very procurable or profitable comment. *Mr. Punch* pointed the moral in his own way by pictorially representing the marked contrast between the well-cared-for pig, and the ill-fed, ill-clad, and neglected peasant. The harvest had been a good one, but it little benefited the impoverished rustic whom philanthropic and

Mr. Punch's rustic poet represents the poor Suffolk countryman urging his children to "the gleania'."

" You'll all wish when the winter come, so' you ha'nt got no bread,

That for all dawtie about so, ye've hurled wrought undone) ;

For all your father 'are most gon old fella'can't reel to pay,

An Marter Lost, the Shoemaker ; so work you hard, I pray ! "

SEPT. 28.

AT this time the Negro Conscription in the North evoked much anger. In July fierce riots against the conscription had taken place in New York, many negroes had been murdered and much property destroyed. After the trial and conviction of the rioters the conscription was carried on more quietly, though not with subdued dissatisfaction. *Mr. Punch* thought he saw in the calling of the emancipated slaves into

Oct. 12.

J. S. Copley, Lord Lyndhurst, the Nestor of the House, as Punch had several times called him, died at the advanced age of 91.

Oct. 13.

The course of the British Government at this moment with reference to the contest in the United States was an extremely difficult one. The policy of neutrality which England had proclaimed she endeavoured to adhere to, giving offence thereby, as it seemed, to both belligerents in the States. Meanwhile in the country, although the larger portion of the community probably sympathised with the supposed anti-slavery North, there was a considerable section in favour of recognizing the South; a desire supported and strengthened by the daily increasing sufferings in the cotton districts.

(See Cartoon, " Scylla and Charybdis, or the Modern Ulysses.")

ULYSSES.

Freely translated from the Twelfth Book of the Odyssey of Homer, whether he was, or they were.

Then spoke Jackides, England's bravest Peer,
" Have no vain terrors, friends, for I Am Here,

SCYLLA AND CHARYBDIS, OR THE MODERN ULYSSES.

Oct. 24.

The Polish insurrection still continued, and the means for suppressing it adopted by the Russians led to lamentable horrors which excited great though fruitless indignation in this country. "Never perhaps" (says Molesworth) "had British sympathy for the misfortunes of that unhappy country been more energetically manifested than by the representatives of the British people in the earlier part of the Session of this year." The Government however decided upon non-intervention. Public agitation was entered upon, indeed, and a great indignation meeting was held in the Guildhall, but this was all, and our "moral aid" however sympathetic did not materially assist the suffering victims of Muscovite oppression and the brutal Mouravieff.

At this time there seemed to be friendly approximations between Russia and the United States. Mr. Punch's "Notes" say, "The Northern States of America were soft sweltering

"HOLDING A CANDLE TO THE ******." (MUCH THE SAME THING.)

the Emperor of Russia, then engaged in putting down the Poles, struggling for their nationality," and again, "The Federals had destroyed a flourishing Southern city by the use of Greek fire, and the insurgent Poles were being subjected to great cruelties on the part of Russia." A subject for satirical comment was found in this *rapprochement* between the great Republic and the huge Autocracy.

[See Cartoon, " ' Holding the Candle to the ***** .'
(Much the same Thing.)"]

HOLDING A CANDLE TO THE *****.

We'll set our Slaves at liberty,
    By Lincoln's proclamation,
Proclaim in every land on earth
    Uniforming emancipation.
Preach up humanity's crusade
    With Beecher Ward, Commander,
A cruelty held, not to old Nick—
    But youthful Alexander!

'Tis true the Poles be darkeneie,
    But then there's Fren==== redoubt 'em.

While England bottom'down to write,
    Though roundly Republic scolds 'em.
So enter France rules', in Mexico,
    And Fagland's rin our dander,
We'd coaxlies hold—e're to old Nick,
    Wark snow young Alexander.

They may say Russia is a bear,
    Because his hide is frisky;
Grave we would carry guns to him
    If he was twice as grizzly,
For I conclude that many for game
    Ain't always sweet for gander.
And coaxlies hold both to old Nick
    And ================

Ocr. 24.

Affairs abroad at this moment presented a menacing aspect; and Mr. Punch, noting the signs of the times, advised Britannia to be on the alert.

(See Cartoon, " The Storm-Signal.")

BRITANNIA HOISTS HER STORM-DRUM.

Up with the drum that storm foretokens,
From the signal rigging down;
Twenty people's homes the smoke
In which to paint the cross—
For upwards rolls of storms from East,
    And downwards from Westward blows.

But if upwards or downwards
    who shall say,
Or opposite comes together,
When clouds on heath and blackens
    each way,
Portending awful weather?
That not the most ship-piercing
    eyes
That Europe holds dare specu-
    late whence,
    Or, still less, prophesy
    whither.

Will the storm come from the
    nor'-nor'-west;
About the Grim Black Eagle's
    nest?
Where red stains fume along
    the snow,
That fain pass Poland's deal
    would hide,
    But up the seething canyon
    show,
With torch set loud as when
    they died,
    With face to Heaven, and
    teeth to foe.
Their hands still clenching scythe
    or spade
Than sword for bayonet or blade.

Where skeleton-like the charred
    beams peep
Out of those sheets of winter's
    sheep,
That look to pure and shroud
    each sin;
Or a little hand shows bone and
    sinew,
Or a silky curl of infant's hair,
    Still clasped the mother's hand
    within,
When died on hand, yet could not
    save,
The little one that shares her
    grave?

The clouds they drew to the nor'-nor'-west,
About the Grim Black Eagle's nest,
So thick, so changed with outguded fire,
So laden with God's own levin-fire,
It seems may be but the storm amid burst
On the nest of the Grim Black Eagle fast.

But further to South and more to West

On Robin's West loud rise,
Spirits of Vikings wake from sleep,
    Who living loved the loud wild roar
Of clamorous upon the deep,
    Or changed so fiercely on the shore,
And Swede and Norseman to Danskar calls,
    And bids be of good cheer,
And forge her glows, and hammer falls,

And the white-hot metal splashing runs
Into the moulds of the mighty guns,
And growling thunder, near and far,
Roll up the sulphurous clouds of war.

Or comes the storm from the Banks of Spree,
    Where " a little game " they're at,
With the Hohenzollern's crown in her jaw,

THE STORM-SIGNAL.

We know not whence the storm may settle,
But its coming's in the air,

And this is the warning of the drum.
Against the storm, PREPARE !

Slow-crossed, to sweep away
The buddie sceptre that bars the path
Of Prussia to breathing day?
Comes the storm from the smouldering fires
Of "Federal" Execution,
The length of the Diet that saves thee
Of its threats of Retribution?

Comes the storm from the clouds in air
Of Pr

NEUTRALITY.

Mr. North. "How about the Alabama, you wicked old man?"
Mr. South. "Where's my Rams? Take back your previous Cottons—there!!!"

We know not whence the storm may come,
And this is the warning of the drum,
Against the worst, Prepare!

Oct. 30.

The neutrality of England (says a "Note" to Vol. XLV.) "pleased neither the North nor the South." Just as the failure to detain the "Alabama" had angered the Federals, so the seizure of the rams in construction at Birkenhead

clamorous upbraiders in America, was neither an easy nor a comfortable one.

"(Sir Cornewall, "Neutrality.")

Nov. 4.

The Emperor of the French addressed letters to the different Sovereigns, proposing a Conference, to assemble at Paris, to consider the general state of Europe. He said, "I have it at heart to prove, by this frank and loyal overture, that my sole object is to arrive, without conval-

patch dated 25 November. It concluded thus: "Not being able, therefore, to discern the likelihood of those beneficial consequences which the Emperor of the French promised himself when proposing a Congress, Her Majesty's Government, following their own strong convictions, after mature deliberation feel themselves unable to accept his Imperial Majesty's invitation."

(*See Cartoon, " The Congress Quadrille."*)

Nov. 18.

HEINRICH VII., King of Denmark, died, and was succeeded by Christian IX., father of the Princess of Wales. Frederick, Duke of Augustenborg, issued a proclamation claiming the succession to Schleswig-Holstein. On the 19th the inhabitants of Kiel petitioned the German Diet in the Duke's favour, and on the 21st the States of Holstein refused to swear allegiance to the new King of Denmark. On the 2nd De-

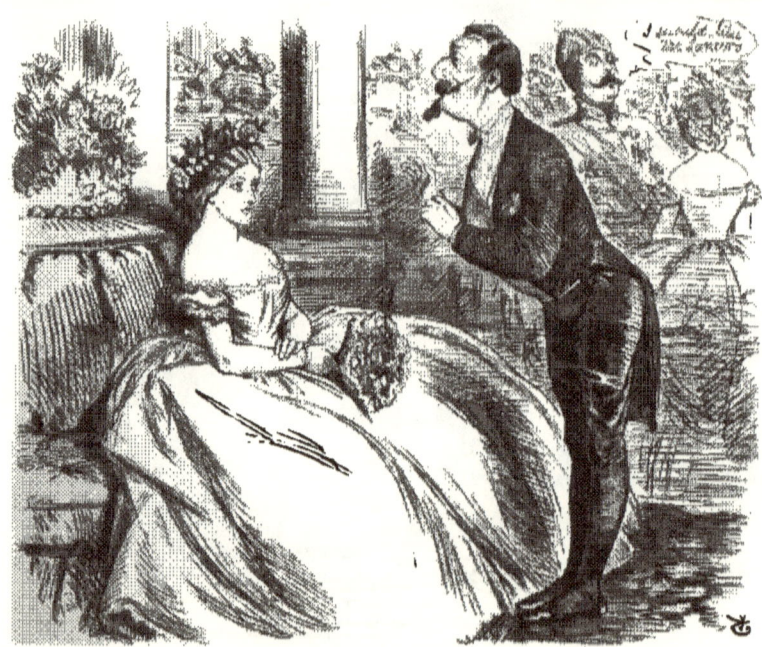

THE CONGRESS QUADRILLE.

RUFFIAN NAPOLEON. "*Vould—vou dance, and mingle?*"
MISS BRITANNIA. "*Thanks, no—I'm not sure of the FIGURE—and I know nothing of the FINALE.*"

cumber the Prussian Chambers, by a majority of 131 to 63, passed a resolution "That the honour and interest of Germany demand that all the German States should preserve the rights of the duchies of Schleswig and Holstein, that they should recognise the hereditary Prince of Schleswig-Holstein-Sonderburg-Augustenburg, and they should lend him assistance in vindication of

Mr. Punch sang:

Oet, Barbsen Datib! all round thy hat
Now weave a wreath of willow—
That hat which crack-brained Prussia flung
Into the Baltic billow.

On the 22nd the Holstein Diet assembled at Hamburg, determined to appeal to the Federal Diet in favour of the Duke of Augustenborg;

Hanoverian troops entered, on the 27th the Prince of Augustenborg was proclaimed Duke of Schleswig-Holstein, with the title of Frederick VIII., and on the 30th he made public entry into Kiel. On the 31st, in a note addressed to the Federal Diet, Earl Russell demanded that a Conference of the Powers who were parties to the Treaty of London, with a representative

to settle the difference between Germany and Denmark, pending which the *status quo* should be maintained.

Nov. 28.

On this date the first Fenian Convention met at Chicago. Sang *Mr. Punch's* Milesian poet:—

WROUP, ochl Eyrin, rouse up from your slumbers,
    burn 'tis we leave the diligent news.
How the Finians are cutting up numbers,
    To make Nassau shake in their shoes !
Their real mind present Milesians,
    Who rack all the "castles in Spain,"
To be backed to their Yankee relations
    When they 've cashed their own blackguenen clan.

Dec. 19.

ENGLAND, as previously explained (see Nov. 4) had declined to join in a Congress proposed by the Emperor Napoleon, and the other European Powers had relinquished the intention of meeting.

(See Cartoon, "Europa carried off by the (John) Bull.")

EUROPA CARRIED OFF BY THE (JOHN) BULL.

Dec. 24.

Once again the close of the year was saddened by the sudden death of a great English writer, William Makepeace Thackeray, author of "Vanity Fair," a man ranking, by common consent, with Fielding, Scott, and Dickens as a master of English fiction, and, in some respects, as least, superior to them all. He had been born in Calcutta in 1811, and was consequently but 52 years of age. His countrymen in general, and *Mr. Punch* in particular, lamented the brilliant satirist, the consummate master of pure English. *Mr. Punch's* first page in the first number for the New Year holds the following tribute to the memory of his great contributor:—

WILLIAM MAKEPEACE THACKERAY.

While generous tributes are everywhere paid to the Genius of him who has been suddenly called away to the fulness of his power and the maturity of his fame, none who have for many years enjoyed the advantage of his association and the delight of his society would simply accord that they have lost a dear friend. As an early tribute to its pages, and he long continued to enrich them, and though of late he had ceased to give other aid than suggestion and advice, he was a constant member of our council, and sat with us on the eighth day from that which has saddened England's Christmas. Let the brilliancy of his tainted humour, the terrible strength of his satire, the subtlety of his wit, the richness of his humour, and the Catholic charge of his calm wisdom, be thrown far others ; the mourning friends who describe three lines to his memory think of the affectionate nature, the cheerful companionship, the large heart and open hand, the simple courteousness, and the endearing frankness of a brave, true, honest Gentleman, whom no pen but his own could depict as those who have him would.

✦ 1864 ✦

JAN. 8.

THE PRINCESS of WALES at two minutes to 9 o'clock this evening was safely delivered of a son.

A WELCOME TO THE BABY PRINCE.

BY THE POET LAUREATE T. P. R.

Twinkle, twinkle, little Star,
That's precisely what you are,
Son of England's hopes, and mine,
Destined on her throne to shine.

Pretty little royal boy,
Father's pride and mother's joy,
How I long to see thee toddle,
And to kiss thy pretty noddle!

Haply if thy praise I sing,
Old England's small but future King!
Pa and Ma will ask me down
To Frogmore, nigh to Windsor town.

Therefore, hail I complete a
child!
Who upon our land hath smiled!
And let thy parents read my
rhymes
A hundred thousand million
times!

JAN. 12.

ON this day, Sir John Lawrence at Calcutta made formal entry upon his office as newly appointed Governor-General of India.

JAN. 16.

"**L**OUIS NAPOLEON," (says a Note to Vol. XLVI.) "was considered to be the prime agitator of the unsettled state of Europe, an impression which he had afterwards endeavoured to remove by inviting a Congress to assemble in Paris."

His endeavours in this direction, as we have seen, had been frustrated.

(See Cartoon, "Miranda and Prospero.")

FEB. 4.

PARLIAMENT was opened by Commission. The Speech referred to the birth at Frog-

MIRANDA AND PROSPERO.

MIRANDA. (Europe). "If by your art, my dearest father, you have put the wild waters in this roar, allay them"

calculated vagueness to the Schleswig Holstein complication, our dispute with Japan, and some other matters. It stated that the condition of the country was on the whole satisfactory. In the debate which ensued, the foreign policy of the Government, especially as regarded the question of Denmark, was subjected to sharp declared that the foreign policy of Earl Russell "so far as the principle of non-intervention is concerned, may be summed up in two truly expressive words — 'meddle' and 'muddle.' During the whole of his diplomatic correspondence wherever he has interfered—and he has interfered everywhere—he has been lecturing.

Russell defended his policy, and asserted that the Danish Minister here had expressly said that Denmark expected no material aid from us, but only sympathy. The Address was ultimately agreed to without a division.

(*See Cartoon, "Dressing the Window."*)

DRESSING THE WINDOW.

QUOTH the Prince of Shop-walkers and Principals, Pam,
    To his head-keeper Gladstone, and John, his head shopman,
"I should know the public, yet puzzled I am,
    What article's best in the window to pop, man.

"Lest your trade run languid; these mound nothing doing,
    Then our stock didn't take, and the public held off it,
Till our striking our balance, for all Gladstone's screwing,
    There appeared on the book-scores a penny of profit.

"From at these unprincipled chaps o'er the way,
    How to dress their own window have managed to learn:

DRESSING THE WINDOW.

PAM (*the Veteran Shop-walker*). "Now, then, MR. RUSSELL! What have we got to put in the Window?"
MR. RUSSELL. "Well, sir, there's some Reform Checks, American Neutral Tints, Foreign Pies, Berlin Worsted, Elder Quiltings, Russian Towelling, French Designs, Lots of Remnants, and any quantity of Red Tape."

And don't mind those our shop to drive custom away;
    That contra-revolution interbond—too know—'name common.'

"What is to be done? Here's the Season beginning,
    And unless we find something the public to fit,
I'm afraid, gents, that so far a fortune from running,
    The concern will be bankrupt, and devilned sta.

"Our book-debts are heavy; on curt'nal examism,
    Thanks to you, Master Johnny, we've largely o'er-bought;
That lot of Reform checks—your recommendation's
    Been on hand ever since; not a penny they've brought.

"There's no useful book-stock, in these pigeon-holes pendia,
    And of bad bills, I know, there's a box at the back full;

How to save the concern when I ask you to ponder,
    All you can suggest to con's, 'Rest and be thankful.'

"As for Gladstone he does try to keep down expenses,
    But he so me's a beggar to argue and reason,
He'll prove black white, spite of a customer's senses,
    And to carry his point, would risk losing the Season.

"If it weren't for my manners, my style of shop-walking,
    And abusing the ladies—or gents, for that matter;
Of Pam & Co.'s smash must the town would be talking,
    Spite of Johnny's smart letters, and Gladstone's glib patter.

"There's one comfort, if people our goods ahi't quite onto,
    They fancy still less that chap's o'er the way;

Though the very same patterns the clearést he puts do,
    And cries all he knows, he can't make the thing pay.

"We do keep a comedown, all it's a runny one),
    But a consolation don't rub Derby, Dizzy & Co. | four,
Their shoddy don't's vnymr than our dip-blown, and fowy
    And where we've one dummy, they spart a whole row!"

FIG. 3.

"GEE Lords" (says *Mr. Punch's* "Essence of Parliament") "like friends (according to a late Poet named Byron), 'mot to part.' But the Judicial Committee of the Privy Council met for an important purpose, namely to deliver judgment in the case connected with 'Essays and Reviews.' The Lord Chancellor gave it, the Bishop of London and some Law Lords being present. The sentence which Dr. Lushington passed upon the Rev. Dr. Williams and the Rev. Dr. Wilson was reversed, and the Bishop of Salisbury was ordered to pay the costs of the appeal."

FEB. 8.

LORD PALMERSTON stated that the English Government had remonstrated with Prussia and Austria for sanctioning the proclamation of the Schleswig - Holstein Pretender, the Duke of Augustenburg, on the ground that their action was inconsistent with the Treaty of 1852, by which those Powers were bound to maintain the integrity of Denmark. This remonstrance however produced no effect. Marshal Wrangel had on the 31st January requested General de Meza to surrender Schleswig, but the Danish Commander replied that he had orders to defend the Duchy. On the 6th February the Danes had been compelled to retreat from the Dannewerke, and on the 16th February the Austrians and Prussians occupied North Schleswig.

Our foreign policy, at this time under the direction of Earl Russell, was scarcely characterised by dignity or decision, and gave little public satisfaction. "Lord Rest-and-be-thankful" (as Punch called the Foreign Minister) seemed always making protests which were disregarded, and implying promises which were not kept. Meanwhile it was suspected that Prussia's aggression upon Denmark would encourage other European Powers, notably France and Italy, in their desire for territorial extension, a suspicion which proved to be well-founded.

NEMESIS.

EMPEROR OF FRANCE. "Ha! Prussia is extending his frontier; why shouldn't I go to the Rhine?"
KING OF ITALY. "Ha! Austria is doing the same; why shouldn't I go to Venice?"

FEB. 9.

IN consequence of our dispute with Japan, Kagosima had been burned by Admiral Kuper. Mr. Buxton made a motion disapproving of this, which after debate was defeated by 164 to 85.

FEB. 11.

DEBATE in the House of Lords on the seizure by Government of the steam ram "Alexandra" at Birkenhead, which seizure was maintained was dictated by too great subservience to the imperative attitude of the American Foreign Secretary. "Arics is giving Tauren a deal of

FEB. 24.

A SUBSCRIPTION was opened in London on behalf of the Danes wounded in the war. The English Government declining to send Denmark material aid, the popular sympathy with her found expression in this form. Denmark had resisted the proposal of England to refer the question of the accession to a Conference of the Powers who were parties to the Treaty of 1852.

MARCH 3.

SIR ROWLAND HILL having resigned his office at the General Post Office, *Mr. Punch*, his admirer, thus genially referred to the incident:—

"Sir Rowland Hill resigns his office. *If every person who has received a letter for one penny would contribute one penny stamp* (an organised collection, in every town, would be a labour of love, not to any fee, for over-employed ladies and gentlemen) we might present Sir Rowland with the most noble parting gift, ever offered in a public man, and assuredly no public man ever deserved a gift so well as the originator of the Penny Postage. He has done more to civilise the country, and to promote its prosperity, than any living man. Will he take a peerage? Probably not, but if he will, he ought to be in the most *Generic* at Lord Queenshead. And the gift, in addition, ought to make him still more like the Rising Sun (as was usually said) than ever. He ought to be able to tip every little Hill and great Hill with gold. If the people do not show their gratitude now, we shall put Britain, and bring Timbuctoo into her place, in the scale of nations. But we won't believe that our teaching and his have been lost. Come, ladies and gentlemen, buy books and cards, and set about your collection of stamps. You may print this paragraph for universal circulation."

(*See Cartoon, "Sir Rowland le Grand."*)

MARCH 7.

MR. PUNCH'S "ESSENCE of Parliament" for this date has the following passage, recording an important stage in the development of legislation for the Working Classes in the Vic-

POST OFFICE SAVINGS BANK

SIR ROWLAND LE GRAND.

"Mr. Gladstone then explained the Government Annuities Bill. He took two hours about it, and his speech was a treat. The object of the Bill is to give the Working Classes a system of safe Life Assurance. They are, to their honour, very earnest in this matter, and have about 30,000 Friendly Societies of various kinds. But these are mostly based upon false principles, and between 5 and 9,000 of them have become bankrupt, while about 800 fail every year. The misery thus caused of their earnings, in the faith that they were making provision for the future, can be understood. Government, in the most legitimate discharge of the duty of a Government, proposes to establish a State Assurance, as it established in the unmistakeable benefit of the people, State Savings Banks. The nation will guarantee the payment of the policy, but as the system will be sound, the nation will have no risk. There is the case, and it seems enough that there can be any objection to so act of common foot approbation of the scheme, but the party make clamours, and in the interest of greedy insurance offices, of inferior type, whose Touts are rampant all over the country, and in the interest of the keepers of public-houses where Friendly Societies convene, there will be a demonstration, in which the virtues of this Monkery will not be ashamed to join. Mr. Gladstone made such a merciless exposure of the views of the present system, and Mr. Dowell, Conservative lawyer, told such tales of cases in which defrauders of the poor had come under the unfavourable notice of a town dozen of their countrymen, that there was an unusual sensation. Lord Stanley applauded the Bill. You can't pull down a dirty old house without disturbing the Vested Interests of rats, but dirty old houses must come down for all that. Mr. Punch advises the Working Classes of the land to address Mr. Gladstone, who is a second time giving them an inestimable boon."

MARCH 8.

"ONE Pears freed up" (says Mr. Punch's "Essence"). "The Germans were waging a war which was wanton and disgraceful beyond any recorded in history. If the Austrians sent a fleet to the Baltic, Lord Shaftesbury hoped that it would be met by a British fleet, with orders to defend Denmark. So spoke the representative of the Religious World. . . . Earl Russell, thus incited, said that noble Lords could not expect him to declare war on his own responsibility, and added that we should not go to war for the Independence of Denmark, IF THAT OBJECT COULD BE OBTAINED WITHOUT WAR. The fleet could easily be got to the Baltic, and he did not think that Austrian and Prussian ships would like to encounter those of Queen Victoria. Having relieved our minds, we noblemen then went to dinner."

MARCH 10.

THE position of the Foreign Secretary, Earl Russell, at this time was not a pleasant

FRIENDLY ADVICE.

PAM. "My dear JOHNNY, the Easter Vacation is a great institution. to—REST AND BE THANKFUL."

one by Mr. Disraeli, Mr. Roebuck and others, against which his chivalrous leader, Lord Palmerston, did his best to defend him. It was suspected, however, that the plucky Premier was not exactly pleased with the restless and resolute literary activity of his colleague at the Foreign Office.

AN EASTER-OFFERING TO LORD RUSSELL.

EASTER not to my Russell!
From Parliament's tussle,
From feuﬁﬁ and blows and baiting;
From Derbyﬁ* exposure,
From cries for " more papers,"
From 'squeezing and 'splashing and *****;

MARCH 11.

On this day occurred a terrible and disastrous inundation at Sheffield, caused by the bursting of the Bradfield reservoir, eight miles above the town. The loosened flood of waters swept everything before it; mills, manufactories, bridges, houses, entire villages. Nearly 300 people were drowned in the appalling catastrophe. A subscription, headed by the Queen, was set on foot for the relief of the survivors.

MARCH 12.

General Ulysses Grant was appointed Commander-in-Chief of the Federal forces in place of Halleck.

MARCH 15.

The Prussians began to bombard Düppel. On the 22nd, in closing the Danish Rigsraad, the King pathetically remarked, "We are still alone, and do not know how long Europe will look with indifference upon the acts of violence perpetrated against us."

MARCH 30.

The Queen this day was present at a flower-show in the Horticultural Gardens, South Kensington. This, her first public appearance since the death of the Prince Consort, was hailed with pleasure and hope by her people.

APRIL 3.

General Garibaldi arrived at Southampton on a visit to England. His reception everywhere was enthusiastic, and his entry into London on the 11th surpassed any Royal progress or Imperial Triumph; the route along which he passed being everywhere densely thronged with multitudes of the excited, admiring, cheering populace of all classes. Never was witnessed such a scene of popular hero-

"THIS IS THE NOBLEST ROMAN OF THEM ALL!"

days he went through a stirring round of receptions, demonstrations, presentations, concerts &c. Then, somewhat suddenly, on the 22nd he left London for Italy, being conveyed to Caprera in the Duke of Sutherland's yacht. The reasons alleged for this rather unexpected

not everywhere received with full credence or complete satisfaction; and neither Government protest nor Parliamentary explanations entirely removed certain vague suspicions that the popular hero had become an embarrassing guest whose "parting" had been politely but de-

APRIL 7.

THE CHANCELLOR OF THE EXCHEQUER introduced the Budget in a speech occupying ten columns of the morning papers. "The great speech" (says *Punch's* "Essence") "was not an adorned one, but was singularly interesting, and where an elevated tone could be adopted, you may be sure Mr. Gladstone improved the occasion. His noble picture of the commercial greatness of England combined the accuracy of a photograph with the colouring of a Turner."

The Budget showed a surplus of £2,370,000. It included a considerable reduction of the Sugar Duties, a penny off the Income Tax, and a lowering of the duty on Fire Insurances from 3s. to 1s. 6d.; altogether a relief from taxation to the amount of some three millions. It did not propose repeal or even reduction of the Malt duties; but later a concession was made to the Anti-Malt-tax party "by the remission of so much of the duty as had hitherto been levied upon malt for the consumption of cattle."

"The loud cheers of the House of Commons as the great orator sat down were nobly earned, and did honour to him and to those whom he had instructed and delighted" ("Essence").

(*See Cartoon, "Goody Gladstone's Gifts."*)

GOODY GLADSTONE'S GIFTS.

(To the Agricultural Party.) *"You've got your 'Sugar,' and your 'Fire Medal,' and there's 'a Penny' for you: and if you're a civil boy, perhaps, some of these days, we'll* THINK *about the 'Malt.'"*

TO MR. GLADSTONE, AFTER HIS BUDGET SPEECH.

POTENT professor! Blondin of debate!
Who, on thy high rope of prose oratorical,
Trundlest a pitch to turn a common pate,
With firm-set feet, and clear brain categorical,
Keeping thy balance, to mankind's amaze,
And ever and anon cracking a joke,
As eggs to make his omelette Blondin broke,
Dropping on heads upturned in breathless gaze,
The empty shells, as thou the well-turned phrase.

Then, all across thy figures' long-stretched line,
A whole attentive Commons House dost bear—
There being, we know, *at least* two parties there—
As blind, if not as brave, as I opine,
As he whom Blondin pick-a-back'd mid-air!

Blondin could juggle but with knives and balls,

While dazzled, doubting, awed, astonished, all
Listen and look, and hold their breath, and say
"Can this go on? This man will surely fall,
That total drop." But no—he holds his way,
His balance kept secure, through all that figure-play!

As Blondin knew to thrill the crowd intense,

So, now and then, will these a
     junne nasty,   [air.
A snorting brainsex, a dumbdel
And Cecil pricks his ears, and
     Dizzy's eye
Warms with slow life, and his
     eye 'gins to glare,
But sum the frint is played, and
     high in air
The proud head shows swayer,
     the first step holds its way!
Mysteplass sled—whose power
     so task cucumbers!
To grasp out many triffnned
     debt is thine,
Or with animals, jaggery and
     Dutch numbers,   Jewelry,
And other nice distractions see :
To play, like una head in the
     grocery line !
What task shows, what task
     below thy power ?
I own a brother, and with
     breathed brunch
Very, as I thee joint Lord
     of the hour,
"I would be Gladstone, if I
     were not Punch."

APRIL 9.

Earl Russell, defending the advice which he had given to Denmark, "to fulfil the engagements it had made to Germany," said that France, Russia, and Sweden were parties to the Treaty of 1852 equally with England, that England was not bound to act alone, and that it would be very unwise for her to do so. A Conference to consider the question was about to meet in London. Lord Granville (on the 11th) said that he hoped good results from the Conference. "So does Lord Punch" (says "Essence of Parliament"), "but as Lord Johnny was not altogether lucky at Vienna, it cannot be offensive to Lord Russell if the other nobleman hints, while Russell is being dressed for the Fair, like Moses in the 'Vicar of Wakefield,' that we shall be a good deal more surprised than delighted if he brings us home a gross of green spectacles, or makes himself a Spectacle of Greenness."

[See Cartoon, "Moses starting for the Conference Fair."]

APRIL 10.

The Archduke Ferdinand Maximilian of Austria received a Mexican deputation at

MOSES STARTING FOR THE CONFERENCE FAIR.

(LET US HOPE HE WON'T BRING BACK " 1 GROSS OF GREEN SPECTACLES.")

Primrose .   . Palmerston.   Mrs. Primrose .   . Britannia.   Moses .   . . Earl Russell.

of "Maximilian the First, Emperor of Mexico." America was opposed to the project, and had already expressed her resolve to discountenance it.

APRIL 12.

Mr. Robert Lowe, Vice-President of the Committee of Council on Education, was with the Reports of Her Majesty's Inspectors of Schools. Lord Robert's resolution being carried against the Government by a majority of 101 to 93, Mr. Lowe resigned his office, but subsequently was fully exonerated by a Committee, the resolution being rescinded. "The Opposition" (said Mr. Punch) "have ejected another good

APRIL 23.

On this day was cele- brated the three hun- dredth anniversary of the birthday of William Shake- speare. The Tercentenary ceremonies centred at Strat- ford-on-Avon, but were also pretty general throughout the country. There was much earnestness doubt- less, but little real impres- siveness about the whole parade of pageants, per- formances, and speeches, held in proper but not very happily conceived glorifica- tion of our great poet's name.

APRIL 25.

The Conference of London held its first sitting. Earl Russell pro- posed a suspension of hos- tilities in the Duchies. On the 6th May it was stated in Parliament that a sus- pension of hostilities had been agreed to for one month from the 12th in- stant, which was subse- quently further extended.

(See Cartoon, " The Aggravated Policeman.")

WHAT TOBY THOUGHT AT THE DOOR OF THE CONFERENCE ROOM.

Toby sits by the Conference-
 room,
The _Vetus-Gricht_ of diplomacy-
 tion' doors. | Hear,
Toby smells at what came on the
From the chink below the Con-
 ference-door.
Toby doesn't know what to
 think ;
It looks like blood, but he hopes
 'tis ink, [which
Toby knows, with ears on the
The bland diplomatists' whispers
 to catch,
But somehow Toby cannot hear,
Such horrible sounds are in his
 ear,
Of booming cannon and harsh-
 ing shells
On the Schleswig foods and the
 wübleven it fells ;
And the groans of the wounded, left to die ;
And the wail of the homeless, forced to fly ;

And Toby thinks—of the party in there,
Each in his gilt and cushioned chair,
And wonders what word they have in their ears,
Thus prevents their hearing the sounds he hears ;
War if their bond, thee terms would do

For bidding that hell of sounds to cease.
And looking most clear at the war on the floor,
That moves and moans under the door,
Toby sees, as it soaks his the wood,
That the stain is not of ink, but blood ;
For blood may by diplomates pass be shed ;
And by protocols more them by bullets are sped.

Her vulture's folly he counts,
Twere well to economise vulture's fare ;
For vultures, when their food they find,
Will gorge themselves both deaf and blind,
Till the wings are weak to lift the carcass
From its carrion perch on skull or haunch,
And, helpless alike to fight or fly,

THE AGGRAVATED POLICEMAN.

Young Bull. A 1. " You're out on my beat, you Savage, or I'd lib you in ! "

MAY 3.

At this time there was fierce and continued fighting between the Federals and Confederates in Virginia, culminating in the severe, though indecisive, tactics at "Wilderness" (on 5th and 6th May), and at Spottsylvania (on the 10th). In these engagements, Generals Lee and Longstreet were opposed to the newly appointed Federal General Grant. The Federal loss was stated to be 40,000 men, killed, wounded, and taken prisoners.

MAY 11.

Mr. Baines moved the second reading of his Bill for lowering the suffrage in boroughs to £6. In the discussion which followed, Mr. Gladstone startled his colleagues in the Ministry, and aroused the country by declaring in favour of a very wide extension of the franchise. "The day," said Mr. Punch ("Essence"), "may be mentioned in history with the days on which Cæsar crossed the Rubicon, Mario went over to the Covent Garden Opera, and Lord

THE FALSE START.

Paw (The Imp). "Hi! Gladstone! Deucedeng! You mean't be seen! You shan't go in!"

Derby abandoned the Reform Ministers. . . . The Chancellor of the Exchequer and M.P. for Oxford University arose, and delivered himself of a very strong speech in favour of Mr. Baines's Bill. 'Parliament,' he said, 'had not done its duty in regard to Reform—there ought to be a sensible increase to the constituency from the working classes—those who would exclude them of that class ought to show why this should be—he believed that if the upper portion of the lower order were admitted, there would not vote for demagogues, and that there was a very good feeling between that class and their superiors' . . . . Mr. Whiteside expressed his astonishment, and wished that Lord Palmerston had been present, as he would have proved to his refractory Chancellor that such a Bill ought not to pass . . . . There was a lengish debate, and the Bill was referred by 276 to 216." Mr. Gladstone's "new departure" in fact excited hopes on one side and fears on the other.

(See Cartoon, "The False Start.")

MAY 15.

Herr von Bismarck openly announced that the Prussian Government could no longer consider itself in any way bound by the obligations it contracted on the 8th May, 1852 (Treaty of London), "under other circumstances."

MAY 28.

The Emperor Maximilian and the Empress landed at Vera Cruz, to assume the throne of Mexico.

MAY 28.

EARL RUSSELL, at the London Conference, submitted a resolution proposing the separation of Holstein, Lauenburg and the southern part of Schleswig from the Danish Monarchy, the line of the frontier, however, not to be drawn more to the north than the mouth of the Schlei, and the line of the Dannewerke. Although Denmark, subject to being only asked to cede Lauenburg on special conditions, consented unhesitatingly to the great sacrifice, Austria and Prussia refused to accept the proposed boundary line.

(*See Cartoon, "The Beadle and the Dane."*)

JUNE 1.

THE Ionian Isles were this day formally ceded to Greece by Great Britain and the other protecting Powers.

JUNE 19.

THE Confederate cruiser "Alabama" (Captain Semmes, commander) was on this day attacked and sunk off Cherbourg by the Federal war-steamer "Kearsage" (Captain Winslow). The "Alabama" had had a dashing career, and had done much damage to the shipping of the United States since her sailing from this country on 19th August, 1862 (which see). The U.S. corvette "Kearsage" had long been in chase of her. The fight was a gallant one, but the "Alabama" was this time overmatched, and, despite the indomitable courage of Captain Semmes and her crew, was, after two hours, found to be disabled and sinking. Mr. Lancaster's yacht, the "Deerhound," which witnessed the fight, succeeded in saving 40 of the "Alabama's" crew, including Captain Semmes and 13 officers, with whom she started for Southampton. The log of the "Deerhound" furnished the public with particulars of this

THE BEADLE AND THE DANE.

Mr. Bull. "Better take it! Half a Loaf's better than no bread, you know!"

JUNE 21.

"ESSAYS and Reviews" condemned in Convocation.

JUNE 22.

THE meeting of the London Conference,

which would be accepted both by Denmark and Germany, and so broke up. Hostilities were resumed in Schleswig next day, but (says "Annals of Our Time") as Denmark saw that the neutral Powers were not likely to aid her in the struggle, she gradually withdrew her armies from the territories in dispute.

JUNE 27.

Interrogations in the House of Commons amounted practically to the question, "Was England to go to war for Denmark?" *Mr. Punch* then summed up the Prime Minister's reply:—

Lord Palmerston said that Denmark had been ill-used, and that the sympathies of the whole English nation were with her.

But in the very origin of the quarrel she had been wrong, though she had completely set herself right.

She rejected the last demand of the Conference, though her acceptance of it might have led to peace.

France and Russia had refused to draw the sword for her.

Therefore, if England interfered, she would have to encounter the whole force of Germany.

The Government of the Queen had not thought it their duty to go to war.

But if Copenhagen were attacked, as the King of Denmark were made a present, their decision might be subject to reconsideration.

Such was the Premier's statement, and Earl Russell's was the same; but he added that we were the most hated to repudiate sword now, as the War in America might end, and then we might have, at any rate, a rupture with a nation possessing an immense army and a powerful navy.

On the 29th the Prussians bombarded and took possession of the Island of Alsen.

(See Cartoon, "The Provisionary Note.")

JULY 4.

Mr. Disraeli moved a vote of censure on the Government to the effect that while the course they had pursued had failed to maintain their avowed policy of upholding the integrity and independence of Denmark, it had lowered the just influence of this country in the capitals of Europe, and thereby diminished the securities for peace.

"Mr. Disraeli" (says *Punch's* "Essence") "moved this resolution in a speech of three hours. His cue was to be tremendously solemn and

tary evidence, and sought to show that we had deceived Denmark, had insulted and alienated France, and had humiliated England. If a dull, decorous statesman had compiled this speech, it would have been complimented, but something more brilliant was expected from the author of 'Coningsby.' On the other hand,

reply, people did not expect much, because the Chancellor's peace-at-almost-any-price policy is not capable of lively illustration. But where Mr. Gladstone, after meeting the documentary evidence, and charging his antagonist with 'falsification' (there was a riot over the word, and over 'calumnies,' and then we had all sorts of

THE PROMISSORY NOTE.

Mr. John Bull (Mr. Punch) having presented the Note for Payment). "Now then, Mr. Koss th and Montagu Premier, what are you thinking of be? Your names are to the Note as well as mine, and you're as much bound to pay your share as I am."

and declared war on Mr. Disraeli, the Chancellor showed himself a terrible gladiator, and showered his blows like wintry rain. The retort of the Ministers is, 'You never have told, and you don't tell now, what you would have done.'"

After a debate ranging over three nights, the vote of censure was negatived by a majority of 18,—295 for, 313 against.

(See Cartoon, "The Fight at St. Stephen's Academy.")

THE GREAT FIGHT.

Described in a Letter from Master Johnny Russell, of Lord Minto's Academy, to Master Thomas Bruce.

DEAR TOM,

I hope you are quite well, I am quite well. I hope your sister is quite well. Give my love to her. There has been a jolly fight between Ben Dizzy and Bill Gladstone, and Ben has got well licked, and I am jolly glad of it, for Ben has been so awful nuisance all this half, and saying nasty things of one, and getting beastly cocky. You know Ben is in the other House, and so he couldn't get at me, for you know I am in the Upper House, among the other Big Boys. But he kept saying spiteful things of me, all behind my back, where he knew I could not answer him, and at last he got so cheeky that he pitched into Old Pam, and said he'd lick him and Bill Gladstone, or any who should be rash. You know Old Pam has been mark of the school for ever such a while, and our fellows all like him, because he is so good-natured, and is such a clever chap at getting fellows out of messes.

Ben was a great deal to think that he could lick Bill Gladstone and Old Pam, for everybody knows that he's not much for either of them. Ben's not a bad hitter, but he's pretty smart in fibbing; but though he's pretty freely in gassing on his legs, you know we all agree that there's no bottom to him, and although his style is showy, he has little real strength. You should have seen just how Bill Gladstone floored him the first round, there never was a fairer knock-down than he gave him. Then he mixed him like a rat, and gave him such a thrashing, and Dizzy looked quite white, and I don't wonder at it. I think I'm more careful now that the contain has been a little taken out of him. He's got such a black eye, and everybody says that he deserved quite what he got, and I know I'm precious glad of it, for he

We broke up in a few days, and I hope that we shan't have to come to school again till February. So I've a jolly lot of holiday before me to write letters, which you know I'm very fond of. And so I must conclude. Believe me,

Your affectionate friend,
JOHNNY RUSSELL.

St. Stephen's Academy, Thursday.

THE FIGHT AT ST. STEPHEN'S ACADEMY.

Mrs. Gamp. "Never mind us dear! You have yer merry bird to win: which that Master Gladstone is such a tremenjous strong boy!"

JULY 8.

To-day the foundation-stone of the Thames Embankment between Westminster and Blackfriars Bridge was laid by the Chairman of the Metropolitan Board of Works, Mr. Thwaites.

JULY 10.

MR. GLADSTONE'S Bill for amending the law relating to the purchase of Government Annuities through the medium of savings-banks, and for permitting the granting by Government of life insurances, received this day the Royal assent. The Bill was conceived in the interests of the working classes, to encourage thrift and facilitate providence.

JULY 15.

TO-DAY there was a long discussion in the House of Lords on the action of Convocation with regard to "Essays and Reviews." Lord Houghton wanted to know if the Government had taken, or would take, the opinion of the law officers of the Crown as to the powers of Convocation to pass a synodical judgment on books written either by clergymen or laymen. Lord Chancellor Bethell, in the course of a blandly bitter reply, which roused the wrath of the Bishops, said, "What is called a synodical judgment is simply a series of well-lubricated terms—a sentence so oily and so saponaceous that no one would grasp it. Like an eel, it slips through your fingers, —it is simply nothing, and I am glad to tell my noble friend (Lord Houghton) that it is literally no sentence at all. . . . As to the question of the noble lord . . . I have only to assure the noble lord that it is not the intention of the Government to take any further steps in the matter."

JULY 20.

THERE was declared between Germany and Denmark, is having been arranged that a Conference should assemble at Vienna, which it did on the 20th instant, with a view to the restoration of peace.

JULY 29.

ON this day Parliament was prorogued by Commission. "The last day of a do-nothing Session," said *Punch's* "Essence." The Royal Speech expressed a hope that the negotiations now opened might restore peace between Germany and Denmark, and referred to the breaking up of peace between the Hospodar of Moldo-Wallachia and the Sultan, the diminution of Lancashire distress, the probability of cotton supply from India, the passage of the Assurance Act, and a sprinkling of minor measures.

(*See Cartoon, "Short Commons, or the Ministerial*

SHORT COMMONS, OR THE MINISTERIAL WHITEBAIT DINNER.

PAM (Head Waiter). "Is that all we've got to put on the Table?"
JOHNNY RUSSELL (the Cook). "Here, we've little o' Fish!"

JULY 31.

GENERAL GRANT on this day made a determined assault on Petersburg, ordering the explosion of a mine by which 150 Confederates were killed. The attack however was repulsed, the Federals retiring with a loss of 10,000 men. About this time the "Tallahassee," a steam vessel belonging to the Southerners, but which had been built in London, attacked and destroyed many of the United States merchant vessels. On the 5th of August, on the other hand, the Confederate fleet near Mobile was defeated and destroyed by Admiral Farragut, the U.S. commander.

AUG. 1.

BY the preliminaries of the Treaty of Vienna, the King of Denmark, yielding to *force majeure*, agreed to the cession of the Duchies to Austria and Prussia. Earl Russell, writing to Bismarck respecting the claims to "moderation" made by the German Powers, said, "If it is said that force has decided this question, and that the superiority of the arms of Austria and Prussia over those of Denmark was incontestable, the assertion must be admitted. But in that case it is out of place to claim credit for equity and moderation."

SEPT. 1.

GENERAL SHERMAN defeated the Confederate leader Hood, and compelled him to retire from Atalanta, which the Federals occupied.

On the same day Mr. McClellan was nominated for the next Presidency by the Democratic Convention at Chicago. His address, however, though declaring for the maintenance of the Union, was thought by some of his supporters not sufficiently uncompromising in its resolution to continue the war. This led to the division of the Democratic party, and

RELIEVING GUARD AT THE VATICAN.

France to Italy. "You mustn't let nobody outside annoy the Party inside; and you mustn't let the Party inside annoy anybody outside."

SEPT. 15.

A CONVENTION was this day concluded between France and Italy, by virtue of which France undertook to withdraw her troops from the Pontifical States in proportion as the army of the Pope should be organised, whilst

of the Holy Father, and prevent by force any attack thereupon from without. It was also decided that Florence should be substituted for Turin as the capital of the Italian Kingdom.

(See Cartoon, "Relieving Guard at the Vatican.")

Oct. 1.

On this day occurred a terrible explosion at Erith of some 1,000 barrels of gunpowder, which completely destroyed and pulverised the buildings of Messrs. Hall, killing ten men and seriously injuring others.

Oct. 29.

"Australia" (says a Note to Vol. XLVII.) "objected to the deportation of criminals from England." The colony had indeed for some time past protested against the continued introduction of convicts from the mother country into their midst, and in this very natural feeling the sympathy of Mr. Punch and the English public was with them.

(Sir Cresswell, "Colonists and Convicts.")

Early in the following year (Jan. 26) it was publicly announced in Melbourne that Australia

COLONISTS AND CONVICTS.

Australian Colonist. "Now, Mr. Party. Don't shed any more of your Burglars here, or you and I shall quarrel."

had ceased to be a colony to which convicts were liable to be sent. ("Annals of Our Time.")

Oct. 29.

On this day Mr. Punch and the whole English-speaking race were saddened by the premature decease of that gifted artist and genial caricaturist of the Victorian Era, John Leech, who died at Hammersmith, at the age of 46. The following was Mr. Punch's heartfelt tribute to the memory of his great contributor:—

JOHN LEECH.

Obiit October 29th, MDCCCLXIV.

ÆTAT. 46.

The simplest words are best where all words are vain. Ten days ago, a great artist, in the noon of life, and with his glorious mental faculties in full power, but with the shade of physical infirmity darkening upon him, took his accustomed place among friends who have this day laid his pall. Some of them had been fellow-workers with him for a quarter of a century, others far fewer years; but to know him at all was to love him dearly, and all in whose name these lines are written mourn as for a brother. (In comparison as in the estimates of a loss to our art and land, and in a hundred works which, at the least, few will not remember were ready than those who have just left his grave. While Leech, whose every phrase he has illustrated with a truth, a grace, and a tenderness known wherever to satiric art, gladly and proudly taken charge of his fame, they, whose pride in the genius of a genial comrade was equalled by their affection for an unselfish friend, would leave on record that they have known no kindlier, more refined, or more generous nature than that of him who has been thus early called to his rest.

Remember the Fourth.

Oct. 30.

The Treaty of Peace was concluded at Vienna between Denmark and Germany. Its main stipulations were that Denmark should give up the Duchies, pay a war indemnity, and assent to a rectification of the Jutland frontier.

Nov. 8.

A<small>BRAHAM</small> L<small>INCOLN</small> was to-day re-elected President for a second term. General McClellan, the other candidate, resigned his command in the U.S. army.

Nov. 10.

A<small>T</small> this time what was called "Spiritualism" was rampant in London society. "The Davenport Brothers," as they dubbed themselves, were performing to crowded audiences their contemptible juggleries. "Three impostors" (says a Note to Vol. XLVII.) "pretended to be

aided by spiritual agency, which released them from their bonds, and played other vagaries in the dark." Spiritualistic "Mediums," female as well as male, pushed a profitable trade by a parade of their absurd pretensions and sham "performances." Mr. Punch lost no opportunity of attacking this peculiarly offensive form

THE AMERICAN BROTHERS; OR, "HOW WILL THEY GET OUT OF IT?"

of folly. One of the tricks of the Davenport Brothers was their extrication, by supposed "spiritual" agency, from rope-bonds in a darkened cabinet. Mr. Punch applied this to the situation in America.

(See Cartoon, "The American Brothers; or, How will they Get Out of It?")

Nov. 25.

A<small>T</small> a Meeting of the Oxford Diocesan Society for augmenting the endowments of small benefices, Mr. Disraeli made a speech

which excited much attention and some amusement. The speech, apart from its Disraelian characteristics of high-flown diction, pungent paradox and adroit epigram, excited interest as presumably embodying "the future Church policy of the Church party." Mr. Disraeli boldly ranged himself with orthodox Anglicanism against heterodox science. "I am not prepared," he said, "to say that the lecture-rooms is more scientific than the Church. What is the question which is now placed before society with

ing? That question is this—is man an ape or an angel? My Lord, I am on the side of the angels. I repudiate with indignation and abhorrence these new-fangled theories. But on the other hand, what does the Church teach us? It teaches us that man is made in the image of his Creator. . . . It is between these two principles that society will have to decide. Upon our acceptance of that divine truth of which the Church is the guardian, all sound and coherent and sensible legislation depends;

is the only guarantee of
real progress."
(*See Cartoon, "Dressing for an
Oxford Bal Masqué."*)

"APE OR ANGEL!"

"On the side of the angels," say
Dizzy?- oh, then [Dr.
How happy the angels should
The ally whom they least could
have looked for of sen
In their array enlisted to see!

The Angelical Doctor's collapsed
in the blow [Dizzy—
Or a new Arch-Angelical
Now that brain big with schemes,
and that tongue glib of
phrase, [Izzy.
On their mission angelic are

Lifting 'gainst the Broad Church
a contempt sans bred,
At Reviewers and Essayists
pointing
The dagger sciens drawn since
you flashed it on Perl,
Wit's edge with Hate's poison
envining.

Port, novelist, journalist, hard-
hip-city trucker,
Capt of Grand - Commission
mystery— 'Exchequer,
Agriculturist, Chancellor of the
New nobles, now actor, of
history—

Yet screen the few mimes can
from Nature escape,
And what's Simham to Nobody
breaks change ill!
Have a may but then then
shouldst be most of the Ape,
When most bent on smoothing
the Angel.

DEC. 8.

The Pope issued an En-
cyclical Letter. An
appendix of eighty propo-
sitions denounced what His
Holiness considered the
chief modern errors and
heresies, religious, scientific
and social. The Papal condemnation included what
are commonly considered
as progress, liberalism and
modern civilization, civil
liberty of worship, freedom
of the press, biblical, so-
cialist, and other secret
societies, and the doctrines
that there was salvation out
of the true Church, and
that Protestantism was only another form of
belief equally pleasing to God.

DEC. 22.

The year ended with the great American
quarrel still unsettled, but to close ob-
servers it became increasingly apparent that in

DRESSING FOR AN OXFORD BAL MASQUÉ.

"*The question is, Is Man an Ape or an Angel? (A Laugh.) Now, I am on the side of the Angels! (Cheers.)*"—MR. DISRAELI's
Oxford Speech, Friday, November 25.

General Sherman, writing to President Lincoln,
said: " I beg to present you, as a Christmas
gift, the city of Savannah, with 300 heavy guns
and plenty of ammunition, and also about
25,000 bales of cotton." Sherman had just
completed his notorious "thirty days' raid"
through Georgia. After destroying Atlanta on
the 15th November, he had marched through

Georgia, a march of 300 miles, capturing cattle,
collecting negroes, horses, mules, waggons, and
foraging freely on the best produce of the
country. On the 30th he appeared at Savannah,
which he took possession of. The feat was a
daring and sensational one, and helped to put
the Federals in good heart after many reverses.
It was indeed " the beginning of the end."

✦ 1865 ✦

JAN. 1.

"THE year 1805," says *Mr. Punch's Political Summary,* "opened with every assurance of 'peace and plenty.' The cotton famine, which had been attended with so much misery during the two preceding years, had now almost vanished, and the Lancashire districts showed indications of returning prosperity. The unhappy contest in America, which had now lasted four years, appeared to be drawing to a close as the Southern States gave signs of exhaustion."

The Pope's Encyclical Letter, reference to which has already been made, caused considerable excitement in France. On the first day of the year the French Minister of Justice addressed a circular to the Bishops of the Church, warning them that as "the Encyclical contained propositions contrary to the principles on which the constitution of the Empire was based," as well as to the liberties of the Gallican Church, its publication was prohibited. Against this a formal protest was raised by thirty-four prelates of the Ultramontane party in France.

[*See Cartoon, "The Imperial Bull-fighter."*]

JAN. 2.

ON this day Mr. John Bright presided at the opening of the new Exchange at Birmingham. He spoke vigorously on behalf of merchants and manufacturers, who he held were not self-assertive in proportion to their importance and their merits. He said that from the commercial classes, and not from monarchs or great lords of the soil, had come whatever there was of social, or civil, or religious freedom to the inhabitants of this country. Speaking of armies, he said they were a "reserve power" not to be also-

THE IMPERIAL BULL-FIGHTER.

L. Nap.—"*You are tired of Bull-fighting, my Bird'un. You shall in no gore my Papal friend yonder the cover the while.*"

JAN. 18.

MR. BRIGHT, at Birmingham, again spoke strongly in favour of Parliamentary Reform, which he declared, if really desired by the excluded five or six millions, must come despite "the 400 easy gentlemen who lounge in and out of that decorated chamber under the same roof," Statesmen, and who does in Downing Street." He claimed for them "the right of admission, through their representatives, into the most ancient and venerable Parliament which at this hour exists among men; and when they are thus admitted, and not till then, it may be truly said that England, the august mother of free nations,

FEB. 3.

PRESIDENT LINCOLN and Secretary Seward met the Confederate Secretary Stephens and a Commissioner at Fort Monroe with a view to negotiate peace. As the Confederate representative, however, refused to treat except on the basis of the recognition of the South, which the President said was wholly inadmissible, the conference was fruitless.

FEB. 7.

PARLIAMENT was opened by Commission. It was (says Mr. Punch's "Essence") "the last session of the Parliament evoked by the Conservatives for their own emersion from office." It had "lived to an unnatural old age, and assumed somewhat of an awful character." "It has a painful consciousness of its own time having been misspent, and therefore it abuses all around it for not bring in a frenzy of energy."

The Royal Speech foreshadowed measures for the revision of the Statute Law, the concentration of the Law Courts, the Relief of the Poor, Public Schools, and the Patent Laws.

A considerable surplus was confidently anticipated, and the advocates of the reduction of the Malt Tax, Fire Assurance, &c., were already clamouring for a share of it.

(See Cartoon, "Back to School.")

MARCH 1.

KING VICTOR EMMANUEL on this day made a triumphal entry into Florence, which city had been selected — until the hoped-for time when Rome should become so — as the capital of the new Italian Kingdom.

MARCH 4.

INAUGURATION of Abraham Lincoln and Andrew Johnson as President and Vice-President of America. The Vice-President

BACK TO SCHOOL. THE BOY WITH THE CAKE.

Chorus of Greedy Boys. "Give us a slice! Give us a slice!"
Dr. Pam (Head Master). "Keep back, Boys! Keep back! or it shall not be cut till Easter."

obvious excitement was attributed to intoxication. The incident created great scandal.

MARCH 28.

MR. DILLWYN, in the Commons, moved — "That the present position of the Irish Church Establishment is unsatisfactory, and

Government." Mr. Gladstone spoke in the debate, saying that though he was not prepared to submit the remedy required, he could not refuse his consent to so much of Mr. Dillwyn's resolution as declared that the condition of the Irish Church was unsatisfactory. He said that "if the condition upon which the ecclesiastical

was altered at the Reformation, that alteration was made mainly with the view that these endowments should be conferred to a body ministering to the wants of a great majority of the people." He avowed his belief that "those who directed the government of this country in the reign of Queen Elizabeth ... would probably be not a little surprised if they could look down the vista of time and see that in the year 1865 the result of all their labours had been that after 300 years the Church which they had endowed and established ministered to the religious wants of only one-eighth or one-ninth part of the community."

Like Mr. Gladstone's recent deliverance on the subject of the Parliamentary Franchise, the speech was a significant foreshadowing of things to come. It excited at once the anger and the alarm of the thick-and-thin supporters of all Church Establishments. The debate was adjourned, and was not resumed during this Session.

APRIL 2.

RICHARD COBDEN, the great champion of Free Trade, died this day at his residence in Suffolk Street, at the age of 60. Earnest tributes to the memory of the great Free Trader and advocate of peace were paid in Parliament, by Lord Palmerston for the Government, and Mr. Disraeli on behalf of the Opposition. The latter described him as "not only an ornament to the House, but an honour to England." Mr. Bright, his personal friend and co-worker in many contests, speaking under the influence of great emotion said : "I can only say that after many years of most intimate and more brotherly friendship, I little knew how much I loved him until I found that I had lost him." He was in-

ARBITRATION BETTER THAN EMIGRATION.

PLUTUS AND VULCAN ACCEPT THE DECISION OF JUSTICE.

attended by many distinguished men and a large contingent from the House of Commons.

APRIL 2.

THERE had been prolonged strike and lockout in the South Staffordshire iron districts, which at last came to an end. In consequence of the

ironmasters (says "Annals of Our Time,") had on the 4th March turned out their workmen and blown off their furnaces. About 70,000 men were without work, and £10,000 per week of wages was lost to them. On the 5th the masters in South Staffordshire re-opened their works, having come to terms with the men.

APRIL 2.

On this day occurred the fall of Richmond, which was practically the close of the great and protracted American War. It was a mortal stroke from which the South could not recover.

(See Cartoon, "The American Gladiators—Habet!")

The siege of Richmond had lasted 1,452 days. The defence had been conducted with courage and skill, especially by the gallant General Lee, who only on the 18th February in this year had taken the general command of the Confederate forces. On the 31st March had commenced a furious and sanguinary three days'

fight at Five Forks. On the 1st April Sheridan succeeded in turning Lee's front, totally routing him and compelling him to retire. On the 2nd the Confederates evacuated Richmond, which was at once occupied by Grant. And on the 9th a climax to the series of Southern disasters occurred, for Lee, who had been overtaken by

THE AMERICAN GLADIATORS—HABET!

Sheridan and defeated at Sailor's Creek on the 6th, surrendered with the Army of Virginia to Grant at Appomatox Court House. It was now "Habet!" indeed!

AFTER THE FIGHT.

Habet! The final cast is made,
The well-poised net falls true,
Hampering, alike, the trenchant blade,
And the strong hand that drew
The world-wide Circus holds its breath
Between the lots of life and death;

Recalls the thrilling combat's course

Courage that took no count of force,
But cheered, and charged, and closed;
Prowess that from defeat arose,
And learnt to deal, by baulking blows,

Till Circus-haunters, who had watched
Famed sword-plays, long ago,
And summed those giants, rudely matched,
Felt admiration grow,
As stubborn strife to strength gave shift,
The art to guard, the craft to lift.

While the fight raged, eyes had but even
To watch its changing cheer;
In busy cheers and sudden silent,
Speaking their hope and fear,
While foot to foot, and hand to hand,

Oh, our short-sighted eyes unlearned
The chances of the fight,
Amused to see him turn, who fled,
Him, who pursued, to flight.
But chance and change can shift to sure,
Might is made clear, resistance o'er.

Brows set in joining the round,
As with a single will;
For rashness's temper is keen,
While sympathy is still;
Millions of throats the circus clears,
But let the vanquished claim a tear.

Man's noble God's guidance doth enwrap,
Are reason and ruth are veiled;
But all men are, when blood runs cool,

In him that, spent and scarred, lies low,
Hate o'erleaf upon own a noble foe.

Not always to the swift the race,
Nor to the brave the fight;
But conquest's blest that adds the grace
Of mercy mee might,

Then let the sign that says "We spare,"
Be his that hath, blinding, there.

Let the blessed purge the bitter sin
For which he fought as well.—
The right claimed for the whiter skin
Black his to buy and sell;
Its champion fall'n, that sin is slain,
Never, like him, to rise again.

Thus sunneth these gushes' columns flood,
Brother take brother's hand,

And o'er the stain of kindred blood
Sweep smooth the trampled sand;
The fate, unto your merry green,
Spare, with sachain of Earth and Heaven.

APRIL 14.

TO-DAY America, just rejoicing over the termination of her long internecine struggle,

BRITANNIA SYMPATHISES WITH COLUMBIA.

was struck dumb with horror and grief at the terrible tragedy of the assassination of her President, Abraham Lincoln. The President was in his private box at Ford's Theatre, Washington, where the assassin, a furious fanatic named John Wilkes Booth, son of a once celebrated actor, made his way into the box, and fired, at close quarters, a pistol-shot, which, entering the President's head at the back, passed nearly through. "Sic semper tyrannis!" shouted Booth, jumping on to the stage and brandishing a knife. He then made his escape at the back

only lived until the morning, when he expired, to the bitter and wrathful grief of his country-men, and the sorrow of the civilised world.

At the same time another assassin made his way into the sick-chamber of Mr. Seward, and inflicted upon him with a knife severe and dangerous wounds, from which, however, the Secretary happily recovered.

This ghastly tragedy came as a shock upon the world, and evoked earnest sympathy in every quarter, particularly, as was natural, in this country. The Queen sent an autograph

"From a Widow to a Widow." Mr. Punch, who had made the groan and ungrudgingly, but, as events proved, genuine-souled and brave Abraham Lincoln the butt of some sharp satire, was forward with the expression of his sympathy and his regret.

[See Cartoon, " Britannia Sympathises with Columbia."]

APRIL 26.

TO-DAY Booth, the assassin of President Lincoln, and Harrold, his associate in the murderous conspiracy, were tracked to a barn

taken refuge. Booth lame
from a broken ankle, caused
in his leap from the President's box to the stage.
Harrold surrendered, and
was taken to Washington,
but Booth refusing to do so,
the barn was fired, and in
the end the assassin was
shot dead by a cavalry-ser-
geant named Corbett, whilst
he was trying to extinguish
the flames.

APRIL 28.

Mr. GLADSTONE brought
forward his Budget.
The revenue for the
year he estimated at
£70,170,000, its expendi-
ture at £66,130,000, sur-
plus over four millions. He
proposed to take twopence
off the Income-Tax, reducing it from 6d. to 4d., sixpence off the Tea-Duty,
and to make the Fire-In-
surance Duty a uniform
eighteenpence, altogether a
relief of taxation to the
amount of £3,170,000,
made up thus: Tea-Duty
£3,300,000, Income-Tax
£1,800,000, Fire-Insurance
Duty £350,000. The Bud-
get was well received, and
was thought to strengthen
the chances of the Liberal
Party in the coming Gene-
ral Election.

MAY 3.

Mr. BAINES had intro-
duced his Bill for
reducing the franchise in
boroughs from £10 to £6.
On the motion for second
reading on this date there
was a keen debate, in which
Mr. Robert Lowe made a
slashing speech against the
Bill, warning the Liberals
against an alliance with
Democracy. He spoke dis-
paragingly of the working
classes, saying that any
man could have the suf-
frage if he chose to give up 110 quarts of beer in
the year, that the man who would not make that
sacrifice did not deserve the trust, and that it
ought not to be degraded (Punch's "Essence of
Parliament"). Mr. Disraeli was in favour of a
large extension of the suffrage, and downwards,
but "in a lateral direction." "Lateral Reform"

THE WORKING-MAN, FROM THE ROYAL WESTMINSTER EXHIBITION.

(1) THE WORKING-MAN . . . John Bright. | (3) THE WORKING-MAN . . . Edward Horsman.
(2) THE WORKING-MAN . . . W. F. Forster. | (4) THE WORKING-MAN . . . R. Lowe.

previous question was ultimately carried by 288
to 214, majority 74 for dropping Mr. Baines'
Bill. The debate led to much angry discussion
in party papers and elsewhere concerning the
character and fitness for electoral power of the
working classes. "The Working Man" (said
Mr. Punch) "cannot complain that he is cut

by such divergent authorities as Mr. John
Bright, Mr. W. E. Forster, Mr. Edward Horsman, and Mr. Robert Lowe, furnished Punch
with the subject for a significant Cartoon, showing the incompleteness and the exaggeration of
partisan ideals.

(See Cartoon, "The Working-man, from the Royal

MAY 10.

Mr. Jefferson Davis, late President of the Southern Confederation, was this day captured at Irwinsville, Georgia, by a company of Federal cavalry. He was imprisoned.

MAY 14.

Mr. Villiers (for the Government) had introduced (on the 17th March) what was known as "The Union Chargeability Bill." "Its chief object," said Mr. Punch's "Essence," "was to prevent landowners, farmers, and others who dislike the poor, or, at least, dislike supporting the poor, from turning them out of parishes. .... Of course the country gentlemen (many of them against their own sense of justice) opposed the measure, but the Second Reading was carried by 203 to 131." On May 15 "the Excluders of the Poor rallied for a new fight. . . . The Obstructive Exclusives were defeated by the enormous majority of 166 to 93."

Ultimately, despite much opposition, the Bill passed both Houses, and received the Royal Assent.

"OUT OF THE PARISH."

Sir Giles Overreach. "Now, then, my man! Your work's done, so be off out of the Parish." Agricultural Labourer. "Ah! Sir Giles! It is better not have made it a Town." Sir Giles Overreach. "Can't help that! No 'Union chargeability' for me."

UNION CHARGEABILITY.

SONG OF THE COUNTRY GENTLEMAN.

Tune—Sir Roger de Coverley.

This new Bill's a bore,
Raising land's grumbling,
To make to maintain our own poor
In spite of our humility,
The burden we used to evade
With comfortable facility;

Well we worked the clown,
In his days of juvenility,
When his hair was black or brown,
We taxed his strength and agility,
To his parish we sent him away,
In indigence and senility,
For his keep not forced to pay
By Union Chargeability.

We need the labouring man,
While he had any utility,

He and don't he done;
triumphs in imbecility;
But a clue very hard to shun
Will be Union Chargeability.

Which way now to turn
Will puzzle our versatility,
Though we'd gladly learn,
With studious docility.
But we shall be forced to bow,
In meekness and humility,

Unless we can reduce
This measure to futility,
Regardless of abuse,
And caring, small possibility;
Unmindful of contempt
Expressed with incivility,
And resolve to remain exempt
From Union Chargeability.

(See Cartoon, "Out of the Parish.")

MAY 20.

In view of the impending appeal to the country, Mr. Disraeli issued an address to the electors of Buckinghamshire. He laid emphasis on the necessity for maintaining the National Church, saying that without his conservative our scheme of government would degenerate into a mere system of police. He saw nothing in such a result "but the corruption of nations and the fall of empires." He also reiterated his view concerning what he had previously (see May 3) called "Lateral Reform."

(*See Cartoon, "Dizzy's K'rect Card for the 'Derby.'"*)

MAY 22.

President Johnson proclaimed the opening of the Southern ports. On the 29th he declared an amnesty, with certain exceptions. The new President was indeed in favour of leniency towards the vanquished South to an extent which excited suspicion and distrust in some quarters. On the 26th Kirby Smith, the last of the Confederate Generals in arms, surrendered, thus finally closing the great war.

MAY 31.

The celebrated French horse "Gladiateur," belonging to Count Lagrange, on this day won the "Derby" of 1865.

JUNE 3.

The Princess of Wales, at eighteen minutes past one this morning, was safely delivered of a son, Prince George.

JUNE 9.

Mr. Gladstone, whose increasingly Liberal tendencies had for some time created alarm amongst his Tory and clerical constituents at Oxford, had been questioned by Dr. Hannah

DIZZY'S K'RECT CARD FOR THE "DERBY"(!)

"K'rect Card, my noble Sportsmen!"—"K'rect Card!"—"Church in Danger!"—"Lateral Reform!"—"K'rect Card!"

the meaning of his recent speech on the Established Church in Ireland. He replied "that the question being remote, and apparently out of all bearing on the practical politics of the day, he thought it would be far him far worse than superfluous to determine upon any scheme or basis of a scheme with respect to it." "As far as I clearly the broad distinction which I make between the abstract and practical views of the subject." He added, "I scarcely expect ever to be called upon to share in such a measure," and hoped that Dr. Hannah would "not and approve my reason for not wishing to carry my own mind further into a question lying at a distance I

JUNE 27.

At this time the Cattle Plague, or Rinderpest, as it was called, began to spread in the dairies of Lambeth and Islington, a cowkeeper at the former place losing 100 animals. The pest spread fast in spite of the most stringent measures for prevention. "By the middle of October" (says the Political Summary to Vol. XLIX.) "over 14,000 head of cattle had been either killed or had died from the disease; in November the number increased to over 81,000, and during the last few weeks of the year the Commissioners reported that more than 50,000 head of cattle had perished."

JUNE 28.

News arrived in this country that Mr. Samuel Baker, completing the work of Speke and Grant, had discovered the second and main source of the Nile in the Lake Albert Nyanza, north latitude 2° 17', the other source being the Victoria Nyanza discovered by Speke.

WAITING FOR THE VERDICT.

"*CONSERVATIVE REACTION*" *ON ITS TRIAL.—See Tory Papers.*

JULY 6.

Parliament was prorogued by Commission until the 11th instant, when it was dissolved by Royal Proclamation. The Elections to the new one were issued immediately. Lord Palmerston claimed a renewal of confidence. Mr. Bright, denying his right to it, because his Administration had broken its solemn pledges, urged once more the cause of Parliamentary Reform. Mr. Mill advocated the suffrage "for all grown persons, both men and women, who of three, and who have not, within some small number of years, received parish relief." He could, however, give the vote in such a manner that no class, even the most numerous, could swamp all the others taken together, and he advocated the representation of minorities. He was "prepared to support a measure which would give the labouring classes a clear half of the national representation."

The elections began on the 11th July. The City returned Goschen, Crawford, Lawrence and Rothschild, all Liberals, and Mr. Mill headed lost 33 seats and gained 57, the Liberals returned numbering 387, and the Conservatives 290. Nominal Liberal majority in the new Parliament, 77.

(*See Cartoon,* "*Waiting for the Verdict.*")

JULY 12.

Mr. Bright, at the Birmingham nomination, sharply criticised Mr. Disraeli with special reference to his fancy for "lateral reform," which he declared would fail, as the "fancy franchises" had failed. "We," he said, "who advocate honest, open, clearly understood and

Mr. Gladstone was defeated at the Oxford University election by Mr. Gathorne Hardy, the return being: Heathcote 3,236, Hardy 1,904, Gladstone 1,724. Hardy thus beating Gladstone by a majority of 180.

"Oxford's loss is England's gain," said *Mr. Punch*. "We condole with the University. We congratulate the Chancellor of the Exchequer and the country. He can now throw away the pole, and with unfaltering steps proceed on the path staked out for him. There was a nonconformity between Mr. Gladstone and the old 'Masters,' which no growth of intelligence in the minds of the country clergy and county squires, no softening of the bigotry of the cloister and the common room could ever have abolished. He had outgrown the suit of Oxford Mixture, which will exactly fit Mr. Gathorne Hardy."

Mr. Gladstone had certainly outgrown Toryism of the Oxford type. He said himself, addressing a large meeting in the Free-Trade Hall, Manchester, on the 18th: "At last, my friends, I am come among you— and I am come, to use an expression which has become very famous, and is not likely to be forgotten, I am come among you 'unmuzzled.'" Expressing a very natural regret at being dismissed after eighteen years' service from the representation of the University, "which he had loved with a deep and passionate love," and saying, "I have no complaint to make of the party which has refused me the representation of that place," he continued, "I am aware of no cause for the votes which have given a majority against me in the University of Oxford, except the fact that the strongest conviction that the human mind can receive, that an overpowering sense of the public interest, that the

PEGASUS UNHARNESSED.

my youth Oxford herself taught me to lay open my mind—all these have shewn me the folly, and, I will say, the madness of refusing to join in the generous sympathies of my countrymen, by adopting what I must call an obstructive policy."

As a landmark in Mr. Gladstone's political

length. He was returned for South Lancashire on the 20th July, third on the poll, with 8,786 votes as against 8,806 for Turner, and 9,171 for Egerton, the two Conservatives elected. From that time forward his mind developed rapidly in the direction of Liberalism.

(*See Cartoon, "Pegasus Unharnessed."*)

JULY 23.

T_{HE} "Great Eastern" started to lay the new Atlantic Cable, accompanied by the "Sphinx" and the "Terrible." The first one, as already recorded, had been successfully laid in August, 1858. The insulation of the wire,

however, soon became imperfect, and intelligence could no longer be transmitted. In 1860 a new Company was formed, and in the present year the "Great Eastern" Steamship was engaged to lay down 2,300 miles of wire. On the 23rd July she connected the wire with the shore of Valentia, and sailed for America. For

some days all seemed to go well, but ultimately the insulation proved defective again, and the apparatus for raising the wire being inadequate, the "Great Eastern" had to return to England, arriving in the Medway on the 19th August.

(See Cartoon, " A Word to the Mermaids.")

A WORD TO THE MERMAIDS.

NEPTUNE. "Ah—o-o-o-oy, there! Cut off a that 'ere Cable, can't you—that's the way father and me treated !!!"

AUG. 14.

B_Y the Convention of Gastein the Danish Duchies were partitioned between Austria and Prussia. Kiel was made a harbour for the German Fleet. Earl Russell wrote that in this Convention all rights, sovereign or popular, had been trodden under foot, and the authority of force alone consulted and recognized.

AUG. 15.

T_{HE} English Fleet paid a visit to Cherbourg,

very courteously and hospitably entertained. A little later, on the 26th, the French Fleet paid a return visit to Portsmouth, where their hospitality was heartily reciprocated.

SEPT. 18.

A_T this time what was known as the Fenian Conspiracy, a secret insurrectionary organization of a violently disloyal character, fed with men and money from the Irish party in America, began to give much trouble. Mr. Justice Keogh, describing its character, said, "the object

of the people, but especially the artizans in towns, and the cultivators of the soil; its ramifications existed not only in this country, but in the States of America; supplies of money and of arms for the purposes of a general insurrection were being collected, not only here, but on the other side of the Atlantic; and, finally, the object of this Confederation was the overthrow of the Queen's authority, the separation of this country (Ireland) from Great Britain, the destruction of our present Constitution, the establishment of some democratic or military despotism, and the

a successful civil war."
(*Annual Register*, 1865.)

On this day the *Irish People*, a Fenian organ in the press, was seized by the Dublin police, all the men on the establishment being arrested. Next day a reward of £500 was offered for the apprehension of one James Stephens, a notorious Fenian leader.

SEPT. 16.

HERR VON BISMARCK, whose domination in the councils of Prussia was becoming more and more manifest, was this day created a Count.

SEPT. 23.

SINCE the death of the Prince Consort the Queen had lived a life of almost absolute retirement. *Mr. Punch* at this time published a Cartoon, based upon a familiar incident in Shakespeare's "Winter's Tale," which, as he explained in a note, "was expressive of the loyal aspiration that Her Majesty would again return to the exercise of her public duties."

(*See* Cartoon, "*Queen Hermione*.")

OCT. 7.

ON this day occurred a serious outbreak of the negroes in Jamaica, beginning at Morant Bay, in the district of St. Thomas-in-the-East, about 20 miles east from Kingston. "For some time previously" (says the "Annual Register") "there had been a good deal of discontent amongst the black population, which had been fostered by the harangues of agitators and the addresses of Baptist ministers, who attributed the distress from which the island suffered to the misgovernment of its rulers."

A band of some 150 men, armed with sticks, assembled in the square in front of the Court-house, with the avowed intention of rescuing a man who was to be tried for some offence, in the case of his being found guilty. A man having

QUEEN HERMIONE.

PAULINA (*Restorative*) *Unveils the Statue.* "'Tis Hers! Descend; be Stone no more!"—*Winter's Tale, Act V., Scene 3.*

the Court-house, the mob made a rush and rescued him from the hands of the police, some of whom were bruised and ill-treated.

Warrants were issued for the apprehension of twenty-eight of the rioters. When however an attempt was made to arrest one Paul Bogle, a body of armed men rescued him, and made prisoners made an attack on the vestry at Morant Bay, murdering the Custos and many other white men, and setting fire to the Court-house.

The Governor, General Eyre, fearing the spread of the insurrection, proclaimed martial law, and summarily punished the ringleaders by hanging or shooting. A coloured member of

Gordon, a popular leader among the black people, who was regarded as the chief instigator of the revolt, was arrested, tried by court-martial and hanged.

This and other severe measures adopted by Governor Eyre, excited great indignation in some quarters, both in the Island and at home, and public opinion was sharply and angrily divided on the question. A meeting was held in Exeter Hall to denounce Governor Eyre for undue haste and excessive severity in suppressing the revolt, the Abolition party and certain religious sects being especially loud in their protests. *Mr. Punch*, on the other hand, held that the Governor had been justified by the exigencies of the occasion, and had probably saved the white population of Jamaica, men and women, from butchery and something worse.

(See Cartoon, " *The Jamaica Question.*")

Eventually Governor Eyre was suspended pending inquiry, and Sir Henry Storks appointed temporarily in his place.

Oct. 18.

LORD PALMERSTON died. The venerable and popular Premier, always, from his unfailing courage, his unconquerable cheeriness and his patriotic spirit, an especial favourite with *Mr. Punch* as with the British people, was within two days of completing his eighty-first year. He expired at Brocket Hall, after an illness of a few days' duration, from which at one time his recovery was confidently expected. Henry John Temple, third, and last, Viscount Palmerston, had sat in the House nearly 60 years, namely since 1806, when he was first returned for Horsham. He was interred in Westminster Abbey on the 27th amidst general signs of honour and

memory of him who was affectionately known as " our everyreen Premier ":—

PALMERSTON.

BORN: OCTOBER 20, 1784. DIED: OCTOBER 18, 1865.

He's down, and for ever! The good fight is ended.

He falls, but unvanquished. He falls in his glory,
A noble old King on the last of his fields :
And with death-song we crown, like the Northmen of story,
And tenderly bear him away on our shields.

Not yet are we conquerors. Let proud words be spoken

THE JAMAICA QUESTION.

White Planter. " Am not I a Man and Brother, too, Mr. Stiggins?"

THE DEMON BUTCHER, OR THE REAL RINDERPEST.

His courage undaunted, his purpose unaltered,
His long patient labour, his
exquisite skill,
The tones of command from a
tongue that ne'er faltered
When bidding the Nations to
list to my will;

Let these be remembered; but
higher and better
The witness that tells how he
dwelt with his trust,
In curbing the tyrant, in breaking the fetter,
Lay the pleasure of him we
commit to the dust.

But his heart was his England's,
his idol her honour,
Her friend was his friend, and
his foe was her foe,
Were her mandate despised, or a
scowl cast upon her,
How stern his rebuke, or how
vengeful his blow!

Her armies were sad, and her
honours were tarnished,
And lethargy wrought on her
strength like a spell,
He came to the front, the undisciplined was marshaled—
The rout let a rectified enemy
tell.

As true to our welfare, he did
his own mission
When Progress approached
him with Wisdom for guide;
He cleared her a path, and with
equal derision
Bade quack and fanatic alike
stand aside.

The choice of his country, her
faction despising,
He marched as a leader all
true men could claim:
They came to their fellows, and
held it sufficing
To glory, to a creed, the great
Minister's name.

So, Hesh in recollection of Him,
long departed,
"Who called the New World
up to balance the Old,"
We lay them in earth,—gallant-
souvened, true-hearted!
Break, humble, thy wound, for
his honours are told.

No, let Pride my law story and
cease, for Affection
Stands one with a wealth of
wild tears in her eyes,
And claims to be heard with
more soft recollection
Of one who was ever so kindly
as wise.

We trusted his wisdom, but here drew no answer
Than homage we owed to his strenuously oft,
For never was monument to Englishmen dearer
Than he who had faith in the great English heart.

The frank steady laugh, and the honest eye filling
With mirth, and the jests that so rapidly fell,
Told out the State secret that made us right willing
...

Our brave English Chief"—lay him down for the sleeping
That nought may disturb till the trumpet of doom:
Honour claims the proud vigil—but Love will come
weeping,
And hang many garlands on Palmerston's tomb!

Oct. 31.

This Commission appointed to inquire into
its terrible ravages, issued its report, recommending
the prohibition of transport and other stringent
measures to arrest the contagion. It was
thought that the meat-salesmen made the prevalence of the cattle disease a pretext for needlessly raising the price of butchers' meat.

[See Cartoon, "The Demon Butcher, or the Real

Nov. 6.

It was announced to-day in the *Gazette* that Earl Russell succeeded to the office of First Lord of the Treasury, in place of Lord Palmerston, whilst the Earl of Clarendon became Foreign Secretary.

Nov. 11.

The Fenian head-centre, James Stephens, was this day taken, and confined in Richmond Bridewell, Dublin.

Nov. 24.

James Stephens escaped from Richmond Prison, Dublin, aided by one of the warders. A reward of £1,000 was offered for his recapture.

Nov. 30.

The Fenian trials commenced at Dublin before a Special Commission. A verdict of guilty was returned, Luby and O'Leary were sentenced to twenty years' penal servitude, and a little later, O'Donovan Rossa was sentenced to penal servitude for life.

Dec. 4.

Earl Russell, writing to Mr. Adams the American Minister, some time previous to this had said, " Her Majesty's Government are ready to consent to the appointment of a Commission to which shall be referred all claims arising out of the late Civil War which the two Powers shall agree to refer to the Commissioners." On this day, in his Annual Message to Congress, President Johnson, referring to the claims made by America upon England in consequence of the damage done to American commerce by the Confederate cruisers (the "Alabama" and others) said that he had approved the proposal to submit the question to arbitration, which arbitration, however, had

other hand, the proposition of a joint Commission, which Great Britain desired to substitute for arbitration, had been found unsatisfactory, and therefore declined by the American Government.

(See Cartoon, " The Disputed Account.")

THE DISPUTED ACCOUNT.

Britannia. " Claim for damages against me? Nonsense, Columbia! don't let mum and money matters."

Dec. 10.

On this day died at Laeken, Brussels, Leopold King of the Belgians, in his 75th year. Mr. Punch said of him:—

He used his sway for justice and for truth
The nations sought his voice as well as king's;
The verdict that he spoke all knew as sooth,

+1866+

THE year of the revival of the long-suppressed question of Parliamentary Reform. Lord Palmerston was no longer alive to chaff and checkmate the more zealous advocates of a fresh reduction of the franchise, and, like the Chancellor in the Poet Laureate's "Day-Dream," "smiling, put the question by." Earl Russell, the old champion of Reform, was in power, and his chief lieutenant, Mr. Gladstone, had committed himself, as Lord Palmerston thought prematurely (see Cartoon, "The False Start," p. 96) to the principle of an extended suffrage. Another Reform campaign, long, exciting, full of surprises, and with a wholly unexpected ending, was about to open. On the 3rd January Mr. John Bright, speaking at Rochdale, advised Earl Russell not to listen to the "prophesying Brahmins of the great Whig Houses, which would be fatal to him and his Government. We are endeavouring" (he continued), "by constitutional means to compass a great constitutional end; to make Parliament not only the organ of the will, but the honest and faithful guardian of the interests of all classes in the country." This was felt to be the keynote of the coming struggle; though Mr. Bright's "friendly lead" was in some quarters resented as officious.

[See Cartoon, "The Officious Passenger."]

THE OFFICIOUS PASSENGER.

LORD JOHN. "Excuse me, Friend BRIGHT, but do you command this Ship, or do I?"

JAN. 11.

WRECK of the steam-ship "London." She went down with 220 of her passengers in the Bay of Biscay. The wreck was made memorable by the cool heroism of her commander, Captain Martin, and of a Wesleyan minister, Rev. Daniel Draper, whilst G. V. and unwearying aid to the captain and crew. Dr. Woolley, Principal of Sydney College, and Mr. Palmer, editor of the "Law Times," went down with the vessel. The only survivors were the crew of the pinnace, 19 in number, who were picked up by the Italian barque "Adriamale," and who told the touching story

JAN. 13.

WITH reference to the talk about "Extradition Treaties," Mr. Punch, in his Number for this date, reminded the Emperor of the French that he also had been a refugee in this country, when Prince Napoleon, and might

his own present views than
prevailed in this country.

(*Sir Gorham, " Lord on His
Picture, and ——.*")

Fᴇʙ. 6.

Hᴇʀ new Parliament
was this day opened
by the Queen in person for
the first time since the death
of the Prince Consort. The
Speaker, Mr. Evelyn Deni-
son, had been re-elected on
the 1st inst.

The Speech (says *Mr.
Punch's* "Essence") was
of enormous length, which
the summary of it certainly
will not be. These were
the points :—

1. Our Helena have has arranged Palace Christian of
   Schleswig-Holstein there.
2. Regret at the demise of King
   Leopold.
3. All right with foreign powers.
4. Meeting of French and English fleets promoted amity.
5. Happy that the American
   war is over.
6. Very happy that American
   slavery is over.
7. We have nearly annihilated
   the West African slave
   trade.
8. You shall see the Alabama
   correspondence.
9. Portugal has made it up
   but were so and Brazil.
10. France and we are trying
    to make it up between
    Spain and Chili.
11. Excellent treaty with the
    Mikado, and revision of
    tariff.
12. Commercial treaty with
    Austria.
13. Gumbi-boops, the Com-
    mission, and the new
    Jamaican Government.
14. Nearly all our soldiers are to
    come back from New Zea-
    land.
15. Union of the British North
    American provinces.
16. The Rinderpest. A law to
    be made.
17. Estimates, Economy, Effici-
    ency.
18. The condition of trade is
    satisfactory.
19. The Fenians have caught it.
20. A law about Capital Punish-
    ment.
21. A new Bankruptcy law.
22. Improvement of the Public Audit.
23. And of the law as to certain pensions.
24. A uniform Parliamentary Oath for all religionists.
25. Parliamentary Reform. Lord Russell is nothing in-
    quiries, and what they are made, and he knows his
    own intentions, the energies of Parliament shall be
    called to the result, with a view to such improve-

"LOOK ON THIS PICTURE, AND —"

Bʀɪᴛᴀɴɴɪᴀ. "*That, SOLE, is the Portrait of a Gentleman whom I should have had to give up to the French Government, had I always translated 'Extradition' as your Majesty's lawyers was told.*"

The O'Donoghue wished to have a paragraph
inserted in the Address, to the effect that Members should examine into and remove the disaffection in Ireland, where Fenianism was now
giving great trouble. Said *Mr. Punch*, "An
Irish debate in the Commons elicited a vote, by

A few English Members were in the minority,
and among them Mr. Stuart Mill, who gave his
support to a proposition which Mr. Gladstone,
admitting the necessity of progressive legislation
for Ireland, eloquently condemned. When such
men differ, who shall blame humbler for be-

Government that, in his opinion, the time for the suspension of the Habeas Corpus in Ireland had arrived, as the conspirators (Irishmen imbued with American notions, and possessed of considerable military experience) were "actually organising an outbreak to destroy the Queen's authority."

(See Cartoon, "The Fenian-Pest.")

On the 17th accordingly a Bill for suspending the Habeas Corpus Act in Ireland passed both Houses. Mr. Bright, who said he had never spoken in the House with a deeper sense of shame and humiliation, entreated it not to let the year during which this suspension of the ordinary law was to operate to pass over "till it had done something to rid us of this blot, for blot it is, upon the reign of the Queen and the administration of her statesmen, upon the civilisation and justice of the people of this country."

FEB. 22.

"COUNT VON BISMARCK" (says a newspaper paragraph quoted in *Punch*) "has just communicated to the Chamber of Deputies a Royal decree, ordering both Houses of the Diet to be closed to-morrow, and to remain adjourned until the end of the present session."

This was in consequence of a motion approved by the Government having been rejected by a large majority in the Prussian Chamber. *Mr. Punch's* past song:—

For years, in by-a-weighty cause,
  Opinion's Court has sat
In "Bismarck *versus* Buchanan
  Duffit,"
    Or "Helmet against Hat."
  Opinion bowed, and Law told low,
    Not fearing revolution,
  Now Bismarck with a vanishing blow
    Besmears the Constitution!

FEB. 26.

"... owton's Nightmare, Bumbledom" (says

REBELLION

THE FENIAR-PEST.

HIBERNIA. "O my dear Sister, what shall we to do with these troublesome people?"
BRITANNIA. "Try isolation first, my dear, and then ——

the conflicting jurisdictions of folks who ought to have no jurisdiction at all, and who job, blunder, squabble, and unevenly misgovern the metropolis of the world, was well lectured upon by Lord Robert Montagu. Sir George Grey, who is afraid of everything, is not the man to sweep the whole system of vestries, and boards, and

based on civil representation, and capable of governing; but it is satisfactory to know that the Home Minister is valiant enough to admit that 'the subject is one of great importance.' As he is said to meditate early retirement, we may hope that his successor will go even a step further."

pal Reformer before the days of Mr. Firth. But the step further has not yet been taken.

(See Cartoon, " London's Nightmare.")

MARCH 12.

AT a quarter to five o'clock (says Mr. *Punch's* " Essence of Parliament ") Mr. Gladstone, Chancellor of the Exchequer, rose to introduce THE REFORM BILL.

And what Earl Russell's Government offer in the way of amendment of the Representation (of England and Wales only) is this :—

The County Franchise to be reduced from £50 to £14.

The Borough Franchise to be reduced from £10 to £7.

A Fancy Franchise, giving a vote to any person who has had £50 in the Savings' Bank for two years.

A vote to a Compound Householder whose holding is worth £10 a-year.

A vote to Lodgers who pay £10 a-year.

Abolition of the law that rates must be paid before voting.

Disfranchisement of the men in the Dockyards.

And these changes, and some smaller ones, with which Mr. *Punch* need not trouble the Householders, are expected to result in the adding 400,000 persons, chiefly of the Working Class, to the present number of electors, which Mr. Gladstone estimates at 906,000.

Thoroughly to understand what would be the operation of the proposals, Noterthatllus (who is more interested in the matter than she thanks, for does not Parliament impose the Taxes?) should know that the figures, which have been carefully collected by the Government, show that at present the Working Class, which has been raising itself, and which continues to raise itself, by honourable industry and frugality in the franchise, has already rather more than a Quarter of the representation, the rest being divided among tradesmen, merchants, lawyers, clergymen, physicians, bankers, landowners, fund-holders, and what are termed the Educated Classes generally. The real question before the nation now is, whether it is desirable to ameliorate the process which admits the Working Man, and to lower the franchise to him, instead of encouraging him to rise to it. The meeting the proposed Bill would make the number of Working Men with votes to stand 230,000.

LONDON'S NIGHTMARE.

counts or impressive. To-night his speech, which occupied nearly two hours and a half, was anything but an oration. It was not that the elaborate details into which he had to enter were too small and prosaic for effect. In his Budget speeches, he deals with much smaller things, and lights them up with flashes of wit, or with fortunate allusions. *Mr. Punch* sat very close to the Chancellor of the Exchequer (he swears it by saying that Mr. G.'s attention, and came away with the conviction that Mr. G. had not put his heart into his work.

Then he plunged into the details with admirable lucidity, though without any suspicion. So, on went the speech, never flat, but never rising, or sparkling, and never adorned even by a quotation, until Mr. Gladstone had recapitulated. Then he re-assumed the oratorical tone, and wound up with an allusion to the House

stituency in that *monstrous duplic-
kin,—but to say—

"So multa fidelis members cannot
Fexis armes, unaliquos spessm illa
Init or orbit,"

but to welcome these clauses to
recruits, and thus to begin in
them a new attachment to the
Constitution, the Throne, and
the Laws.

The new Reform Bill,
in which it was suspected
that Mr. Gladstone himself,
acting under the premier-
ship of "Rest and be
thankful" Russell, had
hardly had "a free hand,"
although it alarmed the
timorous foes of Demo-
cracy, hardly enlisted the
ardent support of its en-
thusiastic friends.

MARCH 13.

Mr. Robert Lowe, from
the Liberal Benches,
made a vehement attack on
the Government Reform
Bill. He objected to placing
more power in the hands
of the lower orders. "If"
(he said) "you want ve-
nality, ignorance, drunkenness, and the means of
intimidation—if you want
impulsive, unreflecting and
violent people, where will
you go to look for them—
to the top or the bottom?"
These words, as seeming
to imply sweeping dispar-
agement of the proletariat,
gave great offence to the
working classes and their
champions. Mr. Bright
retorted vigorously upon
Mr. Lowe, Mr. Horsman,
and other Liberal oppo-
nents of the Bill, whom, in
words which have passed
into the political vocabu-
lary, he charged with
having "retired into a political Cave of Adullam, to
which they invited everyone
who was in distress, and
everyone who was discon-
tented. Mr. Horsman had
succeeded in looking the
right honourable gentleman the Member for Calne,
(Mr. Lowe); a party formed of two men so ami-
able, so genial, so both of these right honourable
gentlemen should be a party perfectly harmonious
and distinguished by a mutual and unbroken
trust. But" (he added) "there is one great
difficulty in the way. It is very much like the case

PUDDING BEFORE MEAT.

Lady Constance. "Why, John! Beef before Pudding!"
Dizzy. "Not so! What an absurd idea!"

some years before) "that was so covered with
hair, that you could not tell which was the head
and which was the tail."

It was long before Mr. Lowe and his fellow
Adullamites heard the last of the Cave and the
Terrier.

The Liberal opposition to the Bill was not,

form of objection to the separation of "Franchise" and "Redistribution." Earl Grosvenor,
on the 20th March, moved that the House
should not discuss the Bill for the reduction of
the franchise, until it had before it the whole
scheme of the Government, including their plan
for redistribution of seats.

MARCH 27.

ESTRIA and Italy entered into an alliance offensive and defensive, Italy engaging to assist Prussia against Austria, and Prussia on her side undertaking to aid Italy in obtaining possession of Venetia.

APRIL 5.

HE EMPEROR NAPOLEON announced his intention to withdraw the French troops from Mexico.

APRIL 7.

"THE Fenians in America" (says a Note prefixed to Vol. L. and explanatory of the Cartoon issued April 7th) "had threatened to invade Canada, and an armed party of them crossed over into that country. The Govern-

THE YANKEE FIREMAN.

CANADA. "They say there's fire at Fire-Centre House. If it spreads to my Premises——"
FIREMAN JONATHAN. "Guess it's only smoke, Miss. Wait till it bust 'ned."

ment of the United States (later) zealously co-operated in extinguishing the whole project."

(See Cartoon, "The Yankee Fireman.")

APRIL 9.

HE Commissioners appointed to inquire into the Jamaica insurrection issued their report, which was to the general effect that the insurrection was serious and premeditated, that its speedy termination was largely due to the skill, promptitude and vigour of Governor Eyre

ments indicted were excessive, the punishment of death unnecessarily frequent, the floggings reckless, and at Both positively barbarous, and the burning of 1,000 houses wanton and cruel.

APRIL 12.

"MR. GLADSTONE" (says Punch's "Essence of Parliament") "moved the Second Reading of the Representation of the People Bill, inaccurately described as the Reform Bill, whereas it is part only." . . . "He then adverted

with any other part of the subject until after the Second Reading." (The Government had announced their intention to oppose Earl Grosvenor's amendments and treat it as a vote of Want of Confidence). "Mr. Gladstone concluded thus:—

Enough and more than enough there has been already of brave, idle, mocking words. Deeds are what is wanted. I beseech you to be wise, and, above all, to let war in time.

"Earl Grosvenor then moved his amendment, which is to the effect that we will not discuss the F. D." (Franchise Bill) "until we

APRIL 26.

"SEVENTH night of the Franchise debate" (*Punch's* "Essence of Parliament"). "Its great feature was a speech against the Bill by Mr. Lowe. Mr. Gladstone, our frequent contributor, shall contribute the 'Essence' for us:

"'When I think of the force of the weapons used, the keenness of their edge, and the skill and rapidity with which these weapons were wielded, I am lost in admiration, though I myself was the object of a fair proportion of the cuts and thrusts.'

"Mr. Lowe moreover drew a dread picture of the Democracy to which he said we were hastening, and adjured the Commons not to sacrifice our institutions. The speech was so effective that for a time no Member liked to follow."

APRIL 27.

EIGHTH and last night of the debate on the Second Reading of the Franchise Bill. Mr. Disraeli spoke for two hours and a half against the Bill. He vigorously assailed Mr. Gladstone; his "sudden declaration one fine morning about man's inherent right to be on the register," his inconsistencies, his "pilgrimages of passion," and his introduction of American principles into English legislation.

Then Mr. Gladstone wound up the memorable debate in an eloquent speech of over two hours' duration. He defended himself against Mr. Disraeli's charge of wishing to coerce the House of Commons, giving an account, charged with intense feeling, of his relations with the Liberal party, among whom, he said, "I came as an outcast from those with whom I associated, driven from them by the slow and resistless force of conviction."

"It wound up" (says *Mr. Punch*) "with this happily conceived and gallantly delivered defiance:

"You cannot fight against the future. Time is on our side. The great social forces which move on in their might and majesty, and which the tumult of our debates does not for a moment impede or disturb—those great social forces are against you: they are marshalled on our side, and the banner which we now carry, though perhaps at some distant victory." Then came, soon after the great Clock Tower had sounded Three, the final suspense in the lobbies. When we returned, the account was then given forth—

For the Second Reading 318
Against 313

REST, AND BE VERY THANKFUL.

BRITANNIA. "You've been so good a boy, SMITH, that I hope you won't get into such another muddle!"

APRIL 30.

Mr. Gladstone announced in the Commons that the Government did not intend to resign in consequence of their narrow majority (of five) on the second reading of the Franchise Bill; that he should, on the following Monday, introduce the Redistribution Bill, and the Scotch and Irish Reform Bill, and also more, that on a day to be fixed, the Committee on the Franchise Bill should be taken. He should bring in the Budget in the meantime (*Punch's* "Essence").

MAY 3.

The Budget. Not an interesting one, for Mr. Gladstone had little more than a million to give away. He remitted the rest of the Timber Duties, equalised the duties on Wines in bottle and in wood, reduced the mileage duties on beasts from a penny to a farthing, and also reduced the duty on carriages drawn by horses. Finally, after a piteous description of the condition of ill-treated Pepper, Mr. Gladstone laid Pepper's Ghost by abolishing the duty on that condiment. Next, he proposed that we should pay off the National Debt, and, by way of a beginning, made an arrangement which, if it lasts, will take 39 millions off 800 millions in nineteen years" ("Essence of Parliament"). He calculated the expenditure for the year at £66,115,000, the revenue at £67,575,000.

MAY 7.

Mr. Gladstone introduced the Redistribution Bill. Here be its best features ("Essence of Parliament").

(*See Cartoon, "Business is Business."*)

1. We Disfranchise No Place.
2. We take away one Member from the little boroughs which at present have two Members.

BUSINESS IS BUSINESS.

Mr. Punch. "Business is business, Jack. If you had brought that before, there would have been no trouble to wind it."

3. Now, we have to give away three seats. For we are not going to alter the number of Members in the House of Commons, but preserve the mystic 658.
4. We give Twenty-six Members to the English Counties.
5. We give a third Member to Manchester, Liverpool, Leeds, and Birmingham, and a second to Salford.
6. We split the Tower Hamlets, which get, therefore, two new Members.

10. We give the University of London one.
11. We give one that. One each to Burnley, Staley-bridge, Hartlepool, Middlesborough, Dewsbury, and Shireswees, equally well known as Gravesend
12. We give the other Seven to Scotland, thus:—One each to the counties of Ayr, Aberdeen, and Lanark, one each to Edinburgh, Glasgow, and Dundee, and one to the fourth University.

to the City of Dublin, the County of Cork, and the Queen's University.

This is the Government scheme. Scotch and Irish Reform Bills were brought in by the Lord Advocate and Mr. Chichester Fortescue. In *Scotland* we reduce the borough franchise from £10 to £7, as we propose to do in England, and to reduce the occupation franchise in counties from £50 to £14. The first process will add 26,000 Scotchmen to the register, of whom a third are working men. The second will about double the county constituency. We reduce Scotland's property franchise from £10 to £5. In *Ireland* we shall not alter the County complicated, but shall reduce the borough franchise from £8 to £6.

The Redistribution Bill did not please the Opposition. Mr. Disraeli (on the 14th) vigorously attacked it as crude and unfair, urged the Government to let the Bill go by the board, to obtain, at leisure, trustworthy information, and then to come to Parliament with a complete and well-digested scheme of Reform ("Essence").

Mr. Gladstone announced that, in compliance with what seemed the general wish, he should fuse the Franchise and Redistribution Bills into one Reform Bill. This mixture, this *Tinct: Reform: Comp:* he proposes to ask Mr. Disraeli to swallow, as a constitutional remedy, on the 18th May.

(*See Cartoon, "Tinct: Reform: Comp:"*)

MAY 10.

In consequence of the suspension of Messrs. Overend, Gurney & Co. (Limited), there occurred the great City Panic, one of the most wide-spread disastrous commercial panics on record. The next day (the 11th) was known as "Black Friday." The Bank raised its rate of discount from 8 to 9, and for special advances 10 per cent. On the 11th at midnight in the House of Commons Mr. Gladstone announced that the Government had decided to

TINCT: REFORM: COMP:

Mr. Gladstone. "There, Mr. D.! You'd better help it at once: the more you look at it, the worse you'll like it."

em of numerous failures and great commercial distress.

Among the great Houses and Companies that "went" during this panic were the English Joint Stock for £80,000; Peto & Betts, for £4,000,000; Shrimpton, railway contractor, for

Company. The shares of Agra and Masterman's Bank (says "Annals of Our Time,") which at the beginning of the year were 33 premium, closed this day (the 11th) at 1 discount. Excited crowds thronged Lombard Street, banking houses were crammed with angry customers,

JUNE 12.

ON this day Princess Mary of Cambridge was married at Kew to Prince Teck.

JUNE 12.

TO-DAY there was a cessation of diplomatic relations between Austria and Prussia, followed immediately by a declaration of war on the part of Prussia, whose armies entered Saxony and Hanover on the 15th instant. On the 16th Austria announced her determination to render Saxony military assistance against Prussia, and on the 17th the Emperor of Austria issued a war manifesto, General Benedek was appointed the Austrian commander-in-chief, and General Moltke directed the Prussian plan of campaign.

[See Cartoon, "Honesty and Policy."]

JUNE 18.

"WATERLOO DAY, Monday, June 18," (says "Essence of Parliament") "was solemnised by the overthrow of the Reform Bill." Lord Dunkellin, a Liberal, had moved an amendment to the clause settling the Borough Franchise, proposing to substitute rating for rental as the standard of value. Ministers opposed the change, and there followed (says Mr. Punch) "what proved to be the most important debate of the whole series, for it resulted in the defeat of the Government by a majority of eleven (315 against 304), the annihilation of the Bill, the resignation of the Ministry, and the formation by the Earl of Derby of a new Administration."

On the 26th the Queen sent for Lord Derby, and requested him to form a Ministry.

JUNE 20.

ITALY declared war against Austria. On the 22nd Prince Frederick Charles, who, with the Crown Prince of Prussia, had received orders to march against the Austrians, issued a general order to the army upon their entering Austrian territory. On the 24th the Italian army, which had crossed the Mincio, were met at Custozza by the Archduke Albert and defeated.

JUNE 27.

DEFEAT of the Austrians under Field-Marshal Ramming at Nachod by the Prussians led by the Crown Prince. On the same day, at Trautenau, the Prussian vanguard, under General Grossmann, were repulsed by the Austrians and had to retreat, though the Austrians were not strong enough to pursue. On the 28th the Hanoverian Army of 19,000 men surrendered to the Prussians under General Vogel von Falkenstein.

HONESTY AND POLICY.

BRITANNIA. "Well! I've done my best, if they will smash each other, they can't."
WAR (aside). "Ah! now one may pick up the pieces!"

JUNE 29.

A PUBLIC demonstration in favour of Reform, attended by some 10,000 persons, was held this day in Trafalgar Square.

JULY 3.

IN a great battle at Sadowa, near Königgrätz in Bohemia, the Austrians were disastrously defeated. Up to about half-past one the Austrians held their own, and were pressing the Prussians hard, when the Crown Prince of Prussia, coming up with the First Army, changed the fortunes of the day, and after a most sanguinary fight, the Austrians were utterly routed and fled, losing 30,224 men and 1,147 officers. The Prussians lost in killed and wounded, 8,794 men and 359 officers. The possession by the Prussian troops of a new breech-loading musket, called the needle-gun (Zündnadelgewehr), which enabled them to fire with great rapidity, gave them an immense advantage, and was one cause of the terrible slaughter amidst their foes. The following day the Emperor of Austria asked for an armistice,

THE LION OF ST. MARK.

which Prussia refused. But Austria was vanquished, and accepted readily the offer of the Emperor of the French to bring about a suspension of hostilities, the Emperor of Austria agreeing to cede Venetia, which was handed over to France as a preliminary to its cession to Italy.

[See Cartoon, " The Lion of St. Mark."]

JULY 5.

PRINCESS HELENA was this day married to Prince Christian at Windsor Castle.

JULY 9.

EARL DERBY in the House of Lords made a statement of the circumstances attending the formation of the new Ministry, and gave an outline of its proposed policy. " As to Reform," he said, " nothing would give me greater pleasure than to see a very considerable portion of the class now excluded admitted to the franchise; but on the other hand, I am afraid that the portion of the community who are most clamorous for the passing of a Reform Bill, are not that portion who would be satisfied with any measure such as could be approved of by the two great political parties in the country."

Mr. Punch said (" Essence"), " The Earl of Derby, being a poet, has amused his leisure by composing the following Catalogue of Ministers and their offices :

Know each his own ! Thus, Stanley, wise and cool,
O'er the Affairs called Foreign calmly rule.
As then the proffered Peerage dost decline,
Again Finance, Disraeli, be thine.

Mellifluous Walpole shall not
  melt to Grey,
And the Home Office prime his
  courteous rosy,
While Jonathan, at Peel, in
  War captain,
And grow our soldiers with yet
  deadlier fires.
To cynic Cranborne anxious
  India's needs;
To graceful Chelmsford we as-
  sign the Seals.
Sir John, the British Navy be
  thy care,
See that black turret darken all
  the sea;
And Henry Lennox, thou wilt
  not refuse
Page's and Bernal Osborne's
  moral slaves.
  The Privy Seal so loudly
  Malmesbury gives,
In them our Postman, Graham
  of Montrose;
Carnarvon, take the Colonies to
  thee,
Because their name and shine
  began with C.
And when men cry, "Off with
  the Council's Head!"
My Potents, Buckingham, thy
  doom be told.
Devon will find the Duchy in
  his way,
Nothing to do and nothing less to
  say;
Thou, Stafford Northcote, whom
  great Gladstone made
His scribe, address thee to the
  Board of Trade;
And thou, great Gladstone's
  victor (to be sure
The Dunmow chase shan't lard),
  take the Poor.
Let plebs our tulips not
  inherit do;
John Manners, mind the Parks
  oftenly.
Thou, conqueror on the gay
  French Derby course,
Bagsdart, ride forth, our Master
  of the Horse.
Our Thunderbolt of Law, forth
  cut, Sir Hugh,
Thy second, Rovill, champion
  tried and true.
Not Glasswork, but Glass
  royalty, in tears
Is held, yet help us, friendly
  Abercorn.
Go, proudly o conni—thy grave
  Yorill pay
To out the haddock caught in
  Dublin Bay,
And so tight food is good in
  these hot days,
Let Mayo's Kent bless at Mayo-
  nean.
  The minor posts by minor
  men be filled,
thank heats o whether skilful or undrilled,
While o'er you all my watchful eye is thrown,
Him that each man had better mind his own.
The Forum is with Fate. Come Jack,
At least we'll die with honour on our back!

JULY 20.

Count Bismarck, in a secret despatch to the Prussian Ambassador in Paris, said that

the Emperor of Prussia had agreed to the armistice with great reluctance, and out of regard for the Emperor Napoleon. "I send, you confidentially for your personal information and guidance the following words of his Majesty: I would rather resign than withdraw without acquiring a considerable amount of territory for Prussia." This despatch did not see the

light until 1869, when it led to much bitter dispute.

Bismarck was now becoming a conspicuous figure in European politics, and this, with the aggrandisement of Prussia, was thought to be little welcome to the "Oracle of the Tuileries," Napoleon III.

(See Cartoon, "Rival Arbiters.")

RIVAL ARBITERS.

"In other Laws thought the ford a Bore."

JULY 23.

This was the day of the great riot in Hyde Park. The Reform League having arranged to hold a great political demonstration there, the new Home Secretary, Mr. Walpole, had officially prohibited it, on the ground that the parks "should not be devoted to any purpose which would interfere with the quiet recreation of the people, and might lead to riot and disorderly demonstrations." The Committee of the Reform League determined not to abandon their purpose, the procession of demonstrators marched to the Park, and mustered in thousands around the chief entrances, which were guarded by police. The leaders, Mr. Edmond Beales and others, demanded admittance, which the police refused, and the leaders, with so many of the demonstrators as would follow them, returned to Trafalgar Square. Meanwhile, however, the crowds who remained at Hyde Park forced an entrance by breaking down the railings in Park Lane and other places, and a scene of riot and of conflict with the police ensued. Quiet was only gradually restored, and that with the assistance of the Guards.

"The artisan class" (said Mr. Punch at the time) "attended in large numbers, and of course behaved perfectly well; but equally of course the proceedings were supplemented by a vast mass of roughs who behaved perfectly ill."

[See Cartoon, "No Rough-ism."]

Some arrests were made, and several of the ring-leaders of the riot were fined or imprisoned. Mr. Walpole, on the part of the Government, was generally thought to have shown some want of vigour and discretion. A deputation from the Reform League, headed by Mr. Beales, waited upon Mr. Walpole, and an amicable understanding was come to, the Home Secretary agreeing that on condition that there was no disturbance and no attack on property, there should be no display of military or police in the Park. Mr. Beales on his side proceeded to the Park and gave notice to his followers that no further meeting would be held there, "except only on next Monday afternoon (July 30), at six o'clock, by arrangement with the Government."

NO ROUGH-IANISM.

WORKING-MAN. "Look here, you Vagabond! Right or Wrong, we won't have you's help!"

JULY 27.

The laying of the Atlantic Telegraph Cable between this country and America was successfully completed this evening about 5 o'clock, and congratulatory messages were exchanged between the Queen and the President of the United States, "expressing a hope that it would be an additional bond of union between the two nations."

Aug. 10.

Parliament was prorogued by Commission. The chief subjects referred to in the Royal Speech were the war between Austria and Prussia, the all but suppressed Fenianism in Ireland, the loyalty of Canada and the good faith of the United States, the mitigation of the Monetary pressure, the diminution of the Cattle Plague, the visitation of the Cholera, and the laying of the Atlantic Telegraph.

Aug. 11.

The Emperor Napoleon offered to hand over Venetia to Italy, saying, "My purpose has always been to restore it to itself, so that Italy should be free from the Alps to the Adriatic. Mistress of her own destinies, Venetia will soon be able to express her will by universal suffrage.

Aug. 23.

Terms of Peace between Austria and Prussia were signed at Prague, Austria consenting to her exclusion from the Germanic Confederation, and agreeing to pay a large sum towards the expenses of the war. Prussia, as the result of her success in what had been called the "Ten Days' War," gained (says *Punch's* Political Summary) a great increase of territory, so that "she incorporated into her dominions, Hanover, Hesse-Cassel, Nassau, Hesse-Homburg, the Duchies of Schleswig, Holstein and Lauenburg (these last however had been previously annexed), that part of Hesse-Darmstadt which lies to the north of the Maine, and the little principality of Hohenzollern—the cradle of the Prussian Royal House, situated on the borders of Lake Constance, between Wurtemburg and Switzerland."

In consequence of these large additions to the territory of Prussia, the Emperor of France on the 5th August demanded a rectification of the frontier of France, claiming a territory including Sarrelouis and Landau. This claim Prussia promptly refused, and it was withdrawn by the Emperor.

(See Cartoon, "Peace, and no Pieces!")

On the same day a treaty was signed between Austria and France respecting the cession of Venetia.

KÖNIGSSTRASSE |

PEACE—AND NO PIECES!

Bismarck. "Pardon, mon Ami! but we really can't allow you to pick up anything here."

Nap. (the Chiffonnier.) "Pray, don't mention it, Mons! It's not of the slightest consequence."

Aug. 27.

Great Reform Demonstration at Birmingham, attended, it was estimated, by about 150,000 people. A meeting in the evening was addressed by Mr. Bright and Mr. Beales, the former dealing sharply with Mr. Lowe for his attack on the working classes.

SEPT. 2.

The "Great Eastern" succeeded in raising and splicing the Atlantic Cable of 1865, which had been useless for some time, but was now restored to working order.

SEPT. 27.

Four Reform Demonstrations were just now the order of the day. There was one on this date at Manchester, attended by from 15,000 to 20,000 persons, and one on the 16th of the following month at Glasgow, where the number present was estimated by the *Times* at 150,000. At most of these large assemblies Mr. Bright was the chief speaker, strenuously advocating the cause of Parliamentary Reform, and passionately denouncing Mr. Lowe and others who were opposed to it. At Glasgow Mr. Bright, speaking of the House of Commons as unworthy of the confidence of the people, said :—" If the Clerk of the House were placed at Temple Bar, and had orders to lay his hand upon the shoulder of every well-dressed and apparently clean-washed man who passed through the ancient Bar, until he had numbered 658, and if the Crown summoned those 658 to be the Parliament for the United Kingdom, my honest conviction is that you would have a better Parliament than now exists."

At Birmingham also there had been a monster Reform Demonstration, numbering, it was estimated, nearly 150,000. Speaking there, Mr. Bright urged his hearers to press on their agitation for restoring the British Constitution with all its freedom to the British people. He declared that he had no fear of Manhood Suffrage.

[See Cartoon, "The Brummagem Frankenstein."]

THE BRUMMAGEM FRANKENSTEIN.

John Bright. "I have no preference of Manhood Suffrage!"—Mr. Bright's Speech at Birmingham.

SEPT. 29.

These were the days of new and enormously expensive developments in the Art of War. Armour-plated vessels and colossal guns had completely transformed the navy; and the various nations competed eagerly in arming their troops with the newest and most destructive rifles. Snider being pitted against Chassepot, and both eclipsed by the terrible death-dealing needle-gun. Armstrong and Whitworth, Palliser and Krupp, were rivals in the manufacture of heavy cannon and enormous shot. It was believed that the wars of the future would depend less upon personal bravery than on the possession of huge armaments, and the latest and most destructive weapons of precision.

Mr. Punch, in a suggestive Cut, called attention to this devotion of the mechanic arts to the purposes of War.
(See Cartoon, "Vulcan's Best Customer.")

THE WAR BLACKSMITH.
(After LONGFELLOW.)

Under its sulphurous canopy
Old Vulcan's smithy stands,
And Vulcan, grown a smith of war,
Has as much on his hands,

That stocks run low, and files but slow
War-orders and demands.
His Cyclops whom he needed most,
Of every Cyclops run ;
For why should not a Cyclops do
As mortar working-man,
And take the time when trade is brisk
To twice on all he can ?
So every day and all day long
Poor Vulcan's own it must flow.

Telling for Europe's sovereigns,
And still the orders grow
For breech-loaders, and armour-plates,
Steel-shot and chilled shot.

With Chassepots for the Emperor
(O'er Dreyses they've the pull),
With Remingtons for Austria,
And Sniders for John Bull,
Balls, Cochranes, Moncrieffs, Harvies,
His hands may well be full ?

VULCAN'S BEST CUSTOMER.

PEACE. *"Not much doing, I suppose, Mr. VULCAN?"*
VULCAN. *"Doing? There's to me, Miss, I've a'most more work than I can manage."*

Meanwhile the Emperor writes to us,
And bids us be good boys ;
It does one good to hear him preach,
And see how he enjoys
The shift of weights that turn the Powers
For Europe's equipoise.

How glad he is that Prussia comes
So strong out of the row,
That Italy Venetia gains—
Via France, all allow ;
Pouring "whatever is, is best "—
At all events just now.

And when France calls that East and South
Her neighbours' power increase,

He hints, 'tis not from every smash
Shy one "puch up the pieces,"
While Peace is Peace, although it brings
No flurrys, and no fleas.

Some say 'tis like the rules that enter
Whited Eve in Paradise ;
But it preaches so delightfully,
And gives such good advice,
Bidding France arm, because she's one
Of peace at any price.

So Vulcan all his toil and stock
Must on War's tasks bestow,
And hum, good for spade and chain,
For sword and gun must go ;

For before this the Emperor's word
Has been a word and blow.

Then let us thank the Emperor
For the lesson he has taught,
That it is in the forge of War
The arms of Peace are wrought ;
And if we haven't breech-loaders,
Breech-loaders must be bought.

OCT. 3.

A TREATY of Peace between Austria and Italy was signed at Vienna.

OCT. 6.

Once auctions, and what were known as "knock-outs," were very prevalent at this time in London. The public were fleeced by sham bidders, who would run up the prices enormously, sharing their infamous gains at the subsequent "knock-out" for the division of the spoil.

In a Cartoon *Mr. Punch* applied this to the equally rascally tricks of electioneering.

(*See Cartoon*, "*An Electioneering 'Knock-Out.'*")

"KNOCK-OUTS," TRADE & PARLIAMENTARY.

There's here enough of auction-rooms, these telegraphers, touts and liars,

Their Jews and brokers leagued to fleece poor *bonâ-fide* buyers;

How by much bids 'gainst others they "the groom have put the chest on," [sweat on,

Till he pays five times the value for the lot that he is

And when at this nice little game these rogues have had their innings, [the winnings,

We've heard how, in a snug knock-out they meet to square

Dividing losses, if there's loss, or profits, if there's profit,

Till whichever way the sale has gone, they get their "reg'lars" off it.

AN ELECTIONEERING "KNOCK-OUT."

Noble Local Resident. "Great territorial influence, my dear Sir: can't do without me!" — *Local Publican.* "No sort o' use bidding on yer own account!"

First Local Attorney. "Let me bid for you: leave a rest for £50,000!" — *Local Rival.* "Better square it with us 'locals,' Gad'mus!"

Second Local Attorney. "Engage us—or you won't have it at any price!"

No to bid or buy at auctions of boroughs you make bold, Sir!

'Tis with warning private buyers are the one lot that is sold, Sir!

And if the bargain-hunter with the broker tries conclusions,

'Tis a case of wilful ignorance, in an age of dis-illusions.

But there's another auction-mart where craft and fudge and flam are

Seen in quite as great perfection as in sales under the hammer,

And that's the auction-mart maintained by our election-brokers,

Who to fresh-fledged ambitions of new men act as smokers:

At Mr. Newman's ear they buzz, M.P. before him dangle,

While for his purse with subtle look and well-barbed hook they angle.

Some public cause, with honest will, poor Newman p'raps espouses;

They introduce "pro bono publico" "for the good of

Poor Newman steps into the mart: he's not his heart a-twist on;

No humbug in particular, but any borough sweet on:

Legal expenses must be paid: he don't mean to be shabby, [Dobby!

But of bribery and corruption he is as innocent as a baby.

The touts are hung round him: most respectable of visitors ... [solicitors,

Local grandees, trade magnates, and sharp witted keen

What's wanted in the market is his purse and not his person,

Legal expenses only treat his brokers to disburse on.

The brokers bid, with tongue in cheek, the struggle most intense it ;
And all the principals have got to do, is to pay expenses.

And when the contest's over and Buff has won the borough,
Mum's agents the problem and damned enquiry thorough ;
And Blue and Buff meet pay again, for accusing and defrauding,
And there's another bill run up, and so on without ending !

When the grave's cut, or Blue and Buff will sit stand further bleeding,
The brokers meet, and pleasantly compound, or stay proceeding ;
And at a song "knock-em" terrange their late (mis-)understanding,
And square accounts, the difference one to the other handing.

OCT. 18.

To-day Venice was formally handed over to the municipal authorities, the Italian flag being hoisted on the tower of St. Mark. The voting in Venetia remained, on the 29th, in 641,758 votes being recorded in favour of incorporation with Italy, and only 69 against.

(See Cartoon, "Venetia Victrix.")

VENETIA VICTRIX.

OCTOBER 20, 1866.

Fangs filed, and talons blunted, his eager wide wings clipped low,
The Lion of St. Mark hath been the wonder of a show.
For years on years the crowds have flocked, to see him in his cage,
To note his beauty and his strength, his weariness and rage.

The light of ancient majesty in the man's eye smouldered dim ;
Dreams of old deeds nerved weak to serve each huge but wasted limb.
As hot with hunger of his heart, in that ignoble show,
The show-caged Lion of St. Mark paced, ever, to and fro.

VENETIA VICTRIX.

Yes, Pius, "There, go along with you ! I forbids the Banns. I'm ashamed of you !"
Longing, "Your turn will come next, then."

Now and anon the soft eye lit, the great throat gave a sound,
A growl of warning thunder, that scared the gazers round ;
The huger limbs throbbed, the broad wings shook—then all was as before :
We saw the Lion of St. Mark pacing his narrow floor.

Pacing, as who must pace till death—but lo, what toss we side,

The Lion of St. Mark is loose,—his gaunt limbs stretching free—
Trying with wonder and delight the stiff wings, once so weak,
Free and again, too pacing his cage from side to side !

Free and again, in ecstasy, across the green lagoon,
Where marble glances and colour glow, in cloudless blue of noon,
Looking for the long-waited fat, greeting the swans at [last—

The day that saw white, red, and green on the campanile mast !
VENETIA VICTRIX ! Let the cry of joy swell on the breeze—
Her Victor comes to wed her, his left bride of the sea,
She that was plight of old with Doge and Bucentaur and ring,
Now, rejoicing, to her bosom takes her Italian King !

On the 7th November the King of Italy made a triumphal entry into Venice.

Oct. 30.

MR. Bright attended a Banquet given in his honour by the Dublin Liberals in the Rotunda. He treated at length of the ills of Ireland, which he conceived to spring mainly from the Established Church and the divorce of the Irish people from the soil. He said:—

"You will recollect that the ancient Hebrew in his captivity had his window open towards Jerusalem where he prayed; you know that the follower of Mahomet, when he prays, turns his face towards Mecca; and the Irish peasant, when he asks for food and freedom and blessing, his eye follows the setting sun, the explosion of his heart reaches beyond the wide Atlantic and to quick he grasps hands with the great Republic of the West. If that be so, I say then that the disease is not only serious, but that it is even desperate."

(See Cartoon, "Dr. Dulcamara in Dublin.")

PAT'S WELCOME TO JOHN.

Hurrah, thy bould Quaker!
   Let Erin awake her,
And rush to the halls where
   he bellows away,
And as for vile England he'll
   praise and rake her
Till ready to hide her lone
   head in the say.

And only just hear how the
   Bishops, the darlins,
Is writing him letters of wel-
   come and glee,
And stuffs in their pockets their
   quarrels and snarlins,
And joins all harmonious to
   praise the big B.

It's for lets us know how this
   poor island suffers
Beneath the black Saxon's
   tyrannical rule,
How William of Orange and
   similar duffers
For ages has given and Erin
   her grade.

DR. DULCAMARA IN DUBLIN.

Indeed, it's the knight of repayment to hear him
   Discoursing our wrongs till he moves us to tears,
No wonder the dark aristocracy fear him,
   For singing such songs in their arrogant ears.

No fear but we'll mend all the Birmingham leisons,
   (And mend 'em, anyhow, like the tragedy Jew)
He pumps out our way to get hould of the blessins
   The Saxon has robbed us their Brian Boru.

It's the Land we're to have, boys, and by the same token
   We'll make the proud Brithivrs sell their estates,
Which if they resist, suggested and promisin',
   We'll ask Captain Rook for to shuddle the room.

That bargain completed, it's nothing but candour
   To hint we're a subsequent scheme to produce,
For, boys, a good move for the Englishman's gander
   Won't make a bad move for the Irishman's goose.

There's lands trodden them what's the Saxon, be jabers,
   Might all be the better for selling right cheap,
We'll send our Surveyors inspecting them acres,
   Modest night-walking boys, with their fares in coups.

Meantime we give thanks for the loan of the wedge-end
   He brings us for cleaving the way to the fight,
In his honour we'll either the minimal legend,
   And cry, In thy future, boys, Erin Go Bright.

NOV. 14.

ON this night a meteoric shower of great splendour and unusual duration took place. As many as 1,880 "falling stars" were counted between midnight and one o'clock from Twickenham Observatory. The heavens in fact were at one time completely covered with the swiftly-glancing meteor-shower.

LES ÉTOILES QUI FILENT.

Philosopher puts question,
Of the planet-population,
Their gravities, digression,
Heights, habits, occupations,
Are Mars' doth all belligerent?
Are Venus's all lovers?
Are Pallas, more refrigerant,
And Vesta, old-maidic colours?
Is Mercury the hottest
Of a flameriering race,
Where the Poets' muse is Legion,
And merits no elegance?
Is Jupiter surrendered
To celestial yeofdom's reign;
With a race, of Dalton regenedazed,
And the hardy-nerves for train?
In far-off island Saturn's
Vast starred belty who may
Inhabitants of gay turns ideas?
And miseries as well?
Or let's a lofty London,
Where crew old lumps, so steady,
(play?)
Whist, with steady faces,
If terror makes on him day;
Where the stars wish life is life,
Beyond the stroke of thunder,
And the dart of human life
Can it tell what life's endured
Abroad those meteors fled,
At whose doves we emitted
On the night of Tuesday last?

*   *   *   *

Are they beams far crystaleous,
As quickly squeezed as spoiled;
Greeted with loose inundations,
With open so random asked?
In their rise in Lar reborn
You supporting them the train
Of Lions of the season
That to Lethe take their talk;
Are there lights they vanish o'er
                    (drowned,
Like a dream that we have
One rising young earth's atmosphere;
Of pledges remittance;
    Those Will-o'-the-Wisps that over
    Embroider Heaven's black cope,
    Hounds for London, Clapham Dover
    Lebrecture-holders hope?
Defying the airybless
    Of Planets and fixed stars,
And threatening collision
    With the red planet Mars,
Are they the bright, brief presage
    Of the Commons' coming storm.

Omen at once and message,
    Touching progress of Reform?
Shown by some unknown tallows,
    And kindred at a smoke,
That they see stars, folks tell us,
    And yet they end in smoke,
Can three of chief deterrencies,
    That unusual dash and go,
Be the beams of good intentions,
    For the paving-works below?

POLITICAL "ECONOMY."

MANAGER. "Now, Man, be up there, what have we got for the Opening Scene?"

PROPERTY-MAN. "Well, Sir, here's the old 'Reform Bill.' A little touching up it were is as good as new."

DEC. 1.

IN response to the growing demand for a further instalment of Electoral Reform, the Tory Government of Lord Derby and Mr. Disraeli, it was suspected, were not prepared with anything more satisfactory than some modification of their own abortive measure of 1859.

(See Cartoon, "Political 'Economy.'")

DEC. 3.

To-day a Demonstration in favour of Reform was held under the auspices of the Reform League, in the grounds of Beaufort House, Chiswick. A large procession of over 20,000 workmen, &c., marched thither from their place of muster, the Mall in St. James's Park. Although the affair passed off peaceably, there was a good deal of wild talking indulged in, and claims then looked upon as extreme were freely advanced. Manhood Suffrage, of which Mr. Bright had lately declared himself to be not afraid, was one of these.

(See Cartoon, "*Manhood Suffrage.*")

MEMENTO TO MIS-LEADERS.

Ignorant tho' mine's a drunken lot,
I'll soberly disprove the imputation,
But talk to me as though I were a sot
Myself, and you'll excuse my indignation.
Who calls me fool offends me
and so much
As he who shows me that he thinks me such.

Say we're impulsive, and I little care,
Then charge my smiting calm,
nor shall refuse,
But don't you tell me if you dare
Attempt to play on me as on a fool,
To agitate me with false eloquence,
Meant to excite vexation, not strike sense.

Don't go to work me up with
gross appeals
To pitiful passion and
stupidity,
Which declamation, void of
truth, reveals
That you attribute to your
heart, to me,
Whilst with your tongue, then seem your mind I claim,
You tell me I am all that's good and wise.

Don't stand me, don't batter me, don't mop,
Don't flatter me. I'm neither king nor fool,
Don't think to wield me at your will: don't hope
We wish the repute of your mouth to rule.
A working man a thinking man may be,
Sorry, I'm my own, the mob—but I'll be free.

MANHOOD SUFFRAGE.

Mr. P. u. n. "*I'm not sure to say, my friend, that THIS is the sort of Manhood you ought to be scared of with!*"

DEC. 4.

At a Reform Meeting of the London Trades held at St. James's Hall, Mr. Ayrton, M.P., having uttered some words implying censure upon the Queen for lack of sympathy with the multitudes who had gathered in front of one of her palaces, Mr. John Bright, in eloquent terms and amidst "loud and prolonged cheering," repudiated the charge as "a great injustice done to the Queen in her desolate and widowed condition." "And I venture to say this" (added the great orator), "that a woman, be she the Queen of a great realm, or be she the wife of one of your labouring men, who can keep alive in her breast a great sorrow for the lost object of her life and affection, is not at all likely to be wanting in a great and generous sympathy with you."

Dec. 8.

On this day the last detachments of French troops left Rome. "The Emperor" (said General Montebello to the Pope) "withdraws his troops from Rome, but not his support."

NON PLUS AND NON POSS;

OR, THE POPE BETWEEN SEVERAL STOOLS.

We cannot stay in Rome that once was ours,
And can to Rome that it is ours no more:

We cannot keep our Italy, with flowers,
And loving looks, a comer at the door:
We cannot turn Venetia's sullen well
Into a pall to shroud, a mask to hide
The tale here once so bright, though plucked and pale,
That renders to Roman hope and Roman pride:
And this present we under seal and cross,
And our Pontifical *non ross :, non ross :!*

ROME, 1866.

" *Welcome the Coming, Speed the Parting Guest.*"

We cannot fly from Rome that still has been
The corpse-billed pedestal of Peter's chair:
Nor leave out Vatican, whose earth has seen
One groove grow high in heaven and wide as air.
Nor stamp from English hostelries to erase
A roof for shelter, or a tomb for rest:
Nor act the sovereign, and be the slave,
As Paris' or Vienna's hostage-guest.
And this present we under seal and cross,
And our Pontifical *non ross :, non ross :!*

We cannot be the young Mastaï again,
Who propped that Italy might yet be one
Cannot re-cast the old Pio Nono vein,
Where lay pulse beat and natural blood would run.

We cannot be, as when, alas, unt-blind,
At struggling Italy's new-birth we stood,
With hand reprobant, and reverent head inclined,
To bless her baptism of fire and blood.
And this present we under seal and cross,
And our Pontifical *non ross :, non ross :!*

(See Cartoon, " *Rome, 1866.*")

On the 26th, Mazzini issued a Proclamation to the Italian people. "Concentrate" (he said) "your hearts on Rome," which represents "the mission of Italy among the nations; the word of

our people; the eternal gospel of unification of the people" ("Annals of Our Time").

Dec. 30.

On this day occurred a disastrous fire at the Crystal Palace, Sydenham, by which the Tropical Department and the Natural History Collection and many of the Courts, &c., at that popular place of amusement were seriously damaged, and in some cases entirely destroyed.

✦1867✦

JAN. 2.

THE winter of 1866—7 was a severe one. On this day occurred a very heavy fall of snow, followed by a hard frost which lasted a fortnight. Traffic was at times almost entirely suspended, and the inconvenience caused thereby drew attention afresh to the inefficiency of the Metropolitan Vestries, and their neglect to make any provision for heavy snow-falls.

Suggestions of legislative action were of course plentiful.

This long frost caused much public inconvenience, and led to many serious accidents. The most terrible of these latter was the sudden breaking up (on the 15th January) of the ice on the ornamental water in Regent's Park whilst some five hundred persons were skating thereon. Two hundred or more of these were immersed, and the reserve on duty being quite unequal to the sudden demand upon their services, the scene soon became a terrible one, men, women and children struggling wildly in the chilling water, some clinging desperately to the edges of the broken ice, and crying piteously for the aid which none could render. Forty-two lives were lost on this calamitous occasion.

JAN. 28.

IN view of the coming Paris Exhibition, Mr. Punch suggested that the convenience and comfort of English visitors thereto would be greatly enhanced by an abandonment of the Custom House "right of search."

(See Cartoon, "The Wrong of Search, or the Luggage Question.")

JAN. 31.

AFTER a long delay of nearly a quarter of a century, the four bronze lions designed by Sir Edwin Landseer for the base of the Nelson Column in Trafalgar Square had been com-

THE WRONG OF SEARCH, OR THE LUGGAGE QUESTION.

Various. "Madam, will you, I trust?"

Britannia. "Well, I should be delighted, I'm sure, but I don't like to have my luggage pulled about."

Various. "Ah! I will do my best to prevent it, if that Gentleman is agreeable."

pleted; and were on this day unveiled to the public on their pedestals around the base of the Monument, the foundation stone of which had been laid on September 30, 1840.

FEB. 5.

PARLIAMENT was opened by the Queen in person. "All doubts as to whether the Derby Ministry would introduce a Reform Bill were at once set at rest by the declaration in the Royal Speech that the attention of Parliament would again be called to the state of the representation of the people."

It was announced that a Trades Union Commission had been appointed, and Bills were foreshadowed on the subject of the Factory Act,

Bankruptcy Amendment, the Metropolitan Poor, Compensation for Improvements in Ireland, &c.

(See Cartoon, " Politics of Kidnapping.")

FEB. 8.

THE Home Secretary obtained leave to bring in a Bill to enable Commissioners to take evidence upon oath respecting Trades Union outrages which had taken place at Sheffield. The Bill was subsequently passed.

FEB. 8.

THE States of the new North German Confederation signed a Treaty at Berlin, by virtue of which the troops of the Confederation were placed under the command of Prussia, and a mutual undertaking was entered into to maintain the integrity and independence of the contracting States. On the 24th instant the first Parliament assembled.

FEB. 11.

"BENJAMIN DISRAELI, Chancellor of the Exchequer, did, on the evening of Monday, February 11, make a speech of two hours and a quarter, and did not explain the intentions of the Conservative Government in regard to Parliamentary Reform.

"What he did say was in this wise. The House should direct itself, upon this occasion only, and by the Particular Desire of several persons of Distinction (country play-bills say) of party spirit. Government hoped for the sympathy of the Conservatives. Lord Derby and his colleagues had resolved this Parliamentary Reform was not

POLITICAL KIDNAPPING.

MRS. RUSSELL. " Hi! Help! Florence! She's taken' away my Ch-ild!"

a question that ought to decide the fate of the Ministers. All parties had tried to deal with it and had failed, and therefore the House of Commons itself must settle it. The Reform Act of 1832 had enfranchised large masses of the labouring classes from the franchise, and now, as prognosticated by Sir Robert Peel, those classes were reclaiming their rights. Moreover the increased application of science to social life had greatly elevated the people. We, the Smiths, love not validly opposed them, but have perhaps beset too Epicurean. He thought that before in-

troducing a Bill he had a right to ask the House whether it would not sanction the course recommended by Government. This question he should ask by moving Resolutions, a course he defended at great length. He intended to reconstruct the House on the principles of the British Constitution. Every class and interest had been represented under the Constitution, and hence our prosperity. Neither France, America, nor Germany had such representation. He was far too artificial symmetry. He should know how to deal with before. The country

population was eleven millions and a half, and they had only 164 Members. The borough population was nine millions and a half, and they had 334 Members. Therefore, the country felt ought at least to be allowed to retain their seats without the interference of the boroughs. The Boundaries question would consequently have to be dealt with. There was a scattered population of nine millions who were the Backbone of the country. The backbone was landominant and had sixteen and deep religion, and ought to be consulted in and represented. [He introduced a parenthetical whap at Mr. Goldwin Smith, who has been bothering on politics, and whom Mr. Disraeli described as 'a compact lecturer, and a Wild Man from the Clusters.') Government were not seeking for a policy. They had one. But they would generally accept the will of the House. The course was not faltering to themselves. [Mr. Bright. He, he! Hear, hear! Mr. Disraeli. Yes, Sir, but it is better to work for the public good than to bring forward such measures.] He hoped the House would rise to this occasion. And he ended thus :—

"'Those who take the larger and nobler view of human affairs will, I think, recognise that about in the councils of Europe, England, now far ahead countless precedents, has, by her Parliament, exhibited a fine example of her Constitution. In the midst of this awful corruption of her better herself, she has maintained and cherished that public spirit which is the soul of commonwealths, and without which empire has no glory, and the wealth of nations is a means of corruption."

" Mr. Disraeli proposed to go into a Committee of the whole House on Monday the 25th February. He did not then produce his Resolutions, but they appeared the following morning. They may as well be reproduced here :—

1. Increase of Voters, town and county.
2. Lower the standard of value, and create 'fancy franchises.'
3. No class interest should predominate.
4. Occupation franchise to be based on rating.
5. Let us have Plurality of Voter in boroughs.
6. Revise the existing distribution of seats.
7. Wholly disfranchise no borough.
8. Consider the claims of unrepresented places.
9. Provide against bribery.
10. Liken the county to the borough system of registration.
11. Votes may be given in writing.
12. Some polling places, and all travelling payments illegal.
13. A Commission on the rough boundaries.

" But on this baker's dozen of Resolutions was set before the leader of the Opposition, Mr. Gladstone could only reply with a compliment to Mr. Disraeli's ability, a remark that his proposed mode of proceeding was novel, that Mr. Gladstone's own impression was against it, and a statement that the Opposition would decide upon their course when the whole case should be before them."

(*See Cartoon,* "Heads I win, Tails you lose.")

FEB. 20.

THE PRINCESS OF WALES gave birth to a daughter, the Princess Louise.

"HEADS I WIN, TAILS YOU LOSE!"

"Say, the meaning that we attribute to the words I have just read is, that, under the circumstances in which the House finds itself, it is our opinion expedient that Parliamentary Reform should no longer be a question that should decide the fate of Ministers." (Loud laughter at this capital joke.)—Vide Speech of CHANCELLOR OF EXCHEQUER, Feb. 11, 1867.

FEB. 25.

ON this night the Chancellor of the Exchequer explained the details of the Government Scheme of Reform, to be based on the Resolutions already submitted to the House.

The important items he threw :—

1. Four New Franchises : (1) Educational. (2) £50 deposit in a Savings Bank. (3) £50 in the Funds. (4) One pound a year direct taxation.
2. A £6 Rating Franchise in boroughs.
3. A £10 Rating Franchise in counties.

Whereby Mr. Disraeli guesses he shall add 400,000 voters to the present number, but his assignments allege that he will do nothing of the kind.

4. Great Yarmouth, Lancaster, Totnes, and Reigate to be disfranchised, *pro criminibus,* and their forfeited seats to be given to new places.

5. Members to be given to twelve new places.
6. Towns Members to be cut in two (many *Members* that we have ours and heard deserve this) and two new Members given.
7. Eight counties or divisions to be split again, whereby fifteen new county Members.
8. A Member to the London University.
9. A Member to be taken away from each of twenty-three boroughs.

10. Plan for detecting and punishing Bribery, and for cheapening elections.
11. A Royal Commission on Boundaries.

Then thirty new seats are to be given in all.

Mr. Disraeli praised the Reform Act of 1832, but said that its blemish was the ignoring the rights of the working classes, a fault which he then proposed to remedy.

This is the Derby Reform scheme of 1867. Or it may be, Why *Mr. Punch* writes hypothetically shall be seen.

The Chancellor of the Exchequer was very quietly received, even by his own party, and he had the further discomfort of knowing that at least four of his colleagues were shocked at much his antagonistic to the men whom he countenanced.

Mr. Gladstone duly noted and was glad of the vital statement, complimented Mr. Disraeli on his cleverness, disbelieved in his calculations, and said that the scheme did not propose to introduce the real Working Class. The

BLIND MAN'S BUFF.

"*Turn round three times, and catch whom you may.*"

Bill of last year did. After some minor objections, Mr. Gladstone said that he had no objection to proceed on Resolution, but it must be a Resolution embodying the plan the present Government had arranged. To this they must be pinned. Whereat the Liberals cheered loudly and significantly. He hoped they should not be asked to proceed on the Resolutions of last week. They had better be withdrawn, that a Bill might be brought in.

Mr. Disraeli, one in a way that indicated great delight at this course of things, said he was willing to meet Mr. Gladstone's views, and abandon some of the Resolutions.

VOL. II.

FEB. 28.

Two hundred and eighty-nine Members of the Opposition met at Mr. Gladstone's residence to consider the situation, with especial reference to Reform. It was resolved to defer action until the Resolution had been embodied in a Bill. Next day Mr. Disraeli announced that the Government gave up the method of proceeding by Resolution, and would introduce a Bill on an early day.

The scheme of Reform explained on the 25th was known as "The Ten Minutes' Bill," owing to the brevind manner in which it was said to have been prepared.

On the 2nd of March, the Cabinet resolving to introduce a "real and satisfactory" Reform Bill, three of its members, General Peel, War Secretary, the Earl of Carnarvon, Colonial Secretary, and Lord Cranborne, Secretary for India, resigned their offices.

(See Cartoon, "*Blind Man's Buff.*")

U

MARCH 15.

A Resolution was carried in the House of Commons, by 108 to 107, abolishing flogging in the army in time of peace.

MARCH 18.

The Chancellor of the Exchequer introduced his new Reform Bill. Its main features, as summarised in *Mr. Punch's* "Essence of Parliament," were—

1. Any male occupant of a house in a borough who personally pays rent shall vote.
2. We shall therefore enfranchise 237,000 persons.
3. We shall not give votes to Compound Householders, nor to those whose rates are paid for them.
4. Two pounds' residence necessary to obtain a vote.
5. Every facility to be given to Compound Householders to enable them to register.
6. A vote to every person who pays £1 a year grounded in taxes.
7. If a householder thus, he shall have two votes.
8. The householder shall have a second vote who has £50 in the funds or the savings bank.
9. There shall be an educational franchise, especially for ministers of religion.
10. No two votes in Counties, and the county occupation franchise to be £15 rating, and the other new franchises to apply.

The Redistribution Scheme already announced on the 15th of February to be adhered to. Mr. Gladstone attacked the scheme with much severity, as ill-conceived in its provisions and illusory in its safeguards, and, in particular, avowed his implacable hostility to the Dual Vote. This attack he repeated in detail on the 25th, when the Bill came on for second reading. He said, however, that if a Lodger Franchise were introduced, something done to prevent very poor householders from being used corruptly, and the Dual Vote surrendered, the Bill might with misgivings be allowed to go into Committee.

Mr. Disraeli made a slashing reply. He said he had no other wish "than, with the co-operation of the House, to bring the question of Parliamentary Reform to a settlement." He at once surrendered the Dual Vote. And he

THE LADIES' ADVOCATE.

Mrs. Bull. "Lor, Mr. Mill! what a lovely speech you can make. I do believe I don't the slightest notion no more such miserable creatures. It's on the top of that your foot that the cat broke down."

would consider anything else in reason. "Pass the Bill" (he said), "and then change the Ministry to-morrow if you like."

The Bill was read a second time without a division.

MARCH 30.

Mr. John Stuart Mill, new Member for Westminster, was an ardent advocate of the extension of the suffrage to women, and in the course of the debates on the Reform Bill submitted a motion to the House of Commons to the effect that instead of "Man" the word "Person" should be introduced. This was negatived.

(See Cartoon, "The Ladies' Advocate.")

MARCH 30.

To-day took place in the North German Parliament a discussion concerning the cession of Luxemburg to France by the King of Holland. Count Bismarck said that the Prussian Government did not adopt the opinion that an arrangement had been entered into between Holland and France, but could not on the other hand deny that such was the case. *Mr. Punch* thus summed up the Luxemburg Question: "Luxemburg is a Duchy, and it belongs to the King of Holland. The Emperor of the French wanted to buy it. The King of Holland wanted to sell it. The Luxemburghers did not want to be sold. The Prussians did not wish German territory handed to France. The Emperor has had to give up his Napoleonic Idea. A waker of our failures, eh?"

(*See Cartoon, "To be Sold."*)

The question gave rise to much anxious discussion, and led to a conference in London of European Powers. Ultimately a Treaty was concluded, by which it was agreed that the Duchy of Luxemburg should be considered a neutral territory, and placed under the collective guarantee of all the Powers parties to the Treaty, and that the Prussian garrison should be withdrawn from the fortress, which was to be dismantled to such an extent as would be satisfactory to the King of Holland.

"TO BE SOLD."

Emperor Napoleon. "I . a--have made an offer to my friend here, yonder."

The Man in Possession. "No, have you, though? had rather than I was the party to apply to."

Emperor Napoleon. "Oh, indeed! Ah! Then in that case I'll —— But it's of no consequence."

APRIL 1.

The Paris International Exhibition was opened by the Emperor of the French.

APRIL 4.

The Chancellor of the Exchequer introduced the Budget. "Mr. Disraeli" (said *Punch*) "made the shortest speech ever heard on such a subject. But he really had only to say that having a surplus of £1,206,000 he wished to follow Mr. Gladstone's lead, and reduce the National Debt by means of Life-Annuities. He also reduced Marine Assurances to three-pence per cent., and kept a trifle (a quarter of a million) in hand. The Budget, and the facility of the Chancellor, were alike approved."

APRIL 5.

At a meeting of Liberal Members (about 340) in Mr. Gladstone's house, it was arranged that Mr. Coleridge should propose a Resolution in Committee on the Reform Bill.

"That it be an instruction to the Committee that they have power to alter the law of rating, and to provide that in every Parliamentary borough the occupiers of tene-

mouths below a given rateable
value be relieved from liability
to personal rating, with the view
to this is time for the borough franchise at which all occupiers
should be reserved on the rate-
book, and should have equal
facilities for the enjoyment of
such franchise as a residential
occupation franchise."

There was however a
revolt in the ranks of the
Liberal party against this
instruction. "About half a
hundred Liberals met in
the Tea Room (of the
House) and decided that
they should be spoons if
they stirred in the matter.
The proposal of Mr. Glad-
stone would appear to the
country as restrictive of the
suffrage which the Government Bill offered." Mr.
Gladstone had to give way,
and agreed to limit the instructions to the first clause
of the Resolution.

Later Mr. Gladstone hav-
ing given notice of a series
of Resolutions on Reform
whose points were :—

(1) To reduce the term of occu-
pancy from two years to
one year ;

(2) To let occupiers under £10
have rates in respect of any
tenements, and not look the
franchise to dwelling-
houses ;

(3) To give a £1 franchise instead of one based on personal payment of rates ;

Mr. Disraeli said these
were Mr. Coleridge's In-
structions in a new form,
and if any of them were carried the Government would
give up the Bill.

The Bill then went into
Committee.

APRIL 12.

IN the discussion on Mr.
Gladstone's first amend-
ment, Mr. Beresford Hope
spoke strongly against the
Government Reform Bill,
saying that "he for one
with his whole heart and
conscience would vote against the Asian Mystery." "But Mr. Disraeli" (said *Punch*) "is a
dangerous person to gird at, and in return he
complimented Mr. Hope on his exhibitions, adding sweetly that their Batavian grace took away
their sting. The Hopes are of Dutch descent."
There was a majority for the Ministry of 21, and
the House rose for the Easter Recess.

THE POLITICAL TAILORS.

DIZZY. "Now, then, GLADSTONE, jump up!—You promised to lend a helping hand, you know."
GLADSTONE. "No, I'm in doubt; and you may finish the job as you best can."

APRIL 18.

MR. GLADSTONE, owing to opposition of
certain of his own nominal followers,
announced that he should not proceed with his
amendments to the Reform Bill, and although
"prepared to attempt concerted action" with
the party "when suitable occasion should arise,"
said "prudence requires me to withdraw from
my attempts to assume the initiative in amending a measure which cannot, perhaps, be effec-
tually amended, except by the reversal, either
formal or virtual, of the vote of Friday the 11th."
This was taken as a virtual withdrawal for the
time from the leadership of the Liberal Party in
the House.

(*See Cartoon, "The Political Tailors."*)

MAY 3.

THE Government was defeated in Committee on an amendment moved by Mr. Ayrton, proposing that the period of residence in boroughs at rentals below £10 should be one year instead of two. Vote 176 to 197—81 majority. Mr. Disraeli demanded time to consult his colleagues, but on the next night announced that the Government did not think it inconsistent with their duty to defer to the decision of the House.

MAY 6.

A LARGE but peaceable Reform League Demonstration this day took place in Hyde Park. Mr. Walpole, whose conduct in connection with these demonstrations had been much canvassed, had, on the 3rd, obtained leave to introduce a bill providing that no public meetings should henceforth take place in any of the Royal Parks without the permission of Her Majesty.

"THE CAT OUT OF THE BAG."

HOME SECRETARY. "My dear Mr. PUNCH, what ARE we to do with our great Rabbits and Ruffians?"
Mr. PUNCH. "My dear Mr. HARDY, there's but one remedy—'the harmless, necessary Cat.'"

MAY 7.

"SIR JOHN GRAY initiated a debate on the Church of Ireland, and proposed that the House should commit itself to a declaration that the Establishment in question should be abandoned by the State. The usual see-saw was varied by an outspoken statement by Mr. Gladstone. The time, he said, had not come for a practical plan, but he to a great extent agreed with Sir John Gray. This indication of a measure which will one day be submitted to the Commons by Mr. Gladstone grievously excited the Irish Attorney-General. . . . After much angry talk the previous question was carried by 195 to 183; so the Irish Church survives as yet. But Mr. Punch, as the family doctor, ventures to hint to the eccentric old lady that she may as well begin to think about making her will." (Mr. Punch's "Essence of Parliament.")

MAY 9.

MR. WALPOLE resigned the office of Home Secretary, and was succeeded by Mr. Gathorne Hardy. It was hoped that the change would lead to a more vigorous dealing with riot and ruffianism, Mr. Walpole's action having been generally looked upon as too timid and vacillating.

(See Cartoon, "The Cat out of the Bag.")

MAY 13.

THE Chancellor of the Exchequer introduced the Scotch Reform Bill with a similar franchise to the English, but with some differences of detail.

MAY 15.

THE Emperor Maximilian was to-day betrayed by General Lopez into the hands of the Juarist General Escobedo.

MAY 17.

Mr. Hodgkinson moved "that no person other than an occupier should be rated to any borough. (This meant the abolition of the much-talked-of Compound Householder.) Mr. Gladstone enforced this proposal in the most earnest manner, declaring he accepted it for the sake of peace. Mr. Disraeli not only accepted it, but did so to the extent of saying that such a course was what he had originally designed, and was entirely in conformity with the principle of the Bill."—*Punch's* "Essence of Parliament."

MAY 20.

THE Queen laid the first stone of the new Albert Hall of Arts and Sciences at Kensington.

MAY 22.

THE "Derby," won by Mr. Chaplin's colt "Hermit," was run in a snow-storm.

MAY 27.

THE County qualification was fixed at £12; in the Bill it stood originally at £20. The qualification to be either house and land or house or land. On the 28th, "with Mr. Disraeli's free consent, we wiped out all the Fancy Franchises, Educational, Money in Savings Bank, Money in Funds, £1 taxation. Mr. Disraeli said that having let in the lodger, we had provided for most of these people. The Dual Vote Clause was also withdrawn. The franchise clauses of the Reform Bill were now settled, and Redistribution was taken in hand."

The Reform Bill of the Government had indeed been modified almost beyond recognition, and mainly by the action of Mr. Gladstone and his followers, but marvel at Mr. Disraeli's flexibility of purpose was more than equalled by admiration of his skill of management.

(*See Cartoon,* "*The Political Egg-Dance.*")

THE POLITICAL EGG-DANCE.

VIVIAN GREY. (YOUNG AND OLD.)

(BY AN ANCIENT TORY BLOB.)

Air "*Auld Robin Gray.*"

OLD John Bull loved me well; and when "Church and State!" I cried,
And "King and Constitution!" he clasped at my side;
Till on Test and Corporation Acts I found myself at sea,
And then with other things than Trade there came a making free.

Emancipation gained ; Reform ;
Corn Laws were swept away ;
The angrier I felt the less my
wrath I could display ;
I wanted Peel pitched into, but
no one for that could see,
When young Vivian Grey came
a-courting of me.

Lord George was great at figures,
but a poon he couldn't spin ;
While Vivian Grey had wealth of
words and power of pushing in ;
He made Peel's life a burden,
Derby's right hand I grew to be,
Then said, "Don't you think,
old True Blue, you'd best take
up with me ?"

My heart it said " Nay ; " I hoped
the chalk-hands would go back :
But they didn't ; things grew
worse and worse ; the old
ways began to crack ;
The old True Blue coach ceased
running ; I was left to cry
"woe's me,
"To have seen the things that I
have seen—to see the things I
see !"

With a man who's done one's
dirty work one feels ashamed
to break ;
I knew what dirt young Vivian
Grey had room for my sake,
So I gave him my hand, though
for my heart could wring he,
And Old Vivian Grey was a
harder for me !

His hand I had followed some two
years, less or more,
When I found, one late morning,
a Reform Bill at my door !
I said, "You're come to the
wrong shop : Bankes and
Bright's the farm, but see ;"
But it said, " I'm sent by Vivian
Grey—made too by yonder he."

Oh, long and how I swore,
though little I did say ;
For better and for worse I am
tied to Vivian Grey ;
I wish I was out, but can't be
charmed ; must be ;
And I must do his dirty work,
as he did mine for me.

King Mob to Britain's threshold
room I have invited in ;
I've to eat my words and pledges,
and don't know where to
begin ;
But I must do my best a Household Suffrager to be,
For old Vivian Grey has no
earthed it for me !

JUNE 3.

To-day Messrs. Overend,
    Chance and Barrow.

THE ROAD TO SHEFFIELD.

Examiners appointed by the Trades' Union Commission, began their inquiries into Trade Outrages which were stated to have been committed at Sheffield. The disclosures were very dreadful, a hideous system of intimidation, supported by the most ruthless murder, being shown to have been carried on under the leadership of the man Broadhead. The country was greatly excited by these hideous revelations. The system of intimidation common in Sheffield had spread to other quarters, among the tailors and other trades.

(*See Cartoon, "The Road to Sheffield."*)

JUNE 19.

To-day the melancholy tragedy in Mexico culminated in the shooting of the ill-fated and high-minded Emperor Maximilian at Queretaro, together with Generals Miramon and Mejia. "Tell Lopez that I forgive his treachery ; tell all Mexico that I pardon its crime," were almost the last words of the murdered Maximilian, a victim to French ambition and Mexican treachery.

On the 20th the city of Mexico surrendered to the Juarists after a siege of 69 days.

JUNE 20.

BY a Treaty, America agreed to purchase from Russia for 7,000,000 dollars the territory known as Russian America or Wal-Russia.

JULY 11.

VISIT of some 1,400 Belgian Volunteers to London at the invitation of a committee of English Riflemen.

JULY 12.

THE SULTAN OF TURKEY arrived on a visit to this country. He was well received.

JULY 15.

THE Reform Bill was this evening read a third time.

(*See Cartoon, "The Return from Victory."*)

Lord Cranborne said that this so-called "gift to the people" had "been purchased by a

"THE RETURN FROM VICTORY." (With Mr. Punch's apologies to Mr. Calderon, R.A.)

political betrayal which has no parallel in our Parliamentary annals;" a taunt levelled at Mr. Disraeli. Mr. Lowe in a brilliant speech repeated his denunciations of the measure, and added:—

"I believe it will be absolutely necessary to compel our future masters (by which he meant the newly enfranchised proletariat) to learn their letters. You have placed the government in the hands of the masses, and you must therefore give them education . . . . That England that was wont to conquer other nations, has gained a shameful victory over herself; and, oh, that a man would rise in order that he might set forth in words that could not die, the shame, the rage, the scorn, the indignation and the despair with which the

measure is viewed by every Englishman who is not a slave to the trammels of party, or who is not dazzled by the glare of a temporary and ignoble success."

Mr. Disraeli, replying, said:—

"I do not think that the country is in danger; I think England is safe in the race of men who inhabit her; that she is safe in something much more precious than her accumulated capital—her accumulated experience. She is safe in her national character and her fame, in the traditions of a thousand years, and in that glorious future which I believe awaits her."

Mr. Gladstone did not take part in the concluding debate, "but" (said Mr. Punch) "it

may be assumed that he is tolerably satisfied." Largely by his action the Bill had been so completely transformed that it was said of it that nothing of the original Government measure was left save the preamble. And Lord Cranborne complained that all the precautions, guarantees, and securities with which the Bill had originally bristled, had been swept away at the imperious bidding of Mr. Gladstone.

Mr. Punch said, "The Reform Act, as it emerged at last, gave Household Suffrage to boroughs, brought the County Franchise down lower than was originally intended, increased votes on lodgers, and widened the operation of that portion of the scheme which dealt with the Redistribution of Seats."

In a memorable Cartoon *Mr. Punch* represented the Bill as "A Leap in the Dark;" "a phrase which became historical from its adoption by Lord Derby in his speech in the Lords on the passing of the Reform Bill."

(See Cartoon, "A Leap in the Dark.")

A LEAP IN THE DARK.

A FINE horse, a fine rider,—and first of the steed—
Caucasian Arab, they say, by his head—
Limbs lithe, light, and muscular; with sinew to speed.
And though past mark of mouth, not a single white hair;
Yet his coat seems to change, as 'tis viewed in the light,
Now, a dull Oxford mixture, now dark, and now bright.
Till what its true colour, 'twere purely to say,
Till they found a new name for it— Vivian Grey—

His temper, you'd say, than a quieter horse
Never played in a paddock, or walked a'er a course,
But for all he's not quiet, a look in his eye
Warns 'gainst trusting one's ribs his fine fetlocks too
And if over a brook had a will of his own,
One is feard in that flesh, and was bred in that bone;
Ere you cross this dark horse, let him look ne'er so nice,
See you've nosebag like whip-cord, a hand like a race,
Or else he'll more find with the bit in his teeth,
And the rider, where riders should not lie, beneath.

A LEAP IN THE DARK.

And he who backs this horse, far field, course, or park,
Ten to one, feels he's taken—a LEAP IN THE DARK.
And what of his rider, the lady in blue?
There are fears and forebodings. Britannia, for you!
Through in front of the field 'twas your glory to shew,
There were when your steed by *your* will had to go;
When though sitting your fastest, you sell, as you led,
Kept a hand on your horse, and a watch well ahead;
Never rushed at your fence, your man's eveshot,
Nor galloped o'er ground where 'twas sheer to tisol;
When, if strange to a country, you sent to a guide
Who knew it,—nor trusted by devotion to ride;
When if a big jump, or a blind, crossed your course,
You noted the ground ere you filed your horse;
If the fin of the land blazed danger beyond—
Old quarry, or chalk-pit, mast roadway, or pond—

When your brave would have taken the fence in his
You pulled him together, and turned him aside,
And the chance of a fall and a fracture to baulk,
To the down incognito went at a walk—
Too brave to heed scorners' or scoffers' remark,
And too wise to hazard a LEAP IN THE DARK.
These feelings you've changed, and these rules you've
thrown by;
With no hand on your reins, seems country you fly;
Curb and snaffle hang loose, and your horse has his head,
And to some put cumped him, now he meets you, instead;
Takes a line of his own, you rock sought where or how;
Let him test over pasture, and gallop o'er plough!
Let him lay the old ways, well-known gaps, ancient
rides,
Leave your sides on the chance, smash your knees, bruise

In the rush have let gatepests too sought to pass through,
At sunset walls he can't leap, goes you cannot undo;
Till at last, where your hand you have lost to the run,
When your eyesight is failing, your strength fairly done,
When your few shapes at random, the guide puts on-
ward,
You hazar not an inch of the country ahead.
He goes by Bright and Gladstone, Hughes, Fawcett, and
Mill,
At a thundering gallop, neter with you down-hill,
In his stride takes the fence that, big, bushy, and black,
Throws up its thick sprigs and sharp shorts in your
track,
And over it skims, like a lad in a lark,
And—who knows what will come of this LEAP IN THE
DARK?

JULY 26.

A DEBATE took place in the House of Commons on the Abyssinian captives, and Lord Stanley said that the Government had under consideration a variety of schemes for organising an expedition for their rescue.

These captives were a number of persons, some of them British subjects, and including Mr Cameron, Her Majesty's Consul at Massowah, and Mr Rassam, Her Majesty's Envoy, who had for some time been detained as prisoners by King Theodore, the half-savage monarch of Abyssinia.

[See Cartoon, "The Abyssinian Question."]

AUG. 6.

THE Reform Bill was read a third time in the House of Lords. It received the Royal assent on the 15th.

AUG. 13.

THE Sheffield Saw-Grinders' Society decided not to expel Broadhead and Crookes, refusing to consider their murderous deeds and incitements as "crimes."

AUG. 13.

THE Public Parks Regulation Bill was "talked out" of the House of Commons.

AUG. 21.

PARLIAMENT was prorogued by Commission. The Royal Speech referred chiefly to the peremptory demand made to the King of Abyssinia for the release of the captives, and to the passing of the Reform Bill.

> " And fair Reform (celestial sound)
> Has smiled on thousands, thanks to you,
> I trow the vote franchise fail
> Beneath the throne is sound and true.
> I trow thus those whom you invite
> To the new franchise great and high,
> Will show they prize the holy right,
> And see their mind, and mind their eye."

THE ABYSSINIAN QUESTION.

BRITANNIA. "Now, then, King Theodore! hand about those Prisoners!"

In the shaping of the Conservative Reform Bill, the Liberals and their leaders had taken so important a share, modifying its provisions greatly in the direction of Liberal desires, that *Punch* suggested the claim of Messrs. Gladstone, Bright and others to seats at the Government Whitebait Dinner, held as usual at Greenwich.

A HINT FROM THE WHITEBAIT.

> Diet, whose Caucasian glory
> I took all Eastern lore untold,
> We'll then know'd th' Arabian story
> By Scheherezade told.
>
> How the enchanted fish, defying
> Bewilderment's brown and yellow puke,
> From the pan, where they lay frying,
> Words of truth and warning spoke.

THE WHITEBAIT DINNER; OR, "PARTIES" AT GREENWICH.

DERBY. "Going to 'The Trafalgar,' are we? Why not dine here? All in the same 'Ship,' we trow, hat ha!"
GLADSTONE. "Hm! Well! All things considered, I think you might have invited us."

(See Cartoon, "The Whitebait Dinner; or, 'Parties' at …)

AUG. 22.

The Sheffield magistrates refused to grant a renewal of a public-house licence to William Broadhead, who had to leave England for America.

AUG. 25.

PROFESSOR FARADAY, the great chemist, died at the age of 75.

"A Priest of Truth: his office
to expound
Earth's mysteries to all who
willed to learn—
Who in this book of Science
sought and found,
With love that knew all reverence, but no fear,"

SEPT. 3.

ON this day the London Working Men's Association, who were organising a Reform Banquet at the Crystal Palace, held a meeting at which were read letters from Earl Russell and Mr. Gladstone in reply to invitations to attend their celebration. Earl Russell in declining wrote :—" It would not be candid of me to stop here. I must add, therefore, that I am too uncertain what effects Lord Derby's 'leap in the dark' may produce to be a fit and enthusiastic companion for those who wish to celebrate the passing of the Reform Bill of 1867. Other measures unconnected with the Reform of Parliament appear to me to be necessary to assure the future of the country."

Mr. Beales and Mr. Potter were leaders of the Reform party among the working men.

(See Cartoon, " Declined with Thanks.")

DECLINED WITH THANKS;
OR, THE RIVAL TOUTS.

SEPT. 4.

A TRADES Union Inquiry opened at Manchester. It led to painful revelations respecting the prevalence of tyranny and outrage

SEPT. 8.

UNDER the presidency of General Garibaldi an International Peace Congress assembled at Geneva, but (says " Annals of our Time ")

" the discussions were conducted in such a disorderly manner that the Conference broke up in confusion on the 11th."

SEPT. 16.

AT Manchester to-day, in an attempt to rescue two Fenian prisoners known as " Colonel" Kelly and " Captain " Deasy from a

prison-van, a party, led by a man named William O'Meara Allen, fired on the van and its escort, demanded the keys of Police-Sergeant Brett, and on his replying, " No, I will stick to my post to the last," shot that brave and dutiful officer dead. Allen and two other ringleaders, Larkin and Gould, were subsequently apprehended, but Kelly and Deasy effected their escape.

SEPT. 24.

The Pan-Anglican Synod commenced its sittings at Lambeth Palace. It met to discuss the best way of promoting the re-union of Christendom, and various matters connected with Church extension and discipline. "It seems" (said *Mr. Punch*) "to have been an impression that the practical results of the Synod were inconsiderable."

(See Cartoon, "A Pan-Anglican Oversight.")

SEPT. 24.

Garibaldi was arrested at Sinalunga, Arezzo, by order of the Italian Government, on account of his taking measures for the invasion of the Pontifical territory. He was subsequently allowed to return to Caprera, whence he again made his escape on the 13th October, and joined the insurgent bands on the Roman frontier.

OCT. 2.

Lord Brougham, now ninety years of age, wrote to the *Globe* that "his most important death-bed legacy was the repression of electoral corruption."

OCT. 23.

A Special Commission was opened at Manchester for the trial of the 26 Fenian prisoners charged with being concerned in the attack on the prison van and the murder of Police-sergeant Brett. The Grand Jury returned a true bill against Allen, Larkin, Gould, Maguire, and Shore.

OCT. 25.

The French Government issued a circular to diplomatic agents concerning its position towards Italy, and suggesting a Congress for the settlement of the Roman question. On the 16th a French iron-clad squadron sailed for Civita Vecchia with troops for the assistance of the Pope. On the same day Garibaldi at the head of his volunteers defeated the Pontifical troops at Monte Rotondo. On the 27th the

A PAN-ANGLICAN OVERSIGHT.

Anxious Wife. "And help for our difficulties, dear?"

Reverend Husband. "Oh no, love. We poor Curates are not even mentioned!"

King of Italy issued a proclamation for the suppression of the insurgents.

OCT. 29.

At a Conservative Banquet given in honour of Mr. Disraeli in the Corn Exchange, Edinburgh, the Chancellor of the Exchequer made a sprightly speech in defence of his dealing with the Reform question. One passage in particular greatly tickled the public. He said that on the subject of Reform "I had to prepare the mind of the country, and to educate—if it be not arrogant to use such a phrase—to educate our party. It is a large party, and requires its attention to be called in questions of this kind with some pressure. I had to prepare the mind of Parliament and of the country on this question of Reform."

(See Cartoon, "Fagin's Political School").

FAGIN'S ACADEMY.

"Most much this ; because there are things which you may not have heard in any speech to back but have made in the city of Edinburgh. (*Laughter and cheers.*)—I had—if it be not arranged to use such a phrase—to educate our party. It is a large party, and requires no ambition to be called in questions of this kind with some persons. I had to prepare the mind of Parliament and the country on this question of Reform."— MR. DISRAELI's *Speech at his Edinburgh Banquet.*

Yes—that is yes, my dears, the work o' seven long years,
And little time enough, you must have known, for such a job ;
If you'll think that I'd to teach sleights o' hand to well as speech,
Something more than "frisking till," "making skin," or "fishing lob."

For seven long years I taught 'em, where once I'd learn and brought 'em
To *Fagin's* private school—my own Academy of Arts :
Your Conservers might ride rusty, or your Conkerers cut up crowy,
But most of 'em took kindly to my teachus', bless their 'earts !

First, I taught 'em grave as mutes,
—their own words how to eat,—
But, mind you, not served up with dirt, in a nasty humble pie :
But with pepper and sharp sauce and our finer rocks of course—
And fine words do better paraseps—than so says they don't, they lie.

Then, the nex thing they'd to learn was their coats how to turn,
So as no one mightn't learn 'em, and, perticler, the police ;
How to slip out of one skin, and another to slip in,
And to look at it fixed, close as wax, and slick as grease.

And, if trapped, in quoit the jug, by making up a mug,
After the book, and awearing they'd not changed coats at all ;
That to do's a thing they'd never—that the coat was one they'd worn,
The same side out, from when they was they couldn't say how small.

Then I taught 'em how to twist, with a flourish of the wrist,
Opinions into all shapes, so p'raps you've seen the same,

FAGIN'S POLITICAL SCHOOL.

"*Now, mark this, because there are things which you may not have heard in any speech which has been made in the city of Edinburgh.* (*Laughter and cheers.*) *I had—if it be not arranged to use such a phrase—TO EDUCATE OUR PARTY. It is a large Party, and requires no attention to be called to questions of this kind with some persons. I had to prepare the mind of Parliament and the country on this question of Reform.*"—MR. DISRAELI's Speech at the Edinburgh Banquet.

Who used to fold a paper, slit by an artful caper
It crossword the form of sentry low, but, forwer put, lady's fan ?
Then they had to learn the sleight of making black look white, [joy :
And keeping a grave face while that little game they First contrivedum how to hide : quietus and scruples to o'er-ride : [way.
And to swaller down the ticket, if a pledge stand in the

Lest I had to make 'em fly, see at faking "skin" or "sly,"
But picking a party's pocket of mite of hand and ball,
With faine as sharp and true that the party never knew
Till the trick was done, and the prig was gone, and the swag safe in my till !

OCT. 30.

The French troops under General Dumont entered Rome. They were received without enthusiasm, but also without overt hostility.

See Cartoon, "Brennus-Bonaparte, or the Gaul again in Rome."

On the 3rd November Garibaldi abandoned his position at Monte Rotondo. "We shall now" (he said) "look on as spectators, and await the solution which our troops and the French army will give the Roman problem; and in the event of that solution not being in conformity with the wishes of the nation, the country will find within itself fresh forces to begin again, and solve the vital question by itself." On the 4th Garibaldi was again arrested, but protesting was released on the 26th.

NOV. 1.

At Manchester Allen, Gould, Larkin, Shore and Maguire, the Fenian prisoners, were convicted and received sentence of death. The remainder of the prisoners were a little later acquitted of the charge of murder and liberated. On the 18th a deputation of sympathisers forced their way into the Home Office and demanded of Mr. Gathorne Hardy the commutation of the capital sentence. Mr. Hardy declined to see them, but under the leadership of a man named Finlen the deputation became very noisy and violent, and ultimately had to be expelled by the police. Other demonstrations in favour of the Fenian prisoners were made; but Allen, Larkin, and Gould were on the 23rd November executed at Manchester.

BRENNUS-BONAPARTE, OR THE GAUL AGAIN IN ROME.

CHECK TO KING MOB.

Whatever the leader us follow,
Heates of Maaters, John Bright or Bob Lowe;
Whether "Derry and Derby!" we holloa,
Or huzza for Gladstone & Co.

One leader all parties will have at,
Old Tory or Rad, Swell or Snob,
Merging all shades of platform and ticket
In a general "Check to King Mob!"
What parties we're the stage readier,
Whatever the cry rules the scene,—
"Greatest happiness of Greatest number,"
"Church and State," "Amend Ways," or "Reform";
Through we change creeds an' colours with leaders,
But to vary, mull, muddle, and job.

There's one cry will feed no wonders,
And that's the cry, "Check to King Mob!"
Discontent may be rife, and with reason,
The State and foolery through,
All may know some indictable treason
'Gainst future or rights to undo.
And what evil's his blue this King's Evil,
The State's blood and marrow to rob?
What set's devils like the great devil
Exorcised by "Check to King Mob."

Then rhrue your ranks, friends
of good order,
Whate'er your side, calling, or
creed :
There is left in this England's
wide border,
Work for all men's good ...
and good deed,
That the duty of duties for all
men—
Hand or brain ...
nerve ... weak, rich or poor,
great or small men—
Is in chorus a "CHALK TO
KING MOB."

Many-headed's this king-beast,
and on it
Is more than can crown'd to be
seen—
Fighting-nine's bloody Phrygian
bonnet,
Rough's billy-cock, I voice
... :
Iron ... in hand, ... dis-
... ,
The ... with gore on
its hands,
Yet, in spite of his surplice, he
trembles
When faced with stern
"CHALK TO KING MOB."

NOV. 2.

The International Exhi-
bition which had been
held this year in Paris, was
to-day finally closed.

NOV. 19.

PARLIAMENT was opened
by Commission, being
called together at this unusual time in order to
sanction the expedition
which it had become necessary to despatch for the
relief of the captives in
Abyssinia. £2,000,000
was required at once for
the purpose. Abyssinia
being 160 miles from the
Red Sea. The control
of the Expedition was
entrusted to Sir Robert
Napier, &c a distinguished
General of Engineers, then
commanding the forces at
Bombay, with Sir Charles
Stavely as second in com-
mand. The advance brigade
of the Expedition had left Bombay on the 7th
October. It was thought it might ultimately cost
four millions or even more. The Income Tax
would have to be raised. There was much talk
of a missing letter alleged to have been sent to
the Queen by King Theodore. Mr. Bernal
Osborne said the postage of that letter would
cost £5,000,000. Of course the House granted

the Government what it required, and on the 7th
Dec. adjourned till Feb. 13.

(See Cartoon, "Tuck in yer Twopenny!")

DEC. 13.

TO-DAY occurred another Fenian outrage, the
wall of the Clerkenwell House of Detention
being blown in in an attempt to rescue the

prisoners Burke and Casey. Six people were
killed on the spot, six more died subsequently,
and 120 people were wounded, whilst immense
damage was done by the explosion to houses and
property in the vicinity. Arrests of suspected
accomplices were at once made, and a reward of
£300 was offered for the conviction of the man
who fired the match.

"TUCK IN YER TWOPENNY!"

DISP. "Now, then, Jack, I'm waiting over yer again! Turk is not twopenny."

✦ 1868 ✦

JAN. 4.

SIR ROBERT NAPIER, leader of the Abyssinian Expedition, landed at Annesley Bay, on his way to the front.

JAN. 9.

THE Fenian prisoners, Burke, Casey, and Shore, were this day committed for trial. "In consequence of Fenian outbreaks and alarms," (says a Note to Vol. LIV.) "special constables were sworn in, in London and in all parts of England."

[*See Cartoon, "A Hint to the Loyal Irish."*]

On the 17th, George Francis Train, an excitable and loquacious American, was arrested on the arrival of the "Scotia" at Queenstown, on suspicion of being a Fenian. He was shortly afterwards liberated, however. On the 18th the Fenian leader Clancy was captured, after a sharp struggle, in Tottenham Court Road. On the same day a Fenian placard was found posted on the front of the Mansion House.

AN UNUSUAL LOYAL TOAST.

HERE'S a health to the Army and Navy,
Likewise to the Volunteers!
When the red wine follows the gravy, [*cheers*]
'Tis a toast that oft when hot forget not our best protectors,
Our heroes who fight in peace,
Whose Colonels are their Inspectors,
Let us drink to the brave Police!

From the group of the last gruntter
It is they can thwarts that ever;
They are down on the Fenian plotter,
And coolue the traitor knaves.
Good speed the Policemen's truncheon,
When he biddeth the Roughs turn back,
And they shrink, lest She cudgel of hard on
Their heads it should come down whack!

And good speed the Policeman mounted,
If a robber they must pursue!
We have not too many, all counted,
Of our guardians clad in blue.

Should you not augment their number,
Seeing rowdies so fast increase
In the British Lion's slumber?
Irish "The Bobbies—and more Police!

JAN. 18.

REPORTS having been received, in the early part of the preceding year, of the murder of the great African explorer and missionary, Dr. Livingstone, a search expedition had been organised and despatched on the 9th June, under the command of Mr. E. D. Young. To-day intelligence was received that the expedition had returned, having satisfied itself that the reports of Livingstone's death were untrue.

A HINT TO THE LOYAL IRISH.

"Ah, then, MISTHER BULL! give us the same ould wan o' thim shticks. Sure, there's hundhreds o' the Boys as is ready to help ye. Sor."

JAN. 25.

AT this time Prince Alfred, Duke of Edinburgh, was in Australia, he having started in the "Galatea," on a visit to our colonies, on the 23rd May of the previous year. He had been well received.

[See Cartoon, "Our Australian Cousin."]

A short time previously the Queen had caused to be published a book entitled "Leaves from our Journal in the Highlands," giving an account of the life led by herself and the Prince Consort when in Scotland, which had been read with friendly interest by her subjects.

THE QUEEN'S BOOK.

LET cynics scoff and worldlings sneer,
And cold misdoubters ponder us :
Their censure weighed not in
    her ear,   [them.
Her counsel was not to'en with

A silent, womanlike thought
Whispered within her woman's
    heart :—
"They that my nature would
    have wrought,
They in my grief shall have
    their part.

"The love I mourn, for whom I
    go
In mourning, ever, to the end,
What England lost in him they
    know,   [friend :
How met a guide, how firm a

"But what the loss the wife, and
    Queen,
Had in that nature, pure and
    sweet,   [serene,
That judgment, stately and
That counsel with all needs
    to meet,

"That light of joy within the
    home,   [hearth,
That fount of peace beside the
That gravity, which ne'er was
    gloom,   [mirth—
That glee in pure woman's

"All this my people cannot
    know,
All this I only can make
    known,   [me
Then they may gauge the joy and
I knew with him, now know alone.

"So my past life, my walks and ways,
The wife's and mother's, not the Queen's,
My treasured tale of happier days,
My record of love-hallowed scenes,

"I'll open to my people's eyes,
And therein let them take their part,
That they may weigh the weight that lies
On my lone life and widowed heart.

OUR AUSTRALIAN COUSIN.

PRINCE ALFRED. "Well, Miss Australia, I knew you were a GREAT Girl, but I'd no idea you were so beautiful.

"I'll feeling what my joy has been,
They feel how vast my grief must be :
And, when my treasure they have seen,
May measure what its loss to me."

What Queen like this was ever known
To take her people in her heart ?
When was Queen's household-life so shown
With modest truth and artless art ?

The Royal Widow has done well
Thus on her people's love to call,
Her simple widely tale to tell,
And trust her joys and griefs to all.

Ne'er since Victoria felt the Crown
A weight upon her girlish brow,
Have Heaven's best blessings been called down
About her path, as they are now.

PARLIAMENT, which had adjourned on the 7th December, resumed its sittings on this day. The Chancellor of the Exchequer introduced a Bill to amend the law relating to election petitions, with a special view to the prevention of bribery and corruption. He had originally intended that Election Bribery Cases should be removed from the jurisdiction of the House of Commons, and be tried by the Judges. But the Judges, through the mouth of Lord Chief Justice Cockburn, had vehemently protested against the imposition of "these new and objectionable duties." So Mr. Disraeli proposed a new tribunal, to be composed of three barristers, at £2,000 a year each, to try election petitions, and be appealed to against revising barristers. Also that "any M.P. unseated for bribery should be kept out for seven years, and on a second conviction should be incapable of ever coming in any more." (*Punch's* "Essence.")

(See Cartoon, "A Legal Difficulty.")

Feb. 17.

EARL RUSSELL published a letter to the Right Hon. Chichester Fortescue setting forth his views on the Irish question, recommending amongst other remedial measures the endowment of the Roman Catholic Church and the Presbyterian Church in Ireland, and the reduction of the revenues of the Protestant Episcopal Church there to one-eighth of their existing amount.

Feb. 25.

LORD DERBY, who had been in failing health for some time, announced that he had tendered his resignation to Her Majesty, who had empowered the Chancellor of the Exchequer, Mr. Disraeli, to form a government. On the

A LEGAL DIFFICULTY.

LORD CHIEF JUSTICE. "Nonsense! You mustn't bring that bribery fellow before us;—WE should have to be IN EARNEST!"

17th Mr. Disraeli had an audience with the Queen and kissed hands on his appointment as First Lord of the Treasury. "The Educator" (said *Mr. Punch's* "Essence") "is now formally installed as Head Master, and as at Eton he receives a Rod (Blue Ribbon in good time), which doubtless he will be glad to use as little as possible, but which, we take it, will not

exactly resemble that spoken of by Duke Vincentio:—

Fond fathers

Having bound up the threatening twigs of birch
Only to stick it in their children's sight
For terror, not for use; in time the Rod
Becomes more mocked than feared.

Mr. Punch has fought with Mr. Disraeli many an hour by the Shrewsbury clock, which used to sound the close

of the poll for the honourable
gentleman. It is extremely probable that *Mr. Punch* may have
to fight with him again, many a
time, and oft. He is a foeman
worthy of *Mr. Pam's* steel.
Be this as it may, *Mr. Punch*
hereby presents his best compliments to the Premier of England,
and respectfully reminds him that,
in 1848 Mr. Disraeli said in the
House, "I belong to a party that
can triumph no more." The
words were half true. The party
belongs to Mr. Disraeli, and the
triumph is his. He has
"Waded at will the 'Aristocracy.'"

Whether it shall be peace or
war between us depends upon
the future, not the past. But be
it, which it may, *Mr. Punch*
frankly recognises the genius and
the perseverance which after
thirty years of strife, have been
rewarded with the Premiership.

We shall take an formal leave
of Prince Rupert. We share the
hope of Earl Russell that we shall
often meet Lord Derby in the
House of Peers, and we add,
Democratic, that if he may not
fight, he may come down to the
trenches and raise his voice, like
Achilles.

(*See Cartoon, " The New Head
Master."*)

CHAPEAU BAS!

Air—" Le Marquis de Carabas."

Lo, brains at last we see,
At the top, where brains should
    be!
He's't was place won is rare,
That so seated pleat and pate;
Heaven weighted head
Never ran a course,
Nor e'er came, at the push,
With a fiercer Uhlbery rush.—
To Vivian Grey *chapeau bas*,
My Lord Marquis De Carabas!

Is't England's praise or blame
Such a player wins his game,
Who can press for success
Be't by trick, revoke, finesse?
Is it good or ill,
This adventurer will,
With an india-rubber brain,
And a countenace proof to
    strain?—
To Vivian Grey *chapeau bas*,
My Lord Marquis De Carabas!

On landshore, tour bar,
Still starring by his star;
Island and sand, surf and strand,
Budging with a dext'rous hand;
Passinglove and cool,
And unles his crew to submit,
When weaker pilots quailed,
Through thro' storm the ship he sailed!—
To Vivian Grey *chapeau bas*,
My Lord Marquis De Carabas!

He's in total tangled took
Clieves thalks of their brook;
He's won toil on unlike soil,
Or snow bleakly took to spoil;
But he wrought, hour by hour,
Till knowledge grew to power,

THE NEW HEAD MASTER.

And as his his Tory class
Learns to see how so they pass,—
To Vivian Grey *chapeau bas*,
My Lord Marquis De Carabas!

If workman's worth his hire,
Why should Dizzy not aspire?
He has striven, brain has given,
To the utmost his seam driven.
Must he only think

How soon best may drink?
'Twas his the cup to crave,
Who but he should drain it down?—
To Vivian Grey *chapeau bas*,
My Lord Marquis De Carabas!

Genius or charlatan?
Settle that point who can.
Who shall bring his name to fling
At Little Benjamin, our King?

By what right he rules,—
As the wise men o'er the fools,
Or the one-eyed o'er the blind,—
Let the house's verdict find.—
To Vivian Grey *chapeau bas*,
My Lord Marquis De Combas!

MARCH 2.

The House of Representatives at Washington adopted the Articles of Impeachment against President Johnson. He was charged with violation of the Tenure of Office Act by removing Mr. Stanton from the office of War Secretary without the consent of the Senate, and of the Army Bill by endeavouring to induce General Emory to obey orders which had not been sent through the Commander-in-Chief, General Grant.

MARCH 2.

Mr. Gladstone, in reply to complaints which had been made to him of the extension of the Co-operative movement, which at this time was becoming rife among Civil Service officials, spoke of the credit system in retail trade as a total inversion of the natural order of things.

"This system" (he added) "also aggravates the risk of bad debts, which form an additional charge to a good debtor; and it is connected with a general irregularity and uncertainty which must also be paid for. I do not doubt that we, the consumers, are much in fault. But I cannot help thinking that traders are much to fault also, and that much might be done by a vigorous effort and by combination among traders in favour of ready-money dealings, either absolutely or encouraged by discounts."

The popularity and prosperity of the Civil Service and other Co-operative Stores was becoming a subject of alarm and anger to those interested in retail trading.

(*See Cartoon, "The Real Trade Union."*)

MARCH 5.

On this day the Disraeli Ministry took their seats. Earl Russell, in the Lords, made a vigorous attack upon them for their inconsistency, twitting Mr Disraeli with protesting

THE REAL TRADE UNION.

Cook. "No, Mr Police, there ain't no borders, and things is come to a pretty pass! What with these Co-obbleration Stores—and so provents—what's to be come of hus pore servants—let alone the tradespeople—question gracious only knows!"

against a "degradation of the franchise" at the very time when, upon his own showing, he was "educating his party" to vote for it. On the same day in the Commons, Mr. Disraeli made a statement of his policy, which was to be a "policy of peace, but not peace at any price;" and "a truly liberal policy—a policy that will not shrink from any changes which are required

by the wants of the age we live in, but will never forget that it is our happy lot to dwell in an ancient and historic country, rich in traditionary influences that are the best security for order and liberty, and the most valuable element of our national character and our national strength." Mr. Bouverie complained that the Conservatives were in power not because they were in a majority, but because the Liberal Party at present, instead of being an organized party, was little better than a rabble with "leaders that won't lead, and followers that won't follow."

MARCH 10.

"To-night" (says Mr. Punch's "Essence of Parliament") "began the great Irish Debate." Mr. Maguire had moved that the House resolve itself into a Committee to take the condition of Ireland into immediate consideration. Lord Mayo, Chief Secretary for Ireland, declared, in a three hours' speech, the Irish policy of the Government. — Mr. Punch's "Essence") neatly summed up the statement in three words,

INACTION, PROCRASTINATION, RETROGRESSION.

Nothing was to be done with the Irish Church until the Commission sitting should have reported, and this, said a member of it, might be two or three months.

(See Cartoon, "Dizzy's Difficulty, or Mrs. Erin's Pigs.")

MARCH 12.

Whilst present at a picnic at Clontarf, Sydney, the Duke of Edinburgh was shot in the back by an assassin named James O'Farrel. He was at first reported to be a Fenian agent, but this was afterwards denied. O'Farrel not appearing to have had any accomplices. The Prince, though severely wounded, happily but narrowly escaped mortal hurt, and very quickly recovered, being pronounced convalescent by the 18th March. O'Farrel was tried for the attempt, found guilty, and executed on the 26th April, though the Duke personally interceded in his favour.

MARCH 16.

End of the debate on Mr. Maguire's motion. Mr. Gladstone declared definitely for the disestablishment of the Irish Church, and also

DIZZY'S DIFFICULTY, OR MRS. ERIN'S PIGS.

Dizzy. "I'd like to see any o' 'em drive on!"

went at considerable length into the questions of education and the land law. In conclusion he said:—

"If we are prudent men, I hope we shall endeavour as far as in us lies to make some provision for a contingent, a doubtful and probably a dangerous future. If we be chivalrous men, I trust we shall endeavour to wipe away all those stains which the civilised world has for ages seen, or seemed to see, on the shield of England

in her treatment of Ireland. If we be compassionate men, I hope we shall, once for all, listen to the tale of woe which comes from her, and the reality of which, if our demand to justice, is testified by the continued migration of her people—that we shall 'wipe out the written troubles from her brain, and pluck from her memory the rooted sorrow.' But, above all, if we be just men, we shall go forward in the name of truth and right, bearing this in mind that—when the one is proved, and the hour is come, justice delayed is justice denied.'"

MARCH 23.

Mr. Gladstone gave notice of his intention to move three Resolutions on the subject of the Irish Church. *Mr. Punch's* "Essence of Parliament" said:—

HARET!

1. That the Established Church of Ireland should cease to exist as an establishment, due regard being had to personal interests.

2. That it is expedient to prevent the creation of new interests.

3. That the Queen be asked to hand over to Parliament her interest in the temporalities of the Irish sees and other dignities.

That is the triple cord with which Mr. Gladstone stood up, on *Monday, March 23d* (*dies natales*), unless chalk to your taste), and proposed to cremate the Irish Church.

Mr. Disraeli, counsel for the Irish Church, Religion generally, Faith, the Altar and the Throne, and the Angels, procured stay of execution until the following Monday.

He next day wrote a letter to the Dartmouth Union (and the workhouse of that delightful place, but a Saw-boy calling itself "National," of which Lord Dartmouth is Chairman, and said that "we had heard something lately of the crisis of Ireland." In his opinion

The Crisis of England is at hand!

"For the purpose is avowed, by a powerful party, of destroying that Sacred Union between Church and State which has hitherto been the chief source of our civilisation, and is the only security for our religious liberty."

On the 17th, Lord Stanley moved as an amendment:

"That this House, while admitting that considerable modification in the temporalities of the United Church in Ireland may, after pending enquiry, appear to be expedient, is of opinion that any proposition tending to the disestablishment or disendowment of that Church ought to be reserved for the decision of the new Parliament."

MARCH 30.

Mr. Gladstone (says *Punch's* "Essence") moved his Anti-Irish Church Resolutions. He spoke very moderately, declared his own consistency, urged that the time had come, and dealt tenderly with the rights, real or possible, of all persons in any way interested in the Church. The debate concluded on April 3, when

Mr. Disraeli spoke for two hours and a half. His speech was rather grandiloquent and melodramatic. He denounced the "vast and violent" change proposed. Mr. Gladstone, he suggested, represented "Ritualism and Popery" ("Essence"). "The High Church Ritualists (he declared) and the followers of the Pope have been long in secret combination, and are now in

open confederacy." This was met by mocking laughter, when Mr. Disraeli added that the proposals of Mr. Gladstone were not confined to mere political arrangements, but attacked the Crown itself.

[See Cartoon, "*New Guy Fawkes, or Dizzy's Chef-d'Œuvre.*"]

NEW GUY FAWKES, OR DIZZY'S CHEF-D'ŒUVRE.

"*Under the guise of Liberalism—under the pretence of legislating in the spirit of the age—they are, as they think, about to seize upon the supreme state of the realm.*"—See Mr. Disraeli's Speech, April 3rd, 1868.

Mr. Gladstone, answering on the whole debate, said some parts of the Premier's speech were characterized by irrelevancy, others by himself imagination. It was too late to endow the Catholic Church.

Lord Stanley's amendment was rejected by 330 to 270, majority 60. Mr. Gladstone's Resolutions were carried by 328 to 272, majority 56, and the House adjourned till April 30.

APRIL 10.

TO-DAY the Abyssinian captives were released. The Expedition, under the able conduct of Sir Robert Napier, had successfully pushed forward on its difficult road, and King Theodore, defeated in an engagement on the heights of Islamgie, opened negotiations for the surrender of his prisoners. Mr. Rassam, Dr. Blanc, and Consul Cameron, with the other Magdala prisoners, were liberated on this and the following day. As, however, the King refused to surrender himself, Sir Robert Napier, on the 13th, attacked and captured Magdala, which almost inaccessible fortress remained (to use his own words), "only a scorched rock." King Theodore fell by his own hands. On the 18th the Expedition commenced its return march from Magdala.

APRIL 15.

THE PRINCE AND PRINCESS OF WALES arrived on a visit to Ireland. An address presented by the Corporation of Dublin expressed a hope that the Queen would establish a residence in Ireland, and dwell as frequently as possible among her subjects there.

APRIL 23.

"IN the Commons the new Chancellor of the Exchequer (Mr. Ward Hunt) brought in the Budget which it had pleased Mr. Disraeli and the Departments to give to him. We shall say nothing about it, except that there is a deficiency of upwards of a Million and a Half, and of course the money is taken from the Middle Class, which never defends itself. *The famous Tax is to be raised to Sixpence.*" ("Essence of Parliament.")

APRIL 27.

MR. GLADSTONE moved the first of his three Resolutions, that the Established Church of Ireland should cease to exist as an establishment. The debate thereon was concluded on the 30th, when the Government was placed in a minority of 65—there being 330 votes for the Resolution, and 265 against. Mr. Disraeli saw the vote made it necessary for the Government to reconsider its position, and proposed adjournment until Monday, which was agreed to.

(*See Cartoon,* "*A Crisis!*")

A CRISIS!

FIRST PORTER. "Now, then, BILL GLADSTONE, where are you a-shovin' to?"

SECOND PORTER. "Well, then, stand if one side, can't yer?"

FIRST PORTER. "Oh, ah, MR. STAND-AST side! and make way for you, I suppose? Thanker—not if I know it!"

[And there they are at this moment.

MAY 4.

Mr. Disraeli explained that he had waited upon the Queen, and advised her to dissolve Parliament, but at the same time offered to resign. That Her Majesty, after consideration, had not accepted his resignation, but expressed her readiness to dissolve as soon as public business would permit. That he had informed her he thought dissolution might be arranged for in the Autumn. That he should oppose Mr. Gladstone's two other Resolutions, but without debate.

Mr. Gladstone said there was no need for dissolution, and no hope of reversing the decision of the Commons. The Government should have resigned in an unqualified way. He should proceed with his Resolutions, and a Bill for suspending Irish Church Appointments.

On the 7th Mr. Gladstone's second and third Irish Resolutions were carried in Committee without a division. On the 15th he brought in his Suspensory Bill, suspending for a limited time the exercise of patronage in the Irish Church.

(*Sir Coram, "Steering under Difficulties."*)

MAY 7.

Henry Lord Brougham, the great versatile and eccentric genius who had for so many years formed a salient subject for *Mr. Punch's* sometimes satirical but always appreciative pencil, died this day at Cannes, at the advanced age of 90. He was found dead in his bed, after passing a peaceful day in his garden, and was buried at Cannes. Said *Mr. Punch* of his old admired friend and honoured foeman:—

A Grand old tree has fallen (Cut it by,
    That with so little ado it has come down)
That in the forest scarce a gap its are
    For loss of that great trunk and reverend crown?
The ninety-year old man was part of all,
    Gaunt part of most that's overblown and bred;

STEERING UNDER DIFFICULTIES.

Ship's Captain. "Give up the helm I—resign the command I—never! Come out, come off, I tell to my Craft. Back I wet—ease my forward, and I blow up the ship. Ho, he!!"

Through that long race the one he scarce let fall,
    Scores through that long day's work passed once to rest.
Comes all the triumphs in these fifty years
    By Right and Truth o'er Wrong and Falsehood won,
Of the Good Cause's Paladins and Peers
    A faithfuller than Henry Brougham is none.
The sennet purged ; charity's stream subdued part I
    Slaves freed ; chicane and bigotry put down ;
Knowledge ta ignorance gaining, slow but sure ;
    This was his life's work, in his memory's crown I

MAY 26.

Mr. Disraeli, who was much taunted for (in the words of Earl Russell) continuing in office without having the confidence of the House of Commons, or being able to carry his measures, to-day announced that the Government intended to confine the work of the Session mainly to the Reform Bills and Estimates, Foreign Cattle, and

Telegraph Bills and possibly the Bribery and Bankruptcy Bill.

Like Coronne, " The Political Leotard.")

M. Leotard was a popular acrobat of the day, celebrated for his performances on the trapeze.

JUNE 2.

COMMENCEMENT of the case of ex-Governor Eyre before Mr. Justice Blackburn in the Court of Queen's Bench. On the 3rd General Eyre issued a letter defending his administration in Jamaica. The case excited much public feeling, society being strongly in favour of the ex-Governor, the denominations for the most part bitterly against him.

JUNE 29.

THE debate in the House of Lords on the second reading of Mr. Gladstone's Irish Church Suspensory Bill, which had begun on the 25th, was ended to-night or rather (says *Mr. Punch's "Essence"*) about three in the morning, when the Lords divided.

For the Irish Church . 104
Against her . . . 97

Majority for rejecting Mr. Gladstone's Bill . 95

A General Election was, however, at hand, and was looked upon as likely to reverse the verdict.

Earl Russell spoke in the course of the debate, stating the entire case against the Irish Church with vigour and terseness. *Mr. Punch* spoke of the veneration due to "the honourable little old brave English nobleman, who, true to the convictions of a life, made another appeal on behalf of a principle which he had held so long."

JULY 4.

"THE unsatisfactory state of the Turf" (says the Introduction to Vol. LV.) "is noticed in the following Volume. The young Marquis of Hastings' short and ruinous career, signalized by the extent of his bets and their unsuccessful

result, the inexplicable performance of his mare 'Lady Elizabeth' in the Derby, for which she was first favourite, the scratching of his horse 'The Earl' for the same race and for the Leger, the allurements of the betting offices, the proceedings of betting men, and the outspoken utterances of Admiral Rous on racing matters—all provoked attention to this disagreeable topic."

JULY 6.

THE PRINCESS OF WALES was this morning safely delivered of a daughter—Victoria Alexandra Olga Mary.

JULY 10.

SIR ROBERT NAPIER, who had conducted the Abyssinian Expedition with so much skill

THE POLITICAL LEOTARD.

" It is a very old trick of mine," wrote M. Leotard, " to make the belief to fall, and then to arrive at my fun."—Morning Paper.

and success, had now returned. The thanks of both Houses had, on the 2nd, been voted to him and his army. Mr. Disraeli, in moving the vote in the Commons, presented a graphic picture of the difficulties of the expedition which had led the elephants of Asia, bearing the artillery of Europe, over broken ground which might have startled the trapper, and appalled the hunter of the Alps, at the end of which "we find the standard of St. George hoisted upon the mountains of Rasselas." To-night the House of Commons voted £2000 per annum to Sir Robert Napier and his next heir male, Sir Robert being also raised to the dignity of Baron Napier of Magdala.

JULY 24.

ON this day the Bribery Bill was passed by the Commons. There had been a good deal of cavil at some of its clauses. Mr. Disraeli had declared that he would not advise the Queen to prorogue until the Bribery Bill should be law. On which Mr. Punch cried, "Well said, sir!" An amendment of Mr. Fawcett's, throwing returning officers' expenses upon the local rates, had been carried by 78 to 69, but subsequently negatived by 115 to 97. A proposition of Mr. Mill's to forbid the employment of paid agents at elections was rejected by 116 to 86. Then the Bill passed, much to the discontent, doubtless, of many persons interested actually and prospectively in electoral corruption. But Mr. Punch said, "Well done, Benjamin our Ruler!"

JULY 30.

THE Thames Embankment from Westminster Bridge to the Temple was on this day opened for traffic.

On this same day also was opened the Abbey Mills Pumping Station of the Metropolitan Main Drainage system.

GOING TO THE COUNTRY.

LANDLADY. "Good bye, Sir! Oh, Sir, was you a wishin' as the Lodgin's should be kept for you, Sir?"

DIZZY. "Oh! No! Well! Yes! I shall want 'em for a week or two at Christmas, and then we'll talk about a permanency."

JULY 31.

"BOTH Houses met to part." The last Parliament elected under the Reform Bill of 1832 was this day closed.

(See Cartoon, "Going to the Country.")

Lord Chancellor Cairns read Mr. Disraeli's Speech from the Throne. It was brief, and well written:—

1. Release, with thanks for diligence.
2. Friendliness with Foreign Powers.
3. Brilliant Abyssinian success.
4. Ireland quiet—tax Fenian prisoners.
5. Thanks for Supplies.
6. Reform Scheme complete.
7. Various other laws—Schools—Railways—Fisheries—Telegraphs—Scotch Legal Proceedings.
8. Controller-in-Chief in War-Office.
9. Intention to dissolve "at the earliest day that

will enable my people to reap the benefits of the extended system of representation."

10. Entire confidence in their proving themselves worthy of the high privilege.

11. Trust that under the blessing of Divine Providence the expression of their opinion on those great questions of public policy which have occupied the attention of Parliament, and remain undecided, may tend to maintain unimpaired that civil and religious freedom which has been secured to all my subjects by the institutions and settlement of my realm.

Prorogation till Thursday, October the 8th.

The last clause of course means Mr. Disraeli's hope that the new Parliament will maintain the Irish Church. Not, of course, that he hopes or cares personally about that particular thing, but that particular thing means office or resignation. It may be, however, that the result may be brought about at a different hour. Never mind about that. Sufficient for the day is the Order thereof.

Aug. 5.

MR. GLADSTONE commenced his electoral Campaign in South-west Lancashire. It was plain that the General Election would turn mainly on the question of the maintenance or disestablishment of the Irish Church. Mr. Gladstone said of it, "It is wholly disabled and disqualified for performing the purpose for which it exists; and consequently I spoke in literal truth, and not in rude sarcasm when I said, 'You must not take away its abuses, because, if you take them away, there will be nothing left.'" This plain speaking aroused intense wrath in the Tory Party, and loud indignation and alarm amongst Churchmen and Church dignitaries everywhere. Gloomy forebodings were prevalent that the attack upon the Irish Establishment was but the prelude to an assault upon the English Church itself.

Aug. 6.

THE QUEEN, whose health for some time past had been indifferent, started for Switzerland, reaching Lucerne on the 6th,

REJECTED ADDRESSES.

Doctor Pusey. "And, my dear young lady, if I could induce you and your friends to look kindly upon my proposal——"
Mrs. Methodist. "But you can't, Sir. I don't want to go to Church at all; and if I did, I'm sure I wouldn't go quite you."
[Dr. Pusey appeals for sympathy to the Wesleyan Conference. His sincerity and earnestness conquered a harsh rebuff."—Times.

staying there until the 9th September, when she left for Paris on her return journey.

Aug. 14.

DR. PUSEY addressed a letter to the President of the Wesleyan Conference, seeking their assistance in opposing Mr. Coleridge's Bill for throwing open the honours and emoluments of the Universities to all creeds and denominations. His advances were not sympathetically received by the Wesleyans, and were refused by many in his own Church.

(See Cartoon, "Rejected Address.")

Aug. 18.

GREAT eclipse of the Sun. "To-day" (says "Annals of Our Time") "a shadow such as never before fell on the earth within historic times, swept at the rate of 200 miles an hour from the Straits of Bab-el-Mandel across the two Indian Peninsulas, over Borneo and Celebes, and touching the northern extremity of Australia, passed out many hundreds of miles (before leaving the earth) upon the Pacific Ocean."

SEPT. 12.

In view of the probability of the coming of the Liberals into office, it was thought likely that Mr. John Bright would become a Member of the new Cabinet. As a matter of fact he did, in December, become a Cabinet Minister and Privy Councillor, and was presented to the Queen on taking the oaths of office.

(See Cartoon, "A Dress Rehearsal.")

SEPT. 26.

"This question of the right of women to the Parliamentary Franchise" (says a Note to Vol. LV.)" was at this time much before the public. Several females had sent in their claim to vote, as being rate-payers, and some overseers had included women in their list of persons entitled to vote. The Revising Barrister at Manchester decided against the claims of the ladies (the decision was appealed against in the Court of Common Pleas, but confirmed by the unanimous opinion of the Judge. Miss Becker was one of the foremost champions of her sex in this matter."

A DRESS REHEARSAL.

PALLAS BRIGHT. "Ha! ha! verily these Ministerial Garments won't be so unbecoming, after all!"

[Said, in other words, to his hat oftener.]

HAMLET AND OPHELIA.

Hamlet (on the frantic occasion and by desire of several persons of quality). . . . A REVISING BARRISTER.
Ophelia (by her maid duties) . . . LADY CLAIMANT.

Ophelia. Good my lord,
How does your honour for this many a day?

Hamlet. I humbly thank you, well. But, good my lady,

Lend me no leobs, at least this many a day.

What is your will with me? You have a will,
All women have their will, as I have heard.

Ophelia. My lord—

Hamlet. Again I tell you I'm no lord,
Nor shall be one till I be made a judge,
A thing that may or may not come to pass.
But women never comprehend a case.

Ophelia. I am very sorry you should say that thing,
For I've a case in which you must be judge.

Hamlet. I grant it well. You come to claim a vote?

A vote which you would give at an election?

Ophelia. Nay, who's in error now? My vote is claimed,
And in your hand the claim. I mean to have
That you retain me on the register.

Hamlet. Register stoves and kitchen ranges, Miss,
And all things culinary appertaining.

Were more in what I beg to call your line.

Ophelia. That's your opinion. I stand here for law.

Hamlet. Ha, ha! see you honest?

Ophelia. My lord—I mean, Sir!

Hamlet. Are you fair?

Ophelia. What means your lordship?

Hamlet. That if you be honest and fair, you have no business in a contented election, where there is neither hearsay nor hearers.

Ophelia. Women will introduce both.

Hamlet. Bosh! Get thee to a Nursery. Why would'st thou be a meddler in politics? I am myself indifferent honest——

Ophelia. I chafe not the indelicacy. Advocacy, regardless of right or wrong, perverts the heart and corrupts the understanding.

Hamlet. Get thee to a Nursery, I say. I am, I repeat, indifferent honest, yet I could accuse me of such things that it were better I had never done my vows. I am loquacious, reckless, hard-mouthed, and there is nothing I would not do for a Solicitor-Generalship. What do you want in a corrupt atmosphere? We are arrant knaves all. Keep away from us. Go thy ways to a Nursery. Where's your father?

Ophelia. At home, Sir.

Hamlet. Does he know that you are out?

Ophelia. Ay, my—your lordship.

Hamlet. Go home and tell him to lock you up with the Comfrey-book, that you may play the game nowhere but in his own house. Get thee to a Nursery—Go! Farewell.

Ophelia. Nay if I don't tell Miss Bertha.   [*Exit.*

SEPT. 29.

QUEEN ISABELLA of Spain, in consequence of the revolution which had broken out there, and the defeat of the Royalist troops by the insurgents under Marshal Serrano, fled the country, taking refuge in France, where the Castle of Pau was placed at her service by the Emperor Napoleon. On the 1st October a provisional Government which had been established at Madrid, issued a proclamation deposing Queen Isabella.

OCT. 2.

IN his Address to the electors of Buckinghamshire, Mr. Disraeli vigorously raised the old cry of "The Church in Danger," and not obscurely hinted that the real triumph in case of

BEN AND HIS BOGEY.

MRS. BULL. "I'LL teach you to frighten people, MASTER BENJAMIN."

the disestablishment of the Irish Church would be the triumph of Rome. He said:—

"Amidst the discordant activity of many factions, there moves the supreme purpose of one power. The philosopher may flatter himself he is advancing in the cause of enlightened progress; the sectarian may be roused to exertion by antagonism of the downfall of ecclesiastical systems. These are transient efforts—vain and passing

apotheoses. The ultimate triumphs, save our Church to fall, would be to that power which would substitute for the authority of our sovereign the supremacy of a foreign prince—to that power with whose craftiness, burning, discipline, and organization our Church alone has hitherto been able to cope, and that too, only when supported by a determined and devoted people."

(*See Cartoon,* "*Ben and his Bogey.*")

Oct. 9.

MR. GLADSTONE issued his Address to the electors of South-west Lancashire. He said, "Our path at least lies before you, broad, open, and well defined; our policy has advocates who do not shrink from its avowal. It is the policy of bringing absolutely to an end the civil establishment of the Church in Ireland." In this he saw the discharge of a debt of civil justice, and the disappearance of a national, almost a world-wide reproach.

(*See Cartoon, "Rival Actors."*)

Nov. 3.

GENERAL GRANT was elected President of the United States.

Nov. 8.

MR. BRIGHT was elected honorary member of the Edinburgh Chamber of Commerce, and a his speech on the occasion advised his hearers to press for a "Free Breakfast Table" (by which he meant the abolition of the duties on tea, coffee, and sugar), a phrase which like many of Mr. Bright's was made free use of thereafter in political polemics.

Nov. 10.

A CONVENTION was this day signed between England and the United States, by virtue of one clause of which Commissioners were to be appointed with power to adjudicate upon the class of claims referred to in the

RIVAL ACTORS.

(MR. GLADSTONE as WILLIAM TELL, *has been called before the curtain's "could the deafening plaudits of a house crowded to the ceiling.")*

MR. BRIGHT (*JEREMY DIDDLER*) *"He's got the house with him, that's certain. Ahem! I must give 'em a touch of my art."*

official correspondence between the two Governments as the "Alabama Claims."

It was stipulated, however, that before any of such claims are taken into consideration by them, the two high contracting parties shall fix upon some sovereign or head of a friendly State as arbitrator in respect of such claims, to whom each class of claims shall be referred

in case the Commissioners shall be unable to come to a unanimous decision upon the same."

Some disappointment was felt by the public, who, from some recent utterances of Mr. Reverdy Johnson, had concluded that the differences between this country and America were practically disposed of.

Nov. 16.

BEGINNING of the elections to the new Parliament. "It was" (said *Mr. Punch's* Introduction) "the first election that had been held under the New Reform Act" (the celebrated "Leap in the Dark") which gave Household Suffrage to the Boroughs, and an extended Franchise to the Counties."

The Election resulted in favour of the Liberal Party, and of Mr. Gladstone's Policy.

(See Cartoon, " Pounded !")

The Liberals largely increased their majority in the Boroughs. In Scotland both Borough and County Votes went in their favour, only seven Conservatives being returned for that country. In Ireland they also gained considerably. In the English Counties the Conservatives were more successful.

"The Election was signalised by some remarkable defeats and successes." Mr. Gladstone lost his seat for South-west Lancashire by 260 Votes; but was returned for the borough of Greenwich. The City of London returned three Liberals, but sent one Conservative in place of Baron Rothschild, who lost his seat. In Westminster Mr. W. H. Smith beat Mr. John Stuart Mill by a majority of 1,500 Votes, one of the greatest losses this to the Liberal Party.

The general result was that the Liberals

" POUNDED !"

The Result of the " Leap in the Dark."

[See Punch for August p. 1867

gained about 15 Votes, counting 30 on a division. Their majority in the new House was estimated at about 110, though this was slightly altered subsequently by the results of election petitions, &c.

Mr. Disraeli resigned at once. On the 4th of December Mr. Gladstone accepted Her Majesty's commands to form a Ministry. On the 8th, Mr. Disraeli delivered up the Seals, and Mr. Gladstone and the new Ministry were sworn into office. The Cabinet included Sir W. Page Wood (Lord Chancellor), Lord Granville, Lord Clarendon, the Duke of Argyll, Mr. Lowe, the Marquis of Hartington, Mr. Childers, Mr. Cardwell, Earl de Grey and Ripon, Lord Kimberley, Mr. Fortescue, Mr. Bruce, and last, but by no means least, Mr. John Bright, who now took office for the first time as President of the Board of Trade.

Mr. Disraeli declined the offer of a title for himself, but his wife was elevated to the peerage with the title of Viscountess Beaconsfield, of Beaconsfield.

Mr. Punch paid that lady the following tribute:

TO MRS. DISRAELI

L ady of Hughenden, Punch, drawing near,
A dmiring offers a homage sincere ;
D eign to accept it, —though playful in tone,
Y our heart will tell you it comes from his own.

B attle left all with your Lord he has done,
E ver in fairness and often in fun,
A cknow, as friends and antagonists knew,
C have, when his money struck a good blow,
O pportune moment he finds, nothing lack,
N ow, for a tribute more pleasant to both,
S mile on the circlet a husband prepares
F or her. Unable to the triumph she foresees and shares :
I s it acknowledged what lot's can be paid,
S everal devotion and womanly aid.
L ong may the gems in that coronet shine,
D eriving lustre from who's more proud of his fame.

On the 10th of December the first Session of the eighth Parliament of the Queen's reign was opened by Royal Commission. On the 19th, after the transaction of the necessary formal business, it adjourned till February 16, 1869.

DEC. 20.

LORD MAYO, who had been appointed Viceroy of India in succession to Sir J. Lawrence, arrived in Bombay.

DEC. 26.

THIS year closed with the establishment of more amicable relations between England and America than had prevailed since the close of the great war between North and South. Mr. Reverdy Johnson had been appointed United States Minister in this country, arriving here on the 15th August. On the 22nd October, speaking at a banquet at Liver-

pool attended by Lord Stanley and Mr. Gladstone, he said that two of the questions at issue between the two countries had been all but settled, and expressed his opinion that the question of the Alabama Claims was likely to be settled on terms equally honourable. Later, at the Lord Mayor's banquet on the 9th November, Mr. Reverdy Johnson said that the differences between this country and America were now ended. Although this did not imply, as

TURKEY AND GREASE.

(Scene from the Introduction to the grand new Oriental Pantomime of Harlequin Palophalodei Thalassis and the Bewildered Bashaw of the Beautiful Bosphorus.)

was at first hoped by some, that the question of the Alabama Claims was absolutely settled, yet the signing of the Convention, already referred to on the 10th of November, was evidence that it had been referred to a friendly arbitrament from which it was expected that a full and final settlement would speedily result.

DEC. 29.

A RUPTURE of diplomatic relations having occurred between Turkey and Greece on

account of disputes which seemed to threaten the re-opening of the Eastern Question, it was arranged that a conference of the Great Powers should meet in Paris early in January with a view to their settlement.

(See Cartoon, "Turkey and Grease.")

TURKEY AND GREASE.
(A Song of the Season.)
To keep this Turkey and that Greece
From coming to a flare-up. —

Which might to such wide bloss increase,
As must only maintain once up, —
And, breaking Europe's Christmas peace,
Bid her big engines tear up,

The cooks of Europe, her Great Powers—
(Cooks are great powers, we know)—
Spend anxious and laborious hours,
And their best spdels bestow;
Diplomacy's cold dew he in showers
On this hot Greece to throw.

+1869+

JAN. 1.

ON the first day of the year began the Overend-Gurney prosecution, being the trial of the members of the late firm of Overend, Gurney & Co., on the charge of having "unlawfully and deceitfully conspired together, and by divers false pretences and divers false statements with reference to the affairs and conditions of the Company, induced the complainant, Dr. Thom, of the Canadian Bar, and the public generally, to subscribe and take shares in the said Company, with intent to cheat and defraud them of large sums of money." The trial created much excitement, as the wild speculation and disastrous failure of the firm had caused wide-spread loss and suffering. On the 17th the preliminary inquiry terminated in the committal for trial of all the defendants.

FEB. 13.

IT was now obvious that the attempt to disestablish the Irish Church would be made by Mr. Gladstone. Fears were freely expressed that this would at no distant date lead to similar dealing with the English Establishment, but this view was disavowed by the supporters of the Government, who held that the Irish Church would benefit by disestablishment, whilst the English Church would not suffer.

(*See Cartoon, "Our Siamese Twins."*)

FEB. 16.

PARLIAMENT was opened by Royal Commission. The Queen's Speech (said *Punch's* "Essence of Parliament") was read by Lord Chancellor Hatherley, his first appearance as a reader of Queen's Speeches. Mr. Gladstone had not given him a great deal to do.

OUR SIAMESE TWINS.

MR. BULL. *"You don't think the operation will be fatal to either?"*
DR. GLADSTONE. *"Oh, no!"*
DR. BRIGHT. *"Not a bit!—Do 'em both all the good in the world."*

1. Her Majesty rejoiced in the advice of Parliament so early as Ministerial arrangements had permitted.

2. Did so with special interest, at a time when the Populace branch had been chosen with the advantage of a grossly enlarged enfranchisement of her faithful and loyal people.

3. All right with Foreign Powers. Believed that they desired to keep the peace.

4. Rejoiced that there was nothing serious in the Levant.

5. Hoped to place friendship with America on a firm basis.

6. Grieved at disturbances in New Zealand. Was confident that the Colonies would take care of themselves.

7. The Estimates would show a Diminished Charge upon the Country.

8. We need not continue to suspend Irish Habeas Corpus.

9. Can we have further guarantee for purity and liberty at Parliamentary and Municipal elections?

10. Powers class of Rate-
payers to be relieved.
11. Scotch Education to be
improved.
12. Abse English Endowed
Schools.
13. Invent Financial Board.
to control the County rate.
14. Reform in Bankruptcy.
Abolition of Imprisonment for
Debt.
15. The Ecclesiastical Arrangements of Ireland are to be considered at an early date.
  (a) Regard to be shewn to
    every legitimate interest.
  (b) Welfare of Religion to
    be promoted through
    equal justice.
  (c) Universal feeling of
    Ireland to be secured on
    the side of loyalty and
    law.
  (d) Memory of former con-
    tentions to be effaced.
  (e) Sympathies of so affec-
    tionate people to be
    cherished.

MARCH 1.

MR. GLADSTONE intro-
duced a Bill " to put
an end to the Established
Church in Ireland, to make
provision in respect of the
temporalities thereof, and of
the Royal College of May-
nooth."

(See Cartoon, " The End of the
' Tempest.'")

PUNCH'S ESSENCE OF
PARLIAMENT.

MONDAY, March 1. — The
Great Magician began to miss
the Words of Power that, when
all are said, shall set the Protestant Ariel free, and bid her
fare far better than ever.

New Year's Day, 1871, will
see the Irish and the English
Churches severed.

But the work of Disestablishment and Disendowment is to
begin on the passing of the Bill,
the Second Reading whereof
stands for the 18th of this month.

Then it the present Ecclesiastical Commission for Ireland is
be wound up, and a new one
formed. For this purpose now
before us, the Church is to be
under two Governments, one,
the State's, to last ten years,
one her Own, to last as long as
the Church pleases.

The first is a New Commission, appointed by the
State.

The second is a flourishing Body, elected by the
Church.

No new Vested Interests are to be created after the
passing of the Act, but for the temporary government of
the Church, spiritual appointments may be made.

The Queen loses her prerogative of appointing Bishops;
but, on the prayer of the Church, may nominate them
for spiritual purposes.

The Irish Bishops at once depart from the House of
Lords.

Synodical action is to be restored to the Irish Church,
and it is invited to elect a body which shall fairly represent bishops, priests, and laymen of the Anglican com-
munion, and if the Government shall consider that such
body is properly representative, the Queen will recognise
it, and it will govern the Irish Free Episcopal Church of
the future. This is the Governing Body that has been
mentioned.

To this body, which it will be convenient to call the
G. B. (let us hope the initials will also mean Great Blessing), will be set over so much of the property of the
Church as she is to retain. Careful calculations have
been gone into as to the value of that property, and of
the rightful claims upon it, and it will be seen that provision is made for the clergy of various ranks.

Would you like to know the value of the Public Endowments of the Irish Church? Mr. Gladstone estimates
them at Sixteen Millions.

THE END OF THE "TEMPEST."

PROSPERO. "Be free, and fare thou well!"—SHAKSPEARE.

The Income of the Irish Church is calculated at £700,000 a year.

Of the Fawcum Sum which has to be dealt with, the Eastern Millions:

Eight Millions and a half to go back to the Church, for the purposes which have been mentioned.

There will be upwards of Seven Millions and a half for Mr. Gladstone to deal with, and in a delightful rather says, "What will he do with it?"

We'll tell you what he will not do with it.

It is not to go to any Church. Not the naprenching of religion. Not for Education, or we should vote he in quarrel.

Not for public works, for the Irish would "job," and "grumble," and besides, the arrangement would not be final.

Not for railways, for similar reasons.

But the application should bear Legible Marks of a Christian character. Therefore,

Let us apply the money in aid of that region of want and suffering which lies between the independent part of the population and the purely pauperised population, the region where the Poor Laws touch not.

Let us first, and most largely, provide for Lunatics.

(See Cartoon, "Swift on a Large Scale.")

The other objects of aid are to be the Deaf and Dumb, and the Blind, the Training of Nurses, Reformatories, Industrial Schools, and Infirmaries.

Such is the Magician's scheme. It was expounded in a speech of three hours, a speech in which an Artist, whose praise is well having, Mr. Disraeli, "willingly admitted that there was one phrase too much."

Mr. Disraeli said that his able lord had not changed its opinion, but looked on the Disestablishment as a grave political error, and upon Disendowment, especially for secular purposes, as Confiscation. He bore the tribute (how) he cited, and would not oppose the introduction of the Bill. But notice has since been given that on the 18th he will move that the Bill be read a Second Time that day six months. So we are to have battle.

SWIFT ON A LARGE SCALE.

GHOST OF DEAN SWIFT. "Well, Mr. Gladstone, you spared my Will, but, by Gondregan, we might have given me credit for being the author of your plan. I left my Church Surplus to a Lunatic Asylum.

"To show, by one satiric touch,
No Nation Wanted it so much."

MARCH 18.

To-day took place a partial opening of the Suez Canal, the waters of the Mediterranean being let into the Bitter Lakes.

MARCH 18.

In the Commons the Grand Remonstrance began. Mr. Disraeli, in pursuance of notice, led off with an oration, terminating with a motion that the (Irish) Church Bill be referred." (" Essence.")

Though of course protesting against the Bill as "confiscation and spoliation," Mr. Disraeli's speech was temperate. "The best thing that can be said of it" (said Mr. Punch) "is that it utterly dissatisfied his party, who were consumedly silent, who went away displeased, and whom it was sought to comfort next day by assurances that there was the utmost wisdom in their chief's 'studied moderation.'"

On the 23rd took place the division on the Second Reading, when there was a majority in favour of the Bill of 118 in a House of 618 Members.

MARCH 27.

ONE conspicuous feature of the late General Election was the growth of opinion in favour of vote by ballot, a long-opposed reform which now seemed "within measurable distance" of realisation. "I am very glad to tell you" (said Mr. Bright in a speech on the 31st December), "that when I went up to London last week, I found, I was going to say, almost nobody professing to be on the Liberal side of the House of Commons who was not in favour of the Ballot."

(See Cartoon, "Little Boy Ballot.")

LITTLE BOY BALLOT.

LITTLE Boy Ballot, come blow me your horn,
Many men have you who laughed you to scorn;
Where's the small boy who was ordered to keep
Under the haw'ings, fast asleep?
Bribery and bullies have waked him now,
And Cabinet Members are patting his paw,
Bidding him bring out his musical box,
That echoes the notes of the popular vox.

APRIL 3.

AMONGST other potent and destructive weapons of war, the submarine explosive engine called the Torpedo was now attracting much attention. Mr. Punch gave his views of it in the following humorous verses:—

MOTHER ENGLAND ON THE TORPEDO.

AH lawka-a-daisy, but's good in those times one can often mention;
But one sort thing I will allow to be a capital invention,
'Tis a machine sent, in the sea, to serve our labours for protection,
Which have been by ingenious men brought very nearly to perfection.

I've heard about a Spanish Don famed for his various, one Quervedo,
Discover he never dreamt of this thing which they calls it a Torpedo,

After a fashion as I'm told, that, lackin if you teach it under,
Gives you a strong hydraulic shock, and which they say's the more as thunder.

Likewise by the galvanic spark this apparatus is worked Unplanted,
With marsh-glycerine, gun-cotton, powder, is at will
When if the enemy's above, the ribbles, repillet' crew, ah dear 'em!

It knows their ship up in the air, and sends the wretches to the bottom.
That's how I wish as we could deal with all detestable intruders, Spreraders,
As couldn't be prevailed upon to keep aloof by dint of proper manners,
Leve us the means, I've always said, of blowin up the foes' marines,
Just like the boys days wagons' ends with fireworks, devils, squibs, and crackers.

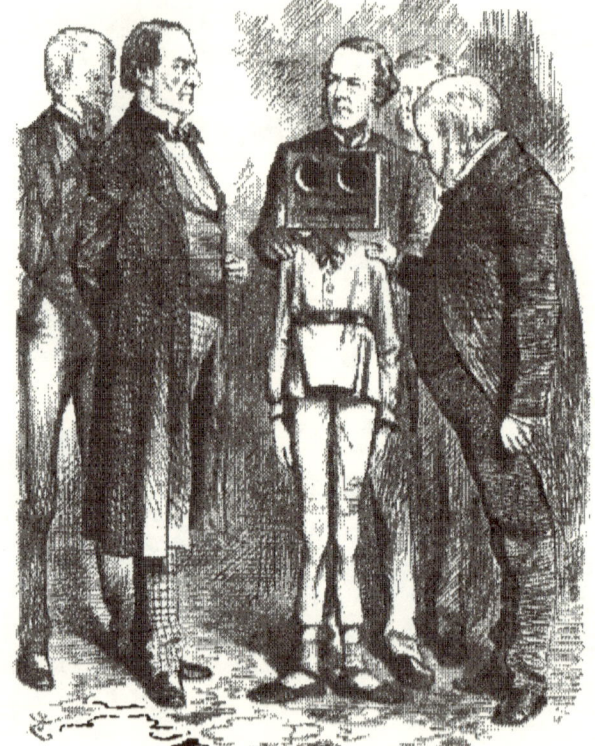

LITTLE BOY BALLOT.

THE HON. R. LOWE. "He's terrible ugly, but he grows tremendous!"

APRIL 6.

The Habitual Criminals Act passed the House of Lords. — "It was designed" (says "Annals of Our Time") "to make further provision for the suppression of crime by ticket-of-leave men and old offenders, and gave authority for their summary apprehension when there was any suspicion that they were obtaining their livelihood by dishonest means." Said *Mr. Punch's* "Essence," "There is no mistake about this bold and salutary measure. It carries the war into the enemy's country. . . . There will be small chance for rascaldom. Honesty, or emigration, are the alternatives if the law be worked vigorously."

[See Cartoon, "The 'Habitual Criminal' Cure."]

OUR HABITUAL CRIMINALS.

VERY ONORED PUNCH,— Aving been a pick pocket almost from my birth I may call myself a member of the criminal persuasion, tho I calls myself a cobbler when I'm brought before the Beak. As sich, I feels a natural interest in the progress of the bill for putting down abitual criminals, and shutting up the shops of those as deals in stolen goods. Well, all as I can say is if you shut up the receivers you'll soon shut up the thieves, for as I says to Charley Clytaker what's the good o' prigging tickers when there's nobody to sell 'em to? We shovellers of industry, as our lively neighbors calls us, in course must find that civil try is all a waste of labour, when there ain't no market open where we can sell the swag. To us old prigs it seems a pity our industry should be wasted, and all our skill and science which has cost us so much trouble be found of no more use. But I spose we must expect ourselves as victims of Society, and if Society have only the pluck to gie the swann up, I shouldn't be surprised at the foldinness of a pumphry I barely see in print —

"You years of earnest legislation, sensible administration and adequate expenditure, real crime as a graduates might be extinguished in Great Britain."

To pass a law to take a crow's bread out of his mouth wot when I consider as "correct legislation." But we poor martyrs must submit to be extinguished if Society insists, and I'm doubtful if Society will give us compensation, though rogues as bad as we have ad a share too.

* *Quory Chirurdors d'Industric.*

But while Society's about it, there are other thieves than us poor prigs is not to be looked after. Pray, mint there thieves in babble companies who prey upon the public quite as much as we do? Aint there habitual criminals in the money-lending line, whom Society would do well to put under surveillance? Aint there rogues in grain who adulterate their bread, or put poison in their beer, and rob people of their health as well as of their money? Aint there rogues who rig the market and trade upon a panic, and care nothing or the widows and the orphans

whom they ruin? Aint there fraudulent directors, and fraudulent promoters, and fraudulent tradesmen, who bury their goods from fraudulent bankrupts, or who swindle poor folks by selling them? Above you brags of the "instinction of crime" by act of parliament, you must hit upon a plan for extinguishing such criminals like those I are named. Why shouldn't money-lending swindlers and rogues who sell short measure have a ticket o' leave given 'em, ever proof of first offence, the same as prigs and burglars who have served their term in quod? They

THE "HABITUAL CRIMINAL" CURE.

BILL SIKES: "Lor, Mus per, I vin't up to nuthin'!" When I was just a-goin' 'ome to my tea!!!"
(A boy nothing, but walks him off)

are all habitual criminals every bit as much as me and Charley Clyfsher, and if Sackey's in earnest about the crushing out of crime it orts to set the crushers on the criminals I've mentioned, as well as on pure pickpockets like Yours truly,

PETER PRIGGINS.

APRIL 8.

THE CHANCELLOR OF THE EXCHEQUER (Mr. Robert Lowe) introduced his Budget.

THE CHANCELLOR OF THE EXCHEQUER, AND HIS BUDGET.

By Jove! Mrs. Grundy, M'm, he takes a Penny off the Income-Tax, one of the two pennies which were laid on by King Theodore.

Also he abolishes the shilling duty on Foreign Corn, and the Poor will benefit.

Also, I've Amusation Duty, after Midsummer.

He modifies the taxes on Locomotion, and specially makes so large a reduction of the duty on Cabs, that a bad cab ought never to be seen again.

Payment for a License to sell Tea is to be done away, as a sacrifice in honour of Temperance.

Hair powder is to fly free.

THE RIVAL CONJURORS.

Professor Bob. "There is no deception—the bag is empty. Hey, presto, pass! (Produces the egg.) SUPPLUS!!!"

Professor Box. "Why, we could ha' done THAT—— (Pause.) If we'd only thought on it."

When do you say to that, M'm? Reads well, doesn't it? Parliamentary Magic, the Honourable Chancellor called it. "Rough Magic," M'm, as *Prospero* observes. How do you think Mr. Lowe gets at the means of doing all these noble things? Then, respected M'm.

The Assessed Taxes are at present collected at a ruining expense, and by instalments. Henceforth they are to be in the nature of Excise Licenses, and are to be collected by trained and disciplined Government officers, who will exact them to the last farthing. Moreover, they are all to be levied in January, in a lump, and we are to pay them all at once. Mr. Lowe says that the poor hate being often bothered for taxes, and the rich like to pay once and have done with it. But how about those who are neither very

our dear very father, and how will they like being called on for a year's taxes in a lump?

By this means, and with the aid of Messrs. Cardwell and Childers' brave savings in Army and Navy, Abyssinia and all is set straight, and we shall have a surplus of £645,000. Mr. Robbin's *tour de force* is brilliant. So was not his speech, but he gave us two characteristic bits, one in which he condoled with his predecessor because the right sort of old people didn't die, to increase the succession duties, though careless old folks were letting rights and left; and the other in reply to a question. He said that if a man married in April, and his matrimonial speculation was unfortunate, and he longed him-self on or before the 19th of December, he would not be asked

to pay taxes. The quaint Budget, quaintly expounded, was received with favour.

(See Cartoon, "The Rival Conjurors.")

APRIL 13.

THE Senate of the United States, by a majority of 54 to 1, rejected the proposed "Alabama" Claims Treaty. Mr. Sumner made a very violent speech against England, saying that "England had done to the United States an injury most difficult to measure," charging

her with giving "her name,
her influence, her material
resources in the wicked
cause, and flinging her
sword into the scale with
slavery;" and saying that
she ought to offer an
apology, and make moral
as well as ample material
atonement.

(See Cartoon, "Humble Pie (?).")

STANZAS TO BUNKER.

Say that an Aristocracy, which
  fears
Perforce rule too much, and
  street-made law,   [jeers.
And rough equality where off are
Well pleased the clerk of your
  Republic new,
And South Secession's
  against North draw ;
Rejoiced to think that chasm
  would never close,
And hope Democracy the
  world o'erran ;
No longer, spht asunder, and at
  blows ;
Withal took not your part, but
  sided with poor foes,

Say that a Government the fact
  too soon
Proclaimed, which it perch-
  ance have, soon or late,
Giving your rebels 'vantage, for
  which boon
From your own act they would
  have had so wid,
So much if you unblushingly
  can state ;
Say that a better work it might
  have kept,
And that you had just cause
  to be brave,
Because a pirate cruiser, while
  it slept,
Out of a British port, the Alabama, crept.

Suppose all this. How speak
  the People's voice ?
Your adversaries did they
  back on you ?
Why, your Bret's hosts hung
  upon their cheers,
Republican would have made
  your Nation two,
Would Englishmen his plan
  have helped him through
Yet not for Manchester and all
  its pens,
Stirred by your conflict, did
  they prove untrue ;
Roaring dire loss with patience,
  they forbore
The cry that would have made
  your Union but too sore.

When's your return for British sympathy,
Squarer and braeis? On wild fiction based
Vain profess in outrageous humble pie,
When meek men only can have earned its taste,
Yielding so much we n err all last disgraced.
Before, before the French Imperial throne,
Let, if you dare, your dainty dish be placed.
There tender kneel to pie in hectoring tone.
Ah, but already clever pun've feared on your own !

HUMBLE-PIE (?)

Jonathan (as interpreted by Mr. Reverdy). "Waal, Reverdy! guess this let 'U about do for your friend John Bull thar."
Reverdy Johnson. "Ha! I've dined with him a good deal lately, and he won't eat THAT, I promise you."

MAY 14.

A PROCLAMATION was issued to the effect
that the old copper coinage would cease
to be current after the end of the present year.

MAY 19.

MR. REVERDY JOHNSON, United States Minister here, returned to America. He was
succeeded by Mr. Motley, who arrived in this
country on the 29th.

MAY 24.

THE French Legislative Assembly had been
dissolved by the Emperor on the 27th
April. There had been riots in Paris, and on
this date the Opposition Candidates were elected

in that city. Thiers, Emile Ollivier, and Jules Favre, being amongst those who were rejected in the first ballot. In other parts of the country also, the elections went in favour of the Opposition.

(See Cartoon, " L'Homme qui Rit.")

The result of the elections was thought to be not too welcome to Napoleon III., to whom *Punch* applied ironically the title of Victor Hugo's lately published romance.

It is probable, however, that it finally decided the Emperor in the direction of contemplated Constitutional Reform, or what had been called "Crowning the Edifice."

NOW CROWN YOU'R EDIFICE.

Napoleon, you have done some
  things, and made some points
  of glory;
The time will write a big book
  who shall duly tell your story;
But, "Ere his death," the
  ancient sage said, "nobody
  call happy;"
A thousand years before by mankind may you be called so,
  Nappy.

Unless him that was before you
  of the Tuileries possessor, —
I do not mean your Uncle, but
  immediate predecessor, —
The purple, weary of his role,
  on one fine day revealed.
He put the mass of foolish upon
  his carpet-ing, and bolted.

Ne'er will it be your fate, I hope,
  in like case to come over,
And, going by the name of
  Brown, tempt shelter at Dover;
Not troubled as the tenure of your
  throne is the conditions
Of Popularity—and in, a grow-
  ing Opposition!

Now will you try to put that
  down by physical repression,
And force of arms ; or turns you
  in disarm it by concession?
You are a clever fellow, Nay,
  I don't intend to flatter,
You can see best the out jumps,
  I should think you'll do the
  latter.

Then, if you fail you'll nobly fall! If you succeed at ma, it

As sure you'll be a boon for historian and for poet.

Nay, you will be immortalised, the Edifice for crowning,
By Tupper and by Tennyson, by Close, and me, and Browning.

MAY 31.

"Hight to be remembered. This night did the Commons read a third time

"*L'HOMME QUI RIT!*"

and pass the Bill for Disestablishment and Disendowing the Irish Church." (*Punch's* "Enemies.")

For the third reading 361 voted; against it, 247. Majority for the Bill, 114.

On the next day Lord Granville laid the Bill on the table of the House of Lords.

In the Lords there was a party led by Lord Derby, who were vehemently opposed to the measure, the most violent and unmeasured denunciations of which were indulged in by clerical advocates and the speakers at indignation meetings held in this country and in Ireland. On the 5th June there was a meeting of Conservative Peers at the Duke of Marlborough's residence, to consider how best to

defeat the Bill, and there Lord Derby and Lord
Cairns strongly inveighed against the Bill; and
it was decided that Lord Harrowby should move
its rejection, though Lords Salisbury, Carnarvon,
and Stanhope were in favour of its being read a
second time and amended in Committee.

*[See Cartoon, "The 'Ram of Derby;' or, Longhead v.
Wronghead."]*

DUKE WRONGHEAD AND LORD LONGHEAD.

(A Peers' Eclogue.)

QUOTH Duke Wronghead, "His own change who will,
    at his cost,
Guide who will, by Bright's compass, his helm—
I've a mind of my own, and that mind I'll make known:
    Are we not an Estate of the Realm?"
    Quoth Duke Wronghead—
      "Am we not an Estate of the Realm?"

Quoth Lord Longhead, "Take care! that error you'll
    impair;
You wise with, not strong, 'tis a man.
If two men ride a horse, one rides hindmost, perforce;
There's nothing like knowing one's place."
    Quoth Lord Longhead—
      "There's nothing like knowing one's place."
      *   *
Duke Wronghead was dumb: e'en his chin pawed his
    thumb—

THE "RAM OF DERBY," OR, LONGHEAD V. WRONGHEAD.

Lord Clotterne. "Hold on, Steady! I will do himself a mischief, as sure as fate."

Quoth Lord Longhead, "Oh 'neath party stress,
The Peers have said 'nay,' when the Country said 'yes,'
But can' 'men' have still ended in 'yes.'"
    Quoth Lord Longhead—
      "But can' 'men' have still ended in 'yes.'"

"Ermined caps crowns may guard; said Peers' heads
    may be bared.
But if to butt betwethe we fell,
The pommeling-match o'er, we shall find, sure for a-er,
We have hurt our heads more than the wall."
    Quoth Lord Longhead—
      "We have hurt our heads more than the wall."

JUNE 14.

MR. BRIGHT, writing in reply to an invitation
to attend a Meeting at Birmingham in
support of the Irish Church Bill, indulged in
some very strong language concerning the
House of Lords. If they delayed the passing of
the Bill for three months, he said, "they will
stimulate discussion on important questions
which, but for their information, might have
slumbered for years." He advised them, instead
of doing a little childish tinkering about life

peerages, to bring themselves on a line with the
opinions and necessities of our day. "In
harmony with the nation," he said, "they may
go on for a long time, but throwing themselves
athwart its course they may meet with accidents
not pleasant to think of."

This letter gave great offence, and was referred to in both Houses of Parliament, where
the Ministers disavowed any official knowledge
of or responsibility for it. It was very generally
thought that considering his own position in
the Cabinet, and the fact that some of his col-

leagues were Members of
the Upper House, Mr.
Bright had gone a little
beyond the bounds of dis-
cretion and courtesy on
this occasion.

*(See Cartoon, " Forgetting his
Place.")*

"HITTING OUT."
Air—" *Jenny Todd.*"

You're an eloquent man, John
Bright, John Bright—
You're an eloquent man, John
Bright—
See the time of your song,
Is still " You are wrong !
There's but one man invariably
right,
And that's Bright ! "—
He's the one man who *always* is
right.

Man of power though you be,
John Bright, John
Bright—
Man of power though you be,
John Bright—
Those who shake fists with
you,
Own, in black and in blue,
There's no foe like a *Friend*
who shows fight
A *la* Bright—
There's no foe like a *Friend* who
shows fight.

So you've whipped your way
up, John Bright, John
Bright—
So you've whipped your way up,
John Bright—
" Hitting out " with a will—
And conquering the still—
As a rule, to your leaders' delight
In John Bright—
As a rule, to your leaders' delight.

Many changes you've seen,
John Bright, John Bright—
Many changes you've seen, John
Bright—
But on the whole view,
Things have come round to
you,
While your cousins' black has
turn'd white,
For John Bright—
Your cousins' black has turn'd
white.

But what change have you seen,
John Bright, John
Bright—
What change have you seen,
John Bright—
Like the right-about-face
That brings you into place,
And bids an Right Hon'rable
write
Plain John Bright—
Bids to you a Right Hon'rable write ?

That change should bring others, John Bright, John
Bright—
That change should bring others, John Bright—
When dignity's due,
Manners should be so too,
And your manners want some setting right,
My dear Bright—
Your manners want some setting right.

You're a Minister now, John Bright, John Bright—
You're a Minister now, John Bright—
And Ministers don't
" Hit out," as we won't—
M.P.'s on their own hooks that fight,
As need Bright—
M.P.'s on their own hooks that fight.

There's the Minister's muzzle, John Bright, John Bright—
There's the Minister's muzzle, John Bright—

And if you can't bear
That muzzle to wear,
To be where you are you've no right,
My dear Bright—
To be where you are you're no right.

JUNE 14.

THE Debate began in the Lords on the
Second Reading of the Irish Church Bill,

FORGETTING HIS PLACE.

John Bright. "*Irish Church coming down !—Pull out o' the way there until that 'infatuated' old Mother of yours—can't yer !*"
(*Voice of the Coachman.* "*John, John, you're FORGETTING YOUR PLACE!—you musn't use that sort of language now.*"

which was moved in a con-
ciliatory speech by Earl
Granville. It was a debate
characterised by the delivery
of great orations of unusual
eloquence and brilliancy.
The Bishop of St. David's
(Dr. Connop Thirlwall,
b. 1797) argued most in-
cidly in its favour, as did
the Duke of Argyll. The
Bishop of Peterborough, Dr.
Magee (an Irishman), made
against it one of the most
dashing harangues ever delivered in the Lords, of
which Lord Derby said,
" Its fervid eloquence and
impassioned and brilliant
language have never in my
memory been surpassed,
and rarely equalled." The
aged Earl Derby himself
argued warmly against the
measure in a speech of
touching earnestness, with
a most pathetic peror-
ation.

" My Lords, I am now an
old man, and, like many of
your Lordships, past the
allotted span of threescore
years and ten. My official
life is at an end ; my political
life is nearly closed, and,
in the course of nature, my
natural life cannot be long.
That natural life commenced at
the period of the great rebellion
in Ireland, which immediately
preceded the union between the
two countries. God grant that
it may not close with the renewal of rebellion. My Lords,
I do not pretend to look at the
prospect of the distant future.
But, whatever may be the result
of your Lordships' consideration
of this measure, for my own part,
if it be for the last time I now
have the honour of addressing
your Lordships, I declare that it
will be to my dying day a satisfaction that I have been able to
lift my voice against the adoption
of a measure the profound im-
policy of which is only equalled
by its moral iniquity."

The Marquis of Salis-
bury made an able speech,
directed against most of the
measure, but in favour of
deferring to the national will and of accepting
the Bill with modifications. Earl Russell delivered a long and interesting historical speech.
He supported the measure, but wished it improved in some particulars. Lord Cairns argued
energetically against it.

The Division took place on the 18th June, in
the fullest House within living memory. 325 peers

DARBY AND JOHN.

(In the Tea-room, after the Division.)

Lord Derby. "I never thought we should live to see this day!"
Lord John. "Ha! I did!"

voting, 179 for and 146 against ; majority for
the Bill, 33.

[*See Cartoon, " Darby and John."*]

JUNE 30.

THE Prime Minister, speaking at a banquet
given by the Lord Mayor, intimated that
the Government would "respectfully consider"

any amendments proposed (in the Lords) to the
Irish Church Bill, subject, however, to the recollection of the position in which the Government
stood, the pledges they had given, and the commission they had received. The Lords, however, set to vigorously to work upon the Bill
they so sincerely hated, that when it left their
hands (on the 12th July) it was scarcely recog-

nimble as the same measure, at least in the opinion of the author and his party.

In the Commons (on the 15th July), Mr. Gladstone announced the Ministry's intentions as regarded the Lords' Amendments, which amounted to a statement (says *Punch's "Essence"*) that he would cut out all the Lords' Amendments of any importance. He likened the Lords to people up in a balloon. He should—

Restore the Preamble.
Put back the date.
Alter the Curate plan.
Reform the Income-Tax abatement.
Agree to protect some Annuitants.
Disagree to the Fourteen Years' clause.

EASING THE CURB.

Emperor Napoleon, "*Here we fret, my boys I shall just drop in curb a little.*"

And the gratis Globe Houses.
And the Ulster lands.
And the Diminution of Poor Rates.
And the Concurrent Endowment.
And the Hobbling up the surplus.

The Commons, by large majorities, supported Mr. Gladstone on the main points to which he declared adhesion. Most of the Amendments inserted by the Lords were again struck out, though on some minor points agreement was found possible.

The measure was then returned for the reconsideration of the Upper House.

JULY 12.

For some time past there had been dissatisfaction and disturbance in France, the Imperial rule gradually becoming unpopular, and the forces of opposition gaining in strength and boldness. On the 27th April the French Legislative body had been dissolved by the Emperor. The newly elected one, in which the Opposition was strongly represented, assembled for the first time on the 29th June. On the 12th July the Emperor found it prudent to announce to it his intention to grant to the Chamber an extension of power not far as compatible with the fundamental basis of the Constitution. "The Emperor" (said the Imperial Message) "has always shown himself disposed to relinquish in the public interest certain of his prerogatives," and the changes now proposed "constitute the natural development of those which have successively been made in the institutions of the Empire."

(*See Cartoon, "Easing the Curb."*)

JULY 20.

A WARM debate upon the returned Irish Bill begun in the Lords. Lord Granville called attention to the fact that of 61 amendments the Commons had adopted 35, recommended 11, and rejected only 13. Lord Cairns retorted that the accepted amendments were slight and mainly verbal, the rejected ones important and essential. After much hot discussion, however, a compromise was agreed to on the 22nd, the Opposition yielding on the point of date, and the Government agreeing to some alteration of the terms of commutation, and the disposition of the surplus, &c. On the 23rd this compromise was agreed to by the Commons.

The House of Commons was suddenly transformed into a Cave of Harmony. Mr. Gladstone, in a most eloquent speech, retraced the history of the Irish Bill, so finally amended, and paid a glowing tribute to the House of Lords. He also complimented the Opposition in the Commons for the manly, but not factious way, in which they had fought for their principles. He wished the Church of Ireland God-speed on her new career. The Bill would, in a few days, become Law.

(See Cartoon, "A Change for the Better.")

DR. GLADSTONE.
Air.—"Nora Creina."

WHEN released from State control,   [seductions,
And cut from Government Orange Boys, yourselves console,
We'll set to work at reconstructions.
Then our Church again will rise
Upon the idea that's clear for action,
Privately yielding to the skies, [time,
And give unbounded satisfaction.
Oh, good Doctor Gladstone, dear,   [Gladstone!
Our darling henry, Doctor
All the pills
For Ireland's ills,
Isn't equal your pill, Dr. Gladstone.

Disestablished, disendowed,
No longer a perpetual blister,
Poor old Ireland we'll corrode,
And wed her with her English sister.
Then, from all restraint exempt
On rolling hard and fast descending,
We, at least, won't earn contempt
By not composing our divisions.

No, good Doctor Gladstone, dear,
Our mental, staunch Churchman, Dr. Gladstone,
Out we'll hack
Each heretic,
And all free-thinkers, Dr. Gladstone.

Hence, with Rumps and Returns,
We'll drive all them that bother us—so!
Ritualism we will refuse
To stand, or tolerate Colenso.

They'll be drummed out to that tune
To which the Rogue, degraded, marches.
Don't you wish their likes, as soon
Got rid of by the Court of Arches?
Oh, good Doctor Gladstone, dear,
High Church, but Liberal. Dr. Gladstone,
We will be
A Church set free,
To rule itself, by Dr. Gladstone.

A CHANGE FOR THE BETTER.

Church to QUEEN ELIZABETH. "Agreed, here then! Ods Boddikins! zouds my life, and marry come up, sweetheart! So let none I'd have knocked all these oddi-poles together till they HAD agreed!"

JULY 26.

To-day the Royal Assent was given, by Commission, to the Irish Church Bill.

(*See Cartoon, "' The Harp that Once,' &c."*)

AUG. 2.

The reforms in the direction of enlargement of popular power and modification of the functions of the Senate and the Legislative Body proposed by the Emperor Napoleon were this day submitted to the Chambers.

AUG. 11.

Parliament was prorogued by Commission. The Royal Speech was thus summarised by *Mr. Punch*:—

1. That negotiation with America has been suspended, and it is hoped that this delay may tend to maintain friendly relations. [*We, if ever persons cut one another, they can hardly quarrel, your disgrace.*]

2. That Parliament has been zealous and assiduous. [*Well deserved.*]

3. The Irish Church Act. [*Fiat Justitia!*]

4. The Re-Creation of the Compound Householder. [*Your health, Mr. Edward!*]

5. The Bankruptcy Act. [*Live within your income, everybody, and (as the shoemaker remarked to his boy, who mentioned that the beast were biting that morning, and was advised by his stern parent to mind his work), "don't the beast won't bite you."*]

6. The Act abolishing Imprisonment for Debt. [*Tradesmen, don't give foolish credit.*]

7. The Endowed Schools Act. [*Now, boys, show your endeavours.*]

8. The Habitual Criminals Act. [*Tremble, ruffians! Well said, Mr. Knox! An admirable warning.*]

9. The Cattle Act. [*Not to Mr. Low's department.*]

10. Repeal of Duty on Fire Insurance. [*Everybody but fools insure.*]

11. Repeal of Duty on Corn. [*No chaff occurs to us.*]

12. The Electric Telegraphic Act. [*Bravo, Mr. Scudamore!*]

The Queen was much obliged for the Supplies, and for the money which has paid the Abyssinian bill.

And this was the highly elegant conclusion:—

"During the recess you will continue to gather that practical knowledge and experience which form the solid basis of legislative aptitude."

" THE HARP THAT ONCE," &c.

BRITANNIA.   "*There, we done, I've turned the string for you that made all the discord, and now I hope we may have something like harmony.*"

HIBERNIA.   "*Ah thin, Sisther dethir', sure there's another sthring as'll have to be tuned by an' by.*"

And so endeth the first Session of the Terrible Parliament, which, elected by the Millions, was to abolish everything except the Gaslighting.

The usual Ministerial Whitebait Dinner at Greenwich did not, for some reason, take place this year, *Mr. Punch* commented upon the omission in the following lines:—

"NO BAIT THIS YEAR !"

The usual Ministerial Whitebait Dinner will not take place this year." —Newspaper paragraph.

What was that said, awful, cry,
That sounded through the Treasury?
And Downing Street thrilled like a sigh—
    "No Bait this Year !"

What paler horror gave Stansfeld's front,
Makes Ayrton's darker than its wont?

The sentence — shrilly, sharp,
and bluat —
"No Raid this Year!"

Won't Gladstone's life, or Grau-
ville's gout,
Leyard's "hot aith," Lowe's
"cold without,"
Or Peter's loathers brought
about,
"No Raid this Year"?

Won't Bright's repugnance to a
dish
That so suggesteth loaves and
fish,
Induced him to put forth the wish
—"No Raid this Year"?

Or won't the want of Rate to kill
(See the Votes on the Irish Bill)
That prompted grateful Glad-
stone's will—
"No Raid this Year"?

Won't Lowe's receipts to his
friends,
His suspense theft of candle-
ends
And cheese-parings, that re-
commends
"No Raid this Year"?

He won't a hint to Treasurer &
Co.,
Vestries and Guardians round to
show
Their letters dimostres can go —
Sans Raid this Year?

Or, sharies of Hart and Quarter-
master ! —
Won't that mark lead three femals
have tale,
All a-ore rejoiced to swell the
stories,
"No Raid this Year"?

Did all, remembering past
"Wonks, Spoke !"
Had nine, stale pfort, and staler
jokes,
Join in the prayer, which soar
provokes—
"No Raid this Year"?

AUG. 13.

An application was
made to-day in the
Court of Chancery for the
appointment of a provi-
sional liquidator for the
Albert Life Assurance
Company, which had failed,
with an aggregate imme-
diate liability of £3,360,000,
and actual assets of only
£810,000, and the possible
produce of calls upon the
shareholders, which, under an absolute liquida-
tion, were estimated to amount to not more
than £100,000.

AUG. 15.

The Emperor Napoleon, "to celebrate the
centenary of the birth of Napoleon I., by
an act which responds to our feelings," pro-

DESTINY AND "FÊTE," OR TIME WORKS WONDERS.

Ghost of Napoleon the First. "*Highly flattered, I'm sure, mon cher!—Does any you're doing what's right!—There is a Nan—but no matter!—At any rate, you're making it safe for YOUNG NUMBER FOUR.*"

claimed a complete amnesty for all political
offenders. Increased pensions were also granted
to survivors of the Grand Army, the troops were
reviewed by the Prince Imperial, and other festivities indulged in.

(See Cartoon, "Destiny and 'Fête,' or Time works
Wonders.")

On the same day there were great rejoicings at
Suez, to celebrate the meeting of the waters of
the Red Sea and the Mediterranean in the
Bitter Lakes on the Suez Canal.

AUG. 24.

The Emperor and Empress left Paris on a
visit to Corsica.

AUG. 27.

To-day occurred an extremely interesting International Sporting event, namely the Boat Race on the Thames between picked representatives from the Universities of Oxford and Harvard. The Race excited much popular interest. The Oxford Crew, consisting of four of the best oarsmen who ever rowed for that University, won by a length and three quarters. *Mr. Punch* thus recorded the event:—

AUGUST 17, 1869.

THE Great International Boat Race is over! Bravo, Harvard! Bravo, Oxford! *Mr. Punch* admires your pluck, skill, and endurance! and thus immortalises you:—

OXFORD.

F. Willan, Exeter (bow).
A. C. Yarborough, Lincoln.
J. C. Tinné, University.
S. D. Darbishire, Balliol (stroke).
J. H. Hall, Corpus (cox.).

HARVARD.

Joseph Story Fay, Boston (bow.).
Francis Ogden Lyman, Ohio (Sandwich Islands).
W. H. Simmonds, Concord, Massachusetts.
Alden Porter Loring, Boston (stroke).
Arthur Burnham, Chicago (cox.).

As you look spring from the outer proven stock—

"Cornelia's own were worthy of their mother—"

there can be no offence in congratulating Oxford on its victory. So let us sing—

Here's a bumper to both the crews,
The Harvards and the Blues.
Ev'ry man!
And when they meet again,
May dark blue its place maintain,
If it can!

[See Cartoon, " Well Rowed All!"]

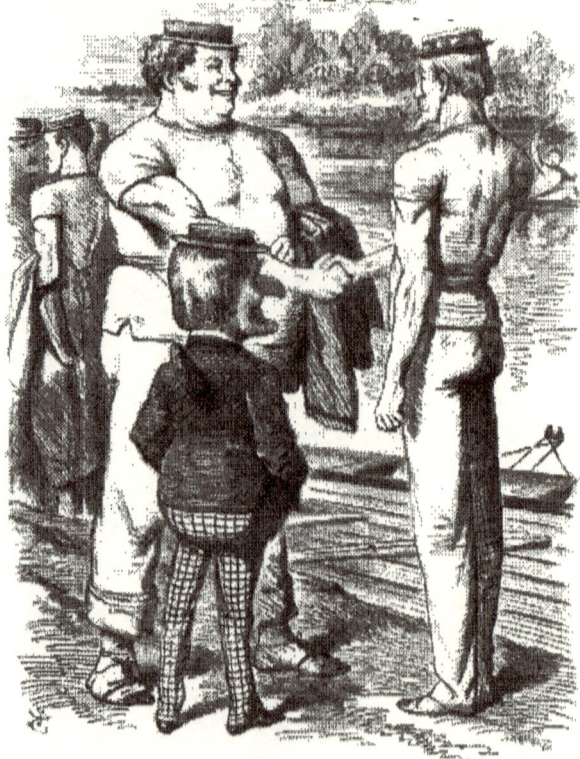

" WELL ROWED ALL!"

Humor. "*Ha, dear Boys, you're able to pull together, in fact all the world!*"

SEPT. 1.

PRINCE NAPOLEON JEROME made an ultra-liberal speech in the Senate, in which he said that the Empire, which had been based upon the personal authority of the Emperor, had now been transformed into an Empire based upon

On the 6th the French Senate, by 134 to 3 votes, adopted the Senatus Consultum modifying the Constitution of the Empire, and on the 8th an Imperial decree was issued giving effect to this resolution.

At this time the Emperor was seriously ill, the condition of his health causing considerable

OCT. 16.

SOME ale was caused about this time by a proposal which had been made by the Chancellor of the Exchequer, Mr. Robert Lowe, to restore the value of the sovereign by one per cent. *Mr. Punch* said, " He wants them kept in

thinks that he can achieve
this by making a sovereign
lighter by one grain than
at present. We prefer our
sovereign *cum grano*."

*(See Cartoon, " Bob and the
Bobby, or only his Fun.")*

OCT. 23.

EDWARD GEOFFREY
STANLEY, fourteenth
Earl of Derby, died to-day
at Knowsley, aged 71.
This high-minded and best-
unveiled nobleman had been
three times Premier, and
had only recently, in consequence of failing health,
resigned the leadership to
Mr. Disraeli. From his
fiery eloquence known as
" The Rupert of Debate "
(a title applied to him
by Lord Lytton), Earl
Derby was a polished
scholar (he had published
an acceptable translation
of Homer) and always a
chivalrous gentleman. *Mr.
Punch* honoured his me-
mory in the following
lines :—

LORD DERBY.

Born, 1799. Died, 1869.

WE THE ANTES show from those
he loved so well,
Autumn's pale morning are him
past away !
Leave them beside their sacred
dead to pray,
Unmarked of strangers. Calmer
memories tell
How nobly Stanley lived. No
braver spirit
Clave to the golden call of all
his days,
Of all their peers. His was the
heart that fires
The eloquent tongue, and lit
the eye whose sun
Alone had quailed his foe. He
wrought for Power,
(And power in England is a
hero's prize)
Yet he could throw it from him;
These whose eyes
See not for tears, remember in
this hour
That he was oft from Homer's page beguiled
To frame some " wonder for a happy child."

NOV. 6.

OPENING by the Queen in state of the new
Blackfriars Bridge and the Holborn Via-
duct. Her Majesty met with an enthusiastic

BOB AND THE BOBBY, OR ONLY HIS FUN.

*BILL . . "Hullo, young feller! If you're a goin' on for "Swindon" the Gold, you'll be gettin' yerself into difficulties."
RECALCITRANT BOB. " Lor' bless yer, Mister Bill, why I'm only a settin' the Hexcise-less lighter!"*

NOV. 11.

DR. TEMPLE was this day elected Bishop of
Exeter in pursuance of Her Majesty's
congé d'élire. A very violent opposition had
been offered to this appointment of Mr. Gladstone's, on account of the share which Dr.

notorious " Essays and Reviews." Dr. Pusey
had called it " a horrible scandal," and suggested
that disestablishment was preferable to the
toleration of such appointments, and " now our
only remedy." Lord Shaftesbury, a leading
light of the Low Church Party, was believed to
be as bitterly opposed to the election of the

the High Church Dr. Pusey and the irascible Archdeacon Denison. *Mr. Punch* said;

TRACTARIAN v. TEMPLE.

MR. GLADSTONE has, in his late episcopal appointments, agreeably disappointed many reasonable Churchmen, who assumed that he was a Puseyite. But he has proved himself anything rather than that. In appointing

Dr. Temple to the See of Exeter, he has disagreeably disappointed Dr. Pusey. But Dr. Pusey would have done wisely, or rather would have refrained from doing unwisely, if he had not proclaimed his disappointment by an indecent opposition to Dr. Temple's preferment. His animosity is calculated to suggest the suspicion that he is more bitterly disappointed than simple people think. Certainly, Mr. Gladstone might have so disposed of a mitre as to satisfy expectations which Dr. Pusey may at one time have, not without reason, entertained. But

then the Premier would have accumulated a row in the Church to which the anti-Temple agitation is a trifle. What would Mrs. Grundy have said, what would the Earl of Shaftesbury have said, what would Exeter Hall have said—and done—if Mr. Gladstone had made a Bishop of Dr. Pusey?

(See Cartoon, "Congé d'Élire-ium. A Case for the Doctors.")

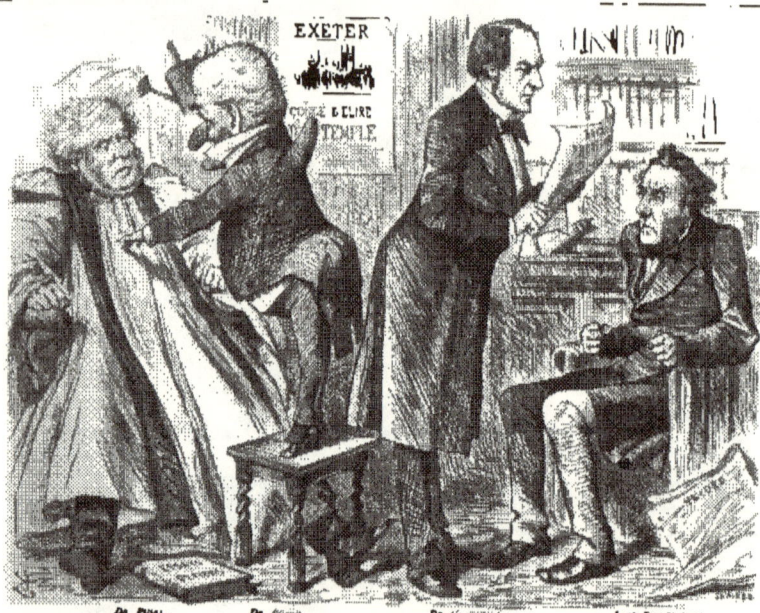

CONGÉ D'ÉLIRE-IUM. A CASE FOR THE DOCTORS.

Nov. 17.

On this day the Suez Canal was formally opened amidst great rejoicings and festivities. The Empress of the French, the Emperor of Austria, the Crown Prince of Prussia, Prince William of Orange, and numerous other notables were present. M. de Lesseps, the projector of this great work, was of course the hero of the hour. As an engineering feat, and as a commercial convenience, everything was to be said in favour of the Canal, but some shared

probable political consequences. *Mr. Punch* had a Cartoon entitled "From the Great Pyramid, a Bird's-eye View of the Canal and its Consequences." The representatives of the Powers are assembled on the top of the Pyramid. "See what it unites!" cries France, pointing to the Canal. "Think what it may divide!" says Britannia, indicating the already perturbed Powers.

LATEST—FROM THE SPHINX.

Still with my many eyes I see,
Still with my many ears I hear.

Thousands of years this resting place
Beneath the Pyramids I hold,
And still these daily shadows trace,
Breathing o'er me, blue and cold,

And many wonders have I known,
And many a race and rule of men,
Since first upon this desert's zone
I fixed my calm, unwinking ken.

'Neath these same orbs that still revolve

But darkest riddle never yet
I framed for Œdipus the wise,
Than those that to the world I set,
Touching three things before
my eyes.

What of this piercing of the masts?
What of this union of the seas?
This group of undaunted heads,
The blending of strange
Banxies?

Arms and Allah too's that flown
From streams and monsigneurs—
These fortifies and robes-fourrure,
*(there—
Those crunches and emblems.*

This far-power of East and West,
Pillars and pomps à la bisque;
Cucumbes belles whom Worth
has drest,
And Parisiennes à l'odalisque?

Riddles that enод as Sphinx to
put,
But more than Œdipus to
read,—
What good or ill from Lesseps'
cut
Eastward and Westward shall
proceed?

Whence love or youth? War or
peace?
festoo healed, or old wounds
oped anew?
Upon the loosing of the seas,
Sicile's blood witless hot house
too?

The Eastern question raised, at
last?
The Eastern question laid for
aye?
Ramdan ambition festered fast?
Or feathered bat for fever play?

Nov. 25.

O'DONOVAN ROSSA, a
reformed Fenian con-
vict, was this day elected
for Tipperary. This was
the culmination of a long-
continued Fenian agitation
in Ireland. Not conciliated
by the passage of the Irish
Church Bill, the extreme
Nationalist faction was
daily growing more violently
seditious and menacing.
The so-called " Manches-
ter Martyrs" were publicly
glorified, and the release
of all Fenian prisoners was
clamorously demanded by
Irish mass-meetings. On

NEIGHBOURS IN COUNCIL.

FRANCE. " Had am I to do with my ' Irreconcilables?' "
BRITANNIA. " I know perfectly well, my dear, what I'm going to do with mine!"

the 25th October an Irish Tenant League
had been formed in Tipperary, with the avowed
object of obtaining fixity of tenure and protection against arbitrary landlords. Mr. Gladstone, in response to urgent appeals, said that
whilst the Government desired to carry
clemency to the Fenian convicts to the farthest

safety permitted, the release of the prisoners
would be contrary to their duty as guardians of
the public security and peace. The result of
the Irish Invincibles was this election of the
of course legally ineligible ex-convict O'Donovan
Rossa.

France at the same time was plagued with

fiery M. Rochefort, one of the candidates for Paris
who had lately been arrested, but released by
order of the Emperor, who directed that he
should have a safe-conduct until the elections
were over. He with two other Irreconcilables,
Cremieux and Arago, were subsequently elected
deputies for Paris.

Nov. 26.

The Princess of Wales was safely delivered of a daughter, the Princess Augusta.

Nov. 29.

Opening of the Legislative Body by the Emperor Napoleon. He referred both to the late concessions to liberty and the recent popular and journalistic excesses. France, he said, wanted liberty, but liberty naked with order. "For order" (he said) "I will answer. Aid me, gentlemen, to save liberty."

On the 5th December a manifesto against the continued personal government of the Emperor was signed by M. Ollivier and 116 members of the Right Centre.

Dec. 6.

At the opening of Congress President Grant expressed a hope that the time might

PENANCE FOR PANCRAS GUARDIANS.

soon come when a solution of the Alabama claims might be successfully approached.

Dec. 13.

Commencement in the Court of Queen's Bench of the trial of the Directors of the Overend-Gurney Co. After a nine days' trial the jury acquitted them.

Dec. 27.

reign of personal government by authorising M. Emile Ollivier to construct a Constitutional Government." He appealed to him to "form a homogeneous Cabinet, faithfully representing the majority of the Legislative Body."

Dec. 31.

The St. Pancras Guardians were at this time in exceedingly bad odour. On the 22nd accelerated by the condition of the infirmary and that it had been overcrowded for the last three years. Also that the Board of Guardians had failed in their duty to the parish in not carrying into effect the recommendations of the Poor Law Board.

Mr. Punch, in a seasonable Cartoon, suggested a suitable penance for these egregious persons.

✦ 1870 ✦

JANUARY.

"THE year 1870, I am sure, cannot but consolidate this general agreement (between France and the other Powers), and tend to the increase of concord and civilisation." So spoke the Oracle of the Tuileries at the annual reception of the Diplomatic Body on the first day of the year. And this was the year of the Franco-Prussian War and of the Siege of Paris!

On the 3rd the Ollivier Ministry was established. On the 10th M. Ollivier said, "We must consolidate a national Government adapting itself to the march of progress in such manner that French democracy may witness the realisation of progress without violence and hurry without revolution." Brave words! A jarring note was struck amidst this optimistic outpouring

MAGNA CHARTA FOR FRANCE.
(A SECOND EDITION OF A GOOD OLD STORY.)

by M. Gambetta, an "Irreconcilable" of great energy and eloquence, then comparatively little known, who declared that a day would come when a majority of the people, without appealing to force, would succeed in establishing a Republic!

(See Cartoon, "Magna Charta for France.")

JAN. 10.

VICTOR NOIR, a Parisian journalist, was this day shot dead by Prince Pierre Bonaparte,

Emperor, in the course of a fracas originating in the visit of Victor Noir and Ulric Fonvielle to the Prince to arrange the preliminaries of a duel with M. Pascal Grousset. The Prince was arrested and ordered to be brought to trial.

JAN. 11.

SPEAKING to his constituents at Birmingham, Mr. John Bright foreshadowed legislation on the Irish Land Question. "If (said he) we are able to banish agrarian crime—if we can unbar the prison doors—if we can reduce all

so tranquil as England and Scotland now are—then, at least, I think we may have done something to justify the wisdom and statesmanship of our time." He also said, "I believe that an alteration of the land laws of England, such as might be made without lessening by sixpence the value of any man's property, would do much to arrest that tide of pauperism which is constantly flowing from the agricultural counties into our great centres of industry." A few days later, in answer to a deputation on the subject of the Fenian prisoners, he said, "I am bound

country than the man who attempts by force of arms to disturb the public peace, and to break down the authority of the law." He also spoke very earnestly in favour of self-help, and the diminution of drinking habits among the labouring classes.

(See Cartoon, "John Bright's New Reform Bill.—" Reform Yourselves!")

BRIGHT STILL BRIGHTER

Bravo, John Bright, bravo once and again!
You were also once a trump in your way—

JOHN BRIGHT'S NEW REFORM BILL.——"REFORM YOURSELVES!"

JAN. 22.

M ESSRS. ROCHEFORT and Pascal Grousset fined and sentenced to six months' imprisonment for publishing seditious articles in the *Marseillaise*.

FEB. 4.

T O-DAY the telegraph lines of the whole of the United Kingdom were transferred to the management of the Post Office department.

FEB. 8.

P ARLIAMENT was opened by Commission. The Royal Speech foreshadowed an Irish Land Bill, an Education Bill, and also measures relating to University Tests, Naturalisation, Rating and Licences. It was foreseen that Irish Land and National Education would be the great subjects of the Session.

FEB. 10.

A NEW WRIT was moved for electing a Member for Tipperary in place of O'Donovan Rossa, who, as a convict, was legally incapable of being elected as a Member of the House of Commons.

TAKING THE (IRISH) BULL BY THE HORNS.

A LESSON FOR IRELAND.

SOME ignorant Irish, old England to fee,
Elected O'Donovan Rossa, Esquire ;
But this Fenian bold is a felon de se,
And, civilly dead, has no life as M.P.
To a maxim, the truth whereof each one allows here,
That you can't make a silk purse out of a sow's ear ;
Of a dunlop truth, too, there needs no debater,
That you can't make an M.P. out of a traitor.

FEB. 14.

national grounds was the object of his increased attention.

FEB. 15.

" I N A splendid speech of three hours " (says *Punch's* " Essence of Parliament "), " the Premier (Mr. Gladstone) introduced his (Irish) Land Bill. . . . Generally its object is to prevent a landlord from turning out a tenant without giving him compensation for eviction. It clearly

Economy. . . . . Law tribunals are to see that no injustice is done either to landlord or tenant."
See Cartoon, " Taking the (Irish) Bull by the Horns.")

Mr. Gladstone discussed the questions of —
1. Leases to occupiers and landlords.
2. The judicial machinery for administering the Act.
3. The different classes of holdings, viz., Usury Customs ; Common analogous to Usury ; Tenancies at Will ; and Leases.
4. Damages for Eviction.
5. Sundries omitted.

minister to the holding The Bill would reverse the present presumption of the law; it would presume all improvement to be the property of the tenant, and it would be for the landlord to prove the contrary."

The Bill was read a first time.

FEB. 17.

Mr. FORSTER, Vice-President of the Committee of Council upon Education, on this day introduced the Government Bill to provide for Public Elementary Education in England and Wales.

It provided for the compulsory attendance of children, each School Board being empowered to make bye laws enforcing the attendance at school of all the children in their district between five and twelve years of age. The Schools constituted under the Bill had to show a certain degree of efficiency before they could claim a Government grant, had to be examined by an undenominational Inspector, and accept a "conscience clause" as a condition of receiving Government aid. The management of the schools to be vested in Boards locally elected. Whilst school fees would not be abolished, the School Boards were to have power to establish free schools in the poorer neighbourhoods where payment was impossible or unlikely, and in paying schools to grant free tickets to parents unable to pay the fees. The additional funds requisite to be provided by local rates, grants from the public treasury and school fees, about a third from each

THE THREE RS: OR, BETTER LATE THAN NEVER.

RIGHT HON. W. E. FORSTER (Chairman of Board). "Well, my little people, we have been gravely and earnestly considering whether you may learn to read. I am happy to tell you that, subject to a variety of restrictions, conscience clauses, and the control of your Vestries—YOU MAY!"

source. If the subsequent charge on the poor rate in any parish should exceed threepence in the pound, a special additional grant was to be made to such parish from the public funds. The Bill as originally framed neither excluded religious instruction nor directed that it should be taught in any particular way. Considerable alterations were however made in Committee; education was not made merely secular, but Local Boards might exclude religious teaching from schools founded on rates. They might not introduce any religious teaching, such as catechism, &c., except the reading and expounding of the Bible. Schools partly supported by voluntary contributions, partly by public grants, to receive nothing from local rates, and to take in the Three Table Commandment Clause

Such in brief outline was the Bill.

[See Cartoon, "The Three R.'s; or, Better Late than Never."]

MARCH 11.

SECOND reading of the Irish Land Bill carried by a majority of 455 to 11.

MARCH 15.

TO-NIGHT Mr. Charles Dickens gave his last "Reading" in St. James's Hall, choosing for his farewell performance "The Christmas Carol" and the "Trial Scene from Pickwick."

MARCH 17.

Mr. CHICHESTER FORTESCUE introduced a strong Coercion Bill entitled "The Peace Preservation (Ireland) Bill." It was read a second time, by 425 to 13, on the 22nd March. On the 15th March the 17th clause, dealing specially with newspapers encouraging or propagating treason and sedition, was carried in Committee by 333 to 56.

(*See* Contents, *" Silencing the Trumpet, after p. 206.*)

The Bill was read a third time and passed on the 16th.

MARCH 18.

The Education Bill, after a three nights' debate, was read a third time without a division.

An amendment moved by Mr. Dixon to the effect "that no measure for the elementary education of the people would afford a satisfactory or permanent solution which left the question of religious instruction in schools supported by public funds and rates to be determined by local authorities," was withdrawn; and Mr. Gladstone intimated that the Government was willing to substitute for the conscience clause a clear and definite line of separation between secular and religious teaching.

MARCH 21.

Prince Pierre Bonaparte tried for shooting Victor Noir. On the 27th the jury returned a verdict of acquittal on the capital charge. Victor Noir's father demanded an indemnity of 100,000 francs (£4,000) for the loss of his son; the Court awarded 25,000 francs (£1,000) to be paid by Prince Pierre to the parents of the slain man.

MARCH 23.

The Burials Bill, legalizing the performance of religious services other than those of the Church of England in parish churchyards, was read a second time in the Commons by 233 to 111 votes.

APRIL 11.

The Chancellor of the Exchequer, Mr. Robert Lowe, introduced the Budget. It showed an estimated surplus of £4,337,000, with which he proposed to reduce the sugar duties

SILENCING THE TRUMPET. (After Æsop.)

Fourth Trumpeter. "Spare me good Sir, I beseech you. I have no arms but this Trumpet only!"

Conqueror. "No, you Vagabond! Without the spirit to fight yourself, you stir up others to war and bloodshed."

Moral.—He who creates the strife is worse than he who takes part in it.

penny (£1,150,000), and abolish some minor imports. The Budget was favourably received.

APRIL 23.

By Imperial decree, the French nation was called upon to vote for or against the following:—"The people approve the liberal

by the Emperor, with the co-operation of the great bodies of the State, and ratify the Senatus Consultum of the 20th April, 1870."

APRIL 24.

An Imperial Proclamation in support of the plebiscitum was issued in France. In it

" By balloting affirmatively you will conjure down the threats of revolution, you will seat order and liberty on a solid basis, and you will render easier for the future the transmission of the crown to my son. Eighteen years ago you were almost unanimous in conferring the most extensive powers upon me. Be now, too, as unanimous in giving your adhesion to the transformation of the Imperial régime. A great nation cannot attain to its complete development without leaning for support upon institutions which are a guarantee both for stability and progress. To the request which I address to you, to ratify the liberal reforms that have been realised during the last ten years, answer 'Yes!' As to myself, faithful to my origin, I shall imbue myself with your thoughts, fortify myself in your will, and, trusting to Providence, I shall not cease to labour without intermission for the prosperity and greatness of France."

MAY 2.

Our literary and fashionable world was much excited by the rather unexpected publication of a new novel, entitled "Lothair," by Mr. Disraeli. It was a sprightly novel of society. In it he sardonically, if not quite originally, described critics as "those who had failed in Literature and Art." "Juventus Mundi" was a book dealing gravely and eloquently with classical themes which Mr. Gladstone had some time before produced.

(See Cartoon, " Critics.")

MAY 8.

The result of the plébiscite in France (including the Algerian vote) was announced. The number of votes recorded in favour of the plébiscitum was 7,336,434, against it 1,560,709. *(See April 23rd).*

"CRITICS."

(WHO HAVE NOT EXACTLY FAILED IN LITERATURE AND ART."—See Mr. D.'s New Work.)

MR. GLADSTONE. "Ha!—Pleasant!"   MR. DISRAELI. "Ha!—Prop!"

MAY 9.

The Postmaster General (Lord Hartington) introduced a Bill to amend the law relating to Procedure at Elections. "You might not guess" (said *Punch's* "Essence") "from its title that—*A Cabinet Minister proposes*

Advocates of Secret Voting have their triumph at last. There is more in this Bill. Nomination day, with all its riot and corruption, is to be done away. . . . Public houses are not to be used as Committee-rooms, and, lastly, and, perhaps, best, any expenditure made by a candidate and not declared on the account for him to give is shall be deemed a Corrupt Payment."

MAY 12.

Mr. Jacob Bright's Bill for giving the Parliamentary franchise to women, which on the 4th had been read a second time by 124 to 91 votes, was to-day rejected by 220 to 94. Mr. Gladstone was in the majority.

[See Cartoon, "An 'Ugly Rush.'"]

MAY 18.

Was read a second time, and sent to a Select Committee, Mr. Buxton's Bill for amending the Government of London. It is the most dangerous and revolutionary project we ever heard of. The Lord Mayor is to be Mayor of all London. . . . The ten boroughs are to be made into ten Municipal Bodies. The City Mayor—hear this, Guildhall, and let your echoes slumber as they answer—is to be called the Deputy Mayor, but may be a Vice-king in the absence of the Great Chief; with other unwise things. Government gasped out that no doubt the present state of things was not perfect, that such a great plan ought to be Ministerial—and that we must Inquire—yes—to point of fact, inquire. Exactly so. Hence the Committee. . . . But Mr. Buxton has no idea of the storm he is Brewing." (Punch's "London.")

AN "UGLY RUSH!"

Mr. Bull. "Not if I know it!"

See Diagram on the Woman's Vote Ball.

On the same night Mr. Russell Gurney's Bill for protecting the Property and Earnings of Married Women was read a second time. On the 21st June it was read a second time in the Lords, and referred to a select Committee.

MAY 23.

To-day Punch sustained a great loss by the death of its first Editor, the judicious and genial Mark Lemon. A tribute to his memory appeared in its pages, from which the following

MARK LEMON,

BORN NOVEMBER 30, 1809. DIED MAY 23, 1870.

He who wrote the first article in this Journal, who from the establishment has been its conductor, and whose prudence and suggestions take effect in the very pages now before the reader, has missed from this and all other earthly care and labour.

"I, past malcontent, old coffin rot i-turn, remnant,
Ex sibi ob, sedis points honors, quies."

There is need that this record of his gone, but of grievous loss to those in whose names this is told, should be prepared too early to permit its being aught but a most important and inadequate expression of our love and

the quiet burial-place by the village church, dear to him in his later years, where he was gladdened by the vestos of his children, joining in the melodies of the religion never forgotten by him when—and it was often—he had friend to aid, or when, and it was rarely—he had enemy to pardon.

Neither to the mental nor the loving nature of the man whom we are mourning, and shall, while we survive him, mourn, do we attempt to do justice here. We do but inscribe a memorial ribbon which we should unfortunately permit our Journal of this date to lose.

But it is of no avenges that we are speaking to friends known and unknown. For simply thirty years he has guided this periodical; and few who read it know not something of him, and of the few, few devote influence

has had the good fortune to be
reunited with habitual advocacy
of truth and justice, if it has
been probed for abstinence from
the less worthy kind of satire, if
it has been trusted by those who
keep good over the purity of
womanhood and of youth, we,
the best witnesses, have for a
moment done our sorrow to hear
the fullest and the most willing
testimony that the high and
noble spirit of Mark Lemon ever
prompted generous championship, ever made unworthy on-
slaught or irreverent jest impossible to the pens of those
who were honoured in being
contributors with him.

Death has been frequent in our
fellowship :
  Where is A'Beckett's Rabe-
    laisian style ;
  Where Jerrold's wrath 'gainst
    wrong, and lightning quip ;
  Where Thackeray's half-sad,
    half-sunny, smile ;

  Where Leech's facile hand and
    faithful brain,
  The truest, truant, cleverest
    of the then ?
  All memories ! And he that
    linked the chain,
  Now thrown of my chimney
    rhyme !

      * * *

His memory will not die out of
  ours.
  For many a year to come : the
    thoughts of him,
  Erewhile musicians with our
    merriest hours,
  Will be a sad one, till all
    thought grows dim.

MAY 24.

MR. AYRTON made
another contribution
to Art.

"He managed something
which a less skilled practitioner
could hardly have accom-
plished. Ministers have the
most powerful majority that
a Government has possessed
since the days of Pitt ; and Mr.
Ayrton to-night actually contrived to leave Mr. Gladstone's
Administration defeated by a
majority of 1 ½. It was on the
Kensington Road question—the
giving away palmecel some valuable land, and removing fine
trees. The House refused to
sanction a Commission on the
Bill. Of course, attempt will be
made to get the Vote rescinded."

Mr. Ayrton, First Commissioner of Works,
was very unpopular, owing to his brusque and
unceremonious manner and his somewhat osten-
tatious disregard of Art and Science as compared
with economy. Even when in the right in principle, he often contrived to put himself in the

A "SAVAGE" WIGGING.

Captain of Ministerial Team. "Look here, Ayrton! We were beat the other day at Kensington returns through poor wild and rubbing batting. You really must ALTER YOUR FORM, or use You know what I mean!'"

ing, and he thus brought considerable oppo-
brium upon Mr. Gladstone's Administration, and
was at least credited with some considerable
share in its ultimate fate. Punch had some time
previously pictured the Art-consuming Ayrton
as "Our New (B). Edile, closely gripping the
Money-Box, and saying, 'I don't know nothink

Harthites, an' Market Gardeners, an' such like.
My dooty's to take care of the Money!'"

(See Cartoon, "A 'Savage' Wigging.")

MAY 25.

The Committee appointed by Convocation
to revise the Authorised Version of the

MAY 25.

Bands of Fenians made a raid into Canada from the United States, but were routed by the regular troops and Canadian Volunteers. The American Government acted with great promptitude, and the Fenian leader, O'Neill, was on the next day arrested by the United States Marshal.

(See Cartoon, "Kick'd Out!!")

MAY 30.

The Irish Land Bill was read a third time in the Commons.

JUNE 10.

To-day the country was shocked and saddened. In no conventional sense, in no ordinary degree, by the announcement that the popular and well-beloved Charles Dickens, the greatest and most humane humorist of the Victorian Era, had

KICK'D OUT!!

Fenian (President Grant). "Well kick'd, British! Come I'll teach the Shami for yer, this side!"

died suddenly at his country house, Gad's Hill, near Rochester. He was only 58 years of age, but the mental strain of his popular "Readings," together with the shock to his nervous system caused by a railway accident some time previously, had sorely shaken his naturally robust constitution. He was on the 8th, while sitting at dinner, suddenly stricken with paralysis, fell from his chair, became unconscious, and died on the 9th at about the same hour. He had directed that he should be buried in Rochester Churchyard, but the public voice was so

minster Abbey that his friends yielded, and there the great novelist was buried, quietly and without ceremony as he would have desired, on the morning of the 14th June.

THE GRAVE OF CHARLES DICKENS.

He sleeps as he should sleep—among the great
　In the old Abbey : sleeps amid the few
Of England's famous thousands whom high state
　Is to lie with her unreproachable too.

His grave is in this heart of England's heart,
　This shrine within her shrine : and all around
Is no name but in Letters or in Art

Of wars, the rulers lie beside his dust,
　Of arms, but mortals heroes and names are here :
But grave of autograph—remains at least—
　They will find place for thee, their latest peer.*

*The noble urn of plain, but solid oak, and it bore the simple inscription—"Charles Dickens, born February 7, 1812, died June 9, 1870." His grave, which is only between five and six feet long, is formed along a pool, or a rock and a puff, keeps that numbers well of Poet's Corner. On spot was adorned by the Dean from among the few voices appear in that language : and our readers will keep well between that all of Cheesy Dickens that is opened lies at the feet of Handel and of the head of Sheridan, with Richard Cumberland resting on his right hand and Macaulay on his left. It is grave is near the feet of Addison's statue : and Thackeray's head had a subtly drawn upon the grave of his old friend : Dr. Johnson and Garrick lie within a few yards of him : and the busts of Shakespeare, Milton, and a host of other worthies, look at their day, are but a little further off.—

Make room, oh peerful Handel, at thy feet;
Make room, oh witty Sheridan, at thy hand;
Shed, Johnson, all thou here hast grave-space meet;
Garrick, whose art he loved, press to him dead.

Macaulay, many-sided mind, receive
By thine, the frame that housed a mind as keen
To take an impress, or an impress leave,
From things, or on things, read or heard, or seen.

Welcome, oh Addison, with calm, wise face;
His coming, who has peopled English air
With types of humour, tenderness, and grace,
Than which thine own nor has dark soul more rare.

Thou, too, his brother of our time, but had,
Thackeray, bend thy brow with kindly cheer
On him, thy comrade, we've more, tempest-tost,
Who, from life's voyage, come to harbour here.

All the more welcome that he sets his art
Without the pumps that follow great ones' ends—
No mourners save the natural ones that pave
About the father's coffin or the friend's.

Humbly they brought him to the uttermost shore,
Humbly and hopefully they laid him down,
And on the plate that tells where dead, where born,
His children's love, the England's, lays a crown.

"OBSTRUCTIVES."

MR. PUNCH (to BULL A 1). "Yes. It's all very well to say, 'Go to School!' How are they to go to School with these purple guarreling in the doorway? Why don't you make 'em move on?"

JUNE 20.

"EDUCATION-OBSTRUCTION" (says PUNCH's "Essence of Parliament") "was then resumed.

"Mr. Richard, rising from Mr. Bright's seat in old days, but not rising to the level of the argument, as Mr. Bright would have done, placed himself in antagonism to the Government, and moved an Amendment, to the effect that

Grants to the present Denominational Schools should not be increased.

Attendance should be everywhere compulsory.

Religious instruction should be provided by voluntary

"Now, on this tortuous Amendment the House debated this night, and on Tuesday, Thursday, and Friday. But Mr. Punch, having controlled his idea of the whole business in a Cartoon so suggestive and so salutic, that while the simplest mind can comprehend it, the profoundest must admire it, has no intention of wasting typography upon a rehash of the blundered tatter-nesped arguments. Mr. Forster announced that Government had come to the end of their concessions. On those who delayed the Bill should rest the responsibility. Admirable was one of Mr. Forster's sentences, and it said, 'It is one of the poor little children that we are shrinking.' "On the last night, there was some good speaking by Mr. Woodolfe, who asked how spiritual instruction was to be infused unless we withhold it...

charing, from his huge personal knowledge, that the prisoners there was hostile to the exclusion of religion; Mr. Walter confessed that tendency, and believed the Bill a wise one, beyond (ironite) : Mr. Harcourt galloped over everybody, but himself came a sound cropper, and Mr. Gladstone finished with a fine and vigorous answer to all antagonists—the result being that the function went out only for, and the united Conservatives and Liberals 421. Mr. Richard's defeat is a comfort for so much magnanimism as Mr. Punch can offer on this subject, while disputants blurb the child's way to school."

(See Cartoon, "Obstructives.")

"Upon the coffin was a square of green baize, and white roses.

JUNE 25.

QUEEN ISABELLA OF SPAIN formally abdicated the throne of that kingdom in favour of her son the Prince of Asturias.

JUNE 27.

THE EARL OF CLARENDON Minister for Foreign Affairs in the present Government, died suddenly, at the age of 70 years. He was succeeded at the Foreign Office by Lord Granville, the Earl of Kimberley becoming Colonial Secretary, Viscount Halifax (formerly Sir Charles Wood) joining the Government as Lord Privy Seal. Mr. Forster's services in the conduct of the Education Bill were recognised by his admission to the Cabinet, he retaining the office of Vice President of the Council.

On the 29th Mr. G. O. Trevelyan resigned his post as one of the Lords of the Admiralty, on the grounds of his inability to vote for the increased grant to denominational schools.

JULY 5.

THE day Lord Granville commenced his duties as Foreign Secretary" (says the Introduction to Vol. LIX.) "he was told by the Permanent Under-Secretary of State that in all his experience he had never known so great a lull in foreign affairs." It was the lull before the storm—before the outburst of the terrible war between France and Prussia.

On the 30th June, M. Ollivier, replying to a question of M. Jules Favre, had said, "At no epoch was the peace of Europe more assured." Nevertheless the great war was on the verge of breaking out.

"Its origin" (says Introduction) "cannot be better told than in the words of the Annual Register :—

"In the beginning of July, an announcement was made by the Spanish Ministers of their intention to recommend Prince Leopold of Hohenzollern-Sigmaringen, a German Prince belonging to a branch of the House widely

A DUEL TO THE DEATH.

FRANCE. "Pray stand back, Madam. You mean well; but this is an old Family Quarrel, and we must FIGHT IT OUT!"

long vacant throne of Spain. . . . Still, no doubt, the King of Prussia was the chef de famille, and the electoral sway served as the ground of a quarrel which just then, for political and dynastic reasons, the governing party in France found it convenient to take up. Ever since the German War of 1866, France, it was well known, had existed in mortal jealousy of Prussian aggrandisement. Foresight and opportunity fixing, met with so formidable a rival in the leadership of continental four years to a considerable section of the French public ; and to this, the Emperor's personal dislike for his dynasty, after the late plebiscitum had revealed a certain amount of dissatisfaction in his army to the Imperial rule ; and it seemed as desirable as it was not difficult to light the flame of public excitement with suggestions of Bonapartism intrigues, and of design on the part of the Prussian monarch to plant a subservient relative on the southern frontier of France."

France complained to Prussia of Prince Leopold's candidature. Prussia said it was no concern of her government. The Duc de Gramont, French Minister for Foreign Affairs, said that France would use her whole strength to prevent the election. Lord Granville directed our Minister at Berlin, Lord A. Loftus, to

appeal to "the wise and disinterested magnanimity" of the King not to support Prince Leopold's candidature, as it would be certain to disturb the peace of Europe. The Duc de Gramont, whilst disavowing any desire to interfere in the internal affairs of Spain, said, "We do not believe that respect for the rights of a

neighbouring people obliges us to suffer a foreign Power, by placing a Prince upon the throne of Charles V., to disturb the European equilibrium to our disadvantage, and thus to imperil the interests and honour of France. M. Benedetti, French Ambassador to the North German Confederation, vainly endeavoured to induce the

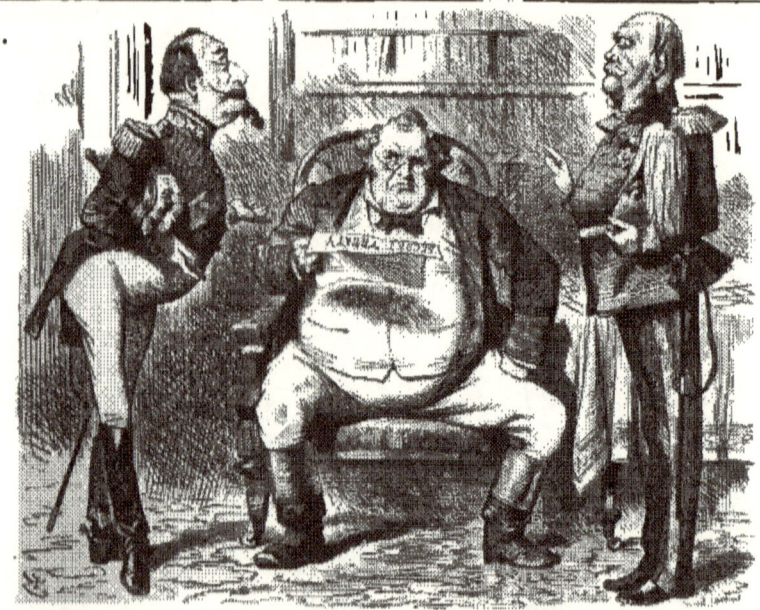

"SIX OF ONE AND HALF-A-DOZEN OF THE OTHER."

JOHN BULL. "'Pon my word, you're a nice couple!"

FRANCE. "Bigum! Mon cher! It is nothing! If I'd wanted Belgium, why have I not taken it any time these four years?"

PRUSSIA. "Mein lieber Johann! You cannot believe that I—a so reputable, so religious friend—connected by marriage also! You cannot believe it!"

King of Prussia to forbid Prince Leopold's acceptance of the Spanish Crown. "Beyond giving his personal sanction as head of the Hohenzollern family, the King said he had no hand in the candidature, and he declined to interfere for its withdrawal. Prince Leopold decided on resigning, but it was too late; public feeling in France was too strong to allow of an accommodation. Both countries prepared for war.

was preparing for war. On the 17th Declaration of War was signed by France.

JULY 21.

MR. GLADSTONE stated that both France and Prussia had given satisfactory assurance of their desire to respect the neutrality of Belgium, Holland, and Luxembourg, assuming that they were able to defend each their own

either belligerents. The Times, however (on the 25th), startled the country with the text of a "Projet de Traité," asserted to have been proposed in 1866 by France to Prussia, by virtue of which France was to recognise the conquests of Prussia, whilst Prussia was to help France to acquire Belgium and Luxembourg.

[See Cartoon, "Six of One and Half-a-Dozen of the Other!"]

JULY 22.

THE Education Bill was read a third time and passed in the Commons.

JULY 23.

WHAT was regarded as the first decisive act of the War took place to-day, the Prussians blowing up the abutment on the Baden shore of the Kehl bridge.

JULY 23.

IN an Imperial Proclamation issued to-day the Emperor of the French charged Germany with having provoked the war, which France entered upon because she wished "to conquer a lasting peace based on the true interests of all peoples." He said, "I am about to place myself at the head of that valiant army which is animated by love of duty and of country. . . . . I take with me my son despite his youth. He knows what are the duties which his name imposes upon him, and he is proud to bear his share in the dangers of those who fight for their country."

Punch had a striking Cartoon entitled "A Vision on the Way," representing the shade of the first Napoleon confronting the Emperor and his son on the war path, and bidding them "Beware!"

THE WARNING BY THE
WAY.

. . . . .

Hard not to call up the shadow of the Uncle, grim and grey, With a hand upraised in warning across the Nephew's way! With eyes that look their lesson, lips that were without a word— How they shot down the sword to smite shall perish by the sword.

TWO MOTHERS.

FRANCE (to the BAVARIAN). "AH, Madame, a mite happiness for both, sooner or later, but there comes dark news of WHILE, taken I shall never see again."

"We addressed the Emperor himself, and provisionally ask him to send back the Prince Imperial to Paris. The presence of the young Prince at the camp is useless. He has been wounded. It is time for him to return to his mother."—Le Libéral, Aug. 7.

JULY 27.

Was Empress Eugénie was appointed Regent during the absence of the Emperor at the seat of war. On the 19th the Emperor, accompanied by the Prince Imperial, left St. Cloud for Metz, where, from the Imperial head-quarters, he issued a proclamation to the army, of which on the 29th he assumed the chief command. The King of Prussia established his head-quarters near Mayence. The two armies by the end of July had concentrated in force along the Rhine frontier. It was estimated that the French were from 250,000 to 350,000 strong, the Germans about 420,000. The campaign on Prussia's side was directed by General Von Moltke, the King of Prussia assuming chief command, and the several divisions being led by General Von Steinmetz, Prince Frederick Charles, and the Crown Prince.

AUG. 1.

"Our House of Lords" (said Punch's "Essence of Parliament") "passed the Irish Land Bill—the second 'Message o' Peace' to Ireland. It is a rather complicated message, and it has been a good deal confused by after-thoughts on the part of the senders, but it is well meant, and, it will, we hope, be accepted in the spirit in which it is forwarded."

AUG. 1.

A debate took place in the Commons on the action of the Government with regard to the war.

"TRUST ME!"

ENGLAND. "All as hope that they won't trouble me, dear friend. BUT IF THEY DO——"

"IS MY POWDER DRY?"

(Emphatically Dedicated to
Mr. CARDWELL.)

Air—"*Coming Through the Rye.*"

Is my powder dry, Cardwell,
  Is my powder dry?
If it isn't, will you let me
  Know the reason why?
With my Army estimates
  At their figure high,
'Tis a shame John Bull must ask
  you
  If his powder's dry?

*   *   *

Don't, in flattery, call a battery,
  What is half a one!
Count to mounted, troops dis-
  mounted,
And I shall feel "done!"
Then is my powder dry, Cardwell,
  Is my powder dry?
For if it's not, *I* pay the shot,
  And I *will* know why!

AUG. 2.

SAARBRÜCK shelled and taken by the French. The Emperor telegraphed to the Empress, "Louis has just received his baptism of fire. He showed admirable coolness, and was not at all affected. . . . . Louis has kept a bullet which fell quite close to him."

On the 4th the first serious engagement between the two armies took place at Weissenburg, the Crown Prince attacking that portion of M'Mahon's corps commanded by General Abel Douay, which was defeated and dispersed. Thus the first important victory of the war fell to the Prussians.

On the 6th the Crown Prince followed up this victory by attacking and defeating the united corps d'armée of Generals M'Mahon, Failly, and Canrobert at Woerth. The King of Prussia telegraphed to Berlin, "Wonderful good fortune! This new great victory won by Fritz. Thank God for His mercy! We have taken 30 cannons, 2 eagles, 6 mitrailleurs, 4,000 prisoners."

On the same day the French were defeated between Saarbrück and Forbach, the Prussians storming the heights of Spicheren, and Frossard being driven back upon Forbach.

Great excitement was caused in Paris by this

the fact that false rumours of brilliant French victories had been spread. The Ministry had to issue a proclamation urging the people to be calm, patient, and orderly.

AUG. 7.

PARIS was declared in a state of siege. The

vague, but sufficient to indicate, as the Empress said in a proclamation issued at midday from the Tuileries, that "the opening of the war has not been in our favour." "Our arms have suffered a check," she added. "Let us be firm under this reverse, and let us hasten to repair it."

PARIS, 1870.

"*THE CRY IS STILL, THEY COME!*"

AUG. 9.

FALL of the French Ministry. It was obvious, as the *Times* said, that the Emperor was never likely to re-appear at the head of affairs. M. Jules Simon, in the course of his speech, said that the Emperor had shewn his incapacity and ought to return to Paris, and that it was necessary that the army should have another chief.

AUG. 10.

PARLIAMENT was prorogued by Commission.

AUG. 10.

STRASBOURG was invested by the Prussians. It had a garrison of 11,000 men, and General Ulrich resolved to defend it. But the French army was beaten and in retreat. On the 14th the French were defeated at Courcelles, and the Emperor's troops driven into Metz. On the 15th the Emperor with his son left Metz for Verdun, and Bazaine withdrew the remains of his army, leaving Metz to its garrison under General Coffinières. On the 17th General Trochu was appointed Governor of Paris, preparations being made for its defense. Bazaine was at Gravelotte with from 110,000 to 130,000 men. On the 18th he was attacked by the Prussians, defeated, cut off from his communications with Paris, and driven back towards Metz. Very soon Metz was completely isolated. On the 30th the army under Marshal M'Mahon was defeated with great loss, and driven back towards the Belgian frontier.

SEPT. 1.

MONDAY began a series of desperate fights around Sedan. The French again and again endeavoured to break through the circle which had been drawn around them by the skill of Von Moltke, but in vain. They were driven

THE DUEL DECIDED.

THE KING. "You have fought gallantly, Sir. May I not hear you say you HAVE ENOUGH?"
THE EMPEROR. "I have been destined about my strength. I have no choice."   [end September, 1870.

city. The town was bombarded. Col. Von Bronsart with a flag of truce demanded the surrender of the army and the fortress. The Emperor in person received him, and referred him to General de Wimpffen. On the 2nd Sedan capitulated, the Emperor surrendering himself to the King of Prussia, whilst the

down their arms. The Emperor, in his conversation with the King of Prussia, declared that he had not desired war, but had been obliged to declare it in obedience to the public opinion of France. The vanquished Emperor was lodged under guard at Wilhelmshöhe.

SEPT. 4.

TO-DAY a revolution broke out in Paris. The Emperor was formally deposed, a Provisional Government of National Defence established under the Presidency of General Trochu, with Gambetta, Jules Favre, and Jules Ferry among its leading members. On the 5th the Republic was officially proclaimed.

(See Cartoon, " France, Sept. 4, 1870.")

EXIT IMPERATOR!

ANOTHER turn of Fortune's wheel,   [how :
That lifts so high, then lays so
Of Life's strange cards another
deal,
Of Destiny's dark dice a throw :
But turn to deal or cast,
Mrthinks, the low !

⁎   ⁎   ⁎   ⁎

That pale and sorrow-stricken
lad,
Too poet baptised with tears
and fire,
Why make his sad young life
more sad?   [this ?
Why in some cover and steal
For love, though it be pain,
L·t him remain.

⁎   ⁎   ⁎   ⁎

Dare not the workman shape his
stock,
Or choose the tools his work
that fit !
While his task needed knave
and fool,
The knaves and fools were
there for it.
But hard was put him out,
And them, no doubt.

Was he the counter Hugo sang?
All dead in him that had stir!
he—
Cavourths, his humble thorp
among,
Who counts blood-gates in
urgie sly,
Jovi : Neupia, Grand Mo-
narque Manice,—
Won't tear or fals ?

Coricarow—how large soe'er
The outline, masterly the hand ;
Strong colour, yes ; here's been
may glaze,
But truth's other lights are
weak to stand,
And this was not the sum
Of Hugo's plan.

Mixed warp and woof in him, as all :
And in this miserable hour,
Soft thoughts come up as breath his fall
So low, from such a height of power,
In Man and Emperor both
Some good found growth.

FRANCE, SEPT. 4, 1870.

" Aux armes, citoyens,
Formez vos bataillons !"—The "Marseillaise."

Maybe, the clear air he ne'er drew,
That comes up with Truth's radiant morn.
Right and wrong fought in him
A battle dim.

But wrong not always conquered, nor
Then right could always wrong defeat :

The false man Hugo drew
To us was true.

But not for pity can we turn
To wish him up out of the dust :
France has done well able to spare
The patriot stay she started to trust.
When the time's need proves weak,

Let those in France that scorned
his aid,
Left comrades to haunt him love
shade,
Nor those whose swift steps vied
for me,
With smiles how far his foot-
stead laid ;
But those who would not
love,
Should buffet now !

If of ruined metal be true wrought,
France, that sheyed him, what
is she ?
After he smoth, her vows he
caught ;
Twice in his yoke she bowed
the knee.
But Paris held aloof—
Lo now, the Proud !

A bas ! with whom, but with
L'Empereur.
Vive ! whm ? What but la
République.
A day—an hour ! La joie doit
foyer,
Should, though it be with
tongue in cheek !
What was up is pulled
down—
Smash Row and Crown !

Whirl, Paris, round from pole
to pole ;
Kiss, curse, laugh, cry, rave,
dance and sing.
Forget the Prussians and their
goal ;
Give Revolution strong and
swing ;
Up with Left ! Down with
Right !
To-morrow fight.

As yesterday to-run to-day—
Swift change, light mood, and
whirling will ;
Abiding never in one stay,
And still be-fooled, and prost-
ing still ;
While the foe at thy gate
harkens swift and strught.

SEPT. 7.

FOUNDERING, off Cape
Finisterre, of the
turret-ship "Captain," with
Captain Burgoyne and
nearly the whole crew, 500
souls in all.

SEPT. 8.

THE KING OF ITALY in-
formed the Pope that
he felt compelled to "as-
sume the responsibility of
maintaining order in the
security of the Holy See." With this view he
resolved to send an army into the Pontifical
States. The Pope protested, and invoked the aid
of the King of Prussia, who declined to interfere,
as not being prepared "to imperil the relations
which exist between Germany and Italy."

ITALY IN ROME.

PAPA PIO (to KING OF ITALY). "I need must surrender the Sword, by me; but I KEEP THE KEYS !"

troops to enter the Papal territory, which they
did on the 20th after a brief resistance from the
Pope's soldiers, soon arrested by His Holiness.
The Pope had to surrender his temporal power,
and "Italy" remained in Rome, which became
the capital of the kingdom.

(The Cannon Match in Rome ?)

SEPT. 9.

THE EMPRESS OF THE FRENCH landed in this
country at Ryde. The Prince Imperial had
already taken refuge here. They took up their
residence at Camden House, Chislehurst.

SEPT. 18.

M. JULES FAVRE held a consultation with Count Bismarck as to the terms of an armistice, but without result, the Chancellor demanding the surrender of Strasburg, Toul, and Verdun, as a preliminary condition of suspension of hostilities, and intimating Prussia's resolve to annex Alsace and Lorraine as far as Metz; terms which France indignantly rejected.

SEPT. 20.

To-day the Crown Prince entered Versailles, and the armies of Prussia began to close around Paris. On the 21st they occupied Melun, on the 23rd Toul surrendered. Count Bismarck was evidently resolved upon exacting to the full the terms of his victories. "It is idle to hope to propitiate France," he was reported to have said. "She will never forgive us for beating her; she will never forgive Sedan. She must therefore be made harmless. We must have Strasburg, and we must have Metz, even if in the latter case we hold merely the garrison, and whatever else is necessary to improve our strategic position against attack from her." Without wishing to discuss to France her form of government, he declined to recognise the action of "the gentlemen of the pavements," as legally superseding the rule of the Emperor.

There was much talk in this country and elsewhere of mediation between the belligerents, in view of the horrors which seemed imminent, but opinion was too divided to admit of decisive action.

SEPT. 28.

STRASBURG surrendered unconditionally, after being reduced almost to starvation. Seventeen thousand men, four hundred officers, 1,100 cannon, 12,000 chassepots, and 6,000 cwt. of ammunition fell into the hands of the Prussians.

VERSAILLES, OCT. 5, 1870.

"The Royal Head-quarters were transferred here to-day."—*Telegram.*

GHOST OF LOUIS THE FOURTEENTH to GHOST OF NAPOLEON THE FIRST. "Is this the end of 'ALL THE GLORIES'?"

all Frenchmen between 21 and 40 to be organised into a Mobilised National Guard.

OCT. 5.

To-day it was announced that the German Royal head-quarters would be removed from Ferrières to Versailles.

OCT. 7.

M. GAMBETTA, leaving Paris in the balloon "Armand-Barbès," passed safely over the Prussian lines and reached Rouen, on a mission from the National Defence Committee in Paris to the Government at Tours. He is-

OCT. 9.

GARIBALDI, who had arrived in France with the generous object of rendering her aid in her extremity, was to-day received by the Government at Tours, and appointed commander of the volunteers.

OCT. 27.

GENERAL BAZAINE with 150,000 troops surrendered Metz to the Germans. The scene of this colossal surrender was a pitiable one, the French troops being described by the *Daily News* correspondent as "demoralised by drink and destitution to an extent which made order or obedience out of the question." "The cavalry seemed to have lost all self-respect; they greeted the Prussians with cheering, and several men broke from the ranks and slunged forward through the mud with the intent to salute with a quietness kiss the Prussian officers standing in front of their Companies."

Bazaine was charged with betrayal of his country in this abject surrender.

On the 31st M. Gambetta issued a proclamation to the army, telling it it had been betrayed by folly and treason, and urging it, under leaders deserving its confidence, to advance and avenge the honour of France, the treason of Sedan and the crime of Metz.

[*See Cartoon, "The 'Niobe of Nations.'"*]

OCT. 31.

TO-DAY insurrection broke out in the beleaguered city of Paris. A Committee of Public Safety and of the Commune of Paris was formed, and the members of the Government were for a time imprisoned in the Hôtel de Ville. The National Guard, however, released General Trochu and his colleagues, dispersed the rioters, and for the time restored order.

the intention of the Emperors be no longer bound by the Treaty of 1856, especially as regarded restriction of his rights of sovereignty in the Black Sea.

NOV. 8.

on the question of supplies, and M. Favre declared later that an armistice without revictualling would have been "equivalent to a capitulation without honour and without hope."

THE "NIOBE OF NATIONS."

on behalf of England to
sanction Russia's right to release herself from a solemn
covenant without consultation with and the consent
of the co-signatory Powers.
He at the same time ex-
pressed the readiness of
Her Majesty's Government
to examine any question
properly raised concerning
any proposed modification
of the Treaty in concert
with the co-signatories
thereto. Prince Gort-
schakoff in response re-
asserted his "august
master's" unchanged reso-
lution. On the 16th No-
vember Count Bismarck
invited the Courts of Vienna,
Constantinople, Florence,
and St. Petersburg to convene in London a Confer-
ence of the Signatory
Powers to the Treaty of
1856. This invitation Earl
Granville accepted upon
the understanding that it
assembled "without any
foregone conclusion as to
its results."

Nov. 28.

GENERAL TROCHU con-
ducted an attack on
the Prussian lines around
Paris, but without success,
the French sorties being
repulsed with heavy loss.
Another great sortie on the
30th was also entirely
driven back.

Dec. 15.

FIRST meeting of the
London School Board.
Mr. Charles Reed was
elected Chairman.

Dec. 20.

MR. JOHN BRIGHT, in
consequence of im-
paired health, retired from
the office of President of
the Board of Trade, and was succeeded by Mr.
Chichester Fortescue.

Dec. 27.

THE Germans opened the bombardment of
Paris by an attack on Mont Avron, which

GERMANY'S ALLY.

Dec. 30.

THE year ended with great distress and
scarcity of food in Paris, the prices given
for ordinary dietary being most extravagant,
whilst horse-flesh, cats, dogs, and even rats were
utilised as articles of food by the starving
residents.

Up to the end of the year the subscriptions
to the National Society in aid of the sick
and wounded French and German soldiers
amounted to £189,674. It had been started
under the patronage of the Queen, in the previous August.

+ 1871 +

Jᴀɴ. 1.

Aᴛ the New Year's Reception at Versailles, the Grand Duke of Baden, on behalf of the other German Princes, whom the King of Prussia had warmly thanked in his speech, spoke of the union of Germany as now happily achieved; he said, "We regard your Majesty as the supreme head of the German Empire, the crown of which is a guarantee of irrevocable unity," and proposed a toast to "King William the Victorious."

Meanwhile the bombardment of devoted Paris was ruthlessly proceeding, and the city was suffering all the horrors of siege, famine, and civic dissension.

Jᴀɴ. 2.

Tʜᴇ question of Army Reform and Reorganization was much debated in this country during the early days of the year. On this day Mr. Cardwell, Secretary for War, who

AFLOAT AND ASHORE.

Nᴇᴘᴛᴜɴᴇ. "I've made all safe outside, Ma'am." Mᴀʀs. "There, and made all safe inside!"

was preparing his Army Regulation Bill, addressing his Oxford constituents, defended the Government with reference to the enlistment of recruits, the supply of arms, the manufacture of powder, &c.

[*See Cartoon, "Afloat and Ashore."*]

Jᴀɴ. 17.

Fɪʀsᴛ meeting of the Black Sea Conference. A special protocol was signed recognising the engagements of a treaty, nor modify the stipulations thereof, unless with the consent of the contracting Powers by means of an amicable arrangement.

Jᴀɴ. 18.

Tᴏ-ᴅᴀʏ, in the Hall of Mirrors at Versailles, surrounded by all the German Princes, King William of Prussia with much stately ceremony was proclaimed Emperor of Germany. Count Bismarck read a proclamation announcing with the re-establishment of the German Empire, to accept the dignity of Emperor, which had been in abeyance for sixty years, he, King William, regarded it as a duty he owed to the entire Fatherland to comply with this call. The German Princes then paid homage to the newly elected Emperor as "deutsche Kaiser."

On the 14th Count Bismarck was announced as Chancellor of the German Empire.

Jᴀɴ. 25.

could hardly reply to the enemy's fire. Hunger was almost universal, the death-rate continually rising. There were serious riots, organised by the " Reds," only suppressed from time to time by the National Guards with difficulty, and considerable loss of life. M. Jules Favre had repaired to Versailles with proposals for a capitulation on conditions of the garrison being allowed to march out with the honours of war. On the 29th the *Times* announced somewhat prematurely that Paris had fallen.

(*See Cartoon, "Her Baptism of Fire."*)

HER BAPTISM OF FIRE.

HER "BAPTISM OF FIRE."

And the warmth in her blood
adding famine to kill,
The winter Frost creeps with
its death-dealing chill.

And at last with the Famine and
Frost has come Fire,
On that hand, stern as thirsty,
its leaps out to pour,
Till her crown of proud towers
topples down in the mire,
And death-smoke are shred
through the crash and the
roar.
Is't despair or defiance then
nerves her to stand,
Though shimmed hilt-high is
the sword in her hand?

Hela her hold her bent brows still
confronting the Foun,
Whose hot hungry tongue licks
her beautiful hair,
As War as fere she would purge
sin and shame,
Draw strength from starvation,
defiance from despair,
Till we ask in amazement
and awe—Can it be?
Is this Dalilah, Queen of
Earth's Wonders, we see?

Is this Athaars, abandt, stricken,
combed, but still proud,
And so staunch in hard steel,
the self-sin-echoed dame,
That with some of her witch-
craft made drunken the
crowd,
Till from men they waved
hosans, and thereof had sore
shame?
Can War's fire so wicked-
ness, wantonnes slay,
That her foul feud shall grow fair,
and her dross through wrong?

JAN. 28.

PARIS surrendered after
a siege of 131 days.

"The inhabitants of Paris
(says Mr. Punch's Introduction
to Vol. LX.), brought down by
famine, sickness and death, their
armies defeated in the field, and
unable to march to the relief of
the capital, and all sorties from
the city proving unsuccessful,
entered into negotiations with
the Germans for a capitulation.
An armistice was concluded for
three weeks, and Paris was at
once provisioned, England un-
grudging towards the supplies
passed in for the relief of the
starving population. Gambetta,
fiercely opposing the negotiations for peace, resigned office
as Minister."

The German Emperor's message to Queen
Augusta said:—

"The troops of the line and the Mobiles will be
increased in Paris on prisoners of war. The Garde
Nationale Sédentaire undertakes the preservation of
order. We occupy all forts. Paris remains invested.
It will be allowed to revictual in soon as the armistice has
been delivered on. The National Assembly will be

EXCESSIVE BAIL.

JUSTICE (to Bismarck). "You should not surrender, and you ask that the defendant 'shall be bound over to keep the peace for seventy years.' But I cannot sanction a demand for exorbitant securities."

armies in the field retain possession of the respective
tracts of country occupied by them, with intervening room
intervening."

The desperate straits to which the doomed
city was reduced before capitulating may be
imagined from the fact that meat other than
horseflesh was absolutely not to be procured.

40 francs a pound, potatoes a francs a pound,
and wretched shrivelled cabbages a francs each.

Negotiations for peace were entered into. It
was pretty generally thought that the terms
demanded by the Germans were harsh and excessive, especially as regarded the amount of the
indemnity.

JAN. 31.

M. GAMBETTA issued from Bordeaux a proclamation in favour of carrying on war at any cost, even to complete exhaustion. The action of the indomitable defier of Germany in this matter, as also in a decree which he was instrumental in publishing, disqualifying certain persons for election to the National Assembly, was denounced by Count Bismarck, and repudiated by M. Jules Favre and his colleagues in Paris. M. Gambetta on the 6th Feb. resigned his post as Minister of the Interior in the Delegate Government of Bordeaux, as being no longer in sympathy with its ideas or hopes.

FEB. 3.

HER first provision train reached Paris on this day. England took a leading part in forwarding food supplies, and M. Jules Favre, telegraphing on the 7th to the Lord Mayor of London, President of the Paris Relief Fund, said, "I have taken charge of the first part of this magnificent and fraternal gift. The City of Paris expresses to the City of London its profound gratitude. In the extremity of its misfortunes the voice of the English people has been the first that has been heard by it from outside with an expression of sympathy."

(*See Cartoon, "The 'Bœuf Gras' for Paris, 1871."*)

FEB. 8.

ELECTIONS for the National Assembly commenced to meet at Bordeaux took place this day throughout France. M. Thiers was returned for the greatest number of seats, and secured the largest number of votes.

FEB. 9.

PARLIAMENT was opened by the Queen in person.

THE "BŒUF GRAS" FOR PARIS. 1871.

every becoming reference to the War between Germany and France, and to a hope that the Armistice would result in a complete Accommodation.

King William has become Emperor of Germany, and we have congratulated him.

We uphold the Neutrality of Prussia. And hence the Black Sea Conference. We regret that France is not present.

A Joint Commission is to endeavour to arrange the American questions.

We have failed in obtaining satisfaction for the Greek murders, but shall persevere.

The anxiety caused by the Chinese murders has ceased. We hope that Parliament will allow China to be treated in a conciliatory meeting.

We are friends with the Sovereigns and States of the civilised world.

"I have assurances of a murderer but trust we deserve

Revenue flourishes, as show Trade, with partial drawbacks. Then came what *Mr. Punch* and the Nation chiefly desired to hear:—

THIS IS THE TIME TO TURN TO ACCOUNT, BY DECISIVE EFFORT, THE LESSONS OF THE WAR. PARLIAMENT WILL NOT GRUDGE THE COST OF A MORE EFFECTIVE AND ELASTIC SYSTEM OF DEFENSIVE MILITARY PREPARATION.

Notwithstanding the interest attaching to foreign affairs, we must attend to Domestic Legislation, and specially to these points:—

1. Abolition of Religious Tests in all the Universities.
2. Ecclesiastical Titles.
3. Disabilities of Tenant Union.
4. Courts of Justice and Appeal.
5. Adjustment of Local Burdens.
6. Liquor Licence Laws.

Government will introduce a Ballot Bill.

Scotland expects a measure on Primary Education.

Ireland, in regard to agrarian outrage, behaves better than she did last winter, but there have have painful enterprises. A period of political calm is desirable for her, after the great measures of last year, so no Irish question is to be raised.

FEB. 9.

A JOINT Commission for settling outstanding disputes between Great Britain and the United States, including the "Alabama" claims, and the Fishery disputes, was announced to meet at Washington.

FEB. 12.

FIRST meeting of the National Assembly at Bordeaux. On the 17th M. Thiers was appointed Head of the Executive Power, and M. Grévy President of the Assembly.

FEB. 17.

MR. CARDWELL, in introducing the Army Estimates, explained the Army Regulations Bill, being the Government scheme for the Reorganisation of the Army, "the object of which was to combine in one harmonious whole all the branches of our military forces." The purchase of Commissions was to be abolished, and the control of the auxiliary forces, the Lords-Lieutenants of Counties to the Crown. Compensation caused by the Abolition of Purchase was estimated to amount to eight millions. The united army of the country, including Regulars, Militia, Yeomanry, two Reserves, and Volunteers, it was estimated would amount to 670,717 men.

"ATTENTION"

MARS. "Look here, CARDWELL. You say YOU can keep things up to the mark? Mind you do, or, by Jingo! I shall advise Her Majesty to sack you both."

FEB. 20.

MR. FORSTER introduced the Ballot Bill securing secret voting at Parliamentary Elections. Public Nominations and Declarations of Poll to be abolished, and the use of public houses as Committee-rooms prohibited.

FEB. 26.

A Treaty of Peace between Germany and France was this day concluded at Versailles. France had to cede Alsace and Lorraine (including Metz) to Germany, and pay a war indemnity of five milliards of francs (£200,000,000).

MARCH 1.

Thirty thousand German troops to-day made triumphal entry into Paris. They remained there three days only. On Prince Bismarck receiving from M. Jules Favre official assurance of the ratification of the Treaty by the Assembly at Bordeaux, the Germans began to leave Paris on their march homeward, and on the 7th the Prussian head-quarters at Versailles broke up, and the Crown Prince of Saxony was left in command of the army which was to occupy France until the completion of the payment of the indemnity.

MARCH 13.

The Black Sea Conference came to an end. It resulted in an agreement to abrogate the restrictions complained of by Russia, and permit the Porte "to receive ships of war of friendly and allied Powers in case the Porte should deem it necessary to do so in order to insure the execution of the stipulations of the Treaty of Paris."

MARCH 18.

To-day, after many premonitory symptoms of revolt, the extreme Red Republicans—discontented with the preliminaries of Peace, the entry of the Prussians into Paris, and the policy of the Government and the National Assembly—broke into open revolution. The Government issued a proclamation declaring its intention to remove public tranquillity, and with this end in view despatched strong bodies of troops, under Generals Vinoy and Lecomte, in the direction of Montmartre to seize the cannon

NATIONAL (BLACK) GUARDS

PARIS. "Murder! Thieves! Help!!"

there and return them to the arsenals. The insurgents, aided by disaffected National Guards, threw up barricades, shot Generals Lecomte and Clement Thomas, induced many of the troops to fraternise with them, took possession of the Hôtel de Ville, the Ministère de Justice, and the military head-quarters in the Place Vendôme, and issued a proclamation, signed by "The Central Committee of the National Guards," calling upon the citizens to resist "the attempts made to impose upon them by force an impossible calm;" and to meet "in their comitia for the communal elections." Paris was in the hands of the Red Republic.

(See Cartoon, "National (Black) Guard.")

MARCH 20.

The Emperor Napoleon arrived in this country, and took up his residence at Chislehurst. On the same day the French Assembly met at Versailles for the first time.

MARCH 21.

To-day the Princess Louise, daughter of the Queen, was married in St. George's Chapel, Windsor, to the Marquis of Lorne, son of the Duke of Argyll.

(See Cartoon, " Over the Ring-fence.")

MARCH 22.

On the occasion of the celebration at Berlin of the Emperor William's 75th birthday, Count Bismarck was created a Prince, and Count Moltke presented with the Order of the Iron Cross.

MARCH 26.

The elections to " The Communal Council of Paris " took place, resulting in a vote of about 140,000 for the men on the lists of the Central Committee, and 60,000 for their opponents. The Committee then dissolved itself, but a few of its leading members formed themselves into a " Sub-Committee."

On the 28th the Commune was proclaimed in front of the Hôtel de Ville. The Red Flag now flew on all public buildings.

On the National Assembly, now at Versailles, headed by M. Thiers, devolved (says *Punch's* Introduction to Vol. LX.), " the terrible task of reducing the capital to submission." Marshal McMahon assumed the command of the Assembly's troops, and the second siege of Paris, conducted this time " by Frenchmen against Frenchmen," commenced.

On the 2nd April an engagement between the troops of Versailles and the Commune took place at Courbevoie. The insurgents were defeated, and M. Thiers issued a manifesto declaring

OVER THE RING-FENCE.

pacified, and that the Commune was already divided, in a doubtful position, and a horror to the Parisians, " who wait with impatience the moment of their deliverance." "The National Assembly, rallying round the Government, is sitting peaceably at Versailles, where it is organising one of the finest armies which France

APRIL 3.

To-day Mr. Bruce, the Home Secretary, introduced a Licensing Bill. The principles it embodied he said were two:—1. That the public have a right to a sufficient number of respectably conducted houses. 2. That all

The Bill proposed to divide the country into districts, and give to the magistrates of each district the right to decide how many public-houses it wants, and to advertise how many licences they will in consequence have. It also regulated the hours of opening and closing in town and country, and imposed punishments for drunkenness and for adulteration.

The Bill was of course opposed by vested interests and the vicious.

(*See Cartoon, " Two Drops of Comfort."*)

On the same day Mr. Goschen, First Lord of the Admiralty at the time, introduced his Bills on the subject of Local Rating and Local Government, designed to popularise local institutions, to provide a uniform system of local government throughout England and Wales (the metropolis excepted) and to secure uniformity of rating. Local expenditure was said to amount to £36,000,000 per annum. The Government proposed to surrender the House Tax (£1,100,000) in aid of Local Rates.

These Bills had to be abandoned later in the session.

APRIL 3.

TO-DAY the eighth decennial Census was taken throughout the United Kingdom.

APRIL 20.

MR. LOWE introduced the Budget. There was a deficiency of £2,713,000. To make it up he proposed to raise the Income Tax from £1 13s. 4d. in the £100, to £1 4s.; to alter the Probate, Legacy and Succession Duty, and to impose a tax on Lucifer Matches, every box of 100 common matches to bear a halfpenny stamp, and every box of 100 wax matches or fusees a penny stamp. He proposed to print the motto " *Ex luce lucellum*," (a small gain out of light) on the box-label, and bound to

realise £550,000 by this tax. This latter proposition after long debate and much chaff was—for the moment—agreed to by the House. But the match-makers protested vehemently, mustered in large numbers at the East-end of London, and marched through the City to Westminster to present petitions against the Match Tax, which Mr. Lowe had to abandon on the 25th

" on account of the dissatisfaction it had excited." The Budget indeed was not a success, the Probate and Succession Duties had also to be abandoned later, " and all the financial schemes of the Chancellor of the Exchequer ended in the simple addition of twopence in the pound to the Queen's Tax, to be levied as before."— (*Punch's Introduction.*)

TWO DROPS OF COMFORT.

PUBLICAN. "'*Pon my word! Things is coming to a pretty pass!*"

CADGER. " *Lor' bless yer, Guv'ner, you won't no call to be afraid. Why, Mr. Bruce he tried to reform the Cads! Well! Ere we are!—here we are!—No better, an' no wuss!!*"

MAY 1.

The new International Exhibition, Royal Albert Hall, was opened this day by the Prince of Wales.

MAY 11.

The great Tichborne Trial, which in one way and another lasted during nearly two years, came on to-day in the Court of Common Pleas before Lord Chief Justice Bovill.

MAY 16.

The Commune, which had day by day increased in violence, disorder and administrative ineptitude, this day carried out its purpose of destroying the Vendôme Column, erected by Napoleon I. chiefly from cannon taken at Ulm, to commemorate the victory of Austerlitz in 1805.

The state of Paris, beleaguered by the troops of the National Assembly, and maddened by the furious folly of the Commune, was now pitiable in the extreme. Among the Communist leaders themselves there was dissension. Their defence of the city against the Assembly's troops was ineffective, though the cause of much bloodshed. They seized the property of M. Thiers, they menaced the life of Monseigneur Darboy, Archbishop of Paris, and others whom they held as "hostages;" they "requisitioned" £80,000 from five railway companies within 48 hours, they suppressed newspapers not favouring them, and announced that all adverse criticism would be treated with the rigour of martial law.

(*The Cartoon, "The Red 'Mokanna.'"*)

On the 21st May, after a siege of nine weeks, the troops of the National Assembly effected their first entry into Paris by the St. Cloud gate and the gate of Montrouge. On the 23rd M. Thiers reported that the Assembly

THE RED "MOKANNA."

"*Here—judge of Hell, wish all its power to damn,*
Can tell one curse to the foul thing I am!"—LALLA ROOKH.

gents, who were estimated to have lost 12,000 killed and wounded and 15,000 prisoners, still held out; but their resistance was declining. On the 24th they set fire to the Tuileries, the Louvre, and other glories of Paris. The conflagrations, the continual cannonading, the mad fury of the desperate Communists, made the 24th the hostages, as they were called—Archbishop Darboy, Father Allard, Father Déguerry, Curé of the Madeleine, Monseigneur Surat, Grand Vicar of the diocese, and others, were ruthlessly shot in the prison-yard of La Roquette, at the instigation of the Procureur-Général of the Commune, Raoul Rigault, and his subordinate Ferré.

Belleville was stormed by the troops of the Assembly. The measures taken by the Versailles troops to suppress the Commune were summary. "No quarter was given," it is said, "to any man, woman, or child found in arms." On the 28th Marshal McMahon issued a proclamation announcing that the struggle was over, the last positions of the insurgents captured, and Paris delivered. On the next day M.

Thiers ordered the disarmament of Paris, and the dissolution of the National Guard of the Department of the Seine. So ended the second siege of Paris.

JUNE 12.

Mr. Cardwell announced that the Government intended to abandon part of the Army Regulation Bill, proceeding only with the

clauses relating to the Abolition of Purchase. This was hotly opposed by the friends of the Army interests.

JUNE 13.

The Lords, by a majority of 129 to 89 votes, agreed with the Commons in rejecting the new Test Clause which Lord Salisbury had desired to introduce into the University Bill.

THE STRONG GOVERNMENT.

Boy (a rude boy). "Now, then, all together!—and be very careful as you don't spoile yerselves!"

JUNE 16.

The German troops engaged in the late war this day entered Berlin in triumph amidst the most enthusiastic demonstrations of national loyalty and jubilation.

JUNE 29.

The Ballot Bill to-day went into Committee. So many of the Government measures had

were received by their opponents with having little to show for the Session but the prospect of passing this minor Bill.

[See Cartoon, "The Strong Government."]

JUNE 30.

The Tichborne Trial was still dragging its slow length along, absorbing the attention and monopolising the talk of gossips and unul-

community. Mr. Punch then expressed his feelings with regard to the "tape-worm" trial:—

GROANS OF THE PERIOD.

Yes Champain in Prospect;
"Highfalutay—Great rapid relict, o!"

With this side the Channel ditch booms,
Can escape the talk of Tichborne!
What would I not give in payment,
To have no more of "the Claimant!"
Rest as Death to poor or rich born,
Comes the inevitable Tichborne

One is fain to choke "the Claimant."
To what realm, by word or warlike terror,
Can I free from talk of Tichborne?
Was life to July from May meant
To be given up to "the Claimant"?

* * * *

With shout lengthic o'er lands and lands borne,
Drops the tape worm ease of Tichborne,
And in nine months' entertainment,

Finds she fighters o'er "the Claimant."
Unto boredom's highest sticha borne,
Three columns the name of Tichborne:
Cæsi : two tongues, appeareat, Manner-o-
Manio, "Argurat on Arthur Claiman?"

JULY 3.

The Army Regulation Bill—narrowed as
before explained mainly to the Abolition

of Purchase, was read a third time in the House
of Commons. It was opposed hotly to the very
end by "the Colonels" and their friends, and
its prospects in the Upper House were regarded
as exceedingly precarious.

(the Cartoon, "Doom'd!")

On the 17th July the Army Bill was thrown

"DOOM'D!"

"THE DOOM'D ONE." SLANG FROM THE GRAND NEW BURLESQUE MILITARY MELODRAMA.
(Congratulatory from the Cavalier. "Soft—he comes!" (Slow Music.)

out by the House of Lords, on the proposal
for second reading, by 155 votes against 130.
This made Army Purchase the question of the
day. Everybody was asking, "What will Mr.
Gladstone do!" On the 20th, in a crowded
House, he announced his intention. He said
that "by means there was no purchase but
what was permitted by the Queen's Regulations.
The House of Commons having condemned
Purchase, and a Royal Commission having
declared that those regulation prices could not
be put an end to except by the valuation of
Purchase as a system, the Government had

resolved to advise Her Majesty to take the
decisive step of cancelling the Royal Warrant
under which Purchase was legal. That advice
had been accepted and acted upon by Her
Majesty. The new Warrant had been framed
in terms conformable with the law, and from
the 1st November next Purchase in the army
would no longer exist. The Government had
no other object in view but simplicity, despatch,
and the observance of constitutional usage."

The Royal Warrant was issued on the same day,
This step led to an angry outburst from the
Opposition against what they called Mr. Glad-

stone's high-handed proceeding, and Mr. Disraeli
charged him with appealing to the Prerogative
of the Crown for the purpose of relieving himself from a difficulty of his own devising.

The Lords, on the 31st, assented to the
second reading, protesting however against
the interposition of the Executive during
the progress of a measure submitted to
Parliament by Her Majesty's Government,
and declaring that they only yielded "in order
to secure the officers of Her Majesty's Army the
compensation they were entitled to consequent
on the abolition of Purchase in the army."

On the 1st of August
the Bill passed the Lords.

*(See Cartoon, " Ajax Defying
the Lightning.")*

AUG. 7.

THE trial of the Com-
munist prisoners be-
gun at Versailles. Assi,
Courbet, Lullier, Groumet,
Verdure, Billioray, Férré,
and Jourde were indicted,
charged severally with in-
citement to civil war, usur-
pation of civil and military
power, assuming Govern-
ment functions, complicity
in massacre, devastation,
pillage, arson and assassination, &c., &c. All the
members of the Commune
were held responsible for
the destruction of property
by fire. The number of
prisoners was estimated to
be 33,000.

AUG. 9.

THE Centenary of Sir
Walter Scott was cele-
brated to-day.

A CENTENARY SALVO
TO SCOTT.

Praise the wise men of Old World
and New, to the Wizard of
the North,
'Tis on Scribner's boldness given that
on Truth's sea put forth,
Turn in honour of the Magus in
mind and beldam grey,
Whose world was a world of
gladness, yet that fadeth not
away!

True Border Scott, d'e've one was,
in big brow and blue eye,
And stalwart frame, and broad
slow speech, and humour
shrewd and sly;
In glow of fervent liberality with
bravely warming rolled,
In passion for a poet's past with
a lawyer's sense empaled.

And march by march, and year
by year, the magic work was
plied,
And all that came within its
range, he to build, imagined and
cried;
And still flowed on without a
check that weird and wondrous stream,
And they who stooped to drink were wanted, till old
things new did seem.

Where sudden on the wizard fell a darkness and a chill
That well-nigh stayed his grammarye, and stopped the
wondrous rill;
But only for a moment; with arm most came new power;
And what had been a day's work once, was one work of

That was the hardest stroke to wage, the dreariest weird
to dree,   [as he;
And the Man showed in the Magus, and a man of pith
Where the work had grown a labour which had been his
delight,   [death a light.
What had love play for hand and brow, for life and

Still toiled he at that labour from rise to set of sun,
And would not rest his summer off until the fight was

And he was nigh to winning when he sank upon the field,
And died in harness knightly, and slept upon his shield.

Almost as much for the life he lived as for the work he
wrought,   [sought;
This gathering from all regions his own genie town hath
And where'er true worth is honoured, our greatest smiles
him,
Reverence for Scott the Writer, blends with love of Scott

AJAX DEFYING THE LIGHTNING.

AUG. 19.

An Admiralty minute on the loss of the "Agincourt," the officers of which had been tried by a Naval Court Martial for stranding that ship on the Pearl Rock at Gibraltar early in the year, stated that in the opinion of their Lordships the primary cause of the disaster was the unsafe course steered by the squadron in obedience to signals from the flag-ship. Vice-Admiral Wellesley and Rear-Admiral Wilmot were in consequence suspended, and Staff Commander Kiddle placed on half pay.

This incident, together with the loss of the "Megæra" troop-ship while on her way to Australia, and other naval disasters, led to grave doubts in the public mind as to the satisfactory condition of our Navy.

(See Cartoon, ".All in the Downs.")

AUG. 21.

Parliament was prorogued by Commission. The Session had not been productive, of all the various measures introduced only seven having been passed; the Army Purchase Act, the Westmeath Crimes Act, the University Tests Act, the Repeal of the Ecclesiastical Titles Act, the Trades' Union Act, the Local Government Act and the Judicial Committee (P.C.) Act. The Licensing Clauses of Mr. Bruce's Bill had been withdrawn, as also Mr. Goschen's Bill for Local Government and Taxation. Mr. Cardwell's Army Organization Bill had been reduced to a mere measure for the Abolition of Purchase; the Ballot Bill, which had passed the Commons, had been thrown out by the Lords. Mr. Gladstone said of it (at Whitby), that "the people's House had passed the people's Bill, and that Bill, when presented again at the door of the House of Lords, as he trusted it would be very early next Session, would be pressed with an authoritative knock which it would not otherwise have possessed."

"ALL IN THE DOWNS!"

Mr. Bull. "That my Army should break down not, to doubt, is to expected; but—Pon my Navy!!!—Zounds! (gloomily—) I this fondly think I was all right with my Navy!"

SEPT. 13.

Opening of the Mont Cenis Tunnel.

SEPT. 20.

Mr. Butt, a Home Rule candidate, was this day returned for Limerick, unopposed.

SEPT. 21.

In conformity with the "Military Manœuvres Act" of last Session, what became popularly known as the "Autumn Manœuvres" had this year been commenced in the open country in Hampshire, the Aldershot Camp forming a centre. Under the command of the Duke of Cambridge 36,000 troops had mustered there.

and the campaign, which
attracted much attention,
was considered to be generally satisfactory in its
results (*Punch's* Introduction).

(*See Cartoon, "Counting the
Cost."*)

THE CHARGE OF THE CAMPAIGN.

A noble and a needful art's the
Art of Self-Defence,
An art which needs I must
have regardless of expense;
For that expense, how e'er great,
may bow much greater more;
I won't begrudge the arms, and
keep, and slashing of the Brave.

I gaze on you unmoved; I in
spect the martial scene;
I own 'tis picturesque, and I'm
involved I won't be mean.
To London if a road foreign far
were on the way,
I'll calculate, with Fancy's aid,
what I might have to pay.

Yet would I could only open my
feet to keep the sea
Which rolls between my neighbours, I am glad to say, and
me;
I'd rather, were I quite secure of
danger from the main,
Watch husbandmen than soldiers
at their work on yonder plain.

SEPT. 26.

MR. GLADSTONE, in
acknowledging the
freedom of the City of
Aberdeen, which was pre-
sented to him to-day, spoke
on the subject of Home
Rule. He said that if
Home Rule were to be
established in Ireland they
would be just as well en-
titled to it in Scotland and
Wales. "Can any sensible
man, can any rational man,
suppose that at this time of
day, in this condition of the
world, we are going to dis-
integrate the great capital
institutions of this country
for the purpose of making
ourselves ridiculous in the
sight of all mankind, and
crippling any power we
possess for bestowing be-
nefits through legislation on the country to
which we belong?"

HOME-RULE.

Too long has fair Erin put up with the Saxon,
His yoke on our shoulders, his scourge our lean backs
on;

COUNTING THE COST.

M_{R.} B_{ULL} (P_{AYMASTER}-G_{ENERAL}). "*H—m—It's a precious expensive experiment; but I do believe it 'll be well worth the money!*"

Since the Lords of the Pale shed the cold blood like
water,
And Cromwell's curse swept on wid fire and wid slaughter,
Thro' William the Dutchman, worse luck, won the rompit,
And busted the Green Isle into Orangemen's ground;
Till her to be Catholic served for a curse
Why they'd skin you alive, another black prent laws,
And they'd put pitch-caps on ye, the bodies to keep

And now Frost laws has been picked to the devil,
They think to hushing us by dressin' in civil;
They our pistols to win, ihmmy-cught by elbowin',
And our Francis by the Protestant Church doctoberin'!
By oppisin' our eyes would they stir the to wid blundness,
And think to cajole us wid jester and kindness?
No, we'll show them the blood in one veins runs in stirrup
Against Saxon right, or against Saxon wrong!

"SAUCE FOR THE GANDER."

"I say, Jan, dear, if you can't enjoy your supper now you have lost your grumble about nine hours—grumble yet no. as I've done footsore, and ain't finished yet."

OCT. 6.

TO-DAY the long strike amongst the engineers at Newcastle-on-Tyne, which had lasted nineteen weeks, came to an end. The strike had been in favour of the Nine Hours' movement. A compromise was effected by which the men agreed after January 1872, for a term (instead of 57 as at present) and overtime where and to what extent might be required by the employers.

[See Cartoon, "Sauce for the Gander."]

OCT. 11.

THERE was much vague talk and party recrimination at this time concerning a new "movement." This was the so-called "Social Alliance" alleged to have been made between "a council of skilled workmen" and certain Carnarvon, and Sandon, Sir John Pakington, Sir Stafford Northcote, Mr. Gathorne Hardy, &c.

"A document" (says a Note in Vol. LXI.) "embodying 'seven points,' sanitary, social, educational, &c., all tending at the improvement of the Working Classes by legislation, was said to have been signed by certain Conservative Peers on the one hand, and certain representative working men on the other, through the mediation of Mr. Scott Russell, the eminent engineer. The scheme of this new 'Social Alliance' was involved in much mystification—several of the Conservative Peers denied that they had signed the document, and seemed to have ended in nothing."

Greenwich constituents at a celebrated open-air meeting on Blackheath, touched upon this among other questions. He said:—

"Those who propose to you—whoever they may be—inform his three seven points of which I have spoken: those who promise to the dwellers in towns that every pint of them shall have a house and garden in free air, with ample space: those who tell you that there shall be markets for selling at wholesale prices small quantities—I won't say are impostors, because I have no doubt they are sincere: but I will say they are quacks."

(*See* Cartoon, "Out of the Bag!")

Nov. 6.

Sir Charles Dilke, in a lecture at Newcastle, made an attack upon Royalty, criticising the expenditure of the Royal Household, and asserted that the Queen, despite a promise given to Parliament, had not been in the habit of paying Income Tax. The latter charge was incorrect, as Mr. Lowe shortly afterwards took occasion to show. Sir Charles Dilke, who declared himself a Republican, incurred considerable odium by this deliverance.

Nov. 7.

Sir Robert Collier was gazetted a Justice of the Court of Common Pleas, in order formally to qualify him for a seat on the Judicial Committee of the Privy Council, an Act requiring that any person appointed to the latter office must be or have been a Judge of one of the Superior Courts of Westminster. He only held the

"OUT OF THE BAG!"

Dizzy. "Eh? Of course he is? Ah, my dear Lord Beaconsfield, you should know this kind of delicate business to your accomplished Leader. Ahem!!"

eldest son and heir of Sir
James Tichborne, who died
in 1861. The plaintiff
declared that he was, and
claimed the Baronetcy and
large estates; the defendants, the trustees of the Tichborne estate, contended that
he was one Arthur Orton,
a butcher, who emigrated
some years back from Wap-
ping to Australia, and that
the real "Roger" had been
lost at sea. Mr. Serjeant
Ballantine was leading
counsel for the plaintiff,
and Sir John Coleridge
(Solicitor - General, and
afterwards Attorney-Gene-
ral,) and Mr. Hawkins,
Q.C., for the defendants.
(Introduction to Vol. LXI.)

(*See Cartoon, "The Old Man
of the Sea."*)

Nov. 10.

MR. HENRY M. STANLEY,
who had been sent
out by the *New York
Herald* in search of Dr.
Livingstone, discovered
him at Ujiji. The meeting
between the great missionary traveller and the energetic Newspaper Corre-
spondent was a striking
scene, which has been so
often described to need de-
tailing here. "Dr. Livingstone, I presume!" said
Mr. Stanley, advancing
quietly to meet the man he
was in search of. "Yes,"
answered the Doctor simply.
The news of the safety of
Livingstone was warmly
welcomed in this country.

Nov. 22.

TO-DAY it was announced
that the Prince of
Wales, then at Sandring-
ham, was indisposed, being
confined to his room with a
feverish cold resulting from
a chill. This developed into
an attack of typhoid fever, and on the 29th the
Queen, whose own health had long been a source
of some anxiety, paid a visit to her sick son.

Nov. 26.

ON this day the session of the Italian Parliament at Rome was opened by King Victor

"THE OLD MAN OF THE SEA."

SINBAD (on representing the British Public). "*I can't be expected to attend to any of YOU, with this 'interesting topic' on my shoulders!*"

VICTOR AT ROME.

"Session of the Italian Parliament was opened yesterday at Rome
by King Victor Emmanuel in person." *Telegraphic Despatch of
Monday, Nov. 27.*

Behold a week drear, and a week to do
From the Quirinal, Italy's crown'd King,
Past Rome's grey ruins, Rome's glad thousands through,
To the Cæsarian Mount his people bring,
Whilst in his own its pride and bravery blest.

His Queen, long wrestled for, now only won,
From hands, from bars, from death-in-life redeemed,
Whose eyes, yet dungeon-deepened, scarce brook the sun,
Whose hopes, that oft for truth took what they dreamed,
Scarcely trust assurance of new life begun,
For fair limbs prison cramped and halter-menaced.

Victor and Italy, bridegroom and bride,
Crown mount for Rome at last! In dusk and dart
Swift to its centre life's tumultuous tide

ROME. 1871.

Nov. 28.

EXECUTION of the Communist Generals Rossel, Ferré, and Bourgeois, who were shot in front of the Artillery Butts at Satory in presence of 3,000 men of the regular army. Much pity was felt for Rossel, a brave and intelligent soldier, though he had been involved in the disorders of the Commune.

Dec. 7.

M. THIERS delivered his first Presidential Address to the National Assembly. "The policy of France," he said, "must be henceforth a policy of dignified and enduring peace. If, contrary to all probability, events should disturb that peace, the deed will not be that of France. ... France will be true to her solemnly pledged word. Moreover the States which took part in the war are fatigued; and those that had been witnesses have become seriously alarmed." The Address went on to say, that France's relations with Spain, Italy and Austria were amicable, whilst with Russia they were most cordial, "the result of an elevated and reciprocal appreciation of the interests of both countries."

Dec. 9.

TO-DAY public anxiety was aroused by the announcement in the bulletin that the Prince of Wales had passed a very unquiet night, with considerable increase in the febrile symptoms. Next day 11th Royal Highness was specially prayed for in the churches throughout the kingdom. The Prince passed a restless night, with farther recurrence of the graver symptoms. On the 13th his fluorws and the public solicitude were at their height. The bulletins were anxiously awaited; the afternoon one on this day was so unfavourable as almost to ex-

SUSPENSE.

was happily a change for the better, the Prince passed a less unquiet evening, as I was said to have recognised the Queen. On the 18th it was announced that he was making satisfactory progress, and thenceforward his course towards recovery, though slow, was assured. On the 26th the Queen, in a letter dated from

"the universal feeling shown by her people during these painful, terrible days, and the sympathy evinced by them with herself and her beloved daughter, the Princess of Wales, as well as the general joy at the improvement in the Prince of Wales's state."

[See Cartoon, "Suspense."]

✦ 1872 ✦

JAN. 1.

AT the annual New Year reception the Emperor of Germany said that he hoped peace was now secured for a long time, and it should be utilised to "strengthen the foundations on which their present greatness had been established."

JAN. 7.

MR. JOHN BRIGHT, who in December, 1870, had been compelled to withdraw from the Presidency of the Board of Trade, owing to impaired health, was now better, and beginning to take an active part in political life. Mr. *Punch* welcomed his return in the following lines :—

COME ABOARD, SIR!

"COME aboard, Sir!" to the Captain
Says John Bright, A.B.,
As he touches his tarpaulin,
Smart and orderly,
And the watch look pleased as Punch is,
Officers and crew,
For A.B.'s like John are always
Welcome back again!

   ＊   ＊   ＊

For the ship has seen hard weather,
And some people say   [The
Captain Gladstone ain't the man
Was the other day;
And if you believe the crankers,
Officers and crew,
Isn't pull with a will together,
As they used to do.

Certain 'tis, since John Bright
left her,
His sick leave to take,
The old craft, in last year's
cruising,
Had an ugly shake.
Made poor day's work, but
much bewray;
Badly fooled her screw;
Scraped her copper, if she didn't
Start a plate or two.

Certain 'tis, with crew and captain,
Officers also,
Things don't go on quite as pleasant
As they used to go.
There's been some high-handed doings,
Some spite the river o';
Some's bunk out, and some's bunk softly;
Some took sail, or worse.

   ＊   ＊   ＊   ＊

Anyway the ship's the better
By a good A.B.,
Now John Bright is all a-taunto,
And comes back to sea.
Be't in talk to the blue-jackets
Like a 'cute old salt;
Con the ship, or call the soundings,
Hale us along a fault,

   ＊   ＊   ＊   ＊

No A.B. in the *Britannia*
Better knows than John;
Which let's hope that Captain G. will
Take his advice thereon.
Well, we know that now John 's buckled
To his work again,
'Twill the officers be better,
And for ship and men!

[See Cartoon, "Off Greenwich."]

"OFF GREENWICH."

JOHN BRIGHT. "Come aboard, Sir!"
CAPTAIN GLADSTONE. "Glad to see you, John. Glad you're A.B. again. If it comes to the blow, we may want your assistance."

JAN. 10.

A^T a Home Rule Demonstration at Limerick, Mr. Butt, the newly-elected Member for that constituency, whilst admitting that the Church and Land Acts had done much good, complained that they had been grudgingly given, and accompanied by Coercion Bills such as would have driven England into rebellion. The question of Home Rule was now being vigorously agitated.

JAN. 14.

O^N this day the last bulletin concerning the Prince of Wales was issued. It reported him as making satisfactory progress, and daily gaining strength. The public relief and pleasure at this cheering announcements were very marked.

JAN. 18.

T^{O-DAY} it was decided at a Cabinet Council that Great Britain would not consent to have what were called the "Indirect Claims" submitted for arbitration. In pursuance of the Treaty signed on the 6th May, 1871, by the High Joint Commissioners at New York, a Board of Arbitration had been formed to consider the "Alabama" Claims, and the Arbitrators were now meeting at Geneva. On the 3rd Feb. Lord Granville informed Mr. Fish that the British Government did not think it to be within the province of the Geneva tribunal to decide the "indirect claims." These were in addition to "the amount of the actual

A STILL BIGGER "CLAIMANT."

and direct damage done by the privateers, whose depredations had given rise to the Treaty," and were intended to cover "the expense that the United States had been put to, and the losses they had sustained in consequence of the failure of our Government to prevent the privateers from quitting our ports"

were not easily definable, and might swell to monstrous proportions.

(See Cartoon, "A Still Bigger 'Claimant.'")

The hearing of the Tichborne case had been resumed on the 15th January, the Attorney-General commencing his speech for the defence.

the unwieldy impostor commonly known as "the Claimant."

JAN. 19.

T^{HE} French National Assembly agreed to the appointment of a Commission to

Budget without taxation of raw material. M. Thiers threatened to resign in consequence.

[See Cartoon, " Too much Pressure."]

A SEAT ON A SAFETY-VALVE.

Are Income tax parties are This re oppose,
O William the Earnest, O Robert the True !
A soul above fear of the Rabble be shows ;
Is that to be said, British Gentlemen, of you ?

Or is it that you, whose enthusiasy doth move
With tribute from all due to lend a part's pura :
Albeit your Honours both one and approve
The better arrangements, do follow the worse ?

How bad are the worse, which your fevered Britons run,
You have often considered ; but declines to advance
On that high path which upright financiers pursue ;
They manage these matters much better in France.

For justice it is what doth [illegible]
these Serve,
Political craft in this mighty firm band,
Whom Rulers perpetual and what impend were fast,
But what impositions tax payers will stand.

It went and enough upon shoulders asked
To pay your whole Budget ;
on fair does oppressed
(As humdrumbers say, the wrong-box to detect)
The Snore has been put ; they are over-instreed.

You fancy your Engine is working to well
By way of a Snum-Rack,
'twill yet move easier,
And best any pressure your force can compel :
You sit on the safety-valve, therefore, in short.

O William the Daring ! O Robert the Rash !
Though dead to remonstrance, to caution give ear,
Ere high pressure bodies burst up with a smash,
And 'three shall Stoker and hoist Engineer.

JAN. 20.

Mr. John Bright having been claimed as an advocate of Home Rule for Ireland, wrote as follows to The O'Donoghue :—

"To have two representative legislative Assemblies of Parliament in the United Kingdom would be, to my

TOO MUCH PRESSURE.

Bob the Stoker. "Lor' bless you, M'mum ! That's the way we 'rein the road ;'—simplest thing in the world !"
M. Thial. "Oh, mon ami ! Pro'en garde ! He shall 'blow op' one day !"

mind can wish for two within the limits of the present United Kingdom who shall not wish the United Kingdom to become two or three unions entirely separated from each other."

FEB. 6.

Parliament was opened by Commission. "The heads of the Speech (said Mr.

1. Thanks for the restoration of the health of the Prince of Wales, and announcement of Thanksgiving therefor, in St. Paul's, on the 27th of February.
2. Foreign relations in all respects satisfactory.
3. The name of the British Empire is dishonoured by slave-trading practices in the South Seas, and a preventive measure is promised.
4. France is objecting to Free Trade, but we are not to quarrel.

" The Arbitrators appointed pursuant to the Treaty of Washington, for the purpose of amicably settling certain claims known as the Alabama Claims, have held their first meeting at Geneva. Cases have been laid before the Arbitrators on behalf of each party to the Treaty. In the case submitted on behalf of the United States large claims have been included, which are understood on my part not to be within the province of the Arbitrators. On this subject, I have caused a friendly communication to be made to the Government of the United States."

6. The "Emperor of Germany" is to arbitrate on the St. Juan Water Boundary.

7. Ireland has been free from Serious Crime. Her trade improved.

8. Crime and the number of criminals in Great Britain have diminished.

9. The Estimates will be suitable to the Circumstances of the Country.

10. Revenue satisfactory, Proportion decreasing.

11. Among the measures of the Session are to be Bills for Scotch Education, Mines Regulation, on the Liquor Question, for improving the Superior Courts of Justice and Appeal, for establishing Secret Voting, for suppressing Corrupt Election Practices, and for doing something in a Sanitary direction.

12. Parliament will be Autumnous, and the Sovereign will rely on its Energy, and on the Loyalty of the People.

Feb. 7.

The Speaker, Mr. Denison, after fifteen years of service, announced his intention of retiring in consequence of the strain upon his strength. He was created Viscount Ossington, but declined the pension usually given to retiring Speakers. He was succeeded in the chair by the Hon. Mr. Brand, long a popular and capital "Whip."

[See Cartoon, " The Old ' Whip'."]

Feb. 8.

To-day Lord Mayo, Governor-General of India, whilst visiting the convict colony at Andaman Island, was assassinated by a convict named Shere Ali, undergoing penal servi-

THE OLD " WHIP."

Hon. Henry Brand (the New Speaker). "My dear Lord Ossington, your advice is invaluable. But I rather like 'late hours;' and as to the 'floors,' I flatter myself as old 'Whip' knows what to do when the 'Rabbits give tongue'!!"

1847, who stabbed him mortally as he was returning to the boat. He had been appointed Viceroy by Mr. Disraeli in 1868, and although the appointment was at the time considered a doubtful one, Lord Mayo had by common consent made an admirable Governor-General, and much sorrow was felt at his untimely decease.

Feb. 22.

Mr. Cardwell moved the Army Estimates (total amount, £14,624,900), and expounded his plan for the Re-organization of the British Army. Briefly (said *Punch's* " Essence "), these lay in heads :—

1. United Kingdom to be divided into Military Dis-

There will be Forty-nine in England, Nine in Scotland, Eight in Ireland, in all, Sixty-six.
3. Each District to be held a Brigade.
3. Each Brigade is to be composed of –
    Two Battalions of the Line,
    Two Battalions of Militia,
    The Volunteers of the District.
4. One of the Line Battalions is always to be on
Foreign Service.

5. The other is, like the pig that did not go to market,
to stay at home, and to be a Depot to its foreign
brother.
6. Qualified Militia officers to be nominated to Battalions.
7. Volunteers to be trained with the rest of the
Brigade, and to be under exclusively Military Control.
8. Buildings to be erected in every District, for Staff
Quarters, Barracks, and Depot.

9. Each Brigade to be commanded by a Lieutenant
Colonel.
10. The Guards to be deprived of their Privileges.
11. Cost, about £1,500,000.
12. The whole of our land forces, if complete, would
give us 467,000 men; but of course we have nothing
like this, at present.
Now, the inviting idea of this scheme is perfectly sound
and good. The House received it with satisfaction.

SMOKING THE "CALUMET."

JO-KE-TE-UP (The Punny Bird). "Come, my Uncle! Let us Smoke the Peace-pipe!"
WIG-WUM-SAM-ASY (The Cheerful Bank). "That is no Peace-pipe! Thy Colon tuned Nail! THAT!"
BEN-TE-FROST (The Wise Buffalo). "Hath not one Uncle 'The Punny Bird' been at the Fire-water of the Pale Fort?"

FEB. 23.

In answer to Lord Granville's "friendly communication," Mr. Fish said that the "indirect
claims" were covered by the Protocol and Treaty,
and that the American Government could not,
therefore, withdraw from the case they had presented for arbitration."

    (See Cartoon, "Smoking the ' Calumet'.")

FEB. 27.

This day was set apart as a Thanksgiving
Day for the recovery of the Prince of
Wales from his late critical illness. The
Queen, the Prince and Princess of Wales and
other members of the Royal Family, with all
the high officers of the Crown, went in state to
St. Paul's Cathedral to join in a Thanksgiving
Service. The public reception of the recovered
Prince was warm and enthusiastic, and the ceremonial at the Cathedral very impressive. On the
29th the Queen, writing from Buckingham
Palace to Mr. Gladstone, said that she was
anxious, as on a previous occasion, " to express
publicly her own personal very deep sense of
the reception she and her dear children met with
on Tuesday the 27th of February, from millions
of her subjects on her way to and from St.
Paul's." And " to convey her warmest and most

heartfelt thanks to the whole nation for this great demonstration of loyalty."

On the same day Her Majesty, when entering Buckingham Palace after a drive, was subjected to annoyance, fortunately unattended by injury, from a lad named Arthur O'Connor, who presented himself at the side of her carriage with a pistol, which proved to be unloaded, and a paper, which turned out to be a petition for the release of the Fenian prisoners.

MARCH 4.

To-day the seemingly interminable Tichborne Case in its first stage came to an unexpected and welcome end, the foreman of the jury submitting the following statement to the Lord Chief Justice. "We have now heard the evidence regarding the tattoo marks, and, subject to your Lordship's direction, and to the hearing of any further evidence that the learned counsel may desire to place before us, I am authorised to state

"THE MONSTER SLAIN."

"And hast thou slain the Waggawock?
Come to my arms, my Beamish Boy!"

(*Vide* "The Jabberwock." in *Through the Looking-Glass.*)

that the jury do not require further evidence. After an adjournment to the 6th (which was the 103rd day of the trial), Mr. Serjeant Ballantine advised his client to submit to a nonsuit. The plaintiff was committed to the next sessions at the Central Criminal Court on a charge of wilful and corrupt perjury. The Government undertook the prosecution.

Sir John Coleridge, Attorney-General, whose days, was credited with a large share in bringing about this welcome result.

(*See Cartoon,* "*The Monster Slain.*")

Mr. Punch, parodying the celebrated well-known poem entitled "Jabberwocky," in Lewis Carroll's delightful "Through the Looking-Glass," expressed his joy at the termination of the huge trial in the following lines:

WAGGAWOCKY.

'Twas Mayday, and she lawyer coves
Did gibe and jabber in the wabe,
All summed were the Tichborne groves,
And their true lord, the Bobe.

" Beware the Waggawock, my son,
The eyelid twitch, the loose' inches.
Beware the magpie hawmock, upon

He took his tun-weight brief in
hand,
Long time the hidden clew he
sought,
Then rested he by the Hawkins
tree,
And sat awhile in thought.

And as in languish thought he
toils,
The Waggawock, now rath or
shapes,
Came lumbering to the wheree-
lee,
And perjured out his Claim.

"Untrue   untrue!" Then,
through and through
The weary works he worked
the task;
But March had youth, eve with
the Truth
He dealt the fatal whack.

"And hast thou slain the Wag-
gawock?   [Boy!
Come to my arms, my Beamish
O Coleridge, J. ! Hoorah !
hooray!"
And chortled in his joy.

MARCH 10.

Joseph Mazzini, the great
Italian patriot, died at
Pisa, aged 72. His funeral
at Genoa, on the 19th, was
followed by 80,000 enthu-
siastic admirers of his elevated character and exciting
career.

MARCH 19.

Sir Charles Dilke's
motion for an inquiry
into the Civil List was rejected by 276 votes against
2. Sir Charles Dilke, whose
attacks upon Royalty and
avowed Republicanism had
made him very unpopular,
only secured the support of
Sir Wilfrid Lawson, Mr.
Auberon Herbert and Mr.
Anderson of Glasgow, two
of the four having to act as
tellers. The scene at the
division was disgracefully
noisy and violent.

MARCH 25.

Mr. Lowe introduced
the Budget. Punch's
"Essence of Parliament"
said :—

1. He had a Surplus of more than £5,500,000. How
he obtained it will be in the remembrance of Mr. and
Mrs. J. Bull.

2. As he makes some sort of Restitution, being, like
Cupid, "a child of remoistenee," in well to of Bingham,
Notts. He takes off Two-Pence from the Income-tax.
John Bull is now John O'Groat.

3. Income-tax payers under £200 were exempted to
the extent of £80. This is extended to payers under

"JEREMY DIDDLOWE."

Mr. Bull. "Yes, Dizzy, you certainly owed me the Twopence; but I hardly like taking it—it looks so uncommonly like your borrowing Fourpence and then!"

4. Half the Coffee duty comes off.

5. Half the Chicory duty comes off. The Grocer's
duty, not to wholesome, is of course encouraged.

6. House-tax to be modified, so as to relieve shops and
offices.

This Budget, unlike the one of the previous
year, was favourably received.

APRIL 3.

Mr. Disraeli, on a visit to Lancashire, spoke
at a large meeting held in the Free Trade
Hall, Manchester. He asserted that the
Crimean War would never have happened had
Lord Derby remained in office, and twitted the
existing Government with "guaranteeing their

and there yielding to the
demands of Russia for the
modification of the Treaty
of Paris, after having first
"threatened war." He
said, also, that it was probably the game of the Radical Party to turn out the
present Ministry and put a
Conservative Government
in a minority in its place,
so as to reconstruct their
own Party on a new plat-
form, pledged to more ex-
treme and more violent
measures, and then have a
Cabinet formed of the most
thorough-going Radicals.
"But (said he), just because
it is their game it ought not
to be ours."

(*See Cartoon, "The Lancashire
Lions."*)

APRIL 15.

THE LORD CHANCELLOR,
in the House of Lords,
moved a resolution declaring it expedient to establish
a new "Imperial Supreme
Court of Appeal, to sit con-
tinuously for the hearing of
all matters now heard by
way of appeal before this
House or before the
Judicial Committee of the
Privy Council, and that the
appellate jurisdiction of
this House be transferred to
such Supreme Court of
Appeal."

APRIL 16.

LORD KIMBERLEY intro-
duced the Govern-
ment Licensing Bill in the
Lords. "The points be
them" (said *Punch's* "Re-
porter ") :—'

Existing rights not to be disturbed.

As regards new licenses, those
granted by County
Magistrates not to be
valid unless confirmed by
a Special Committee of
Quarter Sessions.

In boroughs where there are not more than nine
Justices, they are to have jurisdiction; where
more than nine, they are to appoint a Special
Committee, but its acts are to be confirmed by
the whole body and by the House hereafter.

Various appeals are provided.

London Public-houses to be shut from midnight till
VII. in the morning.

In towns with fewer than 10,000 people, from X. to
VII.

Over that population, from XI. to VII.

On Sundays, no house to open till I. London houses
to shut at VI.; in the second case at IX.; and in
the third at X.

After a very brief discussion the Bill was read

THE LANCASHIRE LIONS.

"You have I heard on holy breed's share,
Another Lion give a louder roar.
And the first Lion thought the last a bore."

ROBERTES PUNCH.

APRIL 27.

CERTAIN judicial decisions at this time had
called public attention once more to the
uncertainty and the inequitable character of
the punishment awarded for crimes of violence

the comparative impunity of ruffianly wife-beaters.

(See Cartoon, " Odd-Handed Justice.")

THE EXTENUATING CIRCUMSTANCE.

(*Respectfully dedicated by Mr. Punch to Mr. Justice Keany.*)

I wallowed my old 'ooman like a sack ;
I broke three cart-whips across her back ;

I kicked her for trying to git away ;
I shoved her under a brewer's dray ;
Yet it's well-beknown three cats o' wives
Has more than a cat's allowance o' lives,
So out of a three-pair front I punched her ;
But the stout-railings went and kinched her ;
Still she bled like a pig, and spoiled her bonnet,
And so the lushinn was down upon it,
And 'gainst the old 'oomans mobbin's speak,
They took and 'ad me afore the Beak,

And blest but the Beak said—" One lark further,
And I should ha' been committed for murder ! "
So he sends me, as no Beak hisn't ort,
To be tried at the Central Criminal Court.

But there I know'd as I'd be all right,
For supple Judges ain't Beaks—to a quite !
So when 'ad up afore My Lord,
I pleads " Not Guilty," and stands unscored.

ODD-HANDED JUSTICE.

First Ruffian. "We was I hop for, and tet 'ere I got ? Well, I floor'd a 'ooman and tuk 'er watch, and I'm got two years and a flogrin'."

Second Ruffian. "He—h flang a 'ooman out o' the top floor winder; an' I'm on'y got three months ! "

First Ruffian. "Ah, but then SHE WAS YER WIFE ! !"

They passes the lushinn, the lushinn, the squash,
As how I'd showed her under the wheels ;
As how, if the ruffinn had not been blunt,
When I pitched her out o' that three-pair front,
They'd likely ha' skivvered her, climbes and all,
Which, in point o' fact they broke her fall.

Says my Lord, " You deserves to go for life,"
" Please your Lordship," says I, " it was only my wife ;—
Which she'd been and chevied me up to my fare."
" Indeed ! " says his Lordship. " That alters the case.
Wives is werry tryin', bless if they ain't—
....

MORAL.

For killing a woman, if tried for your life,
All you 've got to prove is, 't was only your wife.
And if Justice Keany rules the roast,
You 've only to get off with three months at most ?

APRIL 27.

Opening of the International Exhibition at South Kensington.

APRIL 30.

Horace Mayhew died at the age of 55. He was a prominent contributor to *Punch*, having been associated with it from nearly its earliest days. " Henry " (said *Mr. Punch* in his obituary notice) " is the grief that has fallen on those who lived in friendship with the kind, the just, the gentle ' Punny ' Mayhew."

MAY 2.

" IN both Houses" (says *Mr. Punch's* "Essence of Parliament") " we had somewhat mysterious but still satisfactory explanations from Ministers on the Alabama Claims question. Lord Granville and Mr. Gladstone, who had, of course, arranged that their language should be the same, 'had grounds for hoping that an arrangement satisfactory to both countries would be attained.' In other words, the Bonham Wind-Bag has been, as Jonathan all along intended it should do, only, being rather a mischievous —well—playful Jonathan, he wanted to see whether the blatant apparition would disconcert Johnny Bull."

(*See Cartoon, "Busted Up."*)

OVER A DEAD TREATY.

ENOUGH Misunderstandings,
Of Understandings grows :
And Oliver-Twist demandings
By Bonham bellows blows :
We've tried conciliation,
Of concession and fought shy,
Bowed to all humiliation,
Short of downright humble pie;

Yielding never fiercer carried,
Or carried it would be ;
If the Treaty's dead and buried—
Amen to it—say we !

Mean time the Treaty's dear for,
And all's well that ends ;
Till the White House is run for,
Parties meet please their friends.

That fixed in happier season
Fish may resume the float,
And to quiet row by reason
Invite John Bull once more,
Till then, save fume at finishing,
Our terms will stand the same ;
For Indirect Claims—NOTHING :
For Direct ones, HALF TO A CLAIM.

MAY 2.

THE Licensing Bill was read a second time in the House of Lords. The Bishop of Peterborough, in a vigorous speech against tyrannical restrictions, declared that if he had to choose between a free England that drank, and a sober England that abstained in chains, he would vote for Liberty, because that might mean Improvement (*Punch's* " Essence.")

"BUSTED UP!"

MR. BULL. " Ha ! I thought you'd burst him at last !"
JONATHAN. " We'd, old boss ! Guess, it's jist what we meant to do—straight thar—on let's barrer up."

JUNE 17.

THE Ballot Bill passed through Committee in the Lords, with two amendments " designed to trace the voter by marking on the counterfoil his number on the voting register, and to make secrecy only optional " (" Annals of Our Time "). On the 26th it was read a third time and passed. When returned to the Commons on the 28th, the optional ballot was rejected, the scrutiny accepted, and the extension of the hours of polling rejected. Subsequently, after a conference between the two Houses, the Lords withdrew the power of optional secrecy, and the Commons agreed to limit the duration of the Act to 8 years. It received the Royal Assent on the 18th July.

JULY 28.

TO-DAY subscriptions were received for the French Loan of £130,000,000, issued at 84l. 30c. The total amount subscribed was £1,720,000,000.

The quickness with which France rallied from her late terrible disasters and, in particular, the readiness with which she raised the money for the huge war indemnity exacted by her victorious foe, surprised everybody, and, it was suspected, did not entirely gratify the Germans. *Punch* had a Cartoon entitled "Injured Innocence," representing a German soldier reading the news of the colossal subscription, so readily raised for the new Loan. "Von Tausend Six Ondred Million Bounds!!" exclaims the astonished Teuton. "Mein Gott, mein Gott! And dey say ve plondered dem!!!"

LINES ON THE FRENCH LOAN.

How soon has France raised her gigantic loan!

...

THREE MILLIARDS.

A mis-quote title-page now understood, France is the country called "The Great Loan Land."

"ADOLPHE THE ALCHEMIST."
(A TALE OF WONDER AND ENCHANTMENT.)

AUG. 10.

PARLIAMENT was prorogued by Commission. The Royal Speech referred to the termination of the Commercial Treaty with France, which seemed to menace the end of Free Trade with that country, spoke hopefully of America, of the Government's intention to take additional measures for the suppression of the East African Slave-Trade, and made reference to the chief measures of the Session, the Ballot Bill, Municipal Elections Bill, Scottish Education Bill, Licensing Bill, and some others.

AUG. 15.

TO-DAY took place the first Parliamentary Electoral contest under the Ballot Act. Mr. Childers, who had joined the Ministry as Chancellor of the Duchy of Lancaster, was returned for Pontefract by 658 votes as against 578 given to his Conservative opponent, Lord Pollington.

(See Cartoon, "A Good Beginning.")

AUG. 24.

AT this time the importation of tinned beef and mutton, &c., from Australia was greatly increasing, and was thought to give promise of a plentiful supply of cheap food for the poorer classes of the populace. Mr. Punch referred to the subject in the following lines:—

THE SIRLOIN SUPERSEDED.

Once mighty roast beef was the
  Englishman's food.
It has now grown so dear that
  'tis nearly tabooed,
But Australian beef, potted, is
  cheap and is good.
    O, the boiled beef of
      Australia !
    And O, the Australian
      boiled beef !

It is capital cold ; it is excellent
  hot ;
And, if a large number of children you've got,
'Twill greatly assist you in boil-
  ing the pot.
    O, the boiled beef, &c.

First-rate is Australian mutton,
  likewise,
For curries, and rissoles, and
  puddings, and pies.
The thrifty good housewife its
  butcher's meat buys.
    O, the boiled beef, &c.

It will make you a broth that is
  fit for a king ;
And the young ones all like it,
  and that's a great thing.
So Paterfamilias is chosen to sing
    O, the boiled beef, &c.

For the small boys and girls eat the fat with the lean,
Don't leave underdone, but their plates nicely clean—
Where pigs are not kept which helps make all sweet.
    O, the boiled beef, &c.

Australian meat from the home being free,
The more economical meals come it be.
As there are no joints there's no carving, you see,
    O, the boiled beef, &c.

The firstborn of Egypt went once in high fame ;
Australian firstborn have more than the same.
Old England's roast beef is now swallen in name.
    O, the boiled beef, &c.

The privileged victims who Income tax pay,
Whose earnings precarious are taken away,
While coming to deal with a Butcher, can say
    O, the boiled beef, &c.

'Tis true that poor servants, footdden and free,
Australian seem to their faulty decline.
On shillings they hunarder may dine.
    O, the boiled beef, &c.

Now poor out the wine which we could eat afford
Except for Australian' meat on the board.
In (....................................) censored.
    O, the boiled beef, &c.

A GOOD BEGINNING; OR, LITTLE BOY BALLOT'S FIRST STEP IN LIFE.

Successful Candidate. "He may not be pretty to look at, dear Madam, and he may be 'shy;' but he's a TREMENDOUS SUCCESS, I assure you !"

[See Mr. Childers' Speech at Pontefract.

AUG. 24.

A celebrated swimmer, named J. B. Johnson, attempted to swim from Dover to Calais, but after two trials failed, his circulation becoming so low that he had to be lifted into a boat by his friends.

AUG. 24.

The Prince of Wales paid a visit to M. Thiers at Trouville.

AUG. 27.

Mr. Stanley, the discoverer of Dr. Livingstone (he subsequently paid a visit to the Queen at Dunrobin) was presented by Her Majesty with a snuff-box, in recognition of the services of the adventurous young traveller and correspondent in conducting to a successful end the search for the long missing English missionary. (*See* Nov. 10, 1871.)

THE IMPERIAL WITCHES.

Macbeth (Mr. Punch). "Now, then, you wierd, black, and midnight Wigs! What's your little game?"

[Slightly altered from SHAKSPEARE.]

SEPT. 2.

An International Congress of workmen was to-day opened at the Hague.

SEPT. 7.

On this day there took place at Berlin a Conference between the three Emperors, of Germany, Austria and Russia, attended (says "Annals of Our Time") with much military evening. The meeting gave rise to much speculation.

(*See Cartoon,* "*The Imperial Witches.*")

SEPT. 14.

The award of the Geneva Court of Arbitration was issued to-day. The arbitrators unanimously found Great Britain liable for the acts committed by the "Alabama;" by a majority of the Italian, Swiss, Brazilian and United States arbitrators, they found Great Britain liable for majority of the Italian, Swiss, and United States arbitrators, against those of Great Britain and Brazil, they found Great Britain liable for the acts committed by the "Shenandoah" after leaving Melbourne. They decided that Great Britain was not responsible for the acts committed by the "Georgia" or any other of the Confederate cruisers except the three mentioned. They rejected altogether the claim of the United States Government for expenditure incurred in pursuit and capture of the cruisers. They

in gold (about £3,229,116) in satisfaction and final settlement of all claims, including interest. The United States had claimed in all 45,500,000 dollars in gold (about £9,479,166).

The award was signed by all the arbitrators except Sir A. Cockburn, who dissented from it in a very lengthy and elaborate judgment. He agreed with his colleagues as to the "Alabama," though not for the same reasons, but he protested against the allowance of interest, and the amount thereof. He expressed a hope, however, that the decision would be accepted by the British people "with the submission and respect which is due to the decision of a tribunal by whose award it has freely consented to abide."

JONATHAN'S JUDGMENT.

Wal, now we've gained our cause, and the Award,
I guess we can't act nohow but succeed.
It is A triumph; that's a fact: but still,
They have considerably taxed our bill.

Three millions and a quarter.
Come, I say.
We need three hundred millions t'other day.
And, if we had got half of that air sum,
Of Arbitration mumblin' would have come.

John Bull! What's that teemed to that old Horn?
Ourselves won't feel the gain, nor he the loss.
Our claims cut down as close at con-hero's hair,
I guess we shan't make much by that affair.

Bound if we have to be by our own rules,
We shall have made ourselves tarnation fools.
When we air called on to, in after years,
Keep filibusters back, and privateers.

But then we may repudiate the cost:
Not do what we'd have done, but the most.
Meanwhile together in a Lovin' Cup,
Columbia and Britannia liquor up.

(See Cartoon, " The Loving Cup.")

OCT. 2.

TO-DAY a disastrous railway accident occurred, the Scotch express from London

THE LOVING CUP.

"IN THIS WE BURY ALL UNKINDNESS!"—SHAKSPEARE.

running into a mineral train while some waggons were being shunted at Kirtlebridge Station on the Caledonian Railway. The station-master, Currie, was regarded as mainly responsible for the accident, and he was subsequently committed for trial for culpable homicide and wilful violation of duty. He was indeed described as a very careful and hard-worked man; and it was

stated by Captain Tyler that if the particular points the moving of which was the cause of the accident had been interlocked with signals, it would have been impossible for the station-master or anyone else to cause the accident. "(Annals of Our Time"). This led to much public discussion concerning the negligence of Railway Companies in allowing the existence of

distinctive signal arrangements, which in 1871 it
was stated had caused 33
accidents out of 159, and
in 1870, 60 out of 121.

(*See Cartoon, "Muddlery
Junction."*)

A RAILWAY COMPANY'S
QUESTION.

(*Chairman sings.*)

As are there's more collisions more !
Loss killed and maimed ; I
say,   [loss !
My Colleagues, what an awful
There will be much to pay.
* * * *
We want more skilful hands ;
there's no doubt ;
Each pointsman no more
doses ;
How little could we give without
Our having them break down ?

OCT. 2.

Mr. Butt, speaking on
Home Rule at Lime-
rick, said it was the duty
of the Irish people "to present to England the offer of
a federal union under which
they should have the full
right of managing all Irish
affairs, while they were willing to join with England on
equal terms in the management of Imperial affairs."
He thought if they returned
eighty members pledged to
Home Rule, the cause was
won. The great majority of
the Irish people, he be-
lieved, would be perfectly
satisfied with a form of
government that would give
them the perfect and free
management of their own
affairs ; and if the people
of Ireland demanded sepa-
ration, it was because they
thought that was the only
way of gaining indepen-
dence.

Earl Russell, writing on
the 11th, said, " I fear, if an
Irish Parliament is set up
in Ireland, all her energies
will be wasted in political
contention."

These views of Home Rule are interesting
in the light of later events.

OCT. 15.

Lord Hatherley resigned the office of
Lord Chancellor, and was succeeded by

MUDDLERY JUNCTION.

Overworked Pointsman (puzzled). "Let's see'—there's the 'Scorcher' were due at 4'45, and it ain't in ; then, after that, come the 'Mineral.'—No! That must be here the 'Goods,'—nor th' 'Cattle'. No! They were after.—Cattle's shunting now. Let's see—Fast Train come through at —— Confound—must ha' come'd 'the Express' afore its time, and then if I knows which Line she's on!?"

OCT. 21.

Telegraphic communication was this day completed between London and Adelaide, and
messages were exchanged. *Mr. Punch* said,—

" The way to compare Puck's grand feat we've found
In half the time prompt Puck allotted to it ;
A girdle round about the earth we've bound.

OCT. 21.

The Emperor of Germany, who had been
selected as Arbitrator in the dispute
between Great Britain and the United States
regarding the San Juan Boundary Question,
gave his award to-day. It was in favour of the

clared, justly accorded with
the true interpretation of
the Treaty of the 15th
June, 1846.

(See Cartoon, "Humble Pie.")

HUMBLE PIE.

I AM still the same John Bull,
who of glory once supped
full,
   Faced Europe with my rub-
   dubbins, my sabbures, and my
   ships ;
When I'd taken behind my barks,
   when I hit straight at my
   marks,
And found my foes in distress,
   as I found my friends in
   tips :
But now I'm off for a quiet life,
   "jouk, and let the jaw go
   by ;"
Keep my feelings in my pockets,
   and put up with HUMBLE
   PIE.

Once foreigners looked up to me :
   a high brow I could hold :
If my *prestige* cost me millions,
   those millions' worth was
   mine :
Strong and safe were laid my
   bulwarks with British blood
   and gold :
Of a grander kind than Mam-
   mon my island was the
   shrine :
Honour was given to honour, in
   those darksome days gone
   by ;
Now honour's nold for money
   . . . and my dish is HUM-
   BLE PIE.

Then, in dealing with a bully, I
   was game to hold my own :
And the ground once wisely
   taken I stood in, stiff and
   stout :
In smooth tongues I had little
   faith, but much in hands
   well shaven,
And hands as strong to use the
   sword as slow to take it out.
The only kind of fighting I dis-
   liked was fighting shy,
And the one dish I would not
   eat, in those days, was
   HUMBLE PIE!

"If the right cheek's smitten,
   turn the left," was written
   thus to draw,
But the Quakers were the only
   sect wise to that rule would
   agree :
So with so much Christian doctrine waking practice, I
   allow,
I applied that text to friends, not
   foes, and hit them
   who hit me :
Set now it's "Give your coat to
   those who your waistcoat try,"
And the curl is peace and plenty—
   that is, of HUMBLE
   PIE!

How Baxter and Bob Lowe prove
   as plain as tongue can
   speak.

Who cares for the foreigner's laugh in his sleeve, the
   foreigner's tongue in his cheek?
The smaller John Bull sings, 'tis clear, the sweeter he
   flaws his nest.
Once sheare, they say, made him billows and loon, but
   that is all my eye—
There's no meat be so thrives upon (say Baxter) as
   HUMBLE PIE!

"HUMBLE PIE."

MR. BULL. "Humble pie again, WILLIAM!—You gave me that yesterday!"
HEAD WAITER. "Yes, Sir—es, Sir—that was GENEVA humble pie, Sir. This is BERLIN humble pie, Sir!!"

NOV. 8.

ELECTORS for the Presidential contest in
America were chosen for the different
States, the number being equal to the Senators
and Representatives sent by each. Large majorities were found to vote for Grant and Wilson.

against Mr. Greeley's 7
States with 74 votes ("Annals of Our Time"). Gene-
ral Ulysses Grant, the hero
of the American War, an
inveterate smoker, but despite some charges of a tendency to nepotism, still
exceedingly popular, was
elected President for a
second term of office.

(*See Cartoon, "The Return of
Ulysses."*)

Nov. 5.

CHALONS was this day
evacuated by the Ger-
mans.

Nov. 6.

TO-DAY the *Gazette*
published the details
of the new and somewhat
modified Treaty of Com-
merce which had been ar-
ranged with France. The
new provisions with regard
to tariffs were to remain in
force until 1st January, 1877,
and those concerning Navi-
gation till 1st July, 1879.
Lord Granville, at the Lord
Mayor's Banquet on the 9th,
dealt with the new Treaty,
affirming its principle and
substance to be strictly in
accordance with free trade.
M. Thiers, in his Pre-
sidential Message to the
National Assembly at Ver-
sailles on the 13th, also referred favourably to the
new Treaty.

Dec. 9.

FOUR gas-stokers, who
had been lately in the
service of the Commercial
Gas Company at Stepney,
to-day appeared at the
Thames Police Court,
whither they had been
summoned for unlawful
neglect and refusal to fulfil
their contract of service.
The magistrate, Mr. Lush-
ington, sentenced them each to six weeks'
imprisonment with hard labour. On the 2nd
December, 2,400 stokers employed in the
London Gas-works had struck, owing mainly
to the discharge of a "Union" stoker from
the Fulham retort-house. The supply of gas
in the city had in consequence been

THE RETURN OF ULYSSES.

BRITANNIA. "Ah, my dear! I was certain you wouldn't turn away the General. He may smoke too much, and be too fond of his relations; but, at any rate, he's been a good and faithful servant to you!"

inconvenience of the public. The Underground
Railway was to a large extent in darkness,
theatres had to be closed, and postmen had to
carry bull's-eyes.

A little later, on the 19th, five gas-stokers
concerned in the strike were sentenced by Mr.
Justice Brett, at the Central Criminal Court, to

finding them guilty of conspiracy to intimidate,
had strongly recommended them to mercy on the
grounds of their ignorance, their having been
misled, and their previous good character. The
severity of the sentence excited considerable
dissatisfaction in some quarters.

There was at this time what *Mr. Punch*

pollian police had, on the
16th November, mutinied
in consequence of the dismissal of Goodchild, secretary to their movement
for increase of pay; 109
constables had been dis-
missed, and others reduced
in rank and pay. In
August there had been an
extensive strike amongst
the carpenters, and in September amongst the bakers.
It was felt that in the interest of public conveni-
ence, some limitation must
be placed on this tendency.

*(Sir Coresus, " My Old Friend
Homer.")*

THE PESTILENCE OF
STRIKES.

Toastmen of the " Working Men,"
 Not to what your Cant has led.
" Bertha," the Bakers said, " we
  rise;
Struck, and tried to stop our
  bread.

Next the Guardians of the Press,
 Even, struck against us too,
" We will," threatened the
  Police,
" Leave you to the robbers'
  crew."

Then struck Stokers, of a clean
 Public service, at our light;
All they could they did, of gas,
 London to deprive at night.
Mutineers are strikes like these;
 Then its head Rebellion rears
Scabbers, sailors, if you please,
 Next will strike, turned
  mutineers.

DEC. 15.

LADY BEACONSFIELD,
 wife of the Right
Hon. Benjamin Disraeli,
died at Hughenden at the
age of 83.

DEC. 21.

PRINCE BISMARCK re-
 signed the Prussian
Ministry of State, and was
succeeded by Count Von
Roon.

DEC. 21.

ON-DAY the " Chal-
 lenger" started on a
scientific expedition round the world, a voyage
destined to be much heard of hereafter, and
fruitful in results.

THE CHALLENGER HER CHALLENGE.

I'm a spar-decked corvette, hulk of wood not of iron,
I am good under steam, under sail;

"MY OLD FRIEND HOMER."

[" Every day must begin for me with my old friend Homer—the friend of my youth, the friend of my middle age and of my old age
—from whom I hope never to be parted so long as I have any faculties, or any breath in my body."—MR. GLADSTONE, *Dec. 3, 1872.*]

GEORG (*loquit*). " But if a clansman's wit pleases me,
   His wit rejoice he chided, or heard with him,

" *Be likes, wroth, and third and best allowed
   That point of Tydeus, a swarthy Caper.*"

—*THAT IS MR. POPE'S TRANSLATION OF A PASSAGE OF MINE, SIR. WHAT DO YOU MAKE OF IT?*

By my Lords I'm about to be put in commission,
 For a cruise of three years, if not less;
And for all I'm short-handed, I carry provision
 Such as corvette ne'er victualled before.

Mine's no crew to train officers, boys, or blue-jackets,
 Or Britannia's old flag to display;
To observe and report South American stackers,

I beat down plenty-fish at three-fifteen;
 The Challenger new aims at higher dialectics,
 And on different quests sets her crew;

Her task 's to sound Ocean, unmask barnacles or rough in,
 To examine old Nep's deep-sea lord;
Dredge up samples precise of his country's stuffing,
 And the hidden that paves her bank;

A SOP TO CERBERUS.

[*Respectfully dedicated to MM.* Thiers, Gambetta, *and the "Right."*]

DEC. 21.

A value of confidence in the Government was carried by 267 to 117 votes.

✦ 1873 ✦

JAN. 1.

PRINCE BISMARCK, who had retired from the Presidency of the Prussian Chamber, received the Order of the Black Eagle in brilliants conferred, upon him, with a most complimentary letter, by the Emperor of Germany.

JAN. 9.

THE EX-EMPEROR OF THE FRENCH, Charles Louis Napoleon Bonaparte, died to-day at Chislehurst. He had long suffered from a wasting disease, and an operation performed on the 2nd, though at first to be successful, had failed to relieve him. He had been born at the Tuileries on the 20th April, 1808, and so was 65 years of age. He was buried on the 15th January at Chislehurst. It was calculated that nearly 50,000 people congregated to witness the funeral procession, which included the Prince Imperial, Prince Jerome Napoleon, Princess Jenchien and Achille Murat, and M. Rouher as

MRS. TAFFY'S ELIXIR.

"*Ah, Mister! You can bend lustily for your Politics, but if there was a* BALLOT *for '*HUNGER*' you know very well that my Man there would be at work, earning a Dinner for the Children and me, bad you.*"

chief mourners, and between 2000 and 3000 distinguished Frenchmen. In Paris little notice was taken of the death of him who had so lately been their Emperor and oracle.

CHARLES LOUIS NAPOLEON BONAPARTE,
EX-EMPEROR OF THE FRENCH,
BORN AT THE TUILERIES, APRIL 20, 1808. DIED AT CHISLEHURST, JANUARY 9, 1873.

"THE EMPEROR died this morning—half-past ten,"
So runs the telegram, writ-up, short and round,
On sand-splashed windows of each dusty den,
Where, daily, the day's news takes shape and sound.

It was no common life that so could fill
The thought of Europe! 'tis no common death,
Kings, Statesmen, Nations, with such shock to thrill,
As rarely greets an escape of rude's breath.

Already scores of ready pressure draft
Of his life's course to power their bird's-eye view,
Through poverty, and poverty, and craft,
And redder stains that the blurred track imbrue.

Let whoso will come of his faults the root,
And point a moral in his saddened end ;
This is the thought in England's _____ :
He, with his _____ among us, lived our friend.

JAN. 16.

"ONE of the greatest strikes which had as yet been organised." (says a Note to Vol. LXIV.), "took place at the beginning of the year, the strike of 10,000 ironmasters' colliers in Glamorganshire and Monmouthshire, which reduced a population of 60,000 ironworkers to compulsory idleness."

(See Cartoon, "Mrs. Taffy's Elixir.")

"The margin of wages in dispute was inconsiderable, but the ministers refused to negotiate with the representatives of the Trades' Union in the North, who had assumed the direction of the struggle." The strike did not come to an end until March.

JAN. 18.

Edward Bulwer-Lytton, Lord Lytton, the distinguished novelist, died at Torquay, aged 67. He was buried in Westminster Abbey on the 15th. He was a man of versatile talent, and had made his mark in romance, in drama,

in poetry, and in politics, having been Secretary of State for the Colonies from May, 1858, to June 1859.

Mr. Punch wrote of him:—

When wreaths of all set for the victor's prize
In the arena where brain strives with brain,

"KHI-VA LÀ?"

Sentry Granville (to advancing Russian). "Who goes there?"

Has he at once it, in fair knightly guise,
Or, if he lost, to lose, to lose wreved gain.

Novelist, poet, satirist, and sage,
Kept only sovereign of the steely crew and
By witting throstle of his delighted page,
Lord of the theatres' tumultuous pound!

Those from the Stately to the State addrest,
An orator of mark to claim the ear,
Which England's Senate yields but in the lord,
Whose wisdom wise men may be first to heed.

JAN. 25.

The action of Russia in Central Asia was again causing uneasiness in this country. On the 13th January, news had come from

St. Petersburg that an expedition to Khiva had been determined on by a Council of Russian Ministers. Khiva was an independent Turkestan, and the Russian advance thitherwards was regarded as another step in her scheme of conquest, although, when questioned by Lord Granville, she declared that, after exacting retribution for offences alleged to have been committed by the Khan of Khiva and his subjects, the Russian armies would evacuate his territories, which Russia had no intention to annex. These assurances were incredulously received here, and as events shortly proved, not without reason.

(See Cartoon, "Khi-va là?")

QUI VA LÀ?

"You, sentry, at the outposts, beside the line of corral,
On the ridge where Oxus westward, and Indus southward flows,
What are you, an 'twixt Iran as I Turan you look forth,
Oxus Kandahar and Toorkistan to Khiva, East and North?"
The Sentry, to this question, said nothing in reply;
But first for such of his rifle, and then by cocked his eye.

I knew the man I questioned, Private Granville was his name,

A smart and sturdy soldier—of soldier's blood the mass;
A pleasant chap to barter's wares, or raised the cannon fire,
I'm sorry feel to stand to arms, and last on watch in time.
No I thought there was something in it, when, instead of a reply,
He coolly cocked his rifle, and so coolly cocked his eye.

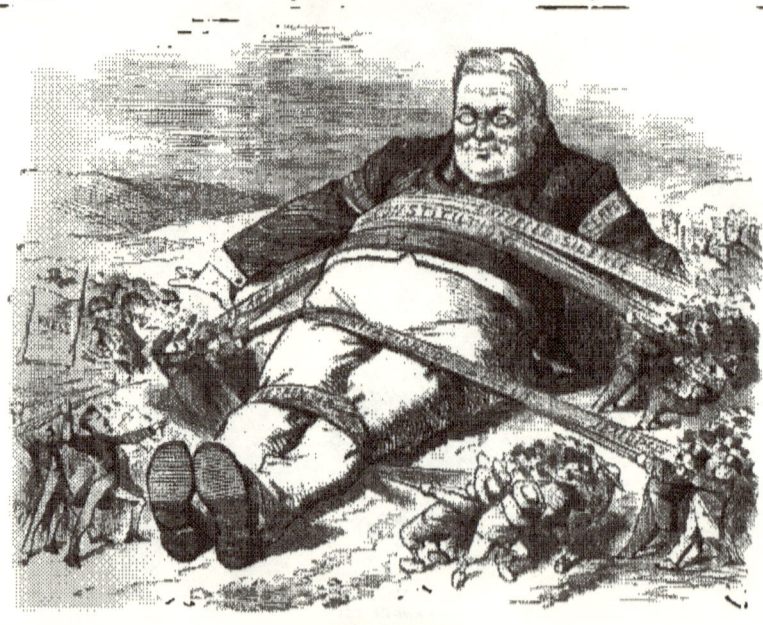

LITTLE GULLIVER.

FEB. 1.

THE PRESIDENT of the French Republic (M. Thiers) was (says a Note to Vol. LXIV.), "carrying on the Government under much opposition and difficulty." The monarchical parties were allied against him, and the "Reds" of the Press attacked him unceasingly.

FEB. 6.

PARLIAMENT was opened by Commission.

The new Lord Chancellor, Lord Selborne, also Sir Roundell Palmer, delivered the Queen's Speech in an admirable manner.

The Speech began with a pleasant phrase :

"I greet you cordially on your re-assembling for the discharge of your committee duties."

Her Majesty was pleased to note the following points :—

Friendship with all Foreign Powers.

Dispatch of Envoy to suppress the Slave Trade in East Africa.

German Emperor's decision in favour of America, as regards the Have Channel.

We submit, and overrate St. Juan.

Geneva Arbitration decision in favour of America, as regards the Direct Claims.

We submit, and you will be asked for the money.

We are very much obliged to the German Emperor and to the Tribunal at Geneva.

(*Sovereigns should be polite, your Majesty, but really*——

Extradition Treaty with King of the Belgians.

New Commercial Treaty with France is in hand.

England and Russia agree that the northern frontier of Afghanistan should be defined. There has been correspondence on the topic.

The Estimates will be as moderate as possible, considering how high certain prices are.

Harvest somewhat deficient, but trade, revenue, and decrease of pauperism and crime generally satisfactory.

A measure will be submitted for settling the question of University Education in Ireland.

Many measures which you have already considered, you will be good enough to consider again. Especially you must create a Supreme Court of Judicature. Also, you still hear of proposals.

For making Land Transfer easier.

For amending Land Taxation.

For amending the Education Act of 1870.

For amending Railway and Canal Law.

BEFORE THE COMITIA.

(*The Two Augurs.*)

In Rome, say the Comitia
To business could be set,
The Augurs and Aruspices
In solemn conclave met ;
The such new, picture, inspector

THE TWO AUGURS.

DIZZAIPUS. "I always wonder, Brother, how we chief Augurs can meet on the opening day without laughing!"
GLADTABER. "I have never felt any temptation to the hilarity you suggest, Brother: and the several mowers of flippancy."

Who, like an able Editor,
Dropped presage from their pens ;
And so by British Parties
Leading oracles are found,
In these oracles in hotchamps—

*   *   *

Tom Cato who the mouthpiece
Of the earlier dared to be—
Some Huxley of the period,

O, Aruspics of our Parties,
Who, without their useful guts,
Predate to read the future,
And forecast its ends or losses,
Perhaps Cato, come to being.

FEB. 11.

KING AMADEUS of Spain to-day announced to the Cortes his intention to abdicate. He had been invited to the throne two years before, but "his earnest efforts to govern on Constitutional principles had been baffled by factious partisans, and among Spaniards of the highest rank the King and his family were exposed to a kind of social excommunication." "My grand wishes" (said the King) "have deceived me, for Spain lives in the midst of a perpetual conflict. If my enemies had been foreigners I would not abandon the task, but they are Spaniards. I wish neither to be the King of a party nor to act illegally; but believing all my efforts to be sterile, I renounce the crown for myself, my sons, and heirs."

(*See Cartoon, "The True Hidalgo."*)

His abdication was unanimously accepted, and on the 11th the Spanish Assembly elected a government of Republicans and Radicals under the presidency of Senor Figueras. King Amadeus and his Queen and family left Madrid on the same day.

FEB. 13.

IN the Upper House the Lord Chancellor (Selborne) introduced a Bill to establish a Supreme Court of Judicature and a Court of Appeal.

In the Lower, Mr. Gladstone introduced his scheme for dealing with Irish University Education.

THE TRUE HIDALGO.

It was quite understood that this was the Measure of the Session, and thus on which it was thought the fate of the Government would turn. It was rather favourably received at first, but as *Mr. Punch's* Introduction to Vol. LXIV. says, "was not destined to run the same prosperous course as *Mr.* Gladstone's two great preceding

schemes for the disestablishment of the Irish Church and the improved tenure of Irish land. *Mr. Punch*, in a celebrated Cartoon entitled " Will he Clear it ? " indicated the danger of the situation by representing *Mr.* Gladstone mounted and going at full speed, having already cleared two stone walls (" Irish Church " and " Irish

Land "), boldly riding for the third—Irish Education.

MARCH 4.

Mr. Plimsoll, in the Commons moved for a Royal Commission to inquire into the condition of, and certain practices connected

THE COFFIN-SHIPS.

Polly. " O, dear Jack! I can't help crying, but I'm so happy to think you're not going in one of those dreadful boats ! "
Jack. " Wbel, Devy Jones's Devy Docks! No! my! Lau—never more!—thanks to our friend Master Plimsoll. God bless him !"

with the Commercial Marine of the United Kingdom.

Simple truth, but yet know what they mean. He argued that, out of 3,700 persons annually drowned, four-fifths were needlessly drowned,—and Noble Lords and Honourable Gentlemen knew why. He is told that to be exploited himself, and indignantly dwelt upon technical practices, the House of Commons cheered him heartily. *Mr. Punch's* cheer is added to his Cartoon this week.

Sir John Pakington seconded the motion, and begged the Government to concede it in the form that would be the most effective. He, too, adduced some terrible statistics.

Mr. Clay wished for a commission that could administer oaths. So did Mr. Samuda, who declared overloading, which was the result of competition, to be the cause of most losses. Now, this gentleman knows all about the subject, and asserts that we lose, every year, as many ships as we build.

Mr. C. Forrescue said something about over-colouring and exaggeration, but entreated the commission, and undertook, for Government, that the Inquiry, which he proposed to extend, should be carried out.

Mr. Bentinck discussed Government, and advised Mr. Plimsoll to draw up his own order of reference.

Mr. G. Hardy said that the charges involved "organised manslaughter" (a good phrase), and wished for evidence on oath.

Finally, the Government proposal was accepted. And now, Mr. Plimsoll, you have a noble work before you, and *Mr. Punch* will back you up against any who may seek to hinder a full investigation into the causes why so many brave fellows are annually drowned.

Mr. Plimsoll's contention was that it was the practice of certain shipowners to send to sea vessels that were either not sea-worthy, or were so laded as to be almost certain to sink, and that this was done for the sake of the Insurance Money.

(*See* Cartoon, " *The Coffin-ships.*")

MARCH 6.

The debate on the second reading of Mr. Gladstone's Irish University Bill was resumed in the Commons. The Bill found few earnest friends, and many bitter enemies. On the same day a deputation of Irish Members had waited on Mr. Gladstone, to inform him that they felt bound by every sense of honour to support religious and denominational education as against Secularisation. On the 9th a Pastoral issued by Cardinal Cullen described Mr. Gladstone's Bill as richly endowing

"Non-Catholic and Godless Colleges," and as "increasing the number of Queen's Colleges, so often and so solemnly condemned by the Catholic Church and by all Ireland," and giving "a new impulse to that sort of teaching which separates education from religion and its holy influences, and banishing God, the author of all good, from our schools."

It was plain that those in whose interests the message was designed, were most angrily hostile to it. On the 11th Mr. Disraeli, as leader of the Opposition, attacked it in a speech full of mocking wit and bitter invective. Mr. Gladstone vigorously and eloquently replied :—

"If," he said, "whom we have manfully sought and toiled for years we find only consternation ; if our tenders of relief are tinted while warm, let us still remember that there is a value which is not heard in the crackling of the first, or in the roaring of the whirlwind or the storm—the still small voice of justice, which is heard after they have passed away . . . . Let us wait we think the hush or pervenment of those whom we are struggling to assist have the dignum effect in turning us from the path on which we have entered."

At 1 A.M. on the morning of the 12th the division took place. The result was a defeat of the Government by 3 votes—287 against and 284 in favour of the Bill. Mr. Gladstone said the vote was of a grave character, and moved the adjournment of the House until Thursday.

Mr. Punch, in a companion Cartoon to "Will he Clear It!" (see p. 262) entitled, "Come a Cropper!" showed Mr. Gladstone and his horse fallen at the foot of the third Irish wall, a party of Irish priests and peasants, "with their sudden waving of flags and crozier," having contributed to his fall.

And we are, through the stones of the wall, in the air,
A rider still in his saddle square :
And we see the Irish fence in a heap
Come rolling over that luckless heap !
And we see that plucky rider down—
With a broken neck, or a fractured crown?
Not yet ! In spite of stun or sprain,
He's off, and up on his legs again,
And shaking his fist at the shouting crew
Who've spoiled his leap with their hullaballoo !
And as ready to ride—thank Squash head—
As if he never had "come to grief!"

[See Cartoon, " What the Doctor says."]

"WHAT THE DOCTOR SAYS."

DOCTOR PUNCH. "Well, it might have been worse! No bones are broken, but you've had a shake, and you must be VERY CAUTIOUS for some time to come."

Mr. Gladstone, on the 13th, announced the resignation of his Government. But Mr. Disraeli, who was not far, informed Her Majesty that he "could not undertake to conduct the Government in the present House of Commons." Mr. Gladstone was therefore again communicated with, and on the 20th it was announced that he and his Cabinet would carry on the Government as formerly.

MARCH 28.

Mᴿ. Chichester Fortescue announced the appointment of a Royal Commission to inquire into and suggest remedies with regard to the alleged unseaworthiness of British shipping.

APRIL 7.

Mᴿ. Lowe introduced the Budget.

Mr. Lowe did not make a very effective speech. Some said that he was not in good frame, having been crammed with his colleagues for not letting him pay off all the Alabama money. Be this as it may, he spoke loftily—little over the hour—and was a good deal bothered with his figures. His points were these :—

1. Unexampled prosperity, in spite of Continental troubles, Suffest, a bad Harvest, and High Prices.

2. We have a surplus of £5,896,000.

3. He hoped we should never have to pay another sum of £3,200,000 in gold, by referring questions to arbitration.

4. We shall pay only one half of that sum out of the revenue of the year, and the rest, without new taxation, by Exchequer Bonds, if finances are unlucky.

5. He takes off half the bogus Duty, after May 8th.

6. He takes One Penny off the Income-tax. Our Income-tax is now to be Two Pence, which, he added, yields quite as much as when Sir Robert Peel laid it on, at Seven Pence, in 1842.

7. He exempts from Taxation Hotel barmans and those "of persons who deal in intoxicating liquors." It must be allowed that the latter have been his generous Benefactors, and from his point of view ought to be rewarded.

Three Millions odd, reduce The Debt by £6,000,000, and relieve taxation by £2,365,000.

Said Mr. Punch, "There's a splendid surplus, Madam, and Drink has produced a very large part of it.—Mr. Lowe will probably say, with the wild fellow in 'Barnaby Rudge,' 'I drink to the Drink.'"

"THE GREAT SELF-TAXED."

Wᴏʀᴋɪɴɢ-Mᴀɴ. "Hi!—Go' mornin'—look here! We're th' People s makes th' Shurplush—now wheer d'you an' our Guv'ment going t'do for th' People I sh'ould like t'know?"

WHERE THE MONEY COMES FROM!

A cheer, a lusty cheer! Six-and-seventy millions this year.

Ne'er never such a revenue by State was raised before. In face of such prosperity, a fico for the fear, boys, Of days when Bull's black-diamond fields their fields shall yield no more!

In spite of strikes and struggles of Capital and Labour,

In Competition's usual game of beggar-my-neighbour,
John Bull has never won so much, and never played
  so high,
that what's this song that, sad and strong, I hear a black-
  bird singing— [fogs and mire,
How, some thing from and shuttle, and more than
'To the Towers and the Limekilns three millions in are
  bringing, — [may burst to shine!
That more in drink, than wealth or work, John Bull

Then the tap-root of our revenue lies deep in sin and sorrow,
  And finds a drain as fatal as Java's Upas-tree!
Then the last part of our surplus from our corruhluous we
  borrow, [to be,
And pay under twenty millions into hearts transferred

APRIL 23.

THE trial of the Tichborne Claimant for perjury came on to-day in the Court of

Queen's Bench before Lord Chief-Justice Cock-
burn, Justice Mellor, and Justice Lush. Mr.
Hawkins opened the case for the Crown, and
Dr. Kenealy defended the Claimant.

APRIL 27.

WILLIAM C. MACREADY, the great and high-
  minded English actor and theatrical

THE "UGLY DUCKLING."

NEPTUNE. "Well, of all the hideous——!"
BRITANNIA. "Ah, she isn't pretty, certainly; but remember, Father Nep, handsome is that handsome does!"

manager, who had done much for the elevation
of the Drama in this country, died at Chelten-
ham, aged 80. Mr. Punch wrote:—

  He was content to shine, and stem the gale
    With which sorrows tempts men on down and up,
  But strove to make the theatre a fane
    I'm noble art, e'en in ignoble days,
          *   *   *   *   *
  Hail and Farewell—thou last of a great line,
    Who in ideal art moved as at home!
  Remember ye bowed at a now empty shrine
    Was your faith false? Lo, the interpret came!

MAY 3.

IRON-CLAD Turret-ships of huge size and
  armed with monster guns were now being
rapidly added to the British Navy. Mr. Punch
had said, à propos of the Navy Estimates introduced by Mr. Goschen on the 25th April, "They
are nearly Two Millions, and exceed last year's
by about £340,000. But who cares about the
money? Look here. We have got twelve ships
so strong that all the rest of the nations of the
world, together, cannot produce a force that can

fight us. In addition, we have another splendid
fleet. Some day the time may come when, in
the beautiful words of the Laureate, we shall be

  'Breaking our mailed ships and armed towers,
  Controlling, by obeying, Nature's powers, Port flowers,'
  And gathering all the fruits of earth, and crowned with all

But it is particularly certain that the time is
not yet come, and anachronisms are bad taste.
So, hooray for the "Devastation" and her terrible Sisters!

(See Cartoon, "The Ugly Duckling.")

MAY 4.

DR. LIVINGSTONE, who had been sinking for some time, breathed his last, it is believed, in the course of this night, in a rude hut at Ulalaenda, attended only by one of his "good boys" (as he affectionately called them in his Diary). Majwara. After much suffering, borne with the calm heroism characteristic of him, the great traveller, who for some days had been unable to take food, to write, or even to see, sank to rest so quietly that Majwara was unable to say when breathing ceased.

MAY 8.

JOHN STUART MILL, the great thinker and writer on Logic and Political Economy, one of the most potent intellectual influences of the Victorian Era, died to-day at Avignon, from erysipelas, at the age of 67. Mr. Punch wrote :—

If e'er man's soul was star-like,
  his was so,
It burned as calmly, in such
  limpid air ;
Gave out to poor and passionless
  a glow,
As wooed our earth's refrac-
  tion seemed to share.

MAY 10.

LORD SELBORNE'S Judicature Bill excited considerable opposition. Said Mr. Punch (in his "Essence of Parliament," under date 10th May):—

"Lord Selborne's Judicature Bill was 'improved,' contrary to his wish. An alteration by Lord Cairns was adopted, purporting to uphold the pre-eminence of the Lord Chancellor. Lord Selborne is a Medea in a new light. He thinks the two ugly little children—Law and Equity, and tosses them into a cauldron, wherein he proposes to fuse them, and to bring out a perfect Angel of Justice. Three respective friends are making a most intolerable row about the operation, and Mr. Punch imputes to more interested motive than patriotism to the demonstration against the measure. But it is certain that those who are most displeased with it are most likely to lose by it."

(See Cartoon, "The New Medea.")

THE NEW MEDEA.

Jason (Mr. Bull). "Goodness gracious !—(aside)—I hope it's all right—but there'll be an awful row!"

MAY 13.

"IN the Commons" (said Punch's "Essence of Parliament ") " we had a capital evening.

" Madam, hear with a brief explanation. Anne Lady Dacre, by will dated December 20th, 1594, left funds which, it is perfectly clear that the good woman meant for the benefit of the poor of Westminster. Never mind details

The Corporation of London got hold of it, in wholly enough, has did not act with faithfulness, and now, out of any children in the school Lady Dacre founded, Westminster has only thirty two. The establishment is called Emmanuel Hospital. Lady Dacre is buried, under a stately monument, in Chelsea Old Church. The Endowed School Commissioners propose to take the Institution out of the hands of Gog and Magog, and to carry out the intention of good Anne. But it is not in G. and M.'s

To-night Mr. Crawford (the excellent M.P. for London) moved for the rejection of the scheme of the Commissioners. He could not say much for his efforts, but he managed unconsciously to represent their grievance as it appears most frightful to themselves. The idea of interfering with the august Corporation of London !

"Now, Mr. Gladstone has plenty of Venomism, but he does not bestow it at random. To-night he bestowed something else. In sober and Homeric truth he stood up to the two-handed measure of Guildhall, and—

"Nay, look at the Cartoon.

"'What ! the City of London, fisted, gorged, not to say Bloated with chuckles—the City of London struggling to hold what was meant for poor, helpless Westminster ! And the City alone, of all the Institutions in England, is not to have a hand laid upon it ! Take that, and that, you —' But where's Homer ?

' And, writh, Vgren dealt a
mighty blow
Full on the Cheek of his vaunty
foe.

Beneath that ponderous arm's
resistless sway
Down dropped he nerveless,
and extended lay.

Like a large fish, when winds
and waters roar,
By some huge billow dashed
against the shore.'

"The death-blow was given, but there was prolonged debate—

' For the prey was strong, and
he strove for life.'

"But the Division came, and Gog and Magog were declared extinct by 386 to 238. They died hard—therefore impenitent. Be it said that Mr. Gladstone never made a better fighting-speech in all his life."

(See Cartoon, "One in the
' Corporation.'")

MAY 13.

EMANUEL OSCAR DEUTSCH, the great Oriental scholar, died to-day at the age of 42 only.

MAY 14.

THE *Times* to-day announced the coming marriage of the Duke of Edinburgh with the Grand Duchess Marie of Russia.

MAY 17.

THE subject of "Ritualism" in the Anglican Church still considerably exercised the public mind, clerical and laic. On the 5th May an Anti-Ritualist Memorial had been presented to the Archbishop at Lambeth Palace, praying

ONE IN THE "CORPORATION."

" *Take that in your charity-basket, you ' fisted, gorged, not to say bloated,' old Grabber!*"

[See MR. GLADSTONE'S Speech à propos of Emmanuel Hospital and the City Aldermen.

the Bishops to exercise all their authority for the active suppression of ceremonies and practices adjudged to be illegal, and to protect the laity and their families from teaching subversive of the principles of Protestantism.

QUESTION AND ANSWER.

SIXTY-TWO thousand Members of the Church of England, and more, have memorialised the Archbishops with

a complaint that Roman doctrine is systematically preached in Anglican pulpits. "If it were so it were a grievous fault," the pleaders for Pseudo-Popery admit ; "but then," they say, "we must settle what is Rome." That may seem an easy thing for anybody to do, and clearly, if the Pope, and no one else, is infallible, Romanism can be defined with certainty by the Roman Pontiff himself when put, if the word of his head-man in this station is to be taken for what is Roman, then, as to the fact that Roman doctrines are preached within the Established Church, it

is only certain that Dr. Manning
has told us, and crushed in his
that is all.

(*See Cartoon, "The Prelates
Puzzled."*)

MAY 18.

In a despatch dated Tiflis,
17th May, published
to-day in the *Daily Telegraph*, it was stated that
Russia had taken Khiva and
made the Khan prisoner.

MAY 24.

Opening of the New
Alexandra Palace on
Muswell Hill. It was de-
stroyed by fire on the
9th of the following June.

MAY 24.

The French Assembly,
by a majority of 360 to
344, adopted an amendment
which was equivalent to a
vote of want of confidence
in the new French Ministry.
It had been reconstructed
on the 18th. M. Thiers,
long the point of attack
for the anti-Republican
factions, thereupon resigned
the office of President, and
was succeeded by Marshal
MacMahon. *Punch*, who
thought M. Thiers had been
ungratefully treated, represented him in a Cartoon as
"Coriolanus" (adapted to
the modern French stage),
addressing his enemies (the
Imperialists, Legitimists
and Orleanists) thus:

*Coriolanus. O most unwise
patricians!
I banish you!
. . . . . .
Let every feeble rumour shake
your hearts!
Your enemies, with nodding of
their plumes
Fan you into despair. Have
the power still
To banish your defenders.*

JUNE 18.

The Shah of Persia
arrived at Dover on a
visit to the Queen. He was
received by the Duke of Edinburgh and Prince
Arthur, on behalf of Her Majesty. On the 19th
he received the members of the Diplomatic Body
and Her Majesty's Ministers at Buckingham
Palace, which had been placed at his service. In
the evening he attended a dinner given in his
honour by the Prince of Wales at Marlborough
House, and on the 20th was received by the
Queen at Windsor. On the 23rd a Naval Review
at Spithead was held in his honour, and on the
following day he accompanied the Queen in a
review of the troops in Windsor Park.

JUNE 30.

The safe arrival of Sir Samuel Baker at
Khartoum was to-day announced (a

THE PRELATES PUZZLED; OR, "WHAT WILL THEY DO WITH IT?"

Archbishop of Canterbury. "If I knew how to deal with the question, say I be—ahem!—Disestablished!"
Archbishop of York. "If I knew what to say in the matter, say I be—ahem!—Disendowed!"

rumour had previously reached this country of
the massacre of himself and his expedition). He
reported that the country as far as the equator
had been annexed to the Egyptian dominion,
and the Slave Trade completely put down.

The celebrated traveller had undertaken in
1869 the command of an expedition to Central
Africa, under the auspices of the Khedive of

Egypt, with the object of annexing the country and putting down the Slave Trade.

SAMUEL BAKER.

Aamost" Belay Ditto."

WENT from his country, far away;
Drove work his time employing;
Had news of him, the other day,
Cairo, happy well-nigh destroying;
That he had been, or would be,
Said some ill rumours' maker;
But now is finded across the worth,
"All right's Sir Samuel Baker."

We get good tidings from Khartoum,
About his expedition—
The vulture's maw is not his tomb,
He has achieved his mission;
Whereof, the slave-trade to suppress,
He was the understaker.
There's no succeeding Sir nature,
Which crowns Sir Samuel Baker.

If he has pushed onto the Line
The realm of modern Pharaoh,
As is avowed, his name will shine
Most brightly at Grand Cairo.
The Khedive'll right well repay
The gain of many an acre.
Sing, fellahs, hey for Baker Bey!
Long live Sir Samuel Baker!

JULY 5.

THE SHAH of PERSIA, who on the 3rd had paid a second visit to the Queen at Windsor, on this day terminated his visit to this country, leaving Dover for France. His visit had created considerable public interest, and was understood to have been satisfactory to Nasir-ed-Din himself, as well as favourable to the political objects in whose interest it was mainly arranged.

The *Times* in its "Annual Summary" for 1873, observed that "the interests of England in the East could only be affected by the partial or total annexation of Khiva, if the aggrandisement of Russia in that part of Central Asia should affect the relations between England and Persia." These "relations" (says a Note to Vol. LXV.) were at this time, in consequence of the Shah's visit to England, apparently of a very friendly character.

(See Cartoon, "Persia Won!")

The Shah had, on the 14th May, granted to Baron Reuter, and any Company which he might establish, a concession of the exclusive right of making and working, for seventy years, throughout the Persian dominions, railways, tramways, and other public works, together with other privileges.

"*PERSIA WON!*"

NASIR-ED-DIN. "*Enjoyed my visit, dear Madam!—Enchanted!—Charmed! And—by the beard of the Prophet, you may rest assured I will allow no trespassers to cross MY GROUNDS into your child Indiana's garden! Mashallah!*" [Exit.

PUNCH WARNS HIS SHAH.

O, SHAH, "may your shadow never be less!"
Though of that but small prospect I see;
Another such week of sight-seeing shows it,
Such riding and roding, curb here and fol-dress,
Such bustling and bustling, parading and press,
Dwindled from a substance with shadow, I guess,
All reduced from a substance with shadow, I guess,
To naught but a shadow you'll be!

That "the commoners eat may
look at a king,"
In England's an ancient saw :
And you, when the light of your
diamonds you fling,
And ubb grave eyes upened as
round as a ring, [bring
Within your spectacles' focus
Our swords, ships, guns, ducks
—everything,—
Will observe, in this land of
sight-seeing, [or a chat.
That the Commons may look

A nine-days' wonder you've been
to John Bull,
And he to you in his turn—
His strength more of beef than
brandED full ; [wool] :
His civilisation [more cry than
His hands that *ought* his hands
to rule : [should be tool :
His hands of his hands that
You've sat in his treaty-making
school, [learn.
And your lesson thereis may

There's Reuter—let's hope 'twill
be Reuter Albert,
Instead of Reuter Comus—
Has set himself, calmly, the gulf
to scan, [rein began,
Which in Persia, since Kadjar
Hath proved with wider and
wider span,
'Twixt dried-up Nature and
dried man.
Where the gold stream — for
Nadir-Shah that suit—
Agent to Nadir has got.

Will Reuter, he Reuter never so
deep
In performing on "the wire,"
Conceive a balance to make, and
keep, [Deep
Of all the concessions which you
On his favoured land, when
you bid him reap
As sinews harvest, and shear
your sheep,
And take thee wool—if any—
dirt-cheap !—
Into that lot investors inquire.

But let this Doctor "Bull's
blood" transfuse
Through Persia's parched-up
veins— [dam—
Let railways bring their rain of
Let Reuter Paradise water anew
To cheat your sands in harvest
hues !—
Suppose prosperity comes
For milk and mines—and Russia
views
And covets your stirling plains ?

Will John Bull's Government
help you guard [you pay ?
That for which he has helped
When Russki comes with his
legal so hard,
Will he find the way to your strong-box latred
By the "Infamy" you sow in Woolwich yard ?
On our arms we trust the Loot and Pard,
For, "moral support" is the adage cited,—
Then's British Lion's play !

The second reading of Mr. Forster's Education Amendment Bill designed to meet

"THE OLD, OLD TUNE."
"PRINCE ALFRED WOULD A WOOING GO".
— There came a fiddler here to play,
And O but he was frisp and gay,
He stole the Lassie's heart away.
And made it all his ain, O."—*Song.*

certain objections raised to the original Act,
especially with regard to the third clause (which
imposed upon Poor Law Guardians, upon certain
conditions, the payment wholly or in part of
school fees for the children of indigent parents)
was moved to-day by Mr. Forster himself, and
carried by 343 to 73 votes.

The Queen in Council formally gave her
assent to the proposed marriage between
the Duke of Edinburgh and the Grand Duchess
Marie, only daughter of the Emperor of Russia.

(See Cartoon, "The Old, Old Tune.")

The Duke, who was then captain of H.M.S. "Galatea," was also a skilful amateur violin player.

JULY 19.

To-day the Right Rev. Samuel Wilberforce, D.D., Bishop of Winchester, met his death in a sudden and shocking manner. He was riding in company with Lord Granville in the neighbourhood of Abinger on a piece of moorland known as "Evershed's Rough" when his horse stumbled, and the Bishop, thrown suddenly forward, fell on his head and dislocated his neck. He was the third son of the celebrated Wilberforce, of anti-slave-trade fame, and had been born Sept. 1, 1805, being then 63 years of age. He was an eloquent speaker, an astute prelate, a winning man of the world.

On the next day died of paralysis, at the age of 73, Richard Bethell, Lord Westbury, ex-Lord Chancellor, a most distinguished lawyer, an ardent advocate of law-reform, and one of the most incisive speakers and effective debaters of his generation.

Mr. Punch wrote :—

They pass together from the bustling scene,
Where, opposites, they played their jostling parts,
Bandying was as bright and
words as keen.
Masters of divers arts, but
equal arts.

JULY 23.

Mr. Trevelyan's Household Suffrage in Counties Bill was "talked out" in the Commons. *Mr. Punch's* "Essence" says :—

"Mr. Trevelyan had a Bill for giving votes to the Agricultural Labourers. The question was 'an open one' for the Cabinet, but Mr. Forster, expressing his own approval of the scheme, read a letter from Mr. Gladstone (temporarily ill) who had asked him to inform the House that the Premier's opinion was that such extension of franchise was just and politic, and could not long be avoided. There was much emotion caused by this announcement that a new Reform Bill would soon be

GREAT AUTUMN MANŒUVRE.

Hodge. "Lawk-a-massy, Measter! Be it to be a 'Fanst be I' Strewth'? What be a to get by thecat?"

Mr. G. "That, my good friend, is a mere detail. The question is, what am I to get by it?"

"In the Debate as to giving a vote to the Agricultural Labourer, Mr. Forster read a letter from the Premier, who declared that such extension of franchise was just and politic, and could not long be avoided. The question was then taken up by the Conservatives, which much needs a 'good cry.'"

headed off, and there was some sarcasm about a 'Message from the Minister.' The feeling was that the matter was taken out of Mr. Trevelyan's hands, but the Bill was talked away until the final 5.45."

(See Cartoon, "Great Autumn Manœuvre.")

JULY 23.

A new Treaty of Commerce was this day signed between England and France.

"We are once more a Most Favoured Nation," said *Mr. Punch.*

JULY 28.

The forthcoming marriage of the Duke of Edinburgh was announced in both Houses, and a day fixed for making additional provision for H.R.H.

AUG. 1.

"MR. PUNCH is happy to announce that the Judicature Bill received final sanction from the Lords, who agreed to all the Commons' Amendments. That valuable measure has passed;—

For Law and Equity will fuse,
Or each one wear the other's shoes."

("Essence of Parliament.")

AUG. 8.

PARLIAMENT was prorogued by Commission. This (said *Punch's* "Essence") was—

THE MESSAGE.

We're very glad to let you go
(Thanks for our Alfred's life, you know),
         (mumbled)
We're quite at peace with all
(Fought Admetus,—never asked).
Several good treaties we have made
         [Trade,
For passing down the Mersey
And one with Festus, our friend
         campagnots, (montagnes,
Which commence will find ad-
And lots with other folks, for
     nicking Januory's kicking,
Rogues who'd scrape their
Nor are forgotten British claims
Regarding certain Vanhorgames.

Our Lords and Gentlemen, with
         glee
Reductions in some days we see:
The Sugar, and the Income taxes
Much lighter lie on people's
         backs.
The Judicature Act's a fact,
And Edermin's now complete.
Railways you've handed to a trio
Who'd dare to heard the hared-
         men do. [Act
We hope the Merchant-Shipping
Will save town ships from being
     wrecked.

Our Income powers exporta-
         tion :   [tion.
Pettawed 's Condition of Our Na-
For which, and other matters, pen
I now when to offer tribute due.

The *Standard* said the Speech "fitly closed the record of a barren session, and reflected the enthusiasm of an expiring Ministry." Mr. Gladstone's Adminis- tration was indeed plainly shaken and sinking. The return, on the 2nd August, of the Conservative Candidate at Greenwich (Mr. Boord) by a majority of 745 over all the other five candidates put together, thus giving Mr. Gladstone a Conservative colleague in that constituency, was a suggestive sign of the times, which greatly elated the Tories and proportionately discouraged the Liberals.

"HER MAJESTY'S SERVANTS."

(BEHIND THE SCENES.)

CONFIDENTIAL FELLOW. "I tell you, W'GLLON, you MUST strengthen your Company for next Season."

CHIEFTOP MANAGER. "I've done it, dear boy! I've taken Best out of 'First Robber;' I mean to change the east all round: I'm 'doubling' a part myself; and we'll revive 'The Quaker' for an afterpiece."

Mr. Gladstone was not unconscious of the failing prestige of his Ministry. There were dissensions within the Cabinet. On the 5th a re-arrangement of affairs was announced. Lord Ripon retired from the post of Lord President of the Council, and was succeeded by Mr. Bruce, who was raised to the peerage. Mr. Childers also retired, and Mr. Bright succeeded him as Chancellor of the Duchy of Lancaster. Mr. Lowe left the Exchequer and succeeded Mr. Bruce as Home Secretary. Mr. Ayrton was made Judge-Advocate, and Mr. Gladstone combined the office of Chancellor of the Exchequer with that of First Lord of the Treasury.

(See Cartoon, "Her Majesty's Servants.")

THE SHUFFLE OF CARDS

More changes! more changes!
Political Bards,
Tune your harps, and be-minstrel
the Shuffle of Cards.

First, in place undoubtemost the
fact be expressed—
Ecumenical Baxter spoke "Baxter's Saint's Rest."

Then shows how the Lind has
too pliable frame
Turns Peer, and will go where
he may be of use;

Succeeded at "Home" by the
cynical wag,
Bob Lowe; here our Bobby will
scold, chide, and sting!

Next, sing how John Bright,
having done his epistles,
Comes back, the bold Quaker,
to quell the fanatics.

Then twist up your strings with
your standard anew—
Our William, too strong for our
office, takes two;

As President puts forth his magnificent powers,
And casts up the national book s
at odd hours.

Sing out, singing beggars, and
wish him good luck!
His fiercest opponents most
honour such pluck, [adieu,

Then (wrangle us off all) the little
How Dodson the national book-
keeping shows;

How Arthur, the son of Sir
Robert, comes in
To do what was done by the
glorified Glyn!

And, lastly, play up an opera-
tically rare tune, [of Ayrton
To hail the alleged new comer
Portfaine that our euro and very
much loved men

Abandons the Noble, and puts
on the Poniton,

Sing away, twang your harps, be
your trumpets all blown,
We'll have an Ecumenical, old
belchs, of our own!

And here's the Prize Theme that
we toss to our Bards—
"Who the deuce cares a fig for
this Shuffle of Cards!"

AUG. 19.

SIR GARNET WOLSELEY
was appointed to the
chief command of stations
on the Gold Coast.

"The Ashantees had some time
since overrun the Coast districts
in the neighbourhood of Elmina ;
and either in consequence of a
misunderstanding as to the tribute, or in resentment of the
demand that they should evacuate the Protected Territory, they attacked a handful of English troops and
seamen, by whom they were signally defeated . . . .
The English Government determined to despatch to
the seat of war a force sufficient to penetrate, if necessary, during the cooler season to the Ashantee capital
(Coomassie); and Sir Garnet Wolseley was appointed to
the command of the expedition." (Times Annual
Summary).

" AU REVOIR!"

GERMANY. " Farewell, Madam, and of——"
FRANCE. " No ! We shall meet again !"

SEPT. 9.

THE "Alabama" Indemnity was paid to-day
at Washington.

SEPT. 16.

THE last of the German troops left in occupation till the War Indemnity should be
paid, crossed the French frontier between nine
and ten o'clock this morning. Verdun was the
last fortress evacuated. The payment of the
enormous indemnity exacted by Germany was
completed a year and a half before the appointed
time, mainly through the efforts of M. Thiers,
who was therefore called "the liberator of the
territory."

(Sir Cartney, " An Remote !")

OCT. 1.

To-day died, at the age of 71, Sir Edwin Landseer, R.A., the great animal painter, one of the most popular artists of the Victorian Era. He was buried in St. Paul's Cathedral on the 11th. *Mr. Punch* penned a tribute to the memory of the painter, from which the following are extracts:—

SIR EDWIN LANDSEER.

BORN 1802.   DIED OCTOBER 1, 1873.

Mourn, all dumb things, for whom his skill found voice, Nothing 'twixt them and us too mournful this,

Tell men could in their voiceless joy rejoice, And read the sorrow in their silent eyes.

*   *   *   *   *

His Art has been made tender to his age, Whether of sympathy 'twixt man and brute, Or is won down from Nature's wholesome page, And pleasure that, in truth, has deepest root.

A FRIEND IN NEED.

Mr. Gladstone: "My dear Lowe, I congratulate you." Just in time to write accounts with our Black Friend yonder."
Lord Robert Lowe: "Hm! Fighting is not quite in my line, as the learned Friend William, nevertheless—!"

*   *   *   *   *

Whatever growth of Art may grow our time, His still shall hold its place—apart—above; Others in high by nobler rivals may climb, None can be nobler loved, or worthier known.

OCT. 3.

Mr. Disraeli, writing to Lord Grey de Wilton respecting the pending Bath election, which Mr. Forsyth, Q.C. was contesting in the Conservative interest, made a scathing attack on the Liberal Government. He said:—

"For nearly five years the present Ministers have harassed every trade, worried every profession, and invaded or menaced every class, institution, and species of property in the country. Occasionally they have varied this state of civil warfare by perpetrating some job which outraged public opinion, or by stumbling into mistakes which have always been discreditable, and sometimes ruinous. All this they call a policy, and seem quite proud of it; but the country has, I think, made up its mind to close this career of plundering and blundering."

The Bath election, unlike most bye-elections of the time, went in favour of the Liberal candidate, Captain Hayter, who polled 2210 votes against Mr. Forsyth's 2071.

OCT. 6.

Mr. John Bright, who had accepted the office of Chancellor of the Duchy of Lancaster, issued an address to his constituents on the occasion of his re-election, which took place without opposition. He said, "I hold the principles when in office that I have constantly professed since you gave me your confidence sixteen years ago." As Mr. Bright came into office just as the Ashantee War broke out, some wondered how he would reconcile support of it with his well-known Peace principles.

[See Cartoon, "A Friend in Need."]

OCT. 18.

"**M.** THIERS," (says a Note to Vol. LXV.) "was now ex-President of the French Republic; but his friends thought he was the only man to save France on the one hand from the re-establishment of Monarchy, on the other from the revival of the horrors of Communism."

(Sir Carter, "Between Two Terrors.")

OCT. 20.

SPEAKING at Warrington to-day, Mr. Hatt said that what the Home Rulers wanted was an Irish Parliament, which should have the right of legislating and regulating all matters relating to the internal affairs of Ireland, and have control over Irish resources and revenue, subject to the obligation of contributing their just proportion of Imperial taxes. By internal affairs they did not mean the management of railways or gasworks, but the higher life of the nation—their own system of education, passing their own University laws and grand Jury laws ("Annals of Our Time").

OCT. 25.

THERE had recently been an exchange of correspondence between the Pope and the Emperor of Germany. Pius IX., writing on the 5th August, said that the measures recently adopted by His Majesty's Government aimed at nothing short of the destruction of Catholicism. He said, incidentally, "every one who has been baptised belongs in some way or other, which to define more precisely would be here out of place—belongs, I may, to the Pope." On the 3rd September the Emperor replied courteously but firmly, saying that Catholic Priests in Italy sought by intrigue to disturb the peace which had existed for centuries. The German State Council had, on the 15th May, unanimously resolved upon the expulsion of certain monastic orders, as coming under the law against the Jesuits. Prince Bismarck had carried through the Prussian Parliament a bill relating to the discipline and education of the clergy, which was regarded by the Bishops and the Holy See as an infringement of ecclesiastical independence. Mr. Punch thus summed up the notable correspondence:—

BETWEEN TWO TERRORS.

("WHITE" AND "RED.")

HISTORICAL CORRESPONDENCE.

(*Alarmingly made easy by* "History's Muse, *as material for burying.*")

PIUS & WILLIAM.

YOUR Majesty should be aware,
For 'tis a terrible affair,
That Bismarck and his scholar crew
Are making quite a tool of you,

And struggling hard, by force or
trick,
To railzpose your Catholics.
Sire, really you must mind your
eye,
Or down your throne comes, by-
and-by.
I speak the truth to great and
small,
Heretics, Catholics, and all;
For all who've been Baptised,
you see,
Belong, or more or less, to Me.
You'll come to grief, *justitia*
sum,
So, bless you much, dear WIl-
liam.

Vatican, August 7.   Pius.

WILLIAM de Pius.

Your Holiness must have been
dragged,
Or, say the least of it, hum-
bagged,
No Minister of mine can go
A step ahead if I say No.
But, Holiness, your blessed
Priests,
Joining with Communistic beasts,
Have in here fire, and wildly
fanned it !
And dash my buttons if I stand
it !
How Christian Clergymen can
do
Such things, I neither know nor
care,
But since they choose to put our
back,
I'm to keep order—and I'll do
it.
The best course you can take's
to frown,
And bid your priests to knuckle
down.
As for belonging to a Pope,
I'm duly grateful (I well may),
Not only know one Mediator
Betwixt myself and my Creator.
But, and withstanding *creeds*, still
I am,
Your peaceful and devoted
WILLIAM.

Berlin, September 3.

Nov. 8.

TO-DAY a monument to
Count Cavour was un-
veiled at Turin, in presence
of King Victor Emmanuel,
the Prince of the Royal
Family, and a crowd of distinguished personages and
deputations from civil and
military bodies.   In France
the intrigues of the Mon-
archical parties, and in
Spain the attacks of the Carlists were antagonistic to the attainment of National unity.

[See Cartoon, " The Latin Sisters."]

Nov. 18.

HOME RULE Conference held in London.
The points insisted on in the several

THE LATIN SISTERS.

ITALIA. "My dear GALLI, and my beloved HISPANIA, look at me—happily 'united' and comfortably settled ! When will you follow the example of your younger Sister !"

1. That Irish prosperity was only possible under self-
government.   2. Ireland's right to such self-government.
3. A Parliament composed of the Sovereign, Lords, and
Commons of Ireland.   4. The principle of a federal
arrangement for internal affairs, leaving to the Imperial
Crown and Parliament big duties respecting the Colonies
and other dependencies, the relations of the Empire with
Foreign Powers, and all matters appertaining to the
defence and stability of the Empire at large, as well as

for Imperial purposes.   5. That such a change effects no
change in the Constitution or distribution of the prerogra-
tives of the Crown.   6. The necessity of an Irish Administration in Ireland for Irish purposes, conducted by
Ministers constitutionally responsible to the Irish Parliament.

As formulating with some distinctness the

tions have considerable interest, especially when viewed in the light of subsequent events.

Nov. 27.

The second London School Board was this day elected.

"The London School Board" (says a Note to

Vol. LXV)" was about to be elected for a second time. Religious party spirit entered too much into the various contests. Mr. Forster, as Vice-President of the Committee of Council on Education, was the author of the Education Bill."

(See Cartoon, " The School (Board) Match.")

DEC. 1.

Sir Garnet Wolseley's Despatches from the Gold Coast, whilst praising the gallantry of our officers, spoke of the miserable behaviour of the native auxiliaries, and emphasized the urgent need of reinforcements of English troops.

THE SCHOOL (BOARD) MATCH.

Mr. Forster (Umpire). " Boys, Boys, this is Uphang, and not fair play! You've lost sight of THE BALL!"

"THE RIGHT MAN IN THE WRONG PLACE."

Our Garnet's a jewel—'twere sad, in the stand
Of a swine such a jewel to see ill-bestowed,
As methinks it will be, if paid carelessly on,
To get Coffee apart and some nasty grounds washed.

Don't let mad-cups triumph, in some's despite;
Our General Routine—that old genius-quarter;
And we haven't a doubt that our Wolseley is fight,
Will turn out a Wellesley, to all but the letter.

He has shown in abundance on shore—or at sea—
Nor yet past the chances of Afoghships and gunboats;

And, in absence of red-coats, his last trust must be
In a few—would he'd more—of brave British taxjackson.

Of advisers at home he has some more than enough,
And of critics in newspaper-columns and clubs;
And - so many ranks' breath, to a proverb, 's sad stuff—
It won't be their fault if the 'labourers he drubs.

In short, he has all things a General should have,
And a great many things which a General should not;
But, while rubbish in tons we cast over the wave,
Our trifle—nk away—we somehow forget.

In our deep penny wisdom, and heaven of trust,
We shipped off the General minus his men,
So that if in a fix he should find himself placed,
He might scarcely lose time writing home back again.

But if we have kept back the red-coats awhile,
Till the Fantees have been undeniably whipped,
No reverse, railway sharpens and mules by the mile,
In advance both of General and troops we have shipped.

So fair Garnet, at sweet Cape Coast Castle arrived—
'Mid fever and Fantees and Scamptees and foes,

Finds the rids he don't want on the bench smugly hired,
And to where is left for the embryos he dost.

We're a promised people—that truth's moved sleep—
And the work of our practical War Office wights
In to pile all the blunders they run in a heap,
And then set our Gen'rals to set them to rights.

DEC. 8.

AT this time there was a serious famine in Bengal and Behar. On this date the Governor-General of India informed the Secretary for India that supplies of rice were now being pushed forward to the districts affected by the scarcity. A large Relief Fund was raised in England.

"HUNGRY, AND YE FED ME."

GAUNT, ghost bands of Famine and of Plague
Uplifted over India's cowering head,
And their black shadow broad'ning, vast yet vague,
More awful for the doubt blent with the dread!

"MENDING THE LESSON."

POLITICAL ECONOMY. "Take care, my dear JOHN. Don't interfere with the laws of supply and demand."
JOHN BULL. "I don't, Miss PRUDENCE. She remains and I victul."

Between the cloudless heavens, blue brass, on high,
And the baked earth, so iron hard, below,
From Ryot's up to Viceroy's, every eye
Wonders, unless, for rain that will not flow.

Yet sure His love is working, in the glow
Of brotherhood that stirs the nation's heart,
In the resolve of all once, high and low,
With hand or brain or purse to bear their part—

That none, whom we can feed, unfed shall go,
No life, that care of ours can save, be lost;
That e'en if parbluod doctrine thrust her "NO,"
On helpless hands, we will not count the cost.

But manly prove, with wealth's and wisdom's aid,
Betwixt poor India and His doom of dearth,
Knowing great means for great occasions made,
And prove God-given to shew man's helpful worth.

(See Cartoon, "Mending the Lesson.")

DEC. 10.

MARSHAL BAZAINE, who had been tried for his conduct in the Franco-German campaign, was this day found guilty on all the counts of his indictment, and sentenced to the penalty of death with military degradation. The sentence was, two days later, on the recommendation of the Court, commuted by President McMahon into 20 years of seclusion on the Isle St. Marguerite.

DEC. 18.

THE Tichborne Case, which had reached the 145th day, was adjourned till after Christmas.

✦1874✦

JANUARY.

"**A**LTHOUGH** civil war still prevailed in Spain" (says a Note to Vol. LXVI.), "a beneficial change in the Government of that country took place, which was principally due to the resolution of General Pavia, who in the first days of the year turned the incapable and factious Cortes out of doors. After the successive miscarriages of Figueras and Salmeron, Señor Castelar had rendered the conduct of public affairs temporarily possible by suspending for six months the sittings of the Cortes, and that impracticable body, when it reassembled on the 2nd of January, refused a vote of confidence to Castelar, who was the only possible Republican President. As Captain-General of Madrid, General Pavia (as has been said) forcibly dissolved the Cortes, and appointed a Provisional Government, of which Serrano, Topete and Sagasta were the principal members. Marshal Serrano, who had a few months before escaped in disguise from Madrid, was soon afterwards raised by his colleagues to the post of Chief of the Executive Power ('Annual Summary' of the *Times*.) Castelar protested against General Pavia's energetic action in dissolving the Cortes."

See Cartoon, "The Paviour of Society."

SPAIN AND HER PAVIOUR.

As the matter of the author of the recent coup d'état should be spoke—(see Mr. Pun.h's Cartoon)—our PAVIA.

Poor Spain! whose search for saviour
Still closes in a crash.
'Twas not too soon for Paviour
Thy Cortes up to smash?

Madrid turn Murcia's schemer:
Whose government scarce varies:
Cortesses, Murcia's outer,
Madrid's rule of contraries.

The moments thus he wasted
Your Don, pissed Donkey, shelves.
For your Republic's planted
You count hours to rule yourselves.

Cortesse, tatterdemalions,
F y Margolls, balmorras,
With Priests and Pronunciados,
All tugging Spain's bare bones.

Thy Paviour's impatience
With Castelar's "good intentions,"
May check paving operations
In a place that no one mentions:

But till fine words Spain's trolving
For restored behaviour,
That place will ne'er want paving,
And Spain will find the Paviour.

THE PAVIOUR OF SOCIETY.

FANCY PORTRAIT OF CAPTAIN-GENERAL PAVIA, OF MADRID (NO MATTER HOW MERE SPANIARDS PRONOUNCE HIS NAME, AS HE APPEARED PERFORMING WHAT THE ELOQUENT CASTELAR STYLES A "BRUTALITY," BUT WHICH EUROPE, SOMEHOW, BELIEVES A NECESSITY.

A POLOGISING for being
unable through in-
disposition to attend a
meeting at St. James' Hall,
"called to express sym-
pathy with the Emperor of
Germany in his conflict
with the Pope," Earl Russell
wrote :—

"The very same principles
which bound me to ask for
equal freedom for the Roman
Catholic, the Protestant Dis-
senter, and the Jew, bind me
to protest against a conspiracy
which aims at confining the
German Empire in chains, never,
it is hoped, to be shaken off. I
hasten to declare, with all friends
of freedom, and, I trust, with
the great majority of the English
nation, that I could no longer
call myself a lover of civil and
religious liberty were I not to
proclaim my sympathy with the
Emperor of Germany in the
noble struggle in which he is
engaged. We have nothing to
do with the details of the German laws; they may be just,
they may be harsh; we can only
leave it to the German people
to decide for themselves, as we
have decided for ourselves. At
all events, we are able to see
that the cause of the German
Emperor is the cause of liberty,
and the cause of the Pope is the
cause of slavery."

(See Cartoon, "Bismarck and
his Backer.")

THE DUKE OF EDIN-
BURGH and the Grand
Duchess Marie Alexan-
drovna of Russia were this
day married at the Winter
Palace, St. Petersburg. The
orthodox ceremony was
performed by Greek eccle-
siastics, and the Anglican
by Dean Stanley.

NEW RUSSIAN BONDS.

(Jan. 22d, 1874.)

"For dark and trees tend smoke
is the marsh."
Thackeray—The Primrose.

PUNCH KRITLALAMPONISK.

Yes, my Alfred, thou sang'st truly,
So said of the Primrose, too :
Wore that "dank" not linked unduly
With the "tender" and the "true."
Witness Russia's shire of splendour,
Stars and streams, more bright yet tenderer,
Than illumine our midnight blue.

Mourn that shine like th we fair maidens
Who o'ercame a fairest brake;

To the wedding-candle's cadence
Moving, stately, side by side—
Virgin queens, with promise laden,
That look latest on the maiden
Ere her nuptial knot is tied,

Mourn, that eahes one of honey—
Tenkey mourn, whose gifts of gold
Prove, too often, fairy-money,
Turned to dust, before 'tis told,

Be this pale to thee beholden
For joys long-lived as they're golden,
Glowing as thy hearts are cold.

Let rude Boreas, balked sterner,
Shake the Winter-Palace door,
For Rose fronts and snows the
                    warmer
Be the Loves for them in store.
Hymen, even in aid of Hymen!

Unless, we know, a finery there is,
Gone the fairest the more free."

(See Cartoon, p. 164, "The Latn' in
'Russia Bonds.'")

* Everybody knows, or ought to know, the
effect of wonna cold in stooping denial to bad
ending.

BISMARCK AND HIS BACKER.

EARL RUSSELL. "Go it, BISMARCK!—Pitch into 'em! I'd hit them it myself, only I've such an AWFULLY BAD COLD!"
[Extract from Newspaper.]

Mr. Gladstone, to the surprise of most people, announced to-day, in an address to the electors of Greenwich, that his Cabinet had resolved to dissolve Parliament. The Government prestige had doubtless been impaired by the events of the previous session, and recent elections had indicated a growing feeling against the Ministry, but this step of the Premier was nevertheless an unexpected one. Mr. Gladstone, in his address, explained his reasons for taking it, and (as the "Annual Register" says) "dexterously threw out his bait for a renewal of confidence, in the shape of a diminution of local taxation, and of an intended total repeal of the Income Tax, for which the surplus he should have to show would afford justification."

Mr. Punch thus summarised the Prime Minister's lengthy address.

MR. GLADSTONE'S DISSOLUTION ADDRESS.

My Greenwich Friends,
    This Parliament

THE LATEST IN "RUSSIA BONDS."

Our Tory friends we banged and
    busted,
And mid the nation's crash they
    wanted.
Well, we're not served such awful
    teams
As we could wish, but there be
    plums—
This year in tune the rhyme's
    our victims,
We'll show a surplus of Six
    Millions.

Ten years have I kept up my
    pecker
As Chancellor of the Exchequer;
No when I paid its prospects
    brightly
You'll know that I'm not speak-
    ing lightly.

Local Taxation, I conceive,
I can reform and eke relieve,
But here's the honey, indeed was,
I will take off the Income-Tax.

Bob Lowe was happy as could
    be,
Who brought it down from six to
    three;
But what is Bobby's joy to his
Who triyes it out? (That's seen
    for life.)

But more I you don't have
    half our gumption ;
We'll cheapen things of Home
    Consumption,
Giving, as fast as we are able,
What Bright has called "Free
    Breakfast Table."

Forty-two years of public life
Have made me rather tired of
    strife,
And I should like my time to
    close
With my friend Howse in repose,
But each must do the thing he
    can,
And for the present I'm your
    Man.
We're told the Liberals are a pest,
"Endangering," "worrying,"
    and the rest.
I will not covertly sling the lie,
But all such charges I deny,
And my oath Insinuation stands
Firmer through work of Liberal
    hands,
And we have given you nobler
    cheer
To reverence the Throne and
    Laws.

Now, chums. I'll serve you,
    If you will,
With all I have of strength and
    skill.
If not, far other old go whistle.
"I'll cheerfully accept dismissal."
        W. E. G.

DEGENERATE DAYS!!

POPKINS. "Call this a General Election? Why it's all over in about a fortnight, and——"
FREE AND INDEPENDENT VOTER. "And not a Popan-note among 'em."

AN ELECTOR'S LAMENT.

Vote by Ballot? Vote be bub-
cred! Vote by Ballot? Vote
be hiccup!
Never for them blessed Liberals
wouldn't ha' voted if I'd
know'd.
Call it Liberal? I say shabby,
not to pay a poor man's vote.
Wot's that worth now when
among 'em all there ain't a
6' penn note?

*   *   *   *   *

Now my vote I can't dispose of
'taint no good no more to
me.
Who the man is for my money
there ain't one as I can see.
And for takin' undtwo trouble I
don't feel I got no call,
Which, if so, would be a reason
my I shouldn't vote at all.

But for me between the parties
though to choose there's
scarce a pin,
They 've a trifle in their flavour
change as always went agin.
There's scarce hopes, however
fickle, if so be they gain the
day.
So the Tories I shall poll for,
though I flings my vote away.

JAN. 26.

PROCLAMATION was to-
day issued for the
dissolution of Parliament,
and writs for the new elections were announced as
returnable on the 9th March.
On the 18th Mr. Gladstone
addressed his constituents
on Blackheath. He was
returned for Greenwich, but
only second on the poll
with 5,968 votes to his
Conservative opponent Mr.
Boord with 6,193. It was
soon seen that the elections
were going against the
Liberals. When they were
over, the Conservatives
found themselves 50 ahead
of their opponents. At
last Mr. Disraeli found
himself the leader of a
substantial Conservative
majority.

(See Cartoon, "Paradise and
the Peri.")

PARADISE AND THE PERI.

"Joy, joy for ever! my task is done—
The gates are passed, and Heaven is won!"—LALLA ROOKH.

PUNCH'S PERI IN PARADISE.

AT LAST!

LEAVE luscious Tom Moore to bewarble the glories
Of Paradise barred to his Peri forlorn—
I'm his Peri, give *Punch* the great teacher of Tories,
And for Eden, long-darkit, the Treasury benches!

In the Tom-Moorish legend, the Peri 'twas given

When she brought them the gift that was dearest to
Heaven—
The tear of a sinner bewailing his sin.

So Ben, *Punch's* Peri, the key talismanic
To the gates of his Downing Street Eden most find,
Through Premier changes, and labours Titanic
In teaching a class, sore to hearts disheartend.

He hath digged for his key-stone—who knows in what

For his talisman dived—in what depths, through what
grief!
Made Tories, bewildered, submit to what Whiggings!
Shewn what faithless polemic of speech, bright as
brief!

For the doubt has found words, win for dull, wind for weary;
His brains, time, and temper to his party has given;
I an brought gift after gift that he thought—patient Peri!—

First, pickback Protection he
  tried on the portal
That best Pitt's Eden to
  dashing desire,
When he brought from the battle
  to Corn Traffic mortal,
The sigh of a Peel, and the
  smile of a Squire.

"The smile of a Squire!" quoth
  the Messenger Angel,
Who does Peter's office at
  Downing Street door,
"Seated since Corn-Law repeal,
  rule's certain evangel,
Is proclaim, on davel, but we
  need something more.

"Thus the sigh of a Peel, from
  the mart of thy sorrow—
Barbed even, oft poisoned, and
  levelled too low—
May prove how, at times, eagles
  suffer from sparrows,
But as passport to Peculiar
  Place is no go."

Away flew the Peri, a fetterless
  rover
O'er the wide-spread domain
  between Chaos and Cosmos,
For Protectionist's doctrine Protection flung over,
And Mohr, at the gate, Household challenge flung down.

But "No," quoth the Angel,
  "Return Befts for pass-keys
Can serve only those who have
  faith in their power,—
As infallible Popes have believed
  in their Manu-keys,—
Not those who adopt them as
  toys of the hour."

Back again flew the Peri, en-
  tombed, undaunted,
Of all cries except the earth
  and she air, far and near,
Then launched at the gate—with
  "At last, see, what's wanted,
Triple Talisman—Ballot, and
  Bible, and Beer!"

The Messenger Angel bowed low
  —at their hinges
The gates flew back meekly,
  constrained to obey,
And the last thing I saw, was
  the Peri's wing-fringes
Into Teetotry Paradise clearing their way!

FEB. 7.

A DESPATCH forwarded
by Sir Garnet Wolse-
ley to the Colonial Office,
stated that the main object
of the expedition had been
fully attained, and that the
troops now on their home-
ward march would em-
bark immediately at Cape
Coast Castle for England. Sir Garnet and
his army had entered Coomassie, the strong-
hold of King Coffee of Ashantee, on the 5th,
after five days' hard fighting. The captives
of the King were liberated, and the English
leader, finding it useless to negotiate with a
nation like the Ashantees, "whose whole scheme

necessary "to leave such a mark of our power
to punish as should deter from future aggression
a nation whom treaties do not bind." He
therefore gave orders for the destruction of the
palace and the burning of the city of Coomassie.
On the 13th, however, the Treaty of Fommarah
was entered into with the King of Ashantee. Its

renunciation of supremacy over certain districts,
and the keeping up of a road from Coomassie to
the coast for purposes of trade.

King Coffee's state umbrella (crimson and
black velvet with gold trimmings) taken at
Coomassie, was brought to England, and presented to the Queen at Windsor.

DEARLY BOUGHT.

SIR GARNET. "It don't look much, Madam, but it has cost good money, and better lives."
BRITANNIA. "And but for you, SIR GARNET, might have cost more of both!"

["King Coffee's Umbrella has been brought to England."—Morning Paper.]

Feb. 17.

Mr. Gladstone to-day tendered his resignation to the Queen, who sent for Mr. Disraeli. On the 20th the latter submitted his Cabinet to Her Majesty. It included himself as First Lord of the Treasury, and twelve colleagues: Lord Chancellor, Lord Cairns; Lord President of the Council, Duke of Richmond; Lord Privy Seal, Lord Malmesbury; Foreign Secretary, Lord Derby; India, Lord Salisbury; the Colonies, Lord Carnarvon; War, Mr. Gathorne Hardy; Home Secretary, Mr. R. A. Cross; Admiralty, Mr. Ward Hunt; Chancellor of the Exchequer, Sir Stafford Northcote; Postmaster-General, Lord John Manners.

In addition to these, the Duke of Abercorn was made Lord-Lieutenant of Ireland, and Sir Michael Hicks Beach Chief Secretary for Ireland.

Feb. 23.

To-day Punch sustained another great loss in the death, at the age of 59, of its Editor, the brilliant and genial Shirley Brooks. Punch contained a tribute to the memory of its well-beloved chief, from which the following is an extract:—

SHIRLEY BROOKS.

Born April 29, 1815.
Died February 23, 1874.

Shirley Brooks has been taken from us in the full force of his buoyant and genial activity. Like so many soldiers of the Pen, he has died, as a good Knight should, in harness, and at his post. His memory will be cherished by all who knew him, and by those most who knew him best. For men have ever brought to the head service of the Periodical Press more nervous intelligence, a mind better equipped for its work, a more self-sustaining purpose to do his best in all he attempted, and a more loyal determination to render true and due service in all he took in hand.

During the years—the too few!—of his Editorship of this Journal, he built up a store of strength in himself, and drew upon others too, as their confidence, trust, and service, grew out of their closer knowledge of the man and master. During the years—the too few!—of his Editorship of this Journal, he Staff have found in him—who was ever the pleasantest of comrades—the most considerate, generous, and kindly of Chiefs.

THE WINNING "STROKE."

Punch. "Come! Glad you're out, Sir."
Dizzy. "Thanks! I knew those SLIDING SEATS would spurt 'em!"

Feb. 28.

To-day, at last, the seemingly interminable Tichborne Trial came to a much-desired end. It was on its 188th day that the Lord Chief Justice concluded his charge to the Jury. After half an hour's absence the jury returned a verdict of guilty, and "The Claimant" was sentenced to fourteen years' penal servitude.

MARCH 19.

The new Parliament was opened by Commission, and Benjamin Disraeli, the astute, the patient, appeared in triumph as Prime Minister.

(See Cartoon, "The Winning 'Stroke.'")

A Note to Vol. LXVI. says:—"The Public ones were believed to have materially helped Mr. Disraeli to the large majority the General Election had given him." (This was the first year of the "sliding seats" being used by University Crews in the Boat Race.)

Parliament had assembled for the election of the Speaker on the 5th, when Mr. Brand had been unanimously elected. The Lord Chancellor read the Royal Message, crowned (says *Mr. Punch's* "Essence of Parliament") by promises so modest as—

1. Simplification of Land-Laws—a bold enough promise, however, as far as probabilities of success go, even with Cairns in office and Selborne out to help him.

2. Extension to Ireland of the judicial re-arrangements and administrative fusion of Law and Equity, already enacted for England.

3. A Royal Commission to inquire into the working of

THE LEVÉE OF THE SEASON.

the Masters and Servant's Act, and the Criminal Offences Act of last Session.

4. A nap in the Pot : Reform of the proved injustices of the Liquor Law.

5. Amendment of the Law as to Friendly and Provident Societies.

Not one "blessing" as heroic undertaking among the lot ; but all sufficiently difficult, and very much wanted—practical improvements, in fact, of a real importance bearing no proportion to the show they make upon paper.

MARCH 30.

THE whole of the troops, 1600 in number, who had returned from Ashantee, were this day reviewed by the Queen in Windsor Great Park.

Sir Garnet Wolseley, who declined titular honours, was made K.C.B. and voted a sum of 25,000*l.*, and Lieutenant Gifford received the Victoria Cross for personal valour. Her Majesty herself fastening it on his breast.

(*See Cartoon, "The Levée of the Season."*)

MARCH 31.

THERE had been a strike among the Farm Labourers in the Eastern Counties for better wages, supported by the Union. The farmers "locked out" those of the men who were members of the "Union." The labourers had to yield in the end. Joseph Arch was the

principal Unionist leader of the movement (Note to Vol. LXVI.).

"BON LOCUTUS EST!"

A LAY OF THE NEW MARKET STRIKE.

He sang it at noon, when the rooks took flight
Over the misty hill ;
He sang it at noon, when the sun was bright
In the drip from the wheel of the mill ;
He sang it at eve, where with weary hand
Under came the ploughing team,
And he sang it at night, 'neath his every mood,
Till his song died off in his dream :
And the song of Hodge was in minor key,
Less of music is it than moan ;
The song of a life that blank of glee
From youth to age had grown.

A NEW ARCH-BISHOP.

JOSEPH ARCH (to BISHOP OF MANCHESTER). "Ah! my Lord, I never expected to find your Lordship on our side!"

[See the Bishop of Manchester's Letter to the *Times* on the Lock-out of the Labourers—"Are the Farmers mad?" &c. &c.

The Bishop of Manchester, in a letter to the *Times*, had expressed sympathy with the Labourers.

(*See Cartoon*, "*A New Arch-Bishop*.")

APRIL 16.

THE CHANCELLOR OF THE EXCHEQUER, Sir

He had the handling of the splendid surplus bequeathed to the Conservatives by Mr. Gladstone. He did not, however, propose to abolish the Income Tax as Mr. Gladstone had suggested, but reduced it by one penny only, abolishing the remaining Sugar Duties and the House Tax.

Says Mr. Punch's "Essence of Parliament:"—

And thus on Thursday, was produced the exciting drama of THE BUDGET—in the most crowded House of the Session. Here is a brief analysis of what we think we are safe in describing as a great success for Sir Stafford Northcote, Bart., the sagacious and ingenious author:—

The piece opens with a Prologue, entitled "Expenditure," in which we are introduced to those very familiar personages, Debt, Consolidated Fund, Army and Navy, Civil Service, Post-Office, Packet Service, Telegraphs, and Collection of Revenue. Their united incomes rise to the imposing dimensions of £74,302,000.

Act 1. introduces a new figure—"Estimated Revenue."

" BLACK SHEEP."

—who, in a struggle with Expenditure, comes out victorious. Estimated Revenue is the father of the child, whose fortunes give the leading interest to the night's performance—Surplus, a lusty young giant of SIX MILLIONS!

In Act II. the Author deals with the efforts of various rival powers—Indian Famine and English Famine, Navy, Mails, Railways, &c., &c.—to get possession of Young Surplus, or to divide his wealth among them.

In Act III. we have the division of the spoil. Debt gets half a million; Local Taxation, for his children, Lunatics, Police, and Government Buildings' Rating, a million and a quarter; Income-tax, close on two millions (by remission of one of the four pennies now levied); Sugar, two millions full; and House Duty half a million.

The piece concludes with a general doom of the Relieved Industries, while the Disappointed Claimants—Beer, Malt, & Co.—scowl, diminished and discomfited,

APRIL 18.

To-day the remains of Dr. Livingstone were interred in Westminster Abbey. The coffin bore the inscription:—" David Livingstone, Born at Blantyre, Lanarkshire, Scotland. March 19, 1813. Died at Ilala, Central Africa. May 4, 1873." Mr. Punch said,

Droop half-mast colours, bare, bare-headed crowds,
As this plain coffin o'er the tide is slung,
To pass by womb of aisles and ratified shrouds,
As erst by Able's breech a hero hung.

Ope the Abbey doors, and bear him in
To sleep with king and statesman, chief, and sage,
The Missionary, come of weaver-kin,

He needs no epitaph to guard a name
Which men shall prize while worthy work is known;
He lived and died the good—he that his fame:
Let marble crumble; this is Living-stone.

APRIL 20.

The Archbishop of Canterbury introduced in the Lords a "Bill for the better Administration of the Law respecting Public Worship." In his speech he referred to existing evils and anomalies, and, in particular, condemned the Romanish practices observed by various Anglican clergymen, which this Bill was designed to check.

APRIL 20.

In introducing the Naval Estimates, which reached the enormous sum of £10,179,485, Mr. Ward Hunt complained of the unsatisfactory state in which the Navy had been left by the late Government, whom Mr. Goschen defended.

BRITANNIA'S CHICKS IN A BAD WAY.

(A Fancy Sketch,—at least, Punch hopes so,—after W. Hunt.)

Air.—"Ten Little Niggers."

Ten British Iron-clads, above and of, the line,
One out her own copper off, then there were nine!

Nine British Iron-clads, much peppered in defence,
One struck a shoal—not in the charts—then there were eight!

Eight British Iron-clads, manœuvring off Devon,
One burst her boilers, then there were seven!

Seven British Iron-clads, fired all through with bricks,
The dry-rot got into one, then there were six!

Six British Iron-clads, anxiously to ride at their's,
One was rammed by all the rest, then there were five!

Five British Iron-clads, sailing round the Nore,
One fouled the Ramsgate light-ship, then there were four!

Four British Iron-clads, for harbour due, not sea,
One grounded on her own barb-hourn, then there were three!

Three British Iron-clads, firing in review,
One blew her turrets through her head, then there were two!

Two British Iron-clads, each with its monster gun,
One burst and blew her ship up, then there was one.

One British Iron-clad, won't stay, wont, won't, nor stirr—
If for him (and he cons back again, p'raps she will disappear.

MAY 13.

The Emperor of Russia, Alexander II., arrived in England on a visit to the Queen. He was well received and considerably fêted, his emancipation of the serfs having inclined the people of this country to regard him with favour.

[See Cartoon, "The New (North) Star."]

THE NEW (NORTH) "STAR."

Freedom and Love, go forth to meet
The Czar on Welcome's wings;
Yours are the smiles the Guest to greet,
With such credentials brings.

In this hand, his and our loved child,
Whom to our Prince he gave;
In that, the collar that he filed
From the neck of the Slave.

JUNE 5.

The Committee on the Licensing Bill, 3 P.M. in and around London. The clause relating to *bonâ fide* travellers, about which there had been much talk, was settled by defining him as a person who had lodged on the preceding night at least 3 miles from the place where he demanded refreshments ("Annals of Our Time"). On the done so much to secure the Conservative victory, and who had expected so much from the Government they had helped to office, were by no means satisfied with the Measure.

HUNG ON HIS BETRAYERS.

We fondly 'oped they did intend
The Licensed Victlers to
befriend;
Instead of which they abandons
And makes the Licensin' Hart
was.   (made.
We're told—fools as us they has
As Moreton says, "We are be-
trapped!"   [Crow;
In change for Bruce we've got a
By which we fools we're gammed
a fence.
The Times with the Liberal side
On that there Bill of his's divide;
The Bill and blake is both a
"do;"   [the two.
To hall a "Cross" between

(See Cartoon, "The Great
"Trick Act.")

JUNE 24.

MR. PLIMSOLL'S Mer-
chant Shipping Bill,
whose object was mainly to
prevent mischief resulting
from overloading, was re-
jected by 173 against 170.

JUNE 25.

THE Public Worship Re-
gulation Bill was read
a third time in the Lords.
On the same day the Su-
preme Court of Judicature
Bill passed in that assembly.

JUNE 30.

MR. BUTT introduced
his motion in favour
of Home Rule in Ireland.
Dr. Ball on behalf of the
Government met it with a
direct negative. On the
2nd July the debate took
place. Mr. Disraeli in a
humorous speech twitted
the Irish with their fondness
for calling themselves "a
conquered race." "No-
thing is to me more extraordinary than the determination of the Irish people
to proclaim to the world
that they are a subjugated
people. I deny that the
Irish people are conquered:
they are proud of it; I
deny that they have any
ground for that pride,"
"England had been sub-
jugated quite as much, but
never boasted of it. The Norman conquered
Ireland, but it was after they had conquered
England. Cromwell conquered Ireland, but
it was after he had conquered England. I
am opposed to it" (he added) "for the sake
of the Irish people as much as for the sake
of the English or for the Scotch. I am

portant crisis of the world—that perhaps is
nearer arriving than some of us suppose—a
united people welded in one nationality; and
because I feel that if we sanction this policy,
if we do not cleanse the Parliamentary bosom
of this perilous stuff, we shall bring about the
disintegration of the kingdom and the destruc-

THE GREAT "TRICK ACT."

RING MASTER (Mr. CROSS). "Now, then, Mr. WITTLES, stand out o' the way!"
CLOWN (LITTLE WITTLES). "Oh oh, of course! Of course I gave 'er a bump, and chill'd 'er short of room, and of
course I'm to get nothing for it! That's what I call Wittles's silliness, now!"   [Exit, disgusted.

Mr. Punch said:—

The truths on the subject are disagreeable ones, but
they lie in a nut shell; and Punch can formulate some of
them which Mr. Michael Hicks Beach and the Marquis of
Hartington and Mr. Disraeli can not put quite so
plainly. They are these:—

Home-Rule means:—

Rome-rule in School legislation: Peasant-rule in Land
legislation: Protectionist-rule in Trade legislation: Job-

HOME-(RULE)-OPATHY.

IRELAND. "Ah, now, then, it's cruel bad I am, intirely; and it's the dacint Gintlemen here knows the stuff to do me good!"

DR. BULL. "No, no, Friend BUTT!—None of your nostrums! We saw her well through the 'Repale' Fever,—and she'll come out of this ould ailint yet!"

"But unto him, as, to his eppi sint inured,
In his red eye the fire of battle burned,
Far-sighted Fronter and grave Gocher's drew,
And their wet blankets on Achilles threw.

Thus worsted, his weapons to the ground he threw
And from the field, with scowling soul, withdrew.

(See Cartoon, "Second Thoughts are Best.")

The much-vaunted Measure, nevertheless, has
not at all answered expectations, and Mr.
Gladstone's opposition, generally blamed at the
time, is thought by many to have been justified
by results.

AUG. 4.

An amendment to the Public Worship
Regulation Bill had been made in the
Commons providing for an appeal being made
to the Archbishop. This produced a conflict
between the Lords and the Commons. The

"SECOND THOUGHTS ARE BEST."

Then up he rode to the coach-window.
And his oak-shooter he popped in:
Says the Archbishop, "Save an egg's in egg's,
This is the bold Tur-pin!"

"Your Grace or your Life," says the Highway-
"You may smile and think it fun.
But that Bill you drop, or else I pop,
With my oak barrels, every one!"

But the Archbishop he made a smile—
"Stand out o' the way," says he,
"And, as for this six-shooter of yours,
'Twill do you more harm than me."

"Second thoughts are best," quoth the Highway.
"There's something in what you say,"
So he loosed his brag, and he turned his nag,
And quietly rode away.

Archbishop conversed, but many of the Bishops
objected vigorously, 9 of them voting against it.
Lord Salisbury spoke of the threat of possible
action by the Commons as "bluster," and the
terror of it as a "bugbear." Ultimately the
appeal to the Archbishop was struck out in the
Lords, by 64 to 23. When the Bill got back
to the Commons, Mr. Disraell, whilst advising
the Commons to agree to the Lords' Amendments, took occasion to retort upon the Marquis
of Salisbury, referring to him as not being

"a man who measures his phrases," as "a great
master of gibes, and flouts and jeers." He
hoped the Commons would not fall into the
Marquis's trap. "I hope we shall show my
noble friend that we remember some of his
manœuvres when he was a simple member of
the House, and that we are not to be taunted
into taking a very indiscreet step, a step refusion
to all our own wishes and expectations, merely to
show that we resent the contemptuous phrases
of one of my colleagues." Lord Salisbury

afterwards protested that he never used the
language attributed to him in the House of
Commons by "a person or persons of considerable authority." When he used the terms
"bluster" and "bugbear" he referred entirely to
what had been said in the House of Lords.
Ultimately the Lords' Amendments were agreed
to.

Mr. Disraell in this debate described the Bill
as one "intended to put down Ritualism,
meaning by Ritualism the practices of a certain

portion of the clergy, symbolical, according to their own admission, of doctrines which they were solemnly bound to renounce."

Aug. 7.

PARLIAMENT was prorogued. It had been "a Session of moderate promise and even more meagre performance" (said *Mr. Punch's "Essence"*), "a Session if not otherwise memorable, perhaps destined to be long remembered as the one to which two Churches may yet have to trace the root of Disestablishment, and in which the anarchy of Her Majesty's Opposition has been reflected in the feebleness and headlessness of Her Majesty's Government."

Friday.—The Queen's Speech of Prorogation. It says nothing but what everybody knew already, and so amounts to the usual sum and substance of Queen's speeches at Prorogation—*nil. Stay*—there is one paragraph in a sombre setting ; that which expresses the belief of H. M.G. that the restoration of peace and order in Spain will be best promoted by a rigid abstinence from interference by other Governments. [*Exit Scene!*]

Or, my Lords and Gentlemen of both sides, *Punch* dismisses you to the relaxation of your pleasure-places or the retirement and reflection of your homes. "Go"—and next Session do not "do likewise."

(See Cartoon, *"A Real Conservative Revival."*)

The Ministerial Whitebait Dinner had been held at Greenwich on the 4th August.

Aug. 10.

MARSHAL BAZAINE effected his escape from the Isle St. Marguerite, where he had been confined since his trial.

Oct. 1.

CRIMES of ruffianly violence were rampant at this time, and *Mr. Punch* suggested that the cat, which had been found so efficacious in the case of the garotters, should be tried upon

A REAL CONSERVATIVE REVIVAL.

"We've been little or no Fish, Gentlemen ; but at least we have revived that great and Conservative institution, THE MINISTERIAL FISH-DINNER !!!"

A WORD TO THE ROUGH.

You ruffian, you scoundrel, you brutal Yahoo !
There 's a good time, be sure of it, coming for you.
You dull, drunken savage, malignantly vile !
You dastard, you blackguard, you criminal and !

You'll be taught to take care how you're they you wreak,

How in fear, wrench, and eyes full with clenched fist you sing ; [sing.
Knock down, stamp on, and smash them with eyes bent-
You shall know, you foul sot, you shall feel to your skin,
What it is to gouge eyes out, and also to bark in ;
Or, in beastial sleep with some wretched temper,
To bite off your antagonist's nose or his ear.

Now you this Learned scourge of time though ugly ? 'Tis the Cat !

On guessing, your fête, with
effect it was tried.
And your bread, too, no doubt
will be reached through
your hide.

(*See Cartoon, "The Demon
'Rough.'"*)

OCT. 2.

Much occurred to-day
a disastrous accident
on the Regent's Canal,
near the Zoological Gar-
dens, caused by an explo-
sion on board the fly-barge
"Tilbury," laden with four
tons of blasting powder,
and six barrels of petro-
leum. The North Lodge
Bridge was blown to pieces,
and much damage done
to property in the neigh-
bourhood. The Coroner's
jury held the Canal Com-
pany guilty of gross neg-
ligence in permitting fires
to be lighted on such
barges, and considered the
existing laws inadequate to
secure public safety.

OCT. 4.

Great surprise was
caused by the arrest
and prosecution of Harry,
Count Von Arnim, lately
German Ambassador at
Paris, on the charge of
retaining State documents
in his possession when he
had been officially dis-
missed from the service of
the State. "In the course
of the proceedings" (says
Mr. Punch's Introduction)
"the publication of a portion of Prince Bismarck's
correspondence on French
affairs proved to be more
interesting than the liti-
gation itself." Count Arnim
was sentenced to two
months' imprisonment. It
was thought that the ami-
able but perhaps not very
discreet Arnim had in-
curred the enmity of the
implacable Chancellor, and that the latter had
resolved upon his ruin.

OCT. 4.

Guizot, the distinguished and venerable
French statesman and historian, died
at Nismes to-day, at the advanced age of 87.

THE DEMON "ROUGH."

Justice. "Look here, you cowardly Ruffian! This has just done Carruthers! We shall soon have to try if it won't just down you!"

GUIZOT.

BORN AT NISMES, OCTOBER 4, 1787; DIED AT VAL
RICHER, SEPTEMBER 12, 1874.

The light, so long tenanted by a band severe,
Dies grave and gradual, without flush or glow,—
No storm cuts short the radiance calm and clear,
That mellowed deedsful but when skies were fair.

Strange hours of Heavenly rule that be

Least lucky in life, was deemed to be
Such People's minister, such Sovereign's tool!

All reverenced the teacher, from whose chair
Truth's trumpet gave forth its unearthly sound;
And when professor's gown for statesman's wear
Was changed, men devoted a better time come round.

Ah me, blind hours of all these wrongs born!

So strong in his own strength, so
  full of scorn,
For others' weakness, mingling
  with the crowd,

Stamped to their littleness his
  stately port,
  Content, as he's hands showed
  to cordial toil :
A man king's scorn grows too
  too high to court,
  He stood by silent while
  knaves shared their spoil,

Deeming mispspaced another
  good enough
For holidays reared on sands
  of hick and torn ;
Till, when the wind rose, and
  the sea waxed rough,
And at the crumbling base upon
  you to yours,

It found me strength above, nor
  ery below, [down,
Just all, a nature calm, toppled
Sweeping away, in sudden
  overthrow, [and Crown.
  Minister, measure, Cabinet,

And whole, crowned and bewildered, he, the chief,
Who had misjudged, labor-
  dered, things and men,
Struggled back to his feet, he
  sought relief
Where lay his strength, in
  thoughts and books and pen,

And was again the man of his
  first fame, [and gable,
The father, sage, philosopher
For whom each day found its
  day's work —a name
  For everyday, love and
  honour, far and wide.

    *   *   *
Why such him there, where he
  had gained and fell,
Emptying work for which he
  was best born ?
Look to that other field in tilled
  so well, [nobly worn,
  To win the wreath so long and

Oct. 10.

CREMATION, as a military
  process for disposing
of the bodies of the dead, was
at this time being strongly
advocated. To-day, in
conformity with her own
previously expressed desire,
the body of Lady Dilke was
subjected to the process in
the furnace of Herr Siemens
at Dresden, and in the
presence of relatives.

Oct. 10.

MR. PLIMSOLL was still engaged in his
  philanthropic efforts to protect our sailors
against the perils of unseaworthy ships. On
the 28th September, the Duke of Edinburgh
had visited Liverpool and had opened a new
Seamen's Orphanage there, and in his speech
had referred to our want of well trained seamen.

OUR MERCHANT NAVY.

Duke Alfred. "Really, Mr. Plimsoll, we're both in the same Boat. You want Seaworthy Ships : I want Seaworthy Men :—and we'd try and get them."

SHIPS AND MEN.

Seaworthy ships we need.
  That's half a truth to tell ;
Seamen we lack, indeed,
  Seaworthy men as well.

But will unworthy men
  Ships unseaworthy chronn ?
And don't unsafe ships, then,

Whole truth unborn with lips,
  And inculcate with pen,
Provide unworthy ships,
  And have unworthy men.

Oct. 31.

THE influence of Prince Bismarck in Cont.

Nov. 21.

Mr. Gladstone (says a Note to Vol. LXVII.) had published "an anti-Papal pamphlet on 'The Vatican Decrees' which caused considerable excitement and elicited numerous replies. In the previous month he had contributed an article to the 'Contemporary Review' on Ritualism, which also had reference to the modern Ultramontane policy of Rome, and occasioned much controversy."

Mr. Gladstone had by certain of his enemies been charged from time to time with cherishing unavowed Romish proclivities. This attack upon Papal dogmas therefore caused as much surprise in some quarters as indignation in others.

[See Cartoon, "An Unexpected Cut."]

THE HAWARDEN WOODCUTTER.

Illustrious Chatham, when the great
Venerated hero every day,
Still hale in hand would prune about
The oaken bolts of Hayes,

AN UNEXPECTED CUT.

Mr. P. "Go it, Gladstone! We didn't expect to find you cutting at THAT Tree, you know."

Mr. G. "All right, Mr. Punch! I chose my own Tree, and my own Time!"

"Mr. Gladstone has been cutting down Trees at Hawarden."—*Morning Paper.*

Enforcing Nature's wise decrees,
Here lopping, felling there,
Whose untrodden boles from younger trees
Usurped the light and air.

So the famed Wizard of the North,
Where hunter skins shone clear,
Made at level, would hinple forth,
With staunch Tom Purdey near,
To summon by Tweed's wimpling tide,
His magic pen flung by,
And bid the minstrel's harp aside,
The Woodman's axe to ply.

Then why should Gladstone prompt the joke,
In Hawarden's forest leisured,
If so the poet's swing and stroke
He fly for health and pleasure?
And for the artist's cant, and call
Of tangled legislation,
Find in the woodman's board and ball
A wholesome recreation?

Proving that he, too, serves the State
Whose toil put to good use is,
On over-growth, for excuse,
Old trees, for old abuses.

When the stout arm thus toppled down
The rotten Church of Erin,
Brings low some dead oak's stagg'y crown,
Room for more saplings clearing,
What wonder if, with equal care,
Brain and axe deal their blow,
If the same lime in felling trees
As fighting Bills he show?
If of no task so tool blunt
That can tax strength and skill,
Upon Rome's oak he turn his blade,
And smite, come what come will!

DEC. 5.

"Mr. Disraeli's Government" (says a Note to Vol. LXVII.), "had agreed to undertake a new Polar Expedition. Sir Henry Rawlinson was President of the Geographical Society,

which lately had been active in procuring the consent of the Government." "The North-West Passage" was a picture by Mr. Millais, R.A., exhibited in this year's Royal Academy. The motto to the Cartoon was the motto of the picture.

THE POLAR EXPEDITION.

Mr. H—y R—wson presents his compliments to Mr. Punch, and will feel obliged by his appending the following correspondence:—

From Sir H—y R—wson—n to Mr. Disraeli.

Dear Diary, you longed to your present control
Of the country by means of a very high Poll ;

"THE NORTH-WEST PASSAGE."

"It can be done, and England ought to do it."

Respectfully dedicated to J. E. Millais, R.A., with Mr. Punch's Apologies for an effort of Memory.

But, if to please all, you yet fain would aspire,
We'll find you a Pole that's enthusiastically higher
Than any you ever have heard of, by far.
Yours faithfully, and to the purpose, H. M.

From Mr. D—sraeli to Sir H—y R—wlins—n.

Dear R—wlins—n, thanks for your letter and quip ;
I can't let a good opportunity slip
Of doing what should have been done when the life
Of a Franklin might perhaps have been spared to his wife.
The North Pole of sense one is to you than to me,
But, by Jingo, we'll find it !
Yours truly, B. D.

(New Cartoon, "The North-West Passage.")

DEC. 9.

A TRANSIT of Venus took place to-day. Great preparations had been made and several expeditions despatched from various countries to observe it.

THE ASTRONOMER AT HOME.

I melt, whatever Proctor writes,
Or Lockyer, or Airy,
Out-door observing, these chill nights,
A want to the unwary.

Long though you gaze into the sky
(Not quite, I hope, cigarless),

What chance of seeing mixtures fly
Through a heaven that hangs starless !

A blazing fire in bright steel bars
first observe, after dining ;
And study—if you must have stars—
These 'neath seathed eyebrows shining.

Transit of Venus simply watch,
With comrades that columns fill ;
There is no place like home to catch
Your Venus in her transit.

Let who will 'mid Exquisites' snare,
Seek freezing-post and thawing-snow,
My Venus one short transit knows—
From dining-room to drawing-room.

✦ 1875 ✦

JAN. 8.

ON the last day of 1874 (says the Introduction to Vol. LXVIII) General Campos in the provinces, and the Captain-

General at Madrid, suddenly proclaimed the son of Queen Isabella, a youth of seventeen, as King, under the title of Alfonso XII. On the 6th January, King Alfonso left Paris to assume the crown, entering Barcelona on the 14th. He was warmly received, and "won favour by his personal conduct and bearing."

The position of the youthful King was, however, a difficult one. The Carlist war still continued, and recognition of the new Royalty was none too ready in some quarters.

(*See Cartoon, "Between Two Fires."*)

"*BETWEEN TWO FIRES.*"

"Prince Bismarck has intimated to the new Spanish Government that its recognition by Germany must be contingent on the withdrawal of the suspension of the two suppressed Protestant Journals, and the re-opening of the closed Protestant Meeting-House."

"When the Pope sent his blessing to King Alfonso, and renewed his Nuncio's commission at Madrid, it was under the assurance that the old ecclesiastical and educational supremacy of the Holy Church would be restored."—*Newspaper Correspondence from Spain.*

JAN. 13.

MR. GLADSTONE, in a letter addressed to Earl Granville, announced his withdrawal from the leadership of the Liberal Party. He described the result in his mind of recent events thus:—

"I see no public advantage in my continuing to act as the leader of the Liberal Party; and at the age of sixty-five and after forty-two years of a laborious public life I think myself entitled to retire on the present opportunity. This retirement is dictated to me by my personal views as to the best method of spreading the

closing years of my life. I need hardly say that my conduct in Parliament will continue to be governed by the principles on which I have heretofore acted, and whatever arrangements may be made for the transaction of general business and for the advantage or convenience of the Liberal Party, they will have my cordial support. I should perhaps add that I am at present, and mean for a short time to be, engaged on a special matter which occupies me closely."

Mr. Punch, commenting on this startling event, said:—

FAREWELL!

Can it be that the time has come for that saddest of sad words?

"Forgo what doth love rulers pal unmen unornband Consilio[?] et cum [?]

Ad propium qui [?] dovetendo ab [?]!"

Or, if Punch may paraphrase Journal,—

Well he who, from Llandudno's calm retreat, Late learnt, at once, on battle and defeat, Well he, though I forwent good, and Granville pray. Himself the Leader's treacheous flag away? Still in his prime of power, unbent by years, Renounce the joy of battle with his peers, Unmoved by Punch's counsel or his prayer, Nor to his ranks relinquished name on heir

Can such a transmogrification indeed by true—from the hearts of the Benches to the heels of the Banks, from Politics to Polemics, from Hansard to Homer?

Yes! He has chosen—and not un all asking, as t'were asked Pompey, but without his livery, "That honey gladsince spoken dum rabit accepted?"—Can such a fighter take his discharge at ween? With Russell still politically combative and controversial, still sensitive to a party row, still hot over the memory of a party defeat and proud in the recall of a party triumph, at eighty-three—! With Hannah, only ten years younger, still in the Head-Master's Chair, still wielding the Head-Master's birchen sceptre over his Tory pupils and subjects—Gladstone thrown up the leadership of the Liberals at fen years over the three score?

It cannot be true that iron has clone this, nor can we try to k the force of that destructive "tide in the affairs of men," which has swept away so much good work—washed out ail traces of so much gratitude.

Can it be that W. E. G., has found Pen a pleasanter or more potent weapon than Tongue? capable of being used with more hummerhaurn in its aim, more precision in its stroke, more pride in the triumphs it secures? But there are so many possible translators in the Comic-myracy of translations from Homer, even of translations as bad as W. E. G.'s of the speech of Achilles that year; so many who could have cut the Churchter by the ears on the Vatican Doctors, and so few who can

"Wield at will the fierce democracy"

which cleaves between it the Benches of the House of Commons; so few who can unite in a party-firm men and minds in for spart as Dilke and Acland, Bright and Grenville, Rylands and Lubbock, Playfair and Peter Taylor; so few under whom all that call themselves "Liberal" can be content to move and club their differences; so few we can all be proud of; so few at whose feet defeated enemies can lay their colours without shame! . . . But if the resurgent emblem, what is Punch to say of the paugust? "Follow my Leader" was a grave banal enough the sense of the livelier Liberals to harp the value of. But "Choose my leader" . . . ! What are these skittish and skipping spts so likely to make of that game?

And when and Alexander—even if he have guessed his ring to Graville—has made no sign to guide the choice of his successor!

But that monument must be found, "Le Roi est mort!" Whom matter is Punch to couple with his "Vive le Roi!"?

"GOOD-BYE!"

DIZZLI. "Sorry to see you look ODEAR with Books: you're cutting with them. Perhaps you're the wiser of the two."

FEB. 3.

It now became necessary to select a new Liberal leader in the House of Commons in place of Mr. Gladstone, and to-day a meeting of Liberal Members was held at the Reform Club for this purpose, presided over by Mr. John Bright. The statesman supposed to be son of the Duke of Devonshire, Mr. W. E. Forster, and Mr. Goschen, some adding the names of Sir William Vernon Harcourt and Mr. Robert Lowe. Mr. Forster, however, sent a letter to be read at the meeting declining candidature. The choice of the meeting fell upon the Marquis of Hartington, who was duly initiated

assuming leadership in the Lords and chief
authority over the party.

(*See Cartoon, "The Row of Ulysses."*)

"THE ROW OF ULYSSES."

" Then, with a manly pace, he took his stand ;
And grasp'd the bow, and tong'd it in his hand.

Three times, with beating heart, he made essay ;
Three times, compel to the task, gave way ;
A modest boldness on his cheek appear'd ;
And thrice he hoped, and thrice again he fear'd ;
The fourth had drawn it. The great one with joy
Behold ; him with a sign forbade the boy,
His ardous straight the clamtrous chief suppress'd,
And, artful, thus the wise train address'd :

" Oh, lay the stone on youth yet immature !
(For heaven forbid, such weakness should endure)
How shall this era, amount to the bow,
Resort an insult, or repel a foe ?
But you ! whom heaven with better nerves has bless'd,
Attempt the trial, and the prize contest."

POPE's *Odyssey*, Book xxi.

THE ROW OF ULYSSES.

" Who now can bend Ulysses' bow, and wing
The well-aim'd arrow through the distant ring ?"

FEB. 8.

PARLIAMENT was opened by Commission.

The Lord Chancellor performed the part of *Queen*
"for this occasion only." He would have pleased
Fchmon. The Speech in his mouth was "well spoken,
with good emphasis and good discretion." Still the performance would have had a better chance of giving his words
with effect, had they been shown into a more rhythmic
and polished form—say something in the fashion—

'Mid peace abroad, prosperity at home,
Gladly once more to the Old House we come !

Our Russian friends won't again catch us slaves.
Spain's latest taw, you see, has " Blood " come down,
Poor Spain may well be thankful for a Crown !
Marley, once chasten'd, so deep in chains or mess,
Japan and t' hath sent a Jerrah have been.
Look out for ourselves when they come to jar—
But Wade (nine both r) came 'twixt them and us,
the Celonies are well as well can be—
Gold Coast, Natal, and, lest, not least, Fiji.
And if Langalibalele we've bade quiet,
Coleman's pleased, and that's no small affair.
In India with foxday we have starve,
And conquered it, thank short limpin and kind Heaven !

MY WORTHY COMMONS,
     You'll be glad to learn
Our trouking-book need glow you no concern.
Sour bills we have to settle, but so small,
You may say they're as good as none at all.
Reform of Judicature, late of Land,
We'll take up where we lost your stayed our hand.
'Foul deer, rank unlooeve, polluted streams,
We're little to deal with—don't say these are devious ?
Friendly Societies and Merchant Shipping
We'll mind, and we those whipped who earn a whipping
For wife-beaters and kicking roughs—it beats
I dole with sour votes to sprinkle brutes ;

We ask leave to keep cats—cats
with nine tails ;
Then Public Prosecutors pleased
shall be,
Till not a crime worshipped of
us go free.
This, with what little pen can
lend to do
For Trade Officers, and Farm
Tenants too,
Will, I think, make a programme
that deals well—
How you'll work out, that let
the Session tell !

The Liberal Party at
this time, discouraged by
recent defeat, divided in
counsel, and further dis-
organised by the loss of
its old leader, was by
no means in a happy or
flourishing condition. The
jeer, "leaders who do not
lead and followers who will
not follow," seemed more
than ever to strike home,
and it was felt that the task
of the new leader, Lord
Hartington, though he had
been unanimously chosen,
and enjoyed in particular
the valuable support of
Mr. John Bright, was by no
means an easy or a thankful
one.

**THE MARQUIS BO-PEEP
AND THE LIBERAL
SHEEP.**

The Marquis Bo-Peep
Herds the Liberal sheep—
If he only knew where to find
them.
Will they ever come home,
And—oplrous Home Rule and
Rome—   [them ?
Bring their Irish tails behind

(*See Cartoon, " The New
Shepherd."*)

FEB. 8.

THE first Cabman's
Shelter or "Rest"
in London was to-day set
up at the stand in Acacia
Road, St. John's Wood
("*Annals of Our Time.*")

**THE CABMAN'S
SHELTER.**

(*Philanthropist sings.*)

O rest thee, my Cabby, this cold and wet night !
Thy radius is here, and thy gas-moons burn bright.
Where's the tavern or pothouse a shelter could be
So cosy, so warm, and so luxurious for thee !

O rest thee, my Cabby ; may even the most cross
When you all will be wooned from your gas, here, and toss.
So rest thee, tire Cabby, from cold, rain, and sleet.

THE NEW SHEPHERD.

Hartington (new hand, just taken on) "Her, but Master !—Wher be th' Sheep ?"

FEB. 16.

JOHN MITCHELL, an escaped convict, was elected
Member of Parliament for Tipperary. He
had been sentenced to transportation for life
for being implicated in the rebellion of 1848,
but had escaped to America. He was a Home-
Ruler.

Then the notorious Dr. Kenealy, late counsel
for the Claimant in the Tichborne Case. His
violent and unscrupulous advocacy in that case
had exposed him to severe rebuke from the
Bench, and he had later on been disbenched,
disbarred and removed from the list of Queen's
Counsel. He had loudly boasted of what he

Common. _Mr. Punch's_
"Essence of Parliament"
thus recorded these
events :—

Tuesday.—A day not to be
marked with a white stone in
the Parliamentary Register, for
it brought news of the return of
Dr. Kenealy (shall we say, as
the _Englishman_ says, the great
and good?) for Stoke-upon-
Trent, and of John Mitchell, the
escaped convict of 1848, for Tipperary. The ill-news was soon
learned through the lobbies,

> "And M. P.'s read aloud,
> Or whispered with white lips, 'The
> _foes_; they come, they come!'"

Thursday.—Very full House,
and all agog for the opening of
Kenealy Act of the evening's
sensation drama. The vessel
which the Stoke Potters have so
strangely freighted to Imm.on
has ran its place in St. Stephen's.

The _Doctor mirabilis_ was attended to the door of the House
by his usual escort of tag-rag and
bob-tail. Let us hope he will
remember that _of that door_ he
leaves them.

The first question is how to
describe the Doctor.

We have what he appears to
our Englishman—the _English-
man_ edited by Dr. Kenealy—as
at once great and good; a mixture of Cromwell, Milton,
Chatham, Mirabeau, and a
Kennymere Baron—the pro-
founded lawyer, purest patriot,
and finest orator of his time;
who is shortly to shrivel Lincoln's
and Gladstone into nothingness
by his scorching eloquence and
crushing contempt, and then to
stay loose both their shoes, and
lead a mighty Party to wield at
will the fierce democracy. What
he appears to the Englishman of
the House of Commons, we may
judge from the fact that he could
not find two of them to introduce
him to the Speaker.

At the suggestion of Mr. Disraeli,—on the subject of the Resolution of February 23, 1848,
which requires such sponsorship,
was the identification of the
Member, and as there could be
no possible mistake about Dr.
Kenealy—who stood strenuously
along in every arena of the word
—the House waived its standing
order, and Dr. Kenealy was
allowed to take the oaths and
his place, without a godfather.

When Mr. Disraeli moved, that John Mitchell,—
having been tried and convicted of treason-felony in 1848,
and having neither survived the Royal pardon, nor
served his sentence,—remains a felon, and is, therefore,
incapable of sitting in Parliament, probably few but barrister M. P.'s could have misjudged the beauty of seasoned
legal hair-splitting before the House. Unluckily the
lawyers knew the hair was there, and determined after
their kind to have it out. In Sir H. James asked the
Attorney-General these questions—by way of hair-off—

and the Attorney-General answered them—by way of
hair-back—and then followed a lively "rouge" or
"scrimmage," in which most of the leading lawyers of
the House took part. In this cheerful little game the
real lawyers in hand thoroughly lost to lose sight of,
till Mr. Disraeli remarked (the players thus what they had
then and there to settle was not, whether Mr. Mitchell
could still be made to serve out the unexpired arm of his
sentence, but whether he could sit in that House, and
insisted that the House could and should settle that

point at once, and without a Committee. Reason being
clearly with Mr. Disraeli, and his being the perfection
of reason, we see no reason to doubt that the House was
right in deciding, by 269 to 102, that John Mitchell,
convicted felon, having escaped before expiration of his
term, and standing unpardoned, is incapacitated from
sitting in the House of Commons.

A NICE DISTINCTION.

DR. KENEALY. "_Very sorry, my dear Mr. Mitchell, I shan't have the pleasure of your company in the House. But we must draw the line somewhere, you know. We draw it—at CONVICTS._"

[_See Cartoon, "A Nice Distinction."_]

MARCH 15.

THE Pope created six new Cardinals. Archbishop Manning was one of them. He took possession of his titular throne in the Church of San Gregorio, Rome, on the 28th March. ("Annals of Our Time.")

A RED STUDY.

Too bitter for blessing, too happy for banning,
See where, Red Hat on knee,
sunny Cardinal Manning.

A RED STUDY.
(WHAT CARDINAL MANNING SAW IN THE FIRE.)

(See Cartoon, "A Red Study.")

APRIL 13.

A Select Committee had been appointed to inquire into the conditions of certain loans raised by South American States, particularly Honduras, in which many persons in this country had misplaced their confidence. While the Committee was still sitting, a curious question of privilege arose.

Mr. C. Lewis averred that the *Times* and *Daily News* have been guilty of a breach of privilege in reporting a letter from Mr. Herran (Honduras Minister at Paris) to the Chairman of the Foreign Loans Committee, read before the Committee but not reported to the House. Mr. Lewis explained that he took this step because the letter contained a libel on a Member of Parliament. Mr. Herran's letter was read by the clerk. Then followed a curious scene. It seemed, for a while, as if Mr. Lewis could find no backer. But a backer was at last found—Biggar could hardly have been desired. Then Mr. Torrens tried to draw Mr. Lewis, and Mr. Lewis would not be drawn. Then there was a fight between Ayes and Noes, and Noes all but had it; but Biggar stood in the breach for the Ayes, and ere the three-minute-glass ran out, the Ayes rallied, and "had it" over the Noes.

Then came Mr. C. Lewis's Rider, "That the printers of the *Times* and *Daily News* be brought before the bar of the House."

This was more serious. Nobody had the presence of mind to meet the previous question.

Mr. Disraeli requested Mr. Torrens's attempt to draw Mr. Lewis—with the same lack of success. The Marquis of Hartington declared Mr. Lewis would not be drawn.

Why, asked Mr. Watkin Williams, try to cripple the Foreign Loans Committee from behind the *Times* and *Daily News*?

Then Sir W. Harcourt dashed into the strife "a big rough noise"—the ugly word "lobbying." Thereupon followed confusion worse-confounded. In spite of Mr. Bright's warning of the absurd position the House would put itself in by calling its own organs of publicity to its bar on a charge of having read the speaking trumpets supplied them by the House's own head, Mr. Hartish was all-advised enough to vote with Mr. Lewis, and the citation of the *Times* to the bar of the House was voted by 204 to 153. There must be more in the matter than meets the eye of the outsider; for 'to that organ it seems to

of itself. There, let them call Mr. Punch to the bar for that—if they like. "*Me, me admove pui fort, ia me conventibile ferrum.*"

[*the Curtins,* — *Tom Thumb the Great.*]

On the matter coming up again for discussion, however, Mr. Disraeli moved that the order

should be read and discharged, which was agreed to.

Also, when Tom Thumb brought his Giants to Bar, The House had resolved Tommy's triumph to mar. So it snubbed the small hero, and cut his cock's comb, And it said to the Giants—"You'd better go home. It was all a mistake; what we wished you to tell, We can get at without you, we find, just as well."

TOM THUMB THE GREAT!

AS REPRESENTED BY MR. C. LEWIS IN THE RECENT "EXTRAVAGANZA" AT THE THEATRE-ROYAL, ST. STEPHEN'S. (BUT THEY ROBBED HIM OF HIS GIANTS, AFTER ALL.)

APRIL 15.

THE CHANCELLOR OF THE EXCHEQUER, Sir Stafford Northcote, introduced the Budget.

Mr. Punch's "Essence of Parliament" said:—

Sir Stafford Northcote got the languid attention of the thinnest House that ever listened to a Budget Speech to the emptiest Budget ever brought forward—shorn of the usual and unbalanced is—in short—

No Surplus;
No Taxes to be taken off;
No Taxes to be put on.

No Surplus, we say, for what is £600,000 surplus on an income of £71,000,000 but only met a deficit? And what is £60,000 Licence duty taken off this little Brewers, but only not absolute stem you of taxation?

Having nothing to say about the Budget proper, Sir Stafford occupied his two hours and a half by developing a plan for paying off the National Debt. His proposer that, from two pence hence, £28,000,000 shall be annually devoted to the Debt. By this means, he calculates that, in thirty years, with the little helps of casual surpluses and terminable annuities, so all present, we may extinguish £11,000,000 of debt. Surprise for Stafford! All Punch can say is, May Sir Stafford live to see it, and may Punch be there to clap him on the shoulder!

MAY 10.

THE EMPEROR OF RUSSIA arrived at Berlin on a visit to the Emperor of Germany. There were rumours just now of disturbed relations between Continental Powers, which for a time created a war scare in this country as well as in the rest of Europe (Introduction, Vol. LXVIII.). "A military party at Berlin affected alarm at a French law which had been passed for the organisation of the Army. It was pretended that the French were preparing for an immediate war, and that it was necessary to anticipate their designs before they were fully ready for the struggle. The crisis was sufficiently menacing to justify diplomatic remonstrances on the part of the English Government, and the personal intervention of the Emperor Alexander of Russia, who paid a visit to Berlin." (*Times* Annual Summary.) (Mr.

"O, LOVELY PEACE."—HANDEL.

BISMARCK (the Peace-Leader). "My Bear always dances to the grandest of tunes."—GOLDSMITH.

(*Continued—Mercury, Sitting.*) Mr. Bourke, in answer to Sir C. Dilke, said that the Government had that morning received from Berlin assurances of a thoroughly satisfactory character, and that the Government was of opinion that there was no further cause for apprehension as to the maintenance of peace in Europe.

The ugly fact remains that there has been such cause. All the more thanks to our Bear, who has danced "to the prettiest of tunes" this time. Perhaps—indeed and he has rendered his tribut accordingly. But which ever made the music, Czar or Chancellor, the right tune seems to have been hit upon.

(*See Cartoon*, "O, Lovely Peace.")

MAY 29.

TO-DAY the New Arctic Expedition started,

"Discovery" (Captain Stephenson) leaving Portsmouth Harbour for the North.

NORTHWARD, HO!

A God-speed to the Arctic Expedition.

Yet once again the fine kings' blood [brood]
Scion in the adventurous island
Yet once again our prankèd prows
Point northward gaily.
And, doing from the fevered shore,
In us right, hearty British zone
As o'er old English echoes mount,
Sounds forth our *Vale* !

Yet not in sad or lost farewell,
Whose sound is like a parting knell,
But as a jubilant God-speed
Our "good-bye" follows
The towering hulls, whose
hopèd-for goal
Is the ice-girded Arctic pole,
And thence when plan'd has won
its meed,
Back, like the swallows.

Northward again, and safe, we
hope [shape,
'In our poor ships' white pinions
Helped by a happy homeward
breeze,
That sacred bearing 'hold.
Which still the chill grey wanders
Spite of all mothers, sweet and
bold, [run
Whom yet the far and frozen
I love first with daring.

Hurrah ! The cry is "North-
ward Ho !" [far,
Chill-numbing wave, and frozen
Are cheerily challenged once again
By keels and muscle
Of British breed ; and now not
night [thought
That Science's far-reaching
Can shape, them beck to arm
the twain
For Titan toash.

We know the North has taken
title [faithe
Of English blood ere now ; yet
In every heart that dares and
shows
The strife, the glory.
On then ! for, hap what happen
may, [awry,—
This chance shall not be cast
To write our names with gallant
In English story ! [Nows

Where stainless Franklin strove
and fell, [well ;
To die was surely more than
And if capricious fortune crown
A blushèd merit,— [then
Though brier put, not greater,—
These is no fear that history's pen
Will miss or mar the fair renown
We shall inherit.

God speed ! may England's parting cheers
Ring high and hopeful in your ears,
'Midst all the unknown fires and fears
Before you lying.
God speed ! We wish you bravely back,
Safe from the frozen Polar pack,
Leaving our British Union Jack

THE INDIGNANT BYSTANDER.

Mr. Gladstone. "Don't you see, Sir, they're doing you ? You won't last !—Really, the Police ought to interfere !"
Dizzy (to foreign Countryman) : "Don't mind him, Sir ! It's all his spite ! He was hef a Table himself !"

JUNE 8.

Mr. Gladstone's Amendment to the Government proposal for reducing the National Debt was rejected by 189 to 112 votes.

(Comments.)—Another Financial Debate on the best way of reducing the National Debt. A good deal like the discussion in *Great Expectations* between *Pip* and his friend over the "reduction of their liabilities." Besides

now comes forward with a third scheme, which Sir Stafford Northcote declares has all the defects of Tomtit-able Annuities with none of the advantages of the Ministerial Sinking Fund. Messrs. Childers and Lowe can't think how a Chancellor of the Exchequer without a surplus can have the impudence to propose paying debts at all. No more can Mr. Gladstone—unless you can manage it in *his* way—Terminable Annuities. On a division, Mr. Gladstone was beaten by 69.

JUNE 9.

THE SULTAN OF ZANZIBAR arrived in London on a touring visit to this country. He was received at Westminster landing by Sir Bartle Frere, who some time before had been sent on a special mission to Zanzibar to negotiate a treaty for the suppression of African Slavery in the Sultan's dominions.

(*See Cartoon, "More Slaveries than One."*)

JUNE 24.

MR. DISRAELI moved the second reading of the Agricultural Holdings Bill.

Agricultural Holdings Bill introduced to the Commons in a terse speech by Mr. Disraeli. Good fight, *à propos* of the Bill, between the "Mays" and the "Musts," the advocates of permissive and compulsory legislation. Rather oddly arranged—Liberal Opposition on the side of "Must," Conservatives of "May." Any landlord may contract himself out of the Bill. All landlords will do so, says Mr. Knatchbull-Hugessen. Yet he objects to the Bill because it is not compulsory. No does Mr. Lowe, though all for freedom of contract. What chance would it have had with the landlords if it *had* been?

Mr. McCombie speaking for the Land of Leases, plainly described the Bill as one of the most innocent ever introduced into the House of Commons. It gave nothing to the tenant-farmers and would take nothing from them. He forgives the difference between Scotch long leaseholders and English tenants at will—as a rule, *Punch* is glad to think, at good-will.

On the whole, Government moves in any of the Bill, to *Sir phonesis* mind of her wound in Thompson's tragedy—

'Our Bill's not great, because it is so small.'

To which the Opposition seems disposed to reply with Thompson's pit-critic.—

"Then 'twould be greater were there none at all."

The Government has, since the Bill passed the Lords, agreed to strike out what Lord Hartington calls its "key notes"—the calculation of compensation on the basis of increase in letting value.

The tenant's compensation is now to be determined by what he has spent—the fairest basis. Mr. Knight, the out-spoken Member for West Worcestershire, has forced that change upon Mr. Disraeli. he modified, no doubt, the Bill will pass. What good it will work is an open ...

MORE SLAVERIES THAN ONE.

RIGHT HON. B. D. "Now that poor Hughson has seen the Member of Freedom, I trust we may rely upon your earnest help in putting down Slavery!"

SULTAN SEYYID BARGHASH. "Ah, yes! Certainly! And remember, O SHAIKH BEN DIZZY, CONSERVATIVE PARTY THAT OTHERS to Zanzibar!"

... willing to admit. But if a chance so good, is can hardly do the harm they prophesy. As yet, *Punch* is bound to say they have not made out a good case against it.

JUNE 26.

"MR. CROSS's Employers and Workmen Bill read a second time to a general chorus of commendation. Never did performer in the Legislative "ground and lofty line" make his bow amid a more brilliant blaze of triumph.

Appreciating the difficulty of getting the Lamb of Labour and the Lion of Capital—or should the brutes and attributes be counterchanged?—to lie down together and honouring good intentions—particularly where they escape consignment to the ravine denominated "down-stairs."

Punch is proud to present
Mr. Cross his compliments
with a cartoon." ("Essence
of Parliament.")

*(See Cartoon, " A Blaze of
Triumph ! ! ")*

JULY 1.

AN insurrection broke
out in the province
of Herzegovina, in European
Turkey," which " (says Introduction to Vol. LXIX.)
" was the beginning of
troubles which led to an
act of quasi-bankruptcy on
the part of Turkey, and to
the revival of the portentous
Eastern Question. Local
grievances were the origin
of the rebellion. The pro-
vocation was given by the
oppressive conduct of the
Mahomedan landowners,
following a deficient
harvest."

JULY. 16.

THIS day was the fifty-
first anniversary of the
funeral of Lord Byron. A
meeting was held at Willis's
Rooms, presided over by
Mr. Disraeli, with a view
to raising funds for a national monument to the
poet. *Mr. Punch* wrote :—

"CREDE BYRON."

" I desire that my body may be
buried in the vault of the garden
of Newstead, without any ceremony or burial service whatever,
and that no inscription, save my
name and age, be written on the
tomb or tablet."—BYRON'S Will.
(*See "Times", July* 14.)

When perils profferment environ
The mighty Poet's radiant
fame
Which fools and scoffers
sought to shame !
The Churchmen, purjolared
and shabby,
Denied him entrance to the
Abbey;
And wherefore so! Because,
forsooth,
In Days of Sham he wrote
the Truth—
Wrote it with Love, indignant
ire,
In letters of eternal fire :
"Crede Byron !"

   *   *   *

Clay mingled with his strength of iron :
But he was greater far than they
Who dare to call him wholly clay.
If England wishes something done
For her last Age's strongest son,
Be it his statue, calm and grand,
By the best sculptor of the land.

A "BLAZE OF TRIUMPH"!!

(With Mr. Punch's Compliments to Mr. Cross.)

JULY 22.

TO-DAY there was an unusual and exciting
scene in the House of Commons. Mr.
Disraeli announced that it was not the intention of Government to proceed further this

ment of the philanthropic object which he
had been ardently pursuing for so long,
lost control of himself, and used language
which, unusual in the circumstances, was a
defiance of the rules of the House, shouting,
"I will unmask the villains who have seat

House, and declining to
withdrew the terms when
called upon to do so.
Mr. Plimsoll subsequently
apologised for this violation
of the rules of the House.
A temporary Bill which it
was said "reflected more
of the spirit of the Member
for Derby than of the
Government Bill" was pre-
pared, brought forward by
the President of the Board
of Trade and passed.

The popular view of the
incident was reflected in
the following lines of *Mr.
Punch* :—

A PLEA FOR PLIMSOLL

What though the passion in
    him tore away
  The dams and dykes of sen-
    torial phrase ?
What though the words that
    spoke his mind outweigh
  The weight of Parliamentary
    decorum ?
What though, brain wrong by
    seven of ruth and rage,
  And sudden-baffled hope of
    help, long nursed,
Against all rules of the St.
    Stephen's stage
  Forth in scorning current
    wrath he burst—:
Of proud that, ghoul-like, feeds
    from a stony grave,
  Of hopes and hearts that
    desolate abide,
Of brave men's lives foredoomed
    for gain of knaves—
  And, in denouncing, flung his
    charges wide,
And gave his comrades a word
    and taunt,
  "Lo ! you, the Sailors' cham-
    pion !" Through their sneers,
Still let his bitter cry ring in our
    ears—
  "They drown by hundreds
    round our England's coast !"

(*See Cartoon, "Doing Penance."*)

JULY 27.

His Right Rev. Connop
Thirlwall, Bishop of
St. David's, one of the
most sagacious and liberal-
minded of Anglican eccle-
siastics, died to-day at the
age of 78.

JULY 31.

What was known as the "Slave Circular"
agitation was now raging. The Admiralty
had issued "Instructions with reference to the
question how far officers in command of Her
Majesty's ships are justified in receiving on

"DOING PENANCE."

board, may claim the protection of the British
Flag." Commanders of the Queen's ships were
directed not only to refuse an asylum to slaves
in foreign waters, but to surrender, on their
return to port, fugitives who might have come
on board on the high seas. This, when it became
known, excited an outburst of popular indigna-

tion. The objectionable circular was suspended, and
later in the year another was issued less open
to criticism.

(*See Cartoon, p. 314, "The Flag of Freedom."*)

BRITANNIA OBJECTS—

*To the Admiralty Circular, of July 31st, to Captains of
H.M. Ships, on the subject of Fugitive Slaves.*

With a look of exceedingly
startled surprise,
— ' Supplementary Slave-
Trade Instructions ' ?
I thought I had settled that
little affair. [I declare !
A pretty *post*-scriptum, my Lord,
But I don't see my countervign-
art anywhere, [doctrines.
To this newest of naval po-

" My will, I conceived, was
made clear to the world,
That, wherever my Union Jack
was unfurled,
The Slave should find freedom
thereunder.
That's a fair and square rule
which all quibblers should
quail.
But, as for this roundabout
' Circular,'—well,
It would tax a Sea-lawyer its
meanings to tell :
One thing, though, is plain,
—it's a blunder !

" No need for gull talk about
ruling the waves,
But, at least, say 'he-ot rule'
does not recognise Slaves,
Whether stretched o'er green
land or blue ocean.
A legalised Serf on a free British
ship [to grip,
Is a moral conception too easy
Re-rivet the chains he has
managed to slip ?
I rather rebel at the notion !

" With Slave-owning gryves my
fine dogs and !
Will find it stiff work to keep
taunt,—if we try.
We hold them in scorn, and
they hate us.
O ! I fancy I see a Committee
of Jacks
On a fugitive wretch coolly
turning their backs,
Or holding palaver, like shear-
going quacks,
With a view to 'determine
his status' !

" Let these look to their ' char-
ters !' my craft were not made
To play any part in the Slave
smuggling trade.
I have spent blood and bullion
to hurt it.
My stand has been taken, and
if it should lead
To some strife of trouble,—as
well may exceed
When Honest lowers counters
Villianous Creed,—
It is not my intention to shirk
it.

" What philanthropists fought
for, and legists confirm,
Shall not be evaded by wriggle and squirm,
Base quibble, or politic pokering.
My Love is writ large for all Nations in one,—
Askers or afront, 'neath my Flag all are Free !
That's a very plain rule, and you'll reckon with me
If you think it requires any shoving !

AUG. 13.

THE "FLAG OF FREEDOM."

FIRST LORD OF THE ADMIRALTY. "A runaway Slave, boys ! You'll have to give him up, you know ! 'Tis our Circular of 31st of July."

JOHN BULL. "Give 'im up, yer Honor !! As well order me to haul down that there Flag at once, Sir !!!"

AUG. 24.

CAPTAIN MATTHEW WEBB to-day achieved the remarkable feat of swimming across the Channel. He started from Dover a few minutes before 1 P.M., and landed at Calais Harbour shortly after half-past ten in the morning, having

SEPT. 1.

ON this day, while the Channel Fleet was cruising off the coast of Wicklow, two of its large iron-clad men-of-war, the "Vanguard" and the "Iron Duke," came into collision in the fog, when the "Vanguard" was sunk, but

captain and officers of the "Vanguard," imputed blame to Vice-Admiral Tarleton in command of the Fleet, dismissed Captain Dawkins, and reprimanded the other superior officers. An Admiralty Minute subsequently exonerated the Admiral from blame, but the public confidence in the management of our Navy was considerably shaken by the incident.

(*See Cartoon, "Loss and Gain."*)

SEPT. 27.

To-day was held at Darlington the fiftieth anniversary of the opening of the Stockton and Darlington Railway, the first one constructed.

The Lord Mayors of London and York, as well as the Mayors of Berwick, Ripon, and many other northern towns, attended the celebration, which comprised the unveiling, by the Duke of

LOSS AND GAIN.

JOHN BULL. "Half a Million of Money gone to the bottom at once!!!"
MR. PUNCH. "Yes, my dear John, it's an expensive experience! But as they were lost, and taught us how what we've got to trust to!"

Cleveland, of a statue erected to the memory of Joseph Pease, a banquet, and a display of illuminations and fireworks.

A GIANT'S JUBILEE.

(Fiftieth Anniversary of the opening of the first Passenger Railway, Darlington, Sept. 27, 1825.)

"Now, my lads, I will tell you that I think you will live to see the day, though I may not live so long, when railways will make to supersede almost all other modes of conveyance in this country—when mail coaches will go by railway, and railroads will become the great highway for the King and all his subjects. The time is coming when it will be cheaper for a working-man to travel on a railway than to walk on foot, I know that there are great and almost insurmountable difficulties that will have to be encountered, but what I have said will come to pass as sure as we live."—STEPHENSON'S prophesied prophecy.

O, a flourishing breed are our latter-day Titans,
The clubbers colossal of Iron and Steam;
Though as black as Old Nex, and as ugly as Shaitans,
These promising pets of Britannia may seem.

One rancorous babe, spite of crushing and snarling,
His Jubilee reaches, still stronger and stout,
And so they at Darlington drink to their darling,
Whom Nephistees dandled, and Harkworth brought out.

He wowed but a rickety knave to his gossips,
His shape was uncouth, and his action but slow

Would he flourish or fade? 'Twas the moment of true-ages,
The quibbizers opined, fifty summers ago.
But his sponsors had faith in their black-visaged bantling,
And now, though a youth, as three Titans count years,
He beats sundeen Bronto in stature and searching,
Bestrews in grasp, and in speed has no peers.

Fifty years! Men are grey who first saw him at play;
His spousers are dead, his detractors are dumb;
And he, to the unyelling young gnome of that day,
throws as huge Harkbhrende as flap-of-cap-Thumb!
Fifty years! and "Owd Neddy," who took him in tow,
The vaunt "Puffing Billy" be fostered might fall
To drivel at the iron-throned Titan we know,
Our Hercules-Puck, with the thousand-leagued tail!

One good-natured glint, he's
    patient and gleam,
Will fresh and will carry at
    anyone's best,
A gracious at fool, of fatigue he's
    defiant,
    A sharpshot Colossus who
    never breaks rest.
No horseman so stout for us
    humble a hive wash,
What snatcher can cheer at
    his Jubilee fête!
And toast him in wine with
    rhetorical fireworks,
    Our standard, steadiest No!
    rest of hints?

Yet gleam we have have there
    trustiness ever,
    Go soft in the carpet, or work
    in the lanes,
And our young Unknown, though
    proven and clever,
    Plays courtsize at cheers little
    likely to please.
Though our huge fate there is
    not vicious or idle,
    Yet to make him run straight,
    and steer close of a spill,
He needs a stout rein, a strong
    hand on the bridle,
    And Arms!—the Batsman!—
    to guide his good will.

Small idioms to the juvenile
    Titan, less trainers
Who hunt of their favourite's
    power and pace,
If they hope of the "National
    Stakes" to be gainers,
    Must learn that good jockey-
    ship counts in the race.
This sturdiest servant of cricket-
    ing
    May stay on the end if they
    handle him well;
But we want fewer "spills" ere
    a satisfied nation
    Claps hands to this chorus of
    whistle and bell.

We may drink to the health of
    our Giant of fifty—
Punch empties his bumper—
    yet gladly would find
His trainers of tale-tale a trifle
    more thrifty,
    While yet in the auto Master
    handicaps blind.
Hours here in our all, our material
    progress ;
    While usual all a stand, shuttere
    there's no rain,
And Civilization an iron-footed
    egress
    Our Titan may not for, her
    cannot restrain.

[See Cartoon, " The Golden
    Wedding."]

THE GOLDEN WEDDING.

(Mr. Punch's present to Values and Values on the 50th Anniversary of their happy Union.)

MR. P. " Let's hope, my dear Friends, that before the next Anniversary you'll have brought Block and Brake both to perfection."

OCT. 11.

THE PRINCE OF WALES left England for a tour in India. He reached Brindisi on the 16th, and proceeded on his journey in the "Serapis," specially equipped for the voyage, accompanied by the Duke of Sutherland, Lord

Russell the celebrated correspondent, and others.

NOV. 2.

THE new High Court of Judicature was opened in Westminster Hall. After many delays the union of Law and Equity was effected.

THE WEDDING OF LAW AND EQUITY.

"This first of November England witnesses their union of Law and Equity."—*Times.*

Union of Equity and Law !
Who such a union ever saw ?
Such Indian must confusion mean !
Can no Queen's Proctor intervene,
Above the plea, yet 'tis here, subserrial—

This happy morn, people say,
Was fitly fixed for All Saints'
Day.
Ye warriors of the Devil's Own,
Was such a blunder ever known?
Ye who in Hall and legal doctors,
Is there an front, that's insaned
All Sinners?

Picture the bride! Bridegroom
great,
Made of the very sternest stuff;
No smile o'er that grim visage
flit;
His wedding coat is lined with
writ;
His honeymoon, no doubt, he
has
Would spend in happy Chancery
Lane.

But O sweet Equity, the bride!
A creature to be deified—
With perfect justice in her eye,
She cannot cheat, she cannot lie;
Behold her, dressed in virgin
white,
An angel of serene delight.

They're wedded! Wonders never
cease;
War in due time will marry
Peace;
To each a husband Truth will
range,
And find him on the Stock Ex-
change;
Religion, joking Controversy—
Her followers long—will wed
with Mercy.

When Law and Equity receive
Their guests, one hardly can
believe
That he, of tyrants quite the
sternest,
Will take her counsel in good
earnest.
But Punch the union won't dis-
parage,
And thanks their long and happy
marriage.

(See Cartoon, " Settled at
Last.")

Nov. 6.

The Prince of Wales
arrived at Bombay,
where he was received in
State by the Governor of
Bombay, the Commander-
in-Chief of India, the Lord
Chief Justice, and upwards
of seventy native princes,
chiefs, and sirdars, in glit-
tering Oriental costumes.
(" Annals of Our Time.")
The Prince laid the foundation stone of the new
wet docks.

The 9th of November, being the Prince's
birthday, was kept at Bombay with abundant
manifestations of loyalty and good-will. On
the 11th the Prince, accompanied by a party
of 400 ladies and gentlemen, visited the

grand procession of elephants, which paraded
through the native city to the old palace, where
the prince was a spectator of wrestlings, fights
between rams, buffaloes, rhinoceroses and
elephants, and other scenes in the arena.

The Prince was everywhere well received, and
the account of his Eastern travels was read with

SETTLED AT LAST!

Nurse. " Bless you, my Children! You haven't 'Married in Haste;' the less likely to ' Repent at Leisure'!"

Nov. 20.

To-day another accident befel the ironclad
" Iron Duke," during the trial of her
machinery in the Channel. The water rushed
into her stokehole to such an extent that the
signal " Sinking" was made to the flagship.
The " Iron Duke" righted and returned to

to our armour-clad fleet caused serious dissatisfaction in the mind of the public, and a strong desire to know with certainty who was in fault.

(*See Cartoon, "Neptune's Warning."*)

ADMIRALTY GUIDE.

(*Out of the Fog.*)

THERE appears to have been considerable misapprehension among officers of the Royal Navy as to the line of conduct to be adopted under certain circumstances. All doubts, however, on these points must have been removed by the decision of a recent Court-Martial, and the Admiralty minute thereupon.

For the benefit of the Service we give a short summary of the Instructions which appear to be conveyed.

For Admirals.

Admirals in command of a squadron will regulate the speed of the ships composing it, but will not be responsible for accidents which may arise from the rate of speed being improper.

On the approach of fog, a gun may be fired from the flagship; care being however taken that the gun used is not heavy enough to be heard by the other ships of the squadron. (Suitable pieces of ordnance for this purpose may be obtained at the Model Dockyard in the Strand.)

For Captains commanding Ironclads in Squadrons.

No alteration of speed or course must under any circumstances be made on the Captain's own authority.

Should a vessel be unfortunately discovered across the bows, the Admiral must be signalled to, and his directions awaited. If, however, the vessel in danger be the Admiralty yacht, carrying their Lordships, the Captain of the Ironclad may, on his own responsibility, order life-buoys to be got ready; that intended for the First Lord being at once decorated with red cloth.

In the event of fog coming on, steam is immediately to be shut off from the whistle, or it might inadvertently be sounded, thus giving notice of your whereabouts to some other ship, and enabling her to get out of your way, or perhaps to run you; in which case, of course, you would be held responsible for the disaster.

Should this however occur, the diver belonging to the ship will immediately resume his dress and descend to inspect the leak.

On his return he will prepare a written report of the loss, &c., and upon this report, countersigned by the Captain, the necessary quantity of cakum, spare sails, and hammocks will be handed to the Carpenter. In order

NEPTUNE'S WARNING.

FATHER NEP. "Look here, my Lass! You are to 'Rule the Waves;' but if you WILL BULL 'em, as you're doing lately, by Jingo there'll be a row!!!"

BRITANNIA. "I'm very I don't know what to blame, Papa dear!"

FATHER NEP. "Don't know!!! Then Pipe all Hands, and find out!!!"

should all endeavours be unavailing, and the ship continue to settle down, the efforts to save her are on no account to cease; but when the ship commences her final plunge, and the decks begin to burst up, boats' crews may be piped away and the boats lowered. The crew must not, however, be allowed to get into them until the water is level with the hammock-nettings. It must be strictly borne in mind that the preservation of the crew is entirely a minor consideration. Men may be had at any

cost both time and money, and the loss of one may even cause the addition of a halfpenny to the Income-Tax.

The above instructions have special reference to ships getting into a fog, and by inducing a corresponding state of mind with them in command, may be of the utmost practical utility.

Nov. 20.

THE Herzegovian insurrection and its conse-

Vol. LXIX.) "caused a drain on the Turkish Exchequer (already impoverished) so exhausting, that a collapse of the Empire seemed imminent, to the grave danger of the peace of Europe. But the Great Powers showed themselves sincerely desirous to avert such a perilous crisis,

and agreed upon a course of Diplomatic action which it was hoped would result in the pacification of the insurgent districts still in active revolution."

(*See Cartoon, "Disinterested Advisers."*)

Nov. 20.

To-day, at Myddleton Hall, Islington, under the auspices of Sir Andrew Lusk, M.P., and Mr. Samuel Waddy, M.P., was introduced an American pastime called a "Spelling Bee" ("Annals of Our Time.") The new game became

DISINTERESTED ADVISERS.

BEARS. "The very best, dear Turkey, our only Object is your Good!"

popular for a season, and allusions to it are plentiful in the literature of the time.

Nov. 25.

It was announced to-day that the British Government had purchased from the Khedive of Egypt the 177,000 shares held by him in the Suez Canal, for the sum of 4,000,000*l.* The policy of this great financial operation, supposed to have been made at the instigation of Mr. Disraeli himself, was much discussed now

MONEY'S WORTH FOR THE MONEY.

"Egyptian Government sold to English Government their Canal shares for £4,000,000 sterling. Minister is authorised to draw on Rothschild at sight."—*Friday's Telegram.*

At our Indian door-key we seem to hold fast,
Britannia's will she has now found a way for;
On our shop-keeping instincts contempt let them cast,
But who'll take what we've forked out four millions to pay for?

Such a sum if it suit John Bull's int'rest to pay,
It is clear it suits Egypt's 'cute Chief to receive.
Now Khedives more Rothschild ones draw now day.

Nov. 27.

This was a very rainy year, and at this season floods and inundations were very prevalent. It was felt that adequate precautions against such dangers were not taken, and Mr. Punch, as usual, gave expression to the public opinion.

THE NEW DELUGE.

'Tis the old, old story o'er again,
We can shower-bath'd now with perpetual rain,
Thames, Severn, and Trent conspire, and this
Would drown our municipalities.

But the sun won't come, and the
rain won't go,
And the housewives your begins
to grow
A mass of dismal cabbies.

Now, can a fellow be jolly and
gay,
And pretty things in his weari-
heart say,
When "the rain it raineth every
day"
With a vicious regularity?

Can you gladden as wit from a
Lady's lip,
When the sound outside is, Drip,
drip, drip?
And icicles bath you on the hip
And a gloom of the Sun's a
rarity?

Why, where's the fun of a merry
lunch?
(As we'll never breid and bacon
munch.)
And where's the radiance of Mr.
Punch?*
(As well read Doctor Ke-
nealy?)

East wind making your throat
throb,
Rain like a school-girl's sulky
sob,—
You drink mulled claret, and sit
by your hob,
And feel like a martyr,
really.

"Rivers, arise!" So Milton
said,†
Fain would we have them keep
their bed,
And down to the sea be safely
led;
But they bring us all this
shiver——

And we cry, "O Mandem for
Greenwich, pity us,
Having disestablished Churches
and trees,
Bring us a little quiet and ease
By disestablishing rivers."

[Sir Cresswell, "A Voice from
the Clouds."]

DEC. 4.

TO-DAY being the eigh-
tieth birthday of
Thomas Carlyle, an ad-
dress in honour of the
occasion was presented to
the venerable "writer of
books," signed by upwards
of one hundred distin-
guished representatives of
literature, science and art.

DEC. 11.

THE purchase by the British Government of
the Suez Canal Shares was still the subject
of much discussion and many conflicting

* Always chose O thyme—Read Punch, and duly rain and all

A VOICE FROM THE CLOUDS.

JUPITER PLUVIUS. "Stop your floods, and Embank your Rivers, and this mercy would prove a Holiday!"

opinions both here and abroad. The Khedive
had first attempted to sell his shares to a French
Financial Company, and on the failure of this
negotiation had offered to transfer them to the
British Government. The promptness with
which Mr. Disraeli, aided by the Messrs. Rothschild, accepted, and made his great financial

tion in some quarters, aroused jealousy and
anger in others. The coup was in this country
generally regarded as clever, though perhaps a
little à la Juive. Mr. Punch, in a memorable
Cartoon, gave pointed expression to this opinion.
The Suez Canal had been called "The Key
of India."

A LOCAL CRITIC.

The Sphinx
She winks
At Drury's rows,
"Yes," think I
The Sphinx,
"I think 'twill do."

(Mr Cartoon, "Mosé in Egitto!!!")

WHAT THEY (AND WE) SAY ABOUT IT.

In France.—That it is worthy of England the perfidious.

That England is now allied to the changing of coats.

That the French Government has neglected to do its duty.

That an angry note should have been sent from Paris to the Court of St. James.

That if this had been done England would have trembled, and the transaction would have been repudiated.

That a further proof has just been given that England is merely a nation of shop-keepers.

That all Englishmen are cowards.

That all Frenchmen are heroes.

That in spite of everything, the incident only increases the glory of France.

In Germany.—That England may (with the kind consent of the Emperor of Germany), do what she pleases in this matter.

That Germany, on account of the relationship existing between the two peoples, will not interfere.

That Germany acknowledges the judicious good feeling displayed by England by disappointing the wishes of that ex-grand nation—the French.

That Germany congratulates England upon having gained the consent of Prince Von Bismarck to the completion of the arrangement.

In Austria.—That England, as an Austro power, of several note importance, may do what she likes with Egypt.

That Austria is, of course, far too grand a country to concern herself with the petty bargains of a nation of cheese selling islanders.

That England need fear no Austrian invasion at present.

That Englishmen should be delighted to hear this piece of good news.

In Russia.—That England is this emergency has done wisely in at last obeying the directions of the late Emperor Nicholas.

That the transaction is worthy of the Stock Exchange, and is consequently characteristic of the British Nation.

That, perhaps, even all the circumstances of the case Russia will defer the annexation of India until next year.

In England.—That Englishmen are not afraid of Frenchmen, Prussians, Austrians, or Russians.

That people living outside the British Empire may say and think what they please.

That the purchase of the interest in the Suez Canal was carried out without the advice, much less the consent, of any foreigner.

with no intention to exclude any other nation from the same advantages.

That England, having got a hold on the Suez Canal, and paid for it, knows how to keep it, and means to keep it, all people and potentates to the contrary notwithstanding.

N.B.—What is said in England, *Mr. Punch* begs to

"MOSÉ IN EGITTO!!!"

DEC. 16.

"A scheme for the mobilization of the army" (says a Note to Vol. LXIX.), "had recently been put forth by the War Office. It was designed to supply deficiencies in the system originated by Mr. Cardwell when Secretary for War. Mobilization had been defined as 'a set of regulations intended to provide for the conversion of the military material of the country into an army as soon as ever it may be required for action.' In the Cartoon the Duke of Cambridge, as Commander-in-Chief, and Mr. Gathorne Hardy as Secretary for War, are explaining a new scheme to Britannia." It is typified by the German "Krieg's-spiel," or War Game.

(See Cartoon, "Our Krieg's Spiel.")

DEC. 22.

The training-ship "Goliath," which was lying in the Thames off Grays, was this day destroyed by fire. Fifteen of the boys lost their lives; but the excellent behaviour of many amongst those rescued, as well as of the captain, officers and sailors of the "Goliath," excited public admiration. Mr. Punch wrote:—

As long as English workhouse lads
Work up to such good stuff,
Britannia still will rule the waves—
Though here and there a scuff
At Whitehall or elsewhere may make
Old John Bull cut up rough!

OUR KRIEG'S-SPIEL.

THE SECRETARY FOR WAR. "Only we have beautifully at Mons!"
BRITANNIA. "Beautifully!—On Paper."

DEC. 23.

The PRINCE OF WALES, whose tour in India was a series of brilliant ceremonies and exciting incidents, who had already visited Bombay, Goa, Ceylon, Madras and other places, was received by the Viceroy, the Commander-in-Chief, the Bishop, the Chief Justice, the Members of the Council, the Judges, as well as by Scindiah and Holkar, the Rajahs of Cashmere and Jeypore, and many other native princes and chiefs. The Prince, attended by a gorgeous procession, round of ceremonies and receptions ensued. On Christmas Day the Prince went to a State Dinner given by the Viceroy in his honour at Barrackpore, after attending service in the Cathedral at Calcutta.

(END OF VOLUME II.)

www.ingramcontent.com/pod-product-compliance
Lightning Source LLC
Chambersburg PA
CBHW020949030726
47496CB00005B/1425